KU-622-369

HANA KHAN
CARRIES ON

UZMA JALALUDDIN

CORVUS

First published in Canada in 2021 by Harper Avenue,
an imprint of Harper Collins Publishers Ltd.

This edition published in paperback and export trade paperback in
Great Britain in 2021 by Corvus, an imprint of Atlantic Books Ltd.

Copyright © Uzma Jalaluddin, 2021

The moral right of Uzma Jalaluddin to be identified as the author of this
work has been asserted by her in accordance with the Copyright, Designs
and Patents Act of 1988.

All rights reserved. No part of this publication may be reproduced, stored in a
retrieval system, or transmitted in any form or by any means, electronic, mechanical,
photocopying, recording, or otherwise, without the prior permission of both the
copyright owner and the above publisher of this book.

This novel is entirely a work of fiction. The names, characters and incidents
portrayed in it are the work of the author's imagination. Any resemblance to actual
persons, living or dead, events or localities, is entirely coincidental.

10 9 8 7 6 5 4 3 2 1

A CIP catalogue record for this book is available from the British Library.

Trade paperback ISBN: 978 1 83895 361 4
Paperback ISBN: 978 1 83895 356 0
E-book ISBN: 978 1 83895 357 7

Printed and bound by CPI Group (UK) Ltd, Croydon, CR0 4YY

Corvus
An imprint of Atlantic Books Ltd
Ormond House
26–27 Boswell Street
London
WC1N 3JZ

www.corvus-books.co.uk

Y041538

The item should be returned or renewed by the last date stamped below.

Dylid dychwelyd neu adnewyddu'r eitem erbyn y dyddiad olaf sydd wedi'i stampio isod.

To renew visit / Adnewyddwch ar
www.newport.gov.uk/libraries

Also by Uzma Jalaluddin

Ayesha at Last

For my parents, Mohammed and Azmat Jalaluddin,
who taught me the importance of community, even as they built one.

Here are the rules:

This is a single-person podcast.

Not a variety show.

No interviews.

Not a comedy hour.

I'm not going to tell you my name or any specific biographical details, except the following: I'm a South Asian Muslim woman in my twenties. I was born and live in the city of Toronto. And I love radio. Really love it.

I also love the free form of podcasts. This particular podcast will be about having a place to ask questions, without worrying who might be listening and judging.

I'm talking about the Big Questions, future friends.

Such as: What do you want out of life?

What do we owe the people we love?

How do our histories and stories influence who we become?

And how do you know that the thing you want is actually the thing you want?

There you have it, listeners: my mission statement. I promise no frills and a clear voice. I promise nothing of substance and nothing but my truth. I promise to take this seriously, but I'm also definitely making it up as I go along.

Whoever and wherever you are, welcome to Ana's Brown Girl Rambles. *I can't wait to start a conversation with you.*

COMMENTS

StanleyP

This popped up in my podcatcher. Nice first episode. I'm always interested in the big questions.

AnaBGR

Is this for real, or are you a catfishing bot?

StanleyP

Real. Just pinched to make sure.

AnaBGR

Wow. Well, thanks for listening.

StanleyP

Sure. I've been asking myself the same questions, so thank you for the company.

AnaBGR

Definitely a bot. You're way too polite. And now we're trapped in a thank-you-cycle.

StanleyP

No escape from the thank-you vortex. This is home now.

AnaBGR

Except I know the safety words: you're welcome.

StanleyP

Bots never give up. Until next time, Ana-nonymous.

Chapter One

StanleyP

Happy five month pod-iversary!

According to inaccuratestatistics.com, most podcasts don't make it past month four, so you've beat the odds! I'd send you flowers, but that would imply I knew your name, mailing address, and flower preference, and that would cause my bot senses to melt into a confused puddle.

AnaBGR

That might be amusing. Okay, my real name is . . .

StanleyP

Wait. What? Seriously?

AnaBGR

Psych. Psych psych psych!

StanleyP

So cruel, when I'm trying to congratulate you. Any news on the mysterious dream-job interview?

No news is good news, right?

StanleyP

Definitely. Especially when you're going after the highly specialized job of . . . unicorn wrangler? toddler exorcist? erotic knitter?

AnaBGR

An erotic knitter can't possibly be a thing.

StanleyP

You're saying you're definitely NOT a paper-folding priestess.

AnaBGR

That's as likely as anyone under the age of 40 actually being
named Stanley.

StanleyP

I've offered to reveal my true identity. Aren't you a little curious
about the incredibly hot, accomplished, muscular man behind
StanleyP?

Was I curious about StanleyP? He had no idea.

I was in the corner booth of Three Sisters Biryani Poutine, the
restaurant my family owned and ran in the heart of the Golden
Crescent neighbourhood, in the east end of Toronto. I was supposed
to be cleaning in anticipation of customers, but instead I was texting
StanleyP, my very first and most loyal listener.

Over the past five months, we had moved from polite commenter and podcaster to friendly acquaintances to genuine friends who texted every day. All without exchanging a single personal detail. Yet when I closed my eyes, I could imagine his smile. It would be shy, tentative. He would be kind—a thinker and listener, with a mischievous glint in his eye. I knew I would love his laugh.

The phone pinged in my hand. I looked down at the direct messaging app we had started using a few months after he first began commenting on my podcast.

StanleyP
I think you might be the person who knows me best in the world right now. And I don't even know your real name.

My fingers hovered over the screen. I could tell him who I really was. I pictured myself typing it out:

My real name is Hana. I'm 24 and I live with my parents in the most diverse suburb in the world—Scarborough, in the east end of Toronto. You already know that I'm a South Asian Muslim, but you don't know that I wear hijab and I work two jobs. One is at Three Sisters Biryani Poutine, the restaurant my mother has been running for the past 15 years, and another at CJKP, a local indie radio station where I intern. Though "work" is a bit of a misnomer—neither position pays me actual money, and both positions have a limited life expectancy. The former because our restaurant is in trouble, and the latter because my internship is coming to an end and I have no idea what comes next. I'm trying not to panic about either situation.

Nope. StanleyP didn't need to know any of that. Better stick with simple biographical details:

I have an older sister named Fazeela and a brother-in-law named Fahim, and in about four months they will make me a khala (that means "aunt," in case you are a non-Urdu-speaking StanleyP). As for my dad . . .

I hesitated.

As for my dad . . .

It had been a long time since I had had to explain about Baba to a stranger. It used to be a daily occurrence as we navigated among hospitals, doctors, nurses, physiotherapists, and personal support workers. As Baba's condition stabilized, his world had shrunk, along with the need for explanations to strangers. In that surreal way that online friendships worked, StanleyP was still, technically, a stranger. A stranger I spoke with daily, one who knew my deepest hopes and fears, but not any details about my real, lived existence.

I picked up my phone and typed carefully.

AnaBGR
It's easier if we keep things the way they've always been. There's a lot going on in my life right now, and I'm not sure I can handle another complication.

Another, longer pause. Imaginary StanleyP had his brow furrowed, but he would understand, and he would respond. He always had a response.

StanleyP
Is this complication . . . relationship-shaped?

I almost laughed out loud at the question—but then my mother would have realized I was goofing off in the dining room and make me help her in the restaurant kitchen.

Things had shifted between Stanley and me over the past month. Lately he had been hinting at more but had never come out and asked. But then, neither had I.

AnaBGR
More what-does-the-future-hold-shaped. A relationship would
be easier to deal with than family and business stuff.

StanleyP
Our lives are running parallel. I have business-and-family-
shaped complications too. That new project I was telling you
about is finally happening. No relationship-shaped complication
for me either.

StanleyP was single too. A flush crept along my collarbone and up through the roots of my hair, which was pulled back neatly under my bright pink hijab. I shifted in my seat. He probably hadn't always been single like me, but still. I knew what he wasn't asking me. And part of me was tempted to not answer back. Instead, I fell back into our usual humour.

AnaBGR
Why can't I be the complicated one? You always have to copy me.

StanleyP

It's what a bot does. The Stanbot is also programmed to give excellent advice and tell hilarious jokes, and is available for revelations of real names or the exchange of pictures/phone numbers. Just say the word. I'd love to get to know you better.

My stomach jolted with awareness at his words. I wanted more too. But it wasn't as easy for me. All the bravery I possessed was currently being put towards other things. I wasn't sure I had the energy to pursue whatever this thing between us was turning out to be.

I didn't know anything about Stanley beyond what he had told me. From hints he had dropped, I knew he lived in Canada and was a second-generation immigrant like me. I suspected he was South Asian, maybe even Muslim, but I didn't know anything for sure, and I wasn't quite ready to venture outside the comfort of our cozy anonymous relationship.

I was saved from responding by his next message.

StanleyP

Message me when you hear you got the job.

I closed the app. Mom emerged from the kitchen a few moments later, ostensibly to deliver my lunch but really to check that I was working. I was distracted from my annoyance by the treat she held in her hand: biryani poutine, my favourite.

"Hana, *beta*, eat fast. Customers could come at any time, *meri jaan*," she said, handing me the steaming plate piled high. My mother, Ghufran Khan, was a curious combination of nurturing and stern. She delivered orders in sharp bursts punctuated with Urdu endearments such as *beta* (child) and *meri jaan* (my life).

I devoured the mixture of fragrant rice, marinated chicken, crispy fries, savoury gravy, and cheese curds. Mom wrinkled her nose and hastily returned to the kitchen. Biryani poutine is . . . an acquired taste. As in, I was the only person who had acquired a taste for our restaurant's namesake dish.

Biryani is a popular north Indian dish, a casserole made from basmati rice layered on top of meat or chicken marinated in yogurt, salt, fresh coriander, a garlic-ginger paste, and garam masala. The dish was topped with ghee and saffron and then baked. Poutine is a regional Canadian dish that first gained popularity in Quebec. It consists of fresh-cut golden fries topped with rich, savoury gravy and fresh cheese curds. Biryani layered with poutine was a strange combination that, so far, appealed only to me. Likely because I dreamt up the dish when I was nine years old.

My sister, brother-in-law, and even random strangers thought biryani poutine was disgusting. Eventually Mom had taken it off the menu after our customers complained, though she still made it for me. It had stuck as the name for the restaurant, probably because Mom hadn't wanted to pay for a new sign.

I put down the plate and, popping in ear buds and cranking my favourite playlist, I began cleaning. After a few minutes I picked up the plate to take another bite of my lunch, swivelling my hips to TSwift's infectious pop and using my spoon as a microphone.

Someone tapped me on the shoulder, and startled, I dropped my plate. Demonstrating lightning-fast reflexes, the someone—a young man, I observed—saved my lunch from disaster. I took out my earbuds, and TSwift's bouncing lyrics blared for a moment into the silence before I hastily swiped the app closed.

The young man half-smiled. *Cute*, I thought.

"Your . . . meal?" he asked, his tone deeply dubious as he handed back the plate. He looked to be about my age or slightly older, wearing a black T-shirt and jeans. A pair of flashy sunglasses with reflective silver lenses dangled from his collar. His hair was dark and curly, and a smile twitched at the corners of his full mouth. A hint of stubble accentuated a square jaw and warm terracotta skin. Large, dark brown eyes regarded me from beneath thick black brows.

Definitely cute, but I didn't appreciate the questioning lilt at the end of that sentence. Or the way the older man standing behind him wrinkled his nose at my lunch.

"*What* is *that?*" the older man asked. Despite the salt-and-pepper hair and the deep frown lines etched into his cheeks, the resemblance between the two was clear. Father and son, I concluded.

"Biryani poutine," I answered, offended. "Only available on the VIP menu."

The older man frowned at my mop, which had fallen to the floor. "You work here? You look about fourteen years old."

I reached up to straighten my wrinkled black tunic and adjust my hijab. The young man followed the movements of my hands with his eyes before looking away with a faint smile. Was Mr. Silver Shades laughing at me?

Welcome to Three Sisters Biryani Poutine, where child labour is encouraged and biryani and poutine are kept segregated, as God intended, I wanted to say. Instead I led them to a booth.

"I don't understand why you insisted on coming here," the older man said loudly, settling into his seat with a look of distaste. "They probably don't even have clean cups."

Charming. A few years ago I might have asked Mr. Silver Shades to take his grumpy dad elsewhere. But they were our first customers of the day, and my family couldn't afford to be picky.

Three Sisters Biryani Poutine had seating for about forty people, spread out among a handful of plastic booths and yellowing square tables paired with wooden chairs. Bright fluorescent lighting painted every smudge and dent in harsh relief, and the walls were an unflattering green. Every year we meant to repaint, but time and money never allowed for it. Some art hung on the walls, mostly prints from IKEA or garage sales; Mom was partial to seascapes and large florals. A counter stood against the back wall, with the cash register in front of a door that led to the kitchen.

"These hole-in-the-wall places sometimes have excellent food, if you can look past the decor," the young man said to his father, not bothering to lower his voice. He caught my eye when I returned with cutlery and glasses, unaware—or uncaring—that I had overheard. The older man immediately reached for his glass and started inspecting it for water blotches.

"Have you worked here long?" Mr. Silver Shades asked.

"A few years," I said shortly, handing them laminated menus. I had officially started serving when I turned sixteen; before that I had helped out as dishwasher, sweeper—any job that needed to be done. Not that Mr. Silver Shades and his designer clothes would have any idea what a struggling family-run business required.

"There aren't any other restaurants in the neighbourhood," he remarked. "This area could use more selection, don't you think?"

"No, I don't," I said. "Things are fine the way they've always been."

Mr. Silver Shades perused the empty dining room dubiously. "I hope you have a backup plan for when this place shuts down. Shouldn't be long now."

I stared at him in shock. Had he really just said that my mother's restaurant was on the brink of closing?

"Bring us some water," the young man said, dismissing me outright. He turned his attention to our comprehensive menu, written in both English and Urdu. I walked away before I did something foolish, like empty the water jug over his head.

When we first opened, Three Sisters had been one of the few full-service restaurants that served halal meat, a fact that had enticed customers from all over the city. As Toronto's Muslim population grew, more halal restaurants began to pop up all over the city. A demographic shift occurred at the same time: second-generation immigrant kids weren't as interested in eating the South Asian staples their parents craved. Mr. Silver Shades was right. Three Sister Biryani Poutine had been open for fifteen years, but now we were in deep trouble.

"Your menu is very extensive. What would you recommend?" Mr. Silver Shades asked when I returned to take their order. Grumpy Dad had pulled out a pair of reading glasses and was examining his fork.

I rattled off our specialties, and the young man frowned at every choice, the notch above his eyebrows deepening with every word. He was contemplating walking out, I could tell. I knew Three Sisters would never win any prizes for beauty, but then, this man and his father would never win any prizes for grace.

"Why don't you just order what you think we'd like," he finally said. "Let's make it four dishes, and some mango lassi."

I chirped, "Sounds good!" and collected their menus. I wasn't sure if I should feel relieved they had stayed to fill our till, or disappointed that they hadn't left and saved me the trouble of serving people I disliked. Then again, they were probably strangers passing through Golden Crescent. I didn't recognize either of them, and I knew most of the people who lived in the neighbourhood. After this meal, I hoped I would never have to see Mr. Silver Shades and his grumpy dad ever again.

Chapter Two

I gave Mom the order: chicken biryani, malai kofta, dal makhani, and naan, then hung around the kitchen while Fazeela, Fahim, and Mom worked.

My sister Fazeela was sous-chef for the day and Fahim was in charge of the large tandoor clay oven that turned dough instantly into soft, crispy naan, while Mom assembled the biryani. Fazee and Fahim were discussing their favourite topic: baby names for the little cantaloupe.

"Hussain is a good choice," Fahim said, smiling. My brother-in-law was always smiling. A tall man with broad shoulders, he was rocking his usual outfit of dark Adidas track pants and hoodie, a perpetual athlete on his way to the gym. "That was my grandfather's name."

Fazeela shook her head. "Hussain is overplayed, like Hassan. Besides, we're having a girl."

"My cousin named her son Hassan. She's the one I was telling you about, the one who just bought a house in Saskatoon. You won't believe how little they paid. We should plan a visit to check it out."

Fahim's family lived in Saskatchewan, nearly three thousand kilometres from Toronto. My sister and brother-in-law had met in culinary school and married the previous year. Ever since Fazeela found out she was pregnant, Fahim hadn't stopped talking about moving west. My sister was less enthusiastic, and I was tired of that conversation.

I opened the messaging app to see if StanleyP had texted again, but Fazeela's teasing voice jolted me back to the kitchen.

"Are you talking to your mystery man again?" she asked, grinning. "It's that internet guy, right? The one from your podcast."

"You don't even listen to my podcast," I said, stashing the phone in my pocket.

"Marvin, or Alan, or Johnny, or—" Fazeela rattled off, ignoring me.

"Stanley," I muttered, instantly regretting it.

"Stanley!" Fazeela crowed. "Some random white dude from who knows where, and you're obsessed!"

"I'm not obsessed," I said, flushing and looking at my mother. "We're just friends. And how do you know he's white?"

Fazeela looked at me in disbelief. "He listens to podcasts."

She had me there. #PodcastsSoWhite.

"You text him more than I do Fahim, and we're married. Should we be concerned, Hanaan?"

My sister was the only one in the family who insisted on calling me by my full name, Hanaan. That's Hana with an extra *an*. At twenty-six she was two years older than me, and with her tall frame and impatient air, she looked like a younger version of our mother. When her athletic body, more used to running on a soccer pitch than standing around the kitchen, had begun to round with signs of new life, the resemblance had become remarkable.

Unlike Fazeela, I hadn't inherited our mother's tall, sturdy build. I was short, with tawny bronze skin and round hips. My eyes were hazel in the sun or after a bout of laughter, I had been told, but otherwise dark brown. My sister and I shared our mother's full, slanting eyebrows and full lips, though mine were set in a small triangular face, in contrast to my sister's more angular features.

"Leave her alone, Fazee," Fahim said, looking over at me with sympathy. "Remember how we used to be when we were first getting to know each other?"

"He's just a friend," I muttered. "I don't even know his real name."

"If the online guy isn't serious, there's always Yusuf," Fahim said to Fazeela. "He's single, he's nice. She could marry him."

"She will decide for herself when and if she wants to marry," I said firmly. "And Yusuf is my best friend."

"They can't all be your friends," Fazeela shot back.

Mom usually stayed out of our low-level bickering, but now she pinned the three of us with a look, and we instantly shut up.

"Hana, *beta*, after you serve the customers, I need you to run home and check on Baba before you leave for the radio station. He isn't picking up the phone," Mom said as I carefully picked up the dishes they had prepared.

My mother thought about everyone and everything, all the time. I wondered how she managed it all. Perhaps if I got my dream job, the income would help take some of the burden from her shoulders.

"Don't forget the mango lassi on your way out," Mom said.

AFTER I SERVED MR. SILVER SHADES and his grumpy father, I moved to the front of the restaurant, delaying my departure. I was waiting for my favourite moment.

I knew Three Sisters Biryani Poutine wasn't fancy. When Mr. Silver

Shades and the old man had insulted the restaurant, I felt defensive because their easy dismissal was often the first reaction of new customers. Until they tasted our food.

Mom had *haat ki maaza*, which is untranslatable Urdu for "magical cooking hands." The men tucked into their buttery dal makhani, lentil stew simmered with garlic and onions and topped with ghee. They soaked up malai kofta, dumplings made from mashed potato and paneer cheese, simmered in a tomato cream sauce, with fresh tandoori naan. They took sips of mango lassi, a fruit and yogurt smoothie, before digging into my mother's signature dish, chicken biryani. She had learned the recipe back home in New Delhi, and I had never tasted that combination of delicate saffron and fragrant spices anywhere else.

As they tasted each dish, their eyebrows rose. They took more bites, unable to believe their taste buds. A slow smile blossomed on Mr. Silver Shades' face, and it seemed real this time, not the polite expression he had worn when he told me to order his lunch. The men passed dishes back and forth. They closed their eyes in ecstasy as the complex flavours danced on their tongues.

Okay, I might have made that last part up. My mother is a good cook is what I mean. She might even be a cooking prodigy. It was how she had sustained the restaurant for all those years. So even though people hadn't been breaking down the door lately clamouring for her Indian staples, she still had *haat ki maaza*.

"Everything all right?" I asked, walking past with a pitcher of water.

The older man kept eating. Mr. Silver Shades, on the other hand, slowed down, a tablespoon heaped with biryani rice paused halfway to his mouth.

"What's wrong, too spicy?"

His father cracked a smile. That's how good my mom's food was: Grumpy Dad actually smiled.

The young man put the spoonful of rice in his mouth and chewed slowly. "It tastes like . . ." He looked disoriented. "Where did the chef learn to cook?" he asked me.

"Secret family recipe," I answered smoothly. "My mother learned from her mother, who learned from her mother."

"Your mother owns this restaurant?" Mr. Silver Shades asked, surprised. "I thought you were just the waitress."

Definitely a jerk.

"It's a family business," I replied, and he looked briefly disconcerted. *Good.*

"Why so much interest?" Grumpy Dad said. "Be quiet and eat the food. Our appointment to inspect the property is in half an hour."

"Are you moving into the neighbourhood?" I asked, filling up their glasses with water. *Please say no,* I thought.

The younger man didn't answer, only shook his head and ate another spoonful of biryani. His eyes fluttered closed and he inhaled deeply.

"What's your mom's name?" he asked. He turned to look at me, and this time I understood the emotion in his eyes. Mr. Silver Shades looked sad.

His father's brows drew together. "What is the problem?"

"This food, it reminds me of . . . the biryani reminds me of . . . Mom." He sounded awkward, as if the word *Mom* was not one he used often.

Grumpy Dad dropped his spoon with a clatter. "Don't talk nonsense. You don't remember what her food tasted like. You were a child when she died." He turned to me, brow thunderous, and I gripped the water pitcher tightly. This conversation felt too intimate. "Bring the bill, girl. Aydin can pay, since he wanted to check out this pile of dirt so badly." He rose and strode out of the restaurant.

Mr. Silver Shades had seemed to shrink at his father's words. Now he uncurled himself and removed a hundred-dollar bill from a sleek leather wallet. He placed it carefully on the table.

"Tell your mother the food was excellent," he said, without looking at me.

Aydin. Mr. Silver Shades' name was Aydin, and he missed his mother. I pocketed the money and began to clear the table.

I DUMPED THE PLATES ON the counter of the kitchen and began emptying the contents into the garbage. I hated that part, throwing away half-eaten food. Sometimes we gave away food that hadn't been served to a shelter.

My mother looked at me, expressionless. "They didn't like it?" she asked.

I hesitated. I wasn't sure what had happened. Instead I took out the hundred-dollar bill, more than double what the food and tip cost together. "They liked it fine. They just had to leave, for an appointment."

Fahim leaned against the counter. "One customer today, and they didn't even finish their food."

Mom picked up another plate and scraped it clean. "A few bad days only. We have run this place for fifteen years. There is no reason why your children will not one day work here during the summertime or after school, as you have done. It will all work out." She said that last part almost to herself. My sister and brother-in-law exchanged a quick glance.

I wasn't in the mood for the same conversation, the one that skirted the real question: How bad was it? Mom remained tight-lipped on the subject of our family finances, so we were all left to imagine the worst.

"I'll be back to help with dinner," I said instead.

They formed a tableau as I walked out: My sister, four months pregnant, her belly round, eyes lowered and eyebrows drawn together. My mother, absently stirring a pot of savoury chicken korma curry as Fahim loaded the dishwasher, his usual smile banished by worry.

That was their life. The life I had opted out of when I chose to pursue broadcast journalism.

Mom was big on choice. She hadn't pushed me to join her full-time in the food business. Baba had never encouraged us to study accounting like him. When my sister decided to go to culinary school, my mother had been happy to welcome her, but only because she came into the restaurant world with eyes wide open, prepared to survive on hope and prayer.

Fifteen years ago, Three Sisters had been the only halal restaurant in the area. That wasn't the case today, though we were still the only restaurant in Golden Crescent. It was ironic, then, that our origin story didn't revolve around food at all.

Three Sisters Biryani Poutine had been conceived by soccer. Premier rep soccer. The kind that costs thousands of dollars a year and had been completely unaffordable on my father's modest salary as a bookkeeper, even before his accident. But my sister Fazeela loved soccer, and she had been very, very good at it—ferocious and ambitious on the field in a way she had never been anywhere else. Mom supported my sister's talent in the best way she knew: she paid for the expensive lessons by starting a catering business. A few years later, Three Sisters Biryani Poutine was born.

Then FIFA, the official governing body for international football, had enacted a new dress code that banned all "headgear." The rule was unsubtly aimed at hijab-wearing Muslim female athletes. Fazeela had decided to stop playing soon afterwards.

I was pretty sure my sister was happy with her choices—she had Fahim, she had the little cantaloupe growing in her belly. But sometimes I wondered if she had made those choices because she felt she had to. Mom had started Three Sisters Biryani Poutine to pay for Fazeela's soccer dreams. And when those dreams died, maybe my sister's career choice had felt more like an inevitability.

Maybe I was the only one who would really get to choose anything. And I had chosen to get out.

Chapter Three

Three Sisters Biryani Poutine was located in a commercial strip surrounded by a dozen storefronts, all owned by first- and second-generation immigrant business owners. Luxmi Aunty ran the Tamil bakery next door, where she sold fresh-baked flatbread and fried savoury snacks such as samosas, chaat, and bhel puri, as well as Indian sweets. Sulaiman Uncle owned the halal butcher a few doors down. A florist shop that specialized in the elaborate garlands used in South Asian weddings and other celebrations stood beside a hair and nail salon that had curtains over the windows to accommodate hijab-wearing women looking for a blowout with some privacy. There was a convenience store that sold lottery tickets and henna cones, and a dry cleaner that knew how to get turmeric and oil stains out of clothes and offered an on-site seamstress.

The street was bookended by a Tim Hortons coffee shop at the north end, run by our business elder, Mr. Lewis, and at the south end by the hollowed-out shell of an abandoned storefront that had long ago been home to another restaurant. A tiny grocery stood directly across the street from Three Sisters, owned by my best friend Yusuf's Syrian family. Beside it was a computer and electronics repair shop that also offered wire money transfers around the world, and a South Asian bridal shop that specialized in bespoke *lenghas* and saris. The stores fronted the residential neighbourhood known as the Golden Crescent, named after its main street. According to local lore, the subdivision also formed the shape of a crescent on Google Maps.

I set off to check on Baba before my shift at the radio station, ducking around the back of the restaurant, through the parking lot, and deeper inside the Golden Crescent. Here the homes were built close together, semi-detached units and blocks of townhouses interspersed with two-storey houses with tiny front lawns. Driveways held two or three cars, usually minivans and older sedans. Extended families lived together, and basement tenants were common.

I turned onto my street, a cul-de-sac that backed onto a ravine. Our home was a split-level detached unit, and I ran up the half-dozen stairs to the front door, eyes resting briefly on the peeling paint that surrounded our large bay window. If Baba was having a good day, he would be dressed and seated in the living room, perhaps reading or working on a jigsaw puzzle. He would greet me with a smile and make a joke about how we worried unnecessarily, and I could text Mom with enough assurances to wipe the strain from her face.

But my father wasn't sitting in the neat living room on his favourite chair. A quick look revealed that he wasn't in the kitchen either, and there was no empty chai mug on the counter. I took the steps two at a time to the room my parents shared at the end of the hall. I knocked once and entered. He was still in bed.

"I tried to get up," Baba said, greeting me with an apologetic smile. "I'm feeling shaky today, and I didn't want to fall again."

Ijaz Khan was a diminutive man, and he seemed even more shrunken under the duvet. His face looked as if it had been assembled from mismatched Mr. Potato Head parts—dark slash of unibrow, large, bulbous nose, full lips, receding hairline—all on a beloved face. He wore oversized reading glasses that magnified his dark eyes. Mom had been right to send me; it was obvious he was in pain.

"Should I get your pills?" I asked gently. He nodded, and I went to the bathroom for his medication. I hated seeing him this way.

Two years ago my father's car had been struck by an SUV making a left turn, his compact sedan pushed into oncoming traffic, legs pinned by the wreckage. For a few weeks afterwards we hadn't been sure if he would ever walk again. Most of the insurance settlement went to paying for extra therapy, medicine, and help after the accident, and he hadn't worked regularly since. Before the accident my father had counted most of the businesses on Golden Crescent among his bookkeeping clients. Now he managed only a handful of storeowners loyal to him. Our family's ability to pay bills in a timely manner rested largely on the success of Three Sisters Biryani Poutine.

While we waited for his medicine to kick in, I switched on the radio he kept on the night table, tuned to the CBC. We listened to the last ten minutes of a tech program until he felt steady enough to grasp the handles of the walker I had moved near.

I helped Baba make his way down the steps, then busied myself in the kitchen, boiling water and heating milk for chai. He hated when I hovered. I buttered toast and brought his meal to the white plastic kitchen table.

"Play one of your podcast episodes, Hana *beta*," he said after taking a restorative sip of scalding hot chai. I had made a mug of the strong, milky tea for myself as well, and we settled down to listen. Baba was the only one in my family who had thought my podcast was a good idea. I scrolled to an episode I thought he would like, and pressed Play.

• • •

Welcome to Ana's Brown Girl Rambles, an anonymous podcast about life as a twenty-something Muslim woman in Canada.

I come from a long line of storytellers. My father loved to tell stories about his family and growing up in India. My sister and I never grew tired of hearing those tales. One of our favourite stories was about my father's oldest brother, who loved to play tricks on his siblings. One day their youngest sister and her friends were play-acting a wedding between their dolls, and my uncle insisted on participating. He would play the part of the imam and marry the dolls. He dressed up in a long robe and prayer cap, and when the time came for the wedding feast, my sister and her friends provided snacks: cakes, and sweet sherbet to drink. Naturally, the minute the nikah was over, my uncle had his friends swoop in and steal all the food, while he kidnapped the newly married dolls and held them for ransom in his hideout on the roof. He didn't let them go until his little sister and her friends agreed to hand over the bride's dowry—three bottles of cola, a toy car, and a handful of rupees.

Baba laughed aloud at my retelling of his mischievous brother's long-ago antics. While he listened to the rest of the podcast, I skimmed the comments.

COMMENTS

StanleyP
I'd like to meet your uncle.

AnaBGR
I haven't seen him in years, but he's a joker even as an adult.

StanleyP
All my relatives are boring.

AnaBGR
Do bots have family?

StanleyP
Only the cool ones, like me. It helps us appear more realistic. How's work going?

AnaBGR
Busy, occasionally soul-sucking, scattered with moments of awesome. You?

StanleyP
I tried pitching my idea the way you suggested. It didn't go over well.

AnaBGR
You need to make your slide deck pop. I told you to add a catchy playlist.

StanleyP
You've never worked in an office before, have you.

AnaBGR
Fine, don't listen to my excellent advice.

StanleyP
Nobody should, actually.

AnaBGR
And yet my listener count is up again. I didn't think anyone would be interested.

StanleyP
Yes, you did. Or you wouldn't have bothered.

AnaBGR
How do you know that?

StanleyP
You got me hooked.

My stomach knotted as I reread StanleyP's words from only a few months ago. This casual flirtation was starting to feel dangerous. What were we doing?

As my podcast self signed off, I looked for Baba's reaction. His wide grin wiped away the lines deeply etched around his mouth, so that he looked almost like the person he had been before the accident. My heart clenched at the sight of his fleeting joy.

Baba had been so happy when I decided to pursue a master's in broadcast journalism, so proud of my internship. He spent so much time at home now, listening to the radio or to podcasts online, that he had become convinced I would soon be given my own show. So far all I had done at my internship was sort archives and research stories. I had graduated the previous June and was still waiting to figure out my next move.

I deposited his empty plate and mug in the sink. "I'll be back late," I said. "I'm at the radio station, and then closing the restaurant afterward."

Baba nodded, hesitating. "How many customers today?" he asked.

I kept my face averted when I answered. "A slow day. Nothing to worry about."

"Things will get better," he said. "Inshallah."

I squeezed his shoulder, then pulled out the tray that held his latest jigsaw puzzle: a Scottish castle, five thousand pieces. I set it up on the coffee table before letting myself out the front door.

My phone pinged with a new email as I stepped onto the sidewalk. It was from the public radio broadcaster—the dream job StanleyP had asked me about earlier. *Please, Allah,* I prayed fervently. My fingers fumbled as I opened the email app. *Please, please, let this be good news.* I read quickly, eyes skimming, heart pounding.

Dear Ms. Khan,

Thank you for your interest in the position of junior producer. We regret to inform you the position has been filled. We thank you for participating in our interview process, as we encourage diverse voices to continue to apply and make a difference in the Canadian media landscape . . .

I deleted the message before reading the rest, and my fingers automatically moved to the messaging app. *I didn't get the job*, I typed to StanleyP, but then my fingers stilled.

Maybe this rejection was a sign that I should focus on what was happening right now, and not worry about dream jobs, or future relationships, that were out of my reach. I erased the message and walked to the bus stop. My dreams could wait a little while longer.

. . .

Welcome to Ana's Brown Girl Rambles, a podcast about the life of a twenty-something Muslim woman in Toronto.

One of the questions I posed in my first episode was about family. What do we owe the people who grew us up, who first made up our entire world?

It's complicated for the kids of immigrants. I'm not talking about the usual "my parents don't understand" thing. My parents believe in the power of choice, and they never asked me to sacrifice my dreams for theirs. Yet I feel like I should anyway. Where does that feeling come from? Is it just loyalty and strong family ties? Is it because, as part of a marginalized community, we all had to stick together to survive, and that sort of experience tends to become habit? Maybe it's about guilt. We are kids who benefited from the sacrifices our parents made when they decided to move to a richer, safer country. If we then grow up to grow apart, have we become ungrateful villains?

My parents would say I'm being dramatic. Maybe I am. Then again, the beauty of running an anonymous podcast is that I can be as dramatic as I like.

I do know that, for all the benefits of being the daughter of immigrants, the one drawback is I've had to establish my own sense of place. All my extended family live elsewhere, on a different continent, and we don't visit often enough to form real ties. There's a lot of freedom in being a pioneer of your family's history in a new place, of course. But there's a lot of loneliness too. I've had to find my own family, to make the sort of friendships that are family. Yet that lack of history means my roots here are shallow, my stories only a few years old.

Maybe that's why I'm feeling so restless today, a little bit stuck. I'm waiting for something, only I'm not sure what. This is when I imagine a different sort of restlessness—the kind my parents felt, the kind that drove them to get on a plane decades ago and leave behind their own world, full of stories and history, for something new.

In so many ways the choices they made have limited mine. No doubt the choices I make will do the same for the generation that follows. I guess we all make peace with that in the end.

Thanks for listening, friends. Let me know if you have similar stories and how you've navigated your own road.

COMMENTS

StanleyP
Great second episode!

AnaBGR
The bot returns.

StanleyP

I subscribed. I guess I'm a fan. My fam isn't as understanding as yours, but I feel you about the loyalty, and the guilt. Can't wait to hear what you come up with next. You should do this for a living.

AnaBGR

Inshallah.

StanleyP

God willing.

AnaBGR

Are you Muslim too?

StanleyP

Anony-Ana, if I answer that question, will you answer some of mine?

AnaBGR

Nope. Withdrawn.

StanleyP

Until next time.

Chapter Four

Radio Toronto was a popular indie station that aired a little of everything. We played local artists as well as Top 40 hits, reported on serious news as well as Toronto street culture. I had beaten hundreds of other applicants to secure my internship position, alongside fellow intern Thomas Matthews. Now that I had lost out on the only other job I really wanted, I was determined to get hired on permanently at the station once my internship ended. To do that, I needed to become indispensable to the station's general manager. Marisa Lake was a sophisticated white woman in her late thirties, tall and willowy, with sleek honey-brown hair pulled into a chignon and a silk scarf draped just so around her neck. Thomas, my fellow intern, thought she was sensitive about her neck.

"You're lucky, you cover all the time," he said now, gesturing at my hijab. We were sitting in our small office, surrounded by boxes of archives that hadn't been touched in decades. Our task was to sort and catalogue, and after two hours, we were both bored.

Thomas's family were Orthodox Christians from south India. He assumed that, as fellow desis, we shared a special connection. He also thought he should be the one offered the permanent job at Radio Toronto at the end of our internship. He was wrong on both counts.

"My neck is fine, thanks," I said.

"Women have all these hang-ups. If it's not their necks or toes, it's their eyebrows."

I peered inside a filing box and tried to tune him out.

"I know what your hang-up is," he said, voice sly. Thomas had dark brown skin and enormous eyes hidden behind circular wire-frame glasses. He favoured slim-fit cardigans and sweater vests, which he thought made him look like a Brown hipster. I knew better; desi Harry Potter would only ever look out for his own interests.

I also knew he wasn't going to let up until I reacted. Next to coming up with strange theories about the people in our office, Thomas loved to tease me.

"Okay, fine. What's my hang-up?" I asked.

He shrugged. "Your hair. That's why you wear that thing on your head."

"Hijab. Say it with me: *he-jab.*"

"The fact that you're so sensitive only proves me right. Tell me the truth. Are you one of those weirdos who can't stop chewing their hair?"

I slammed a file folder onto the desk. "I'm shocked you're still single. What's wrong, Mommy hasn't found you a wife yet?"

"Nobody does the arranged marriage thing anymore, Hana," Thomas said placidly, and I instantly regretted my bout of temper. "Except for crazy conservatives." His eyes lingered on my hijab. "Besides, I have a girlfriend," he said, pulling another folder towards him.

"Virtual girlfriends don't count."

"You would know all about virtual friends," he shot back, gaze resting on the phone in my hand.

I flushed and closed my messaging app. I hadn't been texting Stan-leyP at work, only checking whether he had texted me. He hadn't.

"What are you two talking about?" Marisa had wandered into the storage room. She grabbed a file at random, flicked through it, and put it down on the wrong pile. Today she was wearing light pink lipstick that matched her pale pink scarf, a shade I could never pull off. Marisa dressed more elegantly than her current job demanded. Thomas said it was because she was a woman on the climb.

I wanted to move up too, like Marisa. I even had a scarf collection, though I wore mine on my head instead of around my neck. We weren't so different.

"I'm making great progress with the files, Marisa," Thomas said. "I've got plenty of ideas to keep them organized from now on. I'd love to share them with you later."

I rolled my eyes, but Marisa only smiled faintly in our direction. She was no dummy.

"Thomas was just telling me about his girlfriend," I said, answering her question.

"Oh," Marisa said, a note of disappointment in her voice. "I was hoping to set the two of you up."

Thomas and I looked at each other in dismay and she left us to it.

Marisa called me into her office a few hours later. "I hope you weren't offended, sweetie," she said, indicating that I should take a seat. Her office was small and cramped, but she did have a small window that faced the parking lot. "I thought you and Thomas looked cute together."

I stifled my sigh. Marisa meant well—as much as someone who wanted to match up people by their skin tone could mean well. She didn't get that, although our parents were born in the same country, it didn't follow that we were destined to fall in love. I liked Marisa, so my tone was gentle when I replied. "We don't see each other like that. Also, he has a girlfriend."

"And do you have a boyfriend?" she asked.

My boss was trying to be friendly, but I suspected she also had a bit of a saviour complex, which I could use to my advantage. I thought quickly. "I just dumped him. I'm very committed to my job here at Radio Toronto." I tried to look earnest and deserving of opportunity.

Marisa fingered the scarf at her throat and smiled faintly. "I'm sorry to hear that," she said. "Though it's probably for the best. I'm sure your parents wouldn't approve of you dating before marriage."

I blinked. *What?* "I have no plans to marry until I establish my career," I said firmly.

Marisa looked doubtful. "I didn't know that was an option in your culture," she said. "But if that's the case, I need someone to help me produce *The Wrap-Up* tonight. Interested?"

I decided to let her comments go, because now she had my attention. *The Wrap-Up* was a big deal. A news and pop-culture commentary, it was Radio Toronto's most popular show, aired during our most coveted time slot, the afternoon rush hour, and hosted by our most popular host, Big J. Even my mother listened to the show.

Bonus: Thomas might actually choke with jealousy.

"Sure, I could do that," I said casually.

Co-producing *The Wrap-Up* meant I would miss my evening shift at the restaurant. When I called, Mom said they could manage without me, that I could help close the store after the show. She hesitated for a moment before she hung up. "Hana, we need to talk when you get home. Things are happening," she said carefully.

"What things?" I asked.

Silence. "We will talk tonight after closing."

BIG J WASN'T SO BIG in person, despite his booming voice. He swaggered into the studio an hour before his show began at four p.m., his presence filling the room with a warm, bouncing energy. He looked to be in his late twenties, with a sparse beard that lined full, smiling cheeks. His eyes were an intense blue and he was dressed in low-slung, baggy dark jeans and a white T-shirt that emphasized the slight pudge around his middle. His outfit was topped with a vintage purple Toronto Raptors hat.

Big J greeted Marisa with a quick hug and then, with a discreet glance at my hijab, nodded instead of trying to hug me too. Respectful *and* aware of my religion's practice of not casually touching a member of the opposite sex. I loved this guy.

"Hana is one of our interns, Jonathan. She'll be helping produce today," Marisa explained.

"What's up, my sister?" he said in the deep, melodic voice that would no doubt make him famous one day.

We spent the next hour going over the show, and at four o'clock Big J began with his characteristic catchphrase, "I hear you, Toronto. Are you ready for *The Wrap-Up*?" And then he was off, regaling his audience with local tidbits and anecdotes gleaned from the day's events, cracking jokes about celebrities and reality television one minute and making reference to French philosophers and Canadian history the next. Marisa watched intently, and I helped by keeping an eye on the screens for messages and answering questions posted by listeners on Facebook and Twitter. I posted pictures of the day's viral meme, of Big J drinking coffee from an enormous mug emblazoned with his catchphrase. His fan base had been growing steadily over the years, and he had already attracted the attention of several large broadcasters in the United States and Canada.

The show finished at eight p.m., and Big J flashed me a smile and a thumbs-up as he headed out of the studio. I was grinning so broadly my cheeks hurt, drunk on the rush of producing my first show. When I asked Marisa if she wanted me to help again the next day, she offered an approving smile.

"Of course, sweetie. You're a natural."

Chapter Five

On my walk back from the bus stop, I spotted my best friend Yusuf outside his family's grocery store. He waved and crossed the street, long legs swallowing the distance between us.

Yusuf looked a bit like a Syrian version of Prince Eric from *The Little Mermaid*—dark hair, green-hazel eyes, warm smile. He was ridiculously beautiful, but, save for a brief crush in Grade 6, I was immune to his gorgeous-man superpowers. Besides, his heart belonged to our other best friend, Lily. Yusuf was kind too, always volunteering for the mosque or raising money for his latest activist project. Right now he was finishing up a graduate degree in social work, public policy, and general do-goodery.

"Any aunties hassling you today?" I teased as he approached. Yusuf flushed, making me laugh.

As the local vegetable grocer, his family store was routinely mobbed by people—mostly women, I enjoyed pointing out—buying fresh produce for dinner. His father's customers loved him. Everybody loved beautiful Yusuf.

"Every time I look over, you're not here," he said instead.

"Busy. The restaurant, the radio station, my dad."

Yusuf nodded, his eyes softening. The pitying looks from friends, neighbours, strangers had become hard to bear since my father's accident. Thankfully, Yusuf knew when to change the subject. "It's been a long time since we all hung out. Lily has been working so hard, but she'd come out if you asked her," he said.

Our Three Musketeers gang—the soon-to-be Dr. Lily Moretti, Yusuf, and I—had been friends from childhood, though things had changed when my two best friends started dating. On top of that, we weren't together in school anymore, and our circles no longer intersected so easily. Still, he was right, it had been a while since we all hung out.

I texted Lily after Yusuf returned to the store. *Lil, thinking of you. It's been so long I forget what you look like. Here's a pic of me in case you're having the same problem.* I attached a cross-eyed selfie and ended the message with *I think your boyfriend misses you too. Let me know when you have time to meet. XX*

Yusuf and Lily had been together, on and off, for years. The fact that I wasn't sure if they were currently dating or not said a lot about how long it had been since the three of us spent time together.

The restaurant was about to close, and when I entered the dining room of Three Sisters, only a few customers remained, finishing their meals. I greeted the familiar faces without breaking stride and entered the kitchen, excited to share my news.

"Marisa said I was a natural at co-producing *The Wrap-Up* today!" I announced.

"That's so great, Hanaan," Fazeela said. She looked pale, and there were dark smudges under her eyes I hadn't noticed that morning. "We heard the show. Big J is so funny." Fazee was sitting on a stool, nursing a glass of water.

"I found memes for him of a mountain-climbing baby," I said proudly.

Fazeela smiled faintly and shifted in her seat, wincing. Before I could ask if she was all right, Mom sent me back into the dining room to tend to the remaining customers. She hadn't said a word about my news. I should have stopped off at home first and told Baba; he wouldn't have been too distracted to congratulate me.

Only three tables were occupied when I returned to the dining room. Imam Abdul Bari and his wife were tucked into the corner booth for their weekly date night. Two other tables were in use by single patrons: a lone white woman with frizzy hair and oversized glasses perched on the end of her nose, and Haneef Uncle, who was addicted to my mother's chai.

Abdul Bari greeted me with his habitual smile. "How is the world of broadcasting, Sister Hana?"

Abdul Bari was the imam at the local mosque, the Toronto Muslim Assembly. His smiling presence was a great improvement over our previous imam, whom I had nicknamed "the Gorgon" because of his stern demeanour and boring sermons. I hadn't attended the mosque during the Gorgon's reign, but Imam Abdul Bari had coaxed me back. In his own way, he was as magnetic as Big J.

"I co-produced *The Wrap-Up* today," I said, beaming. I couldn't stop thinking about Marisa's praise—*You're a natural.* After months of tedious research and busywork, I was finally one step closer to learning more about the production part of my job. Baba wanted me to host my own show one day, but my ambitions were more modest. I loved researching stories that meant something to me, then figuring out how to present them in a way that would entice listeners. For me, hosting was secondary. I think that was why podcasting appealed so much. I had complete control and I was free to talk about whatever I liked.

"*Mabrook!* It is important for young Muslims to tell their stories. Your parents must be so proud," the Imam said.

His wife, Nalla, noticed my hesitation and squeezed my hand. "Your mother works so hard. I'm sure she's proud in her own way."

Nalla looked tired, her face thin. Imam Abdul Bari had never said anything, but everyone knew she wasn't well. I had watched her grow weaker with every date night, observed the strain on her face when she walked, the slow way she chewed, as if even the act of eating exhausted her. The Imam, always tender with his wife, had become even more solicitous recently.

The restaurant emptied and I locked the front door and began to clean up, wiping tables, stacking chairs, my mind elsewhere. I pulled out my phone. Still no message from StanleyP. Fazeela was right, I was obsessed.

A knock at the door shook me out of my reverie. Mr. Silver Shades—Aydin—stood framed by the entrance.

We're closed, I mouthed, and made a shooing motion with my hand.

He knocked again, a pleading expression on his face.

I contemplated my options. I could hear laughter from the kitchen, and I knew Mom, Fahim, and Fazeela were in there cleaning up. Besides, Aydin seemed harmless, and I could use the distraction. Plus he had left a massive tip. Maybe he had come back looking for change.

"We don't make change for abandoned meals," I said as I opened the door.

Aydin leaned against the door frame, hands in his pockets. "I'm not looking for change," he said. I waited for him to tell me why he was there, but he only blinked and said nothing.

I left the door propped open and returned to wiping tables. He followed me inside.

"Do you work at the restaurant every day?" he asked. "It's a school night."

I reached for the broom. "I'm twenty-four years old. I have two university degrees and three jobs, if you include having to make small talk with overtippers."

He half smiled. "You look young. It must be the—" He waved vaguely in the direction of my face. "Where else do you work?"

"Radio Toronto," I said, and waited for the inevitable blank look.

Instead he surprised me by grinning widely. The expression was so unexpected I stopped to stare. "I love radio," he said. "Back home in Vancouver, I went to live tapings of some of the local shows. Have you ever been to a live taping?"

"Yes," I replied, dazed. "A few times."

Aydin's grin turned delighted. "My friends call me a vintage nerd, but I don't care. There's something about listening to someone talk, the sound of their voice, sharing their personal stories and dreams . . ."

Our eyes met. Aydin looked away first, embarrassed by his enthusiasm. He passed a hand through thick, dark hair. "I'm twenty-seven but I've only managed one degree. Business and accounting, from UBC," he said, shrugging. "It was what my dad wanted."

I shifted, remembering the autocratic way Aydin's father had spoken to him. Now that I knew he was a fellow radio nerd, I felt myself softening. But that still didn't explain what he was doing there.

"Did you forget something?" I asked.

He stopped his slow pacing. "I came here to say sorry."

Better and better. I appreciated a man who could make amends.

"No matter what happens in the kitchen, never apologize," I said, quoting Julia Child.

Aydin blinked rapidly. I wondered if he knew he did that when he was flustered. "I meant I'm sorry I didn't get to finish the rest of that biryani."

I wasn't sure how to take that, but when I looked at Aydin again, I was pretty sure he was trying to be funny. Plus I'm a sucker for anyone who flatters my mom's food. I left him there without a word, filled up a plate, and headed back to the dining room.

Aydin had taken a seat in the same booth when I returned. I handed him the food before continuing my closing routine, occasionally stealing looks at his face as he slowly, reverently ate the basmati rice and meat. A few times I caught him looking at me.

"It would taste better with cheese curds and gravy," I called over my shoulder.

He smiled, the expression so fleeting I might have imagined it. I moved on with my chores, refilling bottles with Mom's famous mango-lemon-pickle achar, sneaking glances at my unexpected visitor. Had he really returned for another taste of my mother's biryani, or did he also want to talk to me? I examined the thought, turning it over in my mind. He was cute; he liked our food; he had the rudiments of a sense of humour. Maybe he wasn't that arrogant after all.

I looked over at him again, and our gazes tangled. "You keep staring at me," I said.

Aydin immediately glanced away, a slow flush creeping across velvet-smooth skin. "You remind me of someone," he muttered.

I should be wary of him, this strange man I don't know. Except, after a lifetime in the service industry, I had become adept at reading people, and I was pretty sure Aydin was harmless. In fact, there was something comforting about his awkwardness. He seemed younger tonight, more carefree. I noticed his hair was shaggy, curling around the collar of his black shirt; the same silver sunglasses dangled from the front pocket.

"What's your name?" Aydin asked after a few minutes of contented chewing.

"Waitress," I teased.

"No, really."

"Waitress who ordered your lunch."

He made a face.

"Waitress you overtipped and who doesn't make change."

Aydin stood up and placed the wiped-clean plate on the counter. Then he grabbed three bottles and began filling them with achar.

"What are you doing?"

"You'll be done faster if I help you. My name is Aydin, in case you were wondering."

"I heard your dad."

A shadow crossed his face at the mention of his father, but he answered lightly. "You were paying attention."

"I have exceptional hearing."

"I bet you do, *Hana.*"

I stopped. "How do you know my name?"

He nodded at my shirt front, where my name tag was pinned.

"So you can read," I muttered, and he laughed softly.

"Why is this restaurant called Three Sisters Biryani Poutine?" he asked.

I reached for empty salt shakers but paused. They didn't need refilling today; we hadn't had enough customers. To distract myself from that train of thought, I related our origin story and the part I had played in it. "My mom thought 'Three Sisters' sounded better than two. I thought 'Biryani Poutine' made the restaurant sound interesting—a fusion of Indian and Canadian cuisine. Even though we only serve Hyderabadi food."

Aydin smiled widely. "Let me get this straight: there's no third sister and there's no poutine on the menu. I can't believe this place has stayed in business all these years."

"We're a beloved local institution," I protested. I glanced at the full salt shakers. Well, we had been.

He didn't hear me, too busy casting that focused gaze around the interior of the restaurant. "This place isn't completely hopeless," he mused. "A coat of paint, maybe some tablecloths and brighter, bigger lights, would really perk the place up."

"We don't need a makeover," I said, defensive.

Aydin's expression was full of pity as he faced me, a doctor about to deliver bad news. "Your mom's biryani is amazing," he started. "So is the rest of her food, but it's all the usual desi staples—rice and spice. The name of the restaurant is confusing for both your desi and non-desi customers. The first time I walked in here, I nearly turned around and went somewhere else, the interior looked so old and dingy. Your customers have become more discerning. They can pay for better and they expect more."

His words were a slap across the face. It was one thing to know that our restaurant had seen better days, but another to hear criticism from a stranger's mouth.

"The only reason you're still open is because you don't have any competition," Aydin continued. "You're the only halal restaurant in the Golden Crescent. This area is full of South Asian immigrants, and a lot of them eat only halal meat. But it's clear this area is about to change, maybe one day soon. The only thing you can count on is change. You should be getting ready to face it, not hiding behind the same old menu and decor."

His arrogant tone was back, and my shoulders were near my ears now. "I didn't ask for your opinion, Aydin," I said, voice tight. "You don't get to inhale our food and then criticize the way we do things. What do you know about running a restaurant?" Did he think, because he could afford to drop a hundred dollars on food that had cost less than half that, he could lecture me about my family's business? Hell no.

Aydin was surprised at my reaction. "I'm just being honest. Your family clearly needs help."

"We don't want your help." I thought about my mom, and Fahim, and my exhausted-looking sister. They struggled every day to survive in a notoriously difficult business. Who did Aydin think he was?

He examined my face carefully, and I felt that same prickly sensation at the back of my neck under his watchful gaze.

"Your family is stuck in the old way of doing things, Hana," he said. The friendly man of a few minutes ago was gone, replaced by this cold figure who reminded me uncomfortably of his father. Someone who assumed he knew better than me. "Three Sisters may have been running for fifteen years, but you're clearly in trouble now. You seem like a nice enough girl. I'd hate to see your family destroyed because you refuse to look outside your front window."

Girl. I was a *nice girl*, unprepared to face the truth. For a moment I saw red, and he must have seen the fury on my face, because he took one step backwards.

"Who are you?" I asked. Aydin's visit hadn't been so innocent or casual after all, I realized, and my anger was partly at myself for being naive, for thinking a random cute boy would return simply to chat with me and enjoy my mother's cooking. He was there to fish for information, and I had opened up like a mailbox.

Aydin shook his head. "I'm nobody. Thanks for the biryani. I'll see you around."

I closed the door behind him, though I really wanted to slam it shut. My hand stilled on the lock as I remembered Aydin's words. How did he know that Three Sisters had been going for fifteen years?

When I turned around, my mother was framed in the entrance to the kitchen. I didn't know how long she had been standing there, or what she had overheard.

"Hana," she said, "we need to talk."

Chapter Six

Mom wasn't freaked that I had been talking to a boy. I should make that clear, because some people have funny ideas about Muslim women. Let me illustrate: when I was eleven years old, she sat me down and gave me the birds-and-bees talk. Only she used the scientific words and talked about pleasure and responsibility, ending with "That is how babies are made. Yes, even you."

It worked. I was so turned off by her frank discussion of sex that I didn't even think about relationships until I was halfway through high school, when I finally clued in to her plan. But by then it was too late. I was already the nerdy Brown hijabi who didn't date—not to be confused with the nerdy Brown hijabi who did date. That girl wore glasses.

Mom wasn't easily freaked out by anything, is what I mean. Ghufran Khan was the unflappable queen of our family. And now she wanted to talk to me about something serious. I braced myself and followed her to the now empty kitchen. Fazeela and Fahim must have left by the back entrance.

"What do you want to talk about?" I asked.

She seemed distracted, fiddling with a large pot left to soak in the sink. "That was the boy who left before finishing his food. Why did he return?" she asked. She was stalling, which only made me more nervous.

I was still shaken by the abrupt turn my conversation with Aydin had taken, but I didn't want to alarm my mother. "He wants to marry your biryani," I replied.

She smiled faintly. "He can't afford the dowry," she said, and passed a hand over her face. Was there the faintest hint of exhausted despair in her eyes? Impossible. She was Angela Merkel in no-nonsense black hijab.

"Hana, I'm only telling you this so you won't worry," she began, and I tensed. Why did people always say that? *Don't worry about this terrible thing I'm about to tell you.* That really helped calm everyone down.

"Are you sick?" I asked. "Is it Baba?"

She shook her head. "Fazeela has been having a more difficult pregnancy than we anticipated. She has been having trouble keeping up with things. And business has been slowing down lately, so . . ."

My heart clenched. Was Fazeela okay? Had she left early because something was wrong? Or was the restaurant in real trouble this time? Aydin's words floated back to me: *The only thing you can count on is change.* I hated change.

I looked at my mother, so proud, so strong. "What can I do to help? I can work here full-time if Fazeela needs to rest."

She shook her head. "You have your radio internship to finish. I know how important that is, how hard you worked to get that position. But I also can't afford to hire anyone new."

"I can pick up more shifts, learn how to cook things . . ." I trailed off, thinking about the opportunity to co-produce *The Wrap-Up*. That job would go to Thomas now.

"Hana, please stop jumping to conclusions. What I'm trying to tell you is that Rashid will be moving in with us for a few months. You remember, your cousin from India. He wants to study in Canada. His parents are worried he'll get in trouble if he lives on his own. I told Aneesa we would keep an eye on him."

It took me a minute to place Rashid in my large mental catalogue of relations. He must have been eighteen years old by now, the son of my mother's first cousin Aneesa. I remembered a shy boy who hid behind his mother's salwar kameez and had solemnly bested me at tic-tac-toe the last time we visited India.

"You don't even know this kid," I said. "Can he manage in the restaurant?"

Mom shook her head. "He's family. Aneesa would never let him live by himself, and we need the help. This is the best solution for everyone."

Or you could ask for my help, I thought, and instantly felt foolish. Could I really sacrifice my internship now, just when I was getting somewhere?

"Can you get his room ready? Rashid will sleep in the basement," Mom said.

I promised to change the linens and prepare the space for a cousin I barely knew. She also asked if I could pick him up from the airport on Friday after jumah, and I agreed. It was the least I could do.

IT WAS PAST TEN P.M. when we arrived home, and Mom immediately went to her room and closed the door. Baba was likely already asleep.

I was bone-tired, the excitement of the day finally catching up with me. Which was when I discovered that my mother had forgotten to share a second, tiny detail: Rashid wasn't the only one moving in.

The front door of our house opened into a square family room that led to a galley kitchen and attached dining room. There were three bedrooms upstairs. My parents shared the largest room, which had a tiny ensuite bathroom, on the far side of the upper floor, leaving the two smaller rooms and full bathroom on the other side for me and Fazeela.

Fazeela had started sleeping in the basement during high school, ostensibly so she could have a quiet space to study, but I knew it was so she could sneak out of the house to hang with her friends on school nights while our parents worked. In exchange for my silence, she let me have her closet and stored her clothes on a rack in the basement.

I used her empty room to organize my carefully curated hijab-friendly wardrobe—cardigans, long sweaters, flowy dresses, palazzo pants, overcoats, and boxes and boxes of scarves in every print, colour, fabric, and style. Yes, even leopard print. Colourful hijabs were my vice.

So I was surprised when I entered my bedroom to find the contents of my second closet dumped unceremoniously on my bed. Just then Fahim walked in, holding another armful of my clothes.

"Hey, Hana, what's up?" my brother-in-law said, dropping the second pile on top of the first.

"Oh, hey, Fahim," I said, leaning against the door frame. "Need somewhere to store your basketball shoe collection?"

Fahim's smile faded. "I guess your mom didn't tell you. Fazeela is moving back here for a little while. Your dad can keep her company while we're at the restaurant. The obstetrician Lily recommended said she needs to be on bedrest for a while. Fazee's been so worried, and that's not good for the baby . . ."

He kept on talking, but I had stalled on *bedrest* and *Lily recommended*.

"Is Fazee okay? Where is she?" I rushed past my brother-in-law to the small room next door. My sister was curled on the bed, asleep, and I stared at her for a moment. She looked pale but her breathing was even. I removed the final load of clothes from the closet and closed the door gently behind me.

"She's fine, Hana," Fahim said. He was in the hallway, and I could see shadows under his eyes. "She just needs to take it easy for a few weeks."

I wanted to trust Fahim, but what if my family wasn't telling me the whole story? Lily would know what was going on.

I grabbed my phone from my desk. "I'll be right back."

Chapter Seven

clutched my phone tightly and walked in the direction of my old elementary school. It was a warm spring night and the air felt cool on my face, carrying the promise of chlorine-scented rain. A car passed, headlights momentarily blinding me, but I knew the route so well I could walk it blindfolded. I had grown up playing on those streets and riding my bike with friends, pint-sized masters of our small domain. It was past ten, yet I felt completely safe walking alone in the dark. Because of Three Sisters, everyone knew who I was: Ghufran Khan's youngest daughter—not the one who used to play soccer, but the shorter one.

Weather permitting, during the day the streets would be filled with children skipping and playing hopscotch or conducting street-wide games of hide-and-seek, of which I had been the undisputed champion. Yusuf had been heavily involved in rotating local games of basketball and cricket, usually played on the biggest driveway. Lily and I preferred softball, or we would ride our bikes to the local library, where uncles dressed in starched kurtas paired with cardigans lounged on well-worn sofas, reading newspapers from around the world. Older women watched grandchildren while their adult children worked. As a child I had become used to seeing *nanis* and *dadis* dressed in saris, cotton salwar kameez, or long abayas chasing after toddlers and keeping a close eye on all the neighbourhood kids. To be scolded by somebody's grandmother was an almost daily occurrence for me when I was young.

I passed a few families in their garage-turned-gathering-spaces, drinking tea and chatting quietly, a nod to faraway homes with central courtyards. Many of my neighbours had grown up in extended families or small villages; they were used to communal living. My own family was usually too busy to hang out that way. Entire weeks would sometimes go by when we would see each other only while working at Three Sisters. I felt a pang at my neighbours' intimacy, even as I waved to familiar faces.

My late-night stroll ended at a small bungalow beside my old school. I sent a follow-up text to the one I had sent when I left my house. A few minutes later the side door opened and a shadowy form joined me on the front steps of the house.

"I just lost my second closet," I said.

My best friend Lily balanced herself on my shoulder as she stretched one leg and then the other. She was shapely and tall, hair coiled in a neat high bun, face glowing with good health and an excellent skincare routine. "I was sleeping off a twenty-hour shift. So glad you woke me up for this," she said, nudging me gently with her shoulder.

"I hear my family has been asking you for medical advice," I said, my voice unsteady with emotion. My friend knew what I was really asking.

"Fazee is exhausted. She's worried about the restaurant and about being a mom, and she hasn't been taking care of herself. She needs some rest, but she'll be back to normal soon. I promise," Lily said with such calm assurance that I felt better immediately.

Lily had been on rotation at SickKids hospital for the past few months. We had attended the same elementary school, high school, and university, and we'd remained best friends throughout, even though we had nothing in common. She was studious and organized and loved all things science and math; I was into pop culture and radio and considered deadlines as merely suggestions. She had known exactly what she wanted to do with her life from the age of six. It had taken me a little longer: I realized my future was in broadcasting only in my final year of college.

Yet Lily and I had always had each other's back, at least until the past few months. I knew she was busy. The residency program she was applying to was highly selective, and I hadn't wanted to play the needy friend. But then, why hadn't she said anything about my own sister?

"I thought I sent you a text last week so you wouldn't worry," Lily said, anticipating my question. She stretched elegant hands towards the sky and yawned. "When Fahim called, I recommended an ob-gyn I know, someone who specializes in at-risk pregnancies."

"Is my sister at risk?" I asked, worried again.

"Not yet, but she's being monitored closely." She stood up. "Come on. I'm going to fall asleep if we stay here."

We walked next door to the school, slipping past the metal fence into the playground. She took the swing to the left and I took the one on the right, as always.

Lily's curly hair came loose as she swung. At the highest point of the arc, she jumped from the swing, landing lightly on the sand in front of me, high bun unravelled into a dark swirl over her delicate shoulders.

I followed and sailed through the air, landing with such force that

I lost my balance and fell backwards onto my butt; thankfully it was well cushioned from too many onion pakoras, so it didn't hurt. Lily collapsed on the sand next to me, giggling, and I felt a sudden wave of fondness for my friend, the busy doctor who had come outside to play with me.

"I miss you," I said, and her eyes softened.

"How's your dad? The restaurant? Your mom?" Lily got along well with both my parents, but she had a soft spot for my mom. We had spent many hours as kids completing homework at Three Sisters, inhaling whatever food my mom had made for us that day. Lily had a serious addiction to palak paneer—Indian cheese cooked in a spicy spinach curry—and fresh naan.

I shrugged. "She's convinced it's just a slump, but I don't know how much longer we can go on."

Lily reached across and hugged me tight. "Ghufran Aunty is the smartest, most hard-working woman I know. But if the restaurant has to close, maybe that wouldn't be the worst thing . . ." She trailed off as I shook my head slowly, rejecting her words.

"We can't shut down Three Sisters," I said.

"You don't even like working there," she said gently. "Your future is in a sound booth."

"It would kill my mom. Baba isn't healthy enough to work full-time, and I'm just an intern. We'd lose the house. And now with Fazee on bedrest . . ." I closed my eyes, willing myself not to cry, and Lily sat with me in the dark until my breathing steadied.

I opened my eyes and she stared at me, blue eyes steady on my face. "Your family will be fine. Inshallah," she said, smiling. She had picked up some Muslim lingo over the years. When she made a promise, she even added *wallahi*—"I swear to God"—despite being quietly agnostic.

I needed to change the subject. "Yusuf misses you too. What's going on with you two? Are you together again or not?"

Lily shrugged and traced circles in the sand. It was dark, but the street lamp illuminated the faint blush spilling across her cheekbones. I couldn't help feeling proprietary about both of them; I was the one who had introduced them all those years ago.

Lily had been the new girl in Grade 4, and Yusuf hadn't been too happy about the new addition to our twosome. Yusuf and I were already best friends by then because of the proximity of our parents' stores, and we attended the same mosque. Lily hadn't known anyone, and I was determined to adopt her from the moment Mrs. Walker introduced the grave-looking girl to our class.

Lily had been dressed in white tights, a demure plaid skirt, and white blouse buttoned to her chin, her hair in two thick, dark braids. I had been wearing my usual school uniform of black tearaway track pants and a cardigan with a bright red, yellow, purple, and green swirly pattern, a throwback to early 2000s cool. My black hair was wild and frizzy, the neat braid unravelled five minutes after my mother had plaited it that morning. I didn't start wearing hijab until years later, in high school, after Fazeela started wearing it first.

That day on the playground, I introduced Lily to Yusuf. "We're going to be friends," I told him. "Like the Three Musketeers. She doesn't know anyone else here."

Yusuf ground his sneakers into the dirt, not making eye contact. "She can't play in a skirt," he said, voice mutinous.

Lily spoke up. "I can play in a skirt, and I can do it better than you," she said serenely.

We both looked at her in astonishment. She hadn't said a word all day, only listening as our classmates chatted. I had thought she was shy and in need of mentorship. I was delighted to be wrong.

"Boys against girls!" I crowed, grabbing my new friend's hand and running away from Yusuf. He was beautiful even as a child, but when he frowned, he looked like a sulky baby. I laughed back at him. "Baby Yusuf!"

Beside me Lily giggled, and something in Yusuf snapped. He ran after us and we ran away, squealing in delight. Never much of a long-distance runner, I gave up quickly. Yusuf tagged me and then set his sights on Lily. They ran all around the playground, Lily grinning widely, Yusuf looking determined.

"Guys, stop!" I yelled, but they ignored me. "Let's play something else!"

But they only had eyes for each other. I watched them zigzag through children skipping rope and dodge straight through an intense Grade 6 basketball game without breaking a sweat. When Yusuf finally caught up to Lily, he grabbed her hands and swung her around. She tripped and tore her pristine white tights. When I reached them, they were examining her bloody knee and Yusuf was looking sheepish.

"I'm sorry," he said. "You're not going to start crying, are you?"

With a disdainful look, she stood up and tore off her tights, balling them up and throwing them in Yusuf's face. Then she took off again, laughing at our stunned faces.

We had been inseparable since that day on the playground, up until the past year. Maybe growing apart was part of growing up.

My phone pinged, interrupting the silence with a message from StanleyP.

StanleyP
Checking in re: dream job. Is it time to fire the confetti cannons? I have some news to share too!

I fumbled, closing the screen, but Lily had seen. "Your mystery friend?" she asked, and it was my turn to blush.

"Nothing to see here," I muttered.

"It might be time to do something about that whole situation—" she started.

"This from Ms. Indecisive," I countered. "Do you love Yusuf or not?"

"It's not that simple for us. His dad . . . My mom is . . ."

Lily didn't have to fill in the blanks for me. Theirs was an inter-religious relationship frowned upon by both sides. Lily was not religious, but her Italian Catholic family did not approve of her feelings for her childhood best friend who happened to be a practising Muslim and the son of Syrian immigrants. That disapproval was very much mirrored by Yusuf's parents. As a result, my friends' on-again status had mostly been kept secret from both families, as their off-again status was so clearly desired by both. I was the only person either could confide in. Sometimes I wondered why they bothered, whether their feelings for each other were worth all the trouble.

"At least you know who you're dealing with. I know nothing about my online . . . friend," I said.

"If only there were some way to fix that situation," my friend mused in the dark. She snapped her fingers. "I have an idea! Maybe you could try asking him." She giggled as I shoved her. "Come on. What's the worst that could happen?"

I mentally listed my reasons. *What if we started revealing things about ourselves and he turned out to be different from how I imagine him? I would lose someone important to me—a confidant, an accomplice, a well-wisher. The one person who liked my podcasts from the very start.*

I shrugged. "Nothing, I guess. I should . . . I will."

Lily shook her head, smiling slightly. "I know what that means. But you do what feels right, Han. Just let me do the same, okay?"

I hugged her. "Get some sleep, Dr. Moretti," I said. "Try not to forget me while you're busy saving everyone else."

We made plans to meet the next week on her day off. I walked her back home before standing under a street lamp for a few moments, texting StanleyP.

AnaBGR
Didn't get the gig. They went in another direction.

StanleyP
WHAT? Who are these people? They have an angry bot heading their way.

AnaBGR
Nice try.

StanleyP
At least let me do some low-level subtweeting. They're crazy not to hire you.

AnaBGR
You don't even know what the job was. Maybe I wasn't meant to be an Etsy overlord.

StanleyP
I know you applied for a job in radio, Ana. IMO, anyone who has listened to your podcast and doesn't immediately want to see what you can do with actual resources is an idiot.

I stood in the dark for a moment, reading and rereading StanleyP's words. He had no idea how much they meant.

AnaBGR

Thank you. You said you have news too.

StanleyP

It's nothing.

AnaBGR

Friends don't let friends pass up an opportunity to gloat.

StanleyP

When you put it like that . . .

AnaBGR

I insist. Give me some good news.

StanleyP

My project is a go. I signed the contract today. My boss is convinced I know what I'm doing, enough to give me the seed money to take a real leap. We open at the end of the month. I still have some complications to take care of, but I'm excited.

AnaBGR

As my people say, *mabrook*! I remember when you first started talking about this secret project of yours.

StanleyP

It was one of your podcast episodes that inspired me to take the leap.

AnaBGR

I'm almost tempted to break our pact and ask for details. But I won't.

StanleyP

How about this? When my project goes live, I'll send you a picture of what I've been working on, and then you can decide what to do with that information. Deal?

It seemed a neat solution to the problem of moving forward or not. If he sent me a picture of something strange, such as a collection of severed doll's heads, that would be a clear sign not to take the relationship any further. I also liked the idea of a deadline for making a decision about us. End of next month—four weeks away. Far enough away to feel comfortable, yet close enough to stay relevant.

AnaBGR

Deal.

I put my phone away and walked home, contemplative in the humid darkness.

Chapter Eight

Thomas was already in our shared office when I rushed through the door the next day, late and flustered.

"Marisa is looking for you," he said with a cheerful smile.

Shit. My boss was a stickler for punctuality.

"She wanted to talk to you about co-producing *The Wrap-Up*. We agreed that to be equitable, we should both get a chance to produce. My turn is today." Thomas's smile moved into smirk territory. "Marisa also wanted to let you know about a big opportunity."

I was instantly wary. "What opportunity?"

Thomas shrugged. "I'm not your secretary. Ask her yourself."

I shrugged off my jacket and made my way to Marisa's office, knocking once before poking my head in the door.

"Hana! Thank god you came to work." Marisa was dressed in a navy-blue blazer and black jeans, a red and black scarf tied jauntily around her neck. "Thomas said you had some family drama going on. You know you can talk to me about anything, right?"

What was she talking about? I decided to change the subject. "You wanted to speak to me?"

Marisa leaned back in her chair, eyes shining with enthusiasm. "Nathan Davis is coming to our studio in a few days, and he wants to hear more about your fantastic idea for a show."

Nathan Davis was the director of broadcasting for our parent corporation, and every radio station in the province was under his jurisdiction. He was several steps above even Marisa's boss. What was he doing visiting our station, and what fantastic idea was Marisa talking about? She had shot down every suggestion I had made since I started working there, almost a year ago. The confusion must have been clear on my face.

"Thomas told me all about your radio partnership. I am so excited to hear more about this strategic diversity initiative to access multicultural target markets!"

Though I still had no idea what Marisa was talking about, I was pretty sure this was all Thomas's fault. I gritted my teeth, thanked her for the opportunity, and went in search of my "radio partner."

A contrite-looking Thomas was waiting for me in our office. "Don't get mad," he began. "Really, this is your fault for being late all the time. Marisa just burst in, babbling about Davis visiting the station and how it would be a good opportunity to pitch a show to him. Lucky for you, I'm great at thinking on my feet."

Thomas was terrible at thinking on his feet. From the twitchy expression on his face, he knew the next words out of his mouth might very well be his last. "I told her we wanted to host a show that teaches listeners about our different cultures," he said, and braced himself.

I stared at him, appalled. Thomas was a weasel, so I would have assumed he'd be eager to take the opportunity for himself. Then again, he could be strategic when required. I thought I knew the answer, but I asked the question anyway. "You don't like me. Why should we work together on this?"

"If there's two of us, they're more likely to give us a chance to do our own show. I need you for this, Hana!"

He meant *us* as in "two Brown people." He meant *they* as in the higher-ups, who had lately been coming under attack for their lack of diverse programming in one of the most diverse cities in the world. Thomas was taking his shot and dragging me along with him.

I didn't punch him. At heart I'm a pacifist. Instead, I walked out of the office without a word.

WORKING ON A SHOW—ANY SHOW—WAS all I had ever wanted to do. So far, all Thomas and I had done in our internship was file, photocopy, archive, and research other people's stories. The first time I had done a job that excited me had been the day before, when Marisa let me co-produce Big J's show.

Hosting a show about culture and religion was not what I wanted to do. The worst part was, Thomas knew how I felt. We had talked about it before.

"Who is going to tell the stories only we know? We're South Asian, we're second-generation immigrants, you're Indian Muslim and I'm Indian Christian—both minorities within minority communities. We have things to say and diverse perspectives that people would love to hear," he had argued.

"Is that your tag line? *I'm Brown, I'm interesting, listen to me?* The minute I start writing stories about the Muslim or desi community, I'll be put in a box, and that will be all I'll ever do or ever be known for.

I'm too young and interesting to be the 'exotic Brown-person expert' for the next thirty years," I argued back.

"Hana, you could be the person who changes people's minds about Muslims!" Thomas would counter.

That comment always made me laugh. "The bigots are never going to listen to me. And everyone else already likes me because, as an Indian-Canadian, I stand for samosas and maple syrup. I'm good."

The truth was, Thomas had less to lose. When a man talks about politics and religion next to a brown-skinned woman who wears hijab, guess who attracts the misogynist trolls and violent death threats? I come by my cowardice honestly, through the experiences of those braver than myself. I had no desire to be a social justice martyr.

I wanted to follow my instincts and my own interests, not use my faith and skin colour to provide teachable moments to listeners on demand. Thomas knew how I felt, yet he had pitched his stupid idea anyway. He really was the worst.

I took out my phone and messaged StanleyP.

AnaBGR
How good of an advice-giver are you?

StanleyP answered back immediately.

StanleyP
I am regularly consulted by sitting monarchs, regents, prime ministers, and benevolent dictators. Celebrities have me on speed dial.

AnaBGR
Not sure I can afford your consultation fee.

StanleyP

We can work out a payment plan. What troubles you?

AnaBGR

Would you accept a job that helped your career if you had to sell
out on the reasons you got into the field in the first place?

StanleyP

I take it the world of Supreme Etsy Overlord is more fraught
than you first thought. Ah, the naïveté of the untested.

AnaBGR

I'm serious. What would you do if, for example, the only opportunity you had to get a good job was to do work that didn't
interest you and might cause harm to people like you? And
don't tell me I'm being dramatic.

StanleyP

I like dramatic people. They make me feel so grounded.

AnaBGR

Not helping.

StanleyP

Here's what I think: in business, you always have to think about
costs and benefits. What are the benefits you would gain
versus the upfront costs of taking this opportunity? Answer two
questions: (1) Will your employer continue on this path, with or
without you? And (2) Is there a chance that your participation
means the job could be steered in a better direction?

AnaBGR
Yes, and maybe.

StanleyP

Then the cost of leaving is having no input into any of the gains
of staying. And losing any chance you have of being heard.

I put my phone away. I had been hoping StanleyP would advise me
to run for the hills. Instead he was making me reconsider, and I didn't
like it.

MY "RADIO PARTNER" FOUND ME on the front steps outside the station. He took a seat a few feet away and stared down at his shiny
black loafers. I guess he had taken a page out of Marisa's playbook
and was starting to dress for success too.

"Marisa thinks this is a way to keep both of us employed after the
internship is over. She thinks the idea has real potential," he said
quietly.

I didn't even look at him. "This isn't the story I want to tell."

Thomas sighed. "Do you want to get stuck being the most junior
employee at every broadcaster you ever work for? Because you and I,
we don't have contacts in this industry. There's no one we can call for
help, who can give us any advantage. We're pioneers, paving the way
for the kids coming up behind us, and that means we're entirely on
our own. You know we're already swimming against the desi-parent,
socially acceptable career current by not studying something traditional like medicine, engineering, accounting, or law. We need to use
whatever we can to get ahead. And if that means leveraging our culture

and faith to tell the stories we know better than anyone else, that's a win on two levels. This is your duty, your dharma."

I winced at his use of *dharma*, his reference to fate, a concept we both believed in. "I need to take a walk. Don't follow me."

I went to the back of the building, upwind of the Dumpsters, where the smokers used to congregate before someone complained and they were pushed a hundred metres further back. A plain red-brick facade that faced another brick facade. I called it my Thinking Wall.

My father believed that great radio shows are born from passion and authenticity, a place where regular people tell stories that are important to them. I wanted to tell diverse stories that made a difference, that framed personal narratives in a way that allowed people to think about the world in a whole new light. I knew from experience that those narratives needed to be told by people on the inside looking out, because for too long they had been told by people on the outside looking in.

The first time I had heard an outsider explain Islam was in Grade 10 History, when my teacher, Mr. Nielson, delivered a primer on world religions. He was one of the cool teachers at school, a young white man with floppy blond hair, dimples, and chunky square-framed black glasses. He always wore jeans and a button-down shirt paired with a colourful tie. Everyone loved Mr. Nielson; he didn't make a huge deal if we were late and didn't deduct marks for typos. I always looked forward to his classes.

We spent a week studying world religions, part of the intro to his Ancient Civilizations course. We started with Christianity before learning about Judaism, then Hinduism, and finally it was my people's turn. "Islam is a monotheistic religion, meaning that Muslims, the followers of the religion of Islam, worship only one god."

I beamed at him. So far, so good, Mr. N. Then things went horribly wrong.

"Every Muslim believes in the five pillars of Islam. They are (1) belief in one god, (2) praying five times a day, (3) giving in charity, (4) fighting the jihad, and (5) performing the hajj pilgrimage."

I blinked. *Fighting the jihad?* What was he talking about? I raised my hand to correct him. "Um, sir, jihad is not the fourth pillar of Islam. The fourth pillar is fasting during the month of Ramadan."

Mr. Nielson looked at me indulgently. "I know you might not be comfortable with the truth, Hana, but you don't need to feel ashamed. Fighting the jihad is a pillar of Islam."

"No, it's not," I said. I could feel my face flushing. As far as I knew, Mr. Nielson was agnostic. Why wasn't he listening to me, the only Muslim in his class? "The fourth pillar of Islam is fasting in the month of Ramadan. Definitely not jihad."

"Can you prove it?" Mr. Nielson asked. Even years later, I could feel my neck grow hot with embarrassment at the memory of those words. My classmates were snickering by that point, and I just wanted the confrontation to end.

"Because I read in a book that it's jihad," Mr. Nielson continued, his tone hard. "Can you prove that it isn't?"

Could I prove it? Not in a way that would satisfy him. The lesson continued with no more interruptions.

I had plenty of teachers and professors over the years who listened to my opinions and respected my lived experience as a Muslim woman, but that memory rankled still. If there had been more visible Muslims, more South Asians making art and telling their stories, maybe I wouldn't have felt so alone and targeted. I would have been able to point to a character in a TV show or movie, or in a book we had read in school, for my "proof." Instead, all I had was myself, and it hadn't been enough.

Thomas was right. We had to start somewhere.

I looked up at the sky from my spot against the Thinking Wall, tilting my head to take in that beautiful, uncomplicated blue, the same blue as Marisa's eyes.

The man who had hit my dad's car had been Muslim like us, a young man running late for work. He had stayed with Baba, had watched as the firefighters used the jaws of life to pry my father's limp body from his vehicle. The young man's name was Javed, and he had apologized repeatedly to me, my sister, and my mother when we arrived on the scene. He had vowed to give *sadaqah*—money to charity—in my father's name as penance. When I thought about that awful day, what I remembered most clearly was Javed's round, clean-shaven face and the sobs that had shaken his thin frame as they had loaded my father onto the stretcher, in stark contrast to my mother's frozen silence.

Those first few weeks after the accident, my father had been in the hospital, recovering from one surgery or waiting for another. Since Mom had to keep the restaurant running, my sister and I had taken turns spending the day in his room. When it was my turn, I brought earbuds and we passed the time listening to *This American Life*, *Code Switch*, and *Planet Money*. I got a kick out of *Welcome to Nightvale*, while Baba pretended to understand the humour. Together we binge-listened to season one of *Serial*, and after it was over we sat in silence for a long time, each wrapped up in our own thoughts.

My father had always loved radio and now podcasts too. He had cried when I was accepted into the master's program in communications and broadcasting. "Now you will be able to tell your own story, and our stories too," he said. "You have been given a gift, *beta*."

What would he say about this decision right now? My parents had sacrificed so much to help get me where I was. They had helped pay my tuition, and Mom had chosen to import kitchen help from India rather than ask me to give up my internship at Radio Toronto.

If I wanted to work in a corporation, I had to learn how to keep quiet and learn. Maybe this was all part of the process. Maybe I could be a force for good and guide the show away from harmful stereotypes, encourage nuance and variety.

I leaned my head back again as I came to a decision. I would swallow my pride, look beyond my fears, and stay positive. And my father would finally hear my voice on the radio.

THOMAS PUMPED HIS FIST IN the air when I told him I would help pitch his stupid idea to Nathan Davis.

"If we're going to do this, we're doing it my way," I told him. "That means we're not going to talk about samosas, henna, butter chicken, or terrorists on the show. We're going to talk about real issues, not broad stereotypes or overplayed narratives. No honour killings, no bindis, no Bollywood, no discussions about radicalization."

"Whatever you want, Hana," Thomas said. "This is our show. We're in this together."

Minority Alliance activated.

Chapter Nine

On Friday afternoon, Mom reminded me of my promise to pick up cousin Rashid from the airport. "Take Fahim with you," she added.

I told her I was perfectly capable of picking up our future Canadian scholar and present-day kitchen drudge by myself. Also, it would be safer entering an international airport without the company of a six-foot-one bearded, Brown Muslim man; his cheerful face would immediately raise suspicions. But Mom wasn't having it.

Fahim was just as clueless. "Time to catch up with my favourite sister-in-law," he said, smiling at me. He was working on his dad jokes already.

"You'll need help with the luggage," Mom added, ever practical. "No one visits from India without at least ten suitcases."

I insisted on driving, which made Fahim nervous for some reason. I backed our ancient Toyota minivan out of the parking lot and headed for the airport. Fahim flinched when I changed lanes without signalling, cutting off a pickup truck driver, who honked and shook his fist.

"Are you excited about impending daddy-hood?" I asked Fahim.

He clutched the armrest, knuckles white. "If I live that long." He smiled to show he was joking.

"I'm an excellent driver." I slammed on the brakes, and Fahim's head whiplashed forward. "Oops, sorry. The car in front of me stopped."

"They tend to do that at red lights," he said.

His smile was shaky now, but still hanging on. I stomped on the accelerator when the light changed, and zoomed past the snail in the blue Porsche.

"Maybe you should slow down a little," Fahim said.

"Why aren't you living at my house too, with Fazee?" I asked. "She gets grumpy when you're not around."

"That car's coming up really fast. You see it, right? The one with the brake lights?"

Fahim let go of the armrest and was silent. I looked over. His eyes were wide, staring straight ahead. I spotted the car just in time and pounded on the brakes, screeching to a stop inches from a white BMW convertible. The driver gave me the finger. *So rude.*

"*Hanaan!* Are you trying to kill me?" Fahim was breathing hard now. "I didn't move in because there's only a single bed. Fazeela started snoring after the first trimester and I can't sleep."

I mulled over his words. It was true that Fazeela was a bed hog. When we were kids and had to share a bed on road trips, she'd yank all the blankets.

"Your mom told me a customer came by a few days ago after closing. Some young guy," Fahim said, once his breathing had steadied. "You should be careful who you let in after hours. And always let me know first, okay?"

Fahim would freak out if I told him about my conversation with Aydin. I had tried to push it from my mind, with limited success.

There was no reason to worry my brother-in-law too. "Aydin is harmless," I assured him. "He wanted some leftover biryani, that was all. We chatted about the neighbourhood, our jobs. He seemed nice." *Up until the moment he didn't*, I thought.

"Is he cute, this Aydin guy?"

I nearly groaned out loud. "Fahim, drop it."

No wonder my brother-in-law had been so eager to accompany me to the airport. He had been sent on a mission by Fazee to gather intel on my non-existent love life. I wasn't sure why she was interested. Mom and Baba had never asked me about marriage plans; they understood I was too busy, that things were too precarious for me to consider a romantic entanglement.

I had never had a boyfriend, but I had never felt the lack of romance in my life. I was busy with the restaurant, my studies, my internship. In my family and community it was normal to skip the prolonged dating scene and marry quickly once the right guy had been found. Fazeela and Fahim had known they were headed towards a nikah within months of meeting.

My mind wandered to StanleyP and his increasingly intimate, flirty messages. We had settled on a deadline, more or less. In four weeks we would come to some sort of understanding—whatever that happened to be.

"What about you and Yusuf? I'd be happy to talk to him if you're feeling shy," Fahim said.

I nearly slammed on the brakes again. "What? No!"

"Yusuf is practically part of the family, and I can see the two of you together. I could be your love messenger," he said.

Thomas would laugh so hard if he heard that conversation. I could picture Marisa's eyebrows rising at the idea of my brother-in-law "talking to" Yusuf on my behalf. *But why can't you talk to him yourself?* she would ask, puzzled. *In Canada, women are free to pursue their own lovers, darling.*

The thought of trying to explain the rishta proposal process to Marisa made me cringe. In traditional South Asian families like mine, sometimes romantic introductions are made through family, a grown-up version of "Do you like my friend? Check this box for yes and this box for no."

"You know Yusuf and Lily have always been a thing. Why the sudden interest in setting me up?" I asked, suspicious. The fact that my brother-in-law was offering to play matchmaker was laughable. He and Fazeela had figured out things on their own before they informed their respective families about their intention to marry.

"Things are so up in the air right now, with the restaurant and everything else," Fahim said slowly. "Fazee and I want you to find someone who will be on your side, who can help you get through the hard stuff."

I mulled that over, acknowledging the truth of his words. Sometimes it was lonely not having someone who was solely on my side. But that didn't mean I wanted Fahim and Fazeela to interfere in my love life. "Please don't talk to Yusuf, or any other guy, for me, bhai," I said, using the Urdu word for "older brother." I never called him *bhai*, so he knew I was serious.

Fahim was silent for a moment. "Sure, Hana. Just promise you'll be careful with your heart, okay? You deserve someone who puts you first."

THE TERMINAL 1 ARRIVALS LOUNGE at Pearson International Airport was packed. We were surrounded by aunties in saris and salwar kameez trailed by sulky teenagers in ripped jeans and crop tops; young white and Brown and Black men with long beards or goatees or clean-shaven; old men dressed in three-piece suits or lungis; men in turbans, women in hijab; women in long dresses, short skirts, yoga pants, track pants; babies in strollers, children chasing each other through rows of seats—all of the beautiful hues of my city on display. All of us going places and getting stuff done and hauling home souvenirs while we're at it.

Fahim spotted someone he knew, of course. Fahim knew everyone. He picked up friends the way the post office collected packages—constantly, and in strange locations. "Khalid!" he boomed across the arrivals hall, waving enthusiastically at a bearded man in a long white robe. Khalid was holding hands with a pretty, smiling woman in a purple hijab.

I wandered over to the digital bulletin board to check if my cousin's plane had arrived on time. If it was running on Indian Standard Time, the answer would be a hard no.

A young man stood on the other side of the board, head bent over his cellphone. My gaze followed the line of dark stubble on his well-defined jawline, the black hair curling under his collar. Silver sunglasses dangled from his shirt pocket. He lifted dark eyes to mine, and we both froze.

"What are you doing here?" I asked Aydin.

Aydin blinked rapidly before recovering. "I heard one of the airport restaurants has a two-for-one deal on biryani poutine. You know, to scare off the Americans."

I snort-laughed but quickly recovered. "I meant who are you here to pick up?"

Aydin shrugged, the movement casual. "Anyone who will have me."

I gave him a hard look and he smiled, the expression momentarily transforming his handsome face. "I'm here to pick up a friend," he said.

I was confused by his familiarity after our last, heated conversation. Looking for a distraction, I scanned the arrivals board. Rashid's flight was on time, and I made my way to the doors where a small crowd waited for passengers beyond opaque security gates. Aydin fell into step beside me as I unrolled the sign I had scrawled in the parking lot, after I realized I had no idea what my eighteen-year-old cousin looked like. The last time we met, he had been six years old.

Aydin read my sign, eyebrows raised. "Mail-order groom arriving today?" he asked, lips twitching.

"You should take your show on the road," I said.

"Sadly, I'm only this amusing around you."

"You weren't very amusing the last time we met," I said. A strange expression crossed his face, too quickly for me to catch. Regret? Surprise? Irritation? Either Aydin was the moodiest man I knew or there was something else going on behind his hot-and-cold behaviour.

"My restaurant advice was well-meant. You overreacted," he said.

Definitely moody. How could someone so attractive be so dumb? I shook my head. "Nope. Try again."

He pulled a hand through his hair. "I was confused by your smile and your mother's excellent biryani, and I didn't know what I was saying?" A tiny flirtatious gleam in his eye coaxed a smile to my lips, which I immediately suppressed.

"Better, but still not good enough. Let me know when you've figured out the rest of your story," I said. We smiled at each other, and for a moment the air filled with tiny electric sparks.

A tall lady in elegant cigarette pants and flowing black silk salwar top paused and studied my sign. Her dark eyes were coolly assessing, her thin lips painted red and pursed in disapproval. A white dupatta shawl was wrapped tightly around her hair like a 1920s film star.

"Surely you cannot be Ghufran Khan's daughter," the lady drawled in a well-educated Indian accent that denoted an excellent convent education. I blinked, and Aydin took the opportunity to disappear into the crowd.

"Hana Apa!" A burst of motion and I was picked up by a lanky teenage boy. Cousin Rashid, I presumed. His enormous smile engulfed a triangular face similar to mine. His skin was a deep mahogany and his black hair cut close to his head; he wore a red shirt and black dress pants. With skinny wrists he strained to grip two shoulder bags and a carry-on suitcase. Behind him a luggage cart groaned with half a dozen suitcases. I was glad now that Mom had forced me to bring Fahim the Luggage Wrangler.

Rashid whipped out his cellphone and leaned in close. "Smile, Hana Apa!" he said, using the Urdu word for "big sister," and took a selfie. "I have promised Mummy Daddy to send pictures and videos of my experiences in Canada."

He showed me the photo. I looked constipated, but before I could ask him to erase it, he had already sent the offending image to his family. He straightened and began filming the arrivals lounge. I turned to find the older lady still examining me.

"Aunty, I don't know how you know my mother's name, but I don't know you," I said, my voice firm but polite.

Rashid whipped his camera in our direction and started laughing. "This is Kawkab Khala!"

That didn't clear anything up for me. *Khala* meant "mother's sister" according to the specific Urdu accounting of family relationships. But my mom only had one sister, Ghazala, and she lived in India.

"I'm the third sister, *beta*." Kawkab Khala smiled at me, revealing uneven teeth. "Your mother's favourite cousin. I've come to visit my long-lost family in Canada. Surprise!" She sailed past me, Rashid scampering after her like a well-trained puppy, leaving me with his two shoulder bags, the carry-on, and the leaning luggage cart.

What had just happened? I looked around for Fahim, who was still chatting with his friend.

My eyes froze on Mr. Silver Shades. He was in the middle of the lounge, standing close to a raven-haired beauty in a flowing ankle-length red dress gathered at her tiny waist. They were speaking urgently. The young woman shook her head and, with an impatient gesture, stalked ahead of him on stiletto heels. He squared his shoulders and marched after the girl in the red dress.

Anyone who would have him, indeed.

I GRABBED RASHID'S BAGS. I couldn't think about Aydin and his . . . girlfriend? random beautiful stranger? airport hookup? I had to stay focused on one turn of events at a time. Such as Kawkab Khala, my alleged aunt.

She would need a bedroom, and South Asian rules of hospitality were clear. There was no way my mother's older "sister" could be expected to sleep on the couch while there was a bedroom left in the house. As the youngest member of the household, that meant I would be on the couch for as long as Kawkab Khala decided to grace us with her unexpected presence. I eyed her immaculately ironed silk salwar top, the heavy gold chain around her neck, and her discreet gold jhumka ear bobs. She would probably take over my dresser and remaining closet too.

I headed towards Fahim, my cousin and Kawkab Khala trailing behind, and performed the introductions. My brother-in-law nervously raked his fingers through his hair as he looked from Kawkab Khala to Rashid and then back to me, unsure what to do.

The girl in the red dress strode past us on her way to the exit. She was tall and curvy, skin flawless. Her hair, which looked like it had been professionally blow-dried on the plane, fell in soft, cascading waves down her back. She resembled a sultry Bollywood bombshell. Rashid stared open-mouthed, and even the gentlemanly Fahim was having a hard time keeping his gaze modestly lowered.

Aydin caught my eye. "'Whoever will have you'?" I asked, keeping my voice light.

Bollywood Bombshell swayed back to us, trailing a teeny red Louis Vuitton case that was probably stuffed with perfectly tailored dresses, all in a loose-fit size two.

"Hana, this is Zulfa. She flew in from Vancouver for a quick visit," Aydin said, and cleared his throat.

"Well done, brother," Rashid said from over my left shoulder. He stuck out one hand for a high-five. "Perhaps you can give me some tips later on. Or introduce me to her sister?" I shoved my cousin back, colouring at his teenage behaviour.

Zulfa only smiled at Rashid. She was probably used to people acting foolishly around her. "I'm always happy to meet my fiancé's friends," she said.

It took a moment for her words to sink in. *Fiancé?*

"We're not engaged," Aydin said firmly. "She's my publicist."

That was one I hadn't heard before.

Zulfa took his hand. "We'll be together soon enough, sweetie. I can't wait for the grand opening."

What a strange thing to call your engagement ceremony.

Aydin jerked at her words. "You don't have to do that in front of them," he said, voice harsh. He didn't even look at me. "They're not important. We have to go. Now." A faint pink tinged his ears as they left.

Kawkab Khala sniffed at their rudeness, and I ground my teeth. Aydin had flirted with me only a few minutes before. Now he could barely look at me, embarrassed that I had caught him with his fiancée—or, rather, his *publicist*—in the airport. That was twice he had brushed me off after first trying to befriend me. I was done.

Besides, whatever was going on there was none of my business. I had my own drama, featuring Instant Relatives—just add one airport and no advance warning!

Fahim had found a second luggage cart. "Good thing we brought the van," he said, smiling. "Who was that guy?"

"Stand down, love messenger," I said. "That one belongs to Miss Pakistan." I looked at the mound of luggage. "Why do we have baseball bats?"

"Didn't Ghufran Khala tell you? I'm applying for an athletic scholarship." Rashid picked up a bat and swung at an imaginary ball.

"I didn't know baseball was popular in India," I said, quickly taking the bat from his hands before he hit someone.

"What could be more Indian than baseball?" Rashid asked.

We made our way out of the airport. Pensive, Smiling, Disdainful, and Athletic—my family. May God have mercy on us all.

Chapter Ten

Fahim insisted on driving home: something about wanting to live long enough to meet his unborn child. Kawkab Khala claimed shotgun and I was crowded into the back with Rashid and the overstuffed carry-on bags. I wondered how long my cousin and alleged aunt intended to stay. From the looks of it, the answer might be forever.

"How is the, er, family?" I asked. I couldn't recall Rashid's parents' names or if he had any siblings.

"They were sad when I left, but happy I was being accompanied by Kawkab Khala. I have never travelled outside India." Rashid's gaze was fixed on his cellphone, which was pointing out the window as he took video of the ride home. "Everyone is so polite here," he said. A man in a tow truck flipped off Fahim, who, in an effort to restore balance to the universe, was driving ten kilometres below the speed limit.

I stuck my head between the front seats. "Are you sure you know where the accelerator is, Fahim? It's that pedal on the right. The one you're not pressing."

He ignored me.

I settled back against the seat, trying to get comfortable despite the carry-on wheels jabbing into my ribs. "Tell me about your family, Rashid."

"My parents are both accountants, and they have sent me to Canada to learn all about accounting." Grinning, he added, "They don't know about the athletic scholarship."

"And why did you decide to visit Canada, Kawkab Khala?" I asked. "Did you hear about our breathtaking parks? Niagara Falls? Poutine?"

Kawkab Khala didn't reply. Maybe I would let my alleged aunt sleep on the sofa after all.

Fahim parked in the driveway and, together with Rashid, unloaded the luggage. My aunt walked to the door with only a slight curl to her lip and a single "This is where you *live*?" remark.

I helped her inside and, after checking on my father and giving Fazee a quick update, headed back to the restaurant. I had a few questions to ask Mom, specifically about my alleged aunt and where she would be sleeping.

Rashid dashed out the front door and joined me. "Don't you want to rest after your long flight?" I asked hopefully.

He shook his head, his body vibrating with youthful energy. "I want to greet your mother. Also, I must see the restaurant and familiarize myself with the family operation. I don't want to look foolish when I begin my post tomorrow." His eyes were intelligent and took in every detail of the street. "I thought your restaurant was the only one in the neighbourhood."

"It is," I answered. We were approaching the south end of Golden Crescent, passing the lone empty storefront before heading into the strip proper.

"Then what is that?"

Rashid had stopped in front of the abandoned building. Except it was no longer a hollowed-out shell. Various vehicles were parked out front and a construction crew milled around. A large sign was plastered across the front. COMING SOON! WHOLISTIC BURGERS AND GRILL. GOURMET HALAL DONE RIGHT. TRY SOMETHING DIFFERENT!

My world tilted on its axis.

Rashid was still talking, but I heard only Aydin's words from a few nights ago. *The only reason you're still open is because you don't have any competition. You're the only halal restaurant in the Golden Crescent. . . . It's clear this area is about to change, maybe one day soon.* And Zulfa's words at the airport: *I can't wait for the grand opening,* followed by Aydin's abrupt response.

That sneaky spy. He had come to Three Sisters to scope out the competition in the neighbourhood. He had been digging for dirt and then trash-talking our restaurant to my face, once he realized I was the daughter of the owner.

I stalked towards Three Sisters, Rashid trailing after me.

"Assalamu alaikum, Hana!" Yusuf called from across the street. I remembered that Yusuf's dad, Brother Musa, was the president of our local BOA, the Business Owners Association. I gestured him over.

"Whose restaurant is that?" I asked.

A startled expression crossed Yusuf's face before it settled into understanding. He had known, I realized, and he hadn't bothered to warn me, or my mother.

My friend shrugged as if it were no big deal. I wondered if he would have the same reaction if a Whole Foods decided to open beside his father's grocer shop. "Dad said it's someone from outside the neighbourhood. The new owners will be at the BOA meeting tomorrow night." Yusuf looked from me to Rashid, expectant. "Aren't you going to introduce me?"

The problem with living in a close-knit community is that everyone knows everything, or wants to. "We have family visiting from India. This is my cousin Rashid."

Rashid put out his hand to shake. Instead of taking it, Yusuf took a step closer and bellowed, "ASSALAMU ALAIKUM! My. Name. Is. Yusuf. What. Is. Your. Name?"

"Ra-shid," my cousin said, echoing Yusuf's slow pronunciation.

Yusuf nodded and put an arm around my cousin. "WELCOME TO CANADA!" he boomed. "YOU ARE FREE HERE!"

Rashid looked over at me and waggled his brows. I motioned my cousin into Three Sisters and pulled my beautiful, idiotic friend to the curbside. "What's wrong with you?" I whispered to Yusuf, furious. "He's from India, not a time traveller from the 1700s."

Yusuf shifted uncomfortably. "I just thought he might be, you know, too poor for the stuff we take for granted. You don't know the situations I've read about in case studies at school."

I rolled my eyes. My beautiful friend was a bleeding heart. "Rashid will be here for a while. Maybe the two of you can hang out and you can expose him to some of those Canadian values we take for granted," I said.

Yusuf brightened at that, the green of his eyes glowing in the afternoon light. "Bring him to the BOA meeting, so he can see democracy in action."

I had heard tales from my sister and mother about the antics of the Business Owners Association. I only made a noncommittal noise and reminded him that India is already a democracy.

"You know what I mean. Hey, did you hear back from Lily?"

"She's pretty busy with her residency," I said, shifting uncomfortably. I didn't want to be dragged into the middle of whatever was currently going on between them.

"Could you and I hang out without Lily? I really need to talk to someone, and I could use your advice. Coffee sometime this week?" he asked.

I looked across the street to Yusuf's family store, where I could just make out the outline of his father, Brother Musa. Then my gaze drifted diagonally to the future location of Wholistic Burgers and Grill, and my eyes narrowed. I could use Yusuf's advice too, maybe get some more information about the not-so-mysterious owners of the new restaurant, and why my best friend had not thought to give me a heads-up. We made plans to meet the next day.

Inside the restaurant, Rashid was chatting with my mother. When I entered a few moments later, he had begun to sweep the dining room. "Your friend Yusuf is funny," he said.

"I hope you weren't offended. He wants you to come to the Business Owners Association meeting, so he can introduce you around."

Rashid gave me a wicked smile. "I would be honoured to attend. I have the perfect costume to wear: a sherwani suit with curly-toed shoes, a turban, and a string of pearls. Your friend will tell everyone I am a Mughal prince."

The Mughals were a Muslim dynasty that ruled Southeast Asia for over three hundred years. Their empire had dissolved in 1857. I wasn't too sure about my alleged aunt, but Rashid was definitely growing on me.

Chapter Eleven

om knew about the restaurant. Apparently Brother Musa had informed her, and she wasn't bothered. Not by the sudden appearance of Kawkab Khala, not by our new competition, not by anything.

"You've never mentioned Kawkab Khala before," I said.

Mom shrugged. "Yes, I have, except I never called her Kawkab. She started using her given name after her husband died. We know her by another name." Mom looked uncomfortable. "It's a pet name, and I don't think she likes it. We used to call her Billi Apa."

Billi Apa! Billi Apa was legendary. She used to go horseback riding around the neighbourhood in India at a time when demure young women weren't supposed to engage in unladylike physical exertions. She played poker at the men's club. She would smoke hand-rolled cigarettes she bought off the servants. She was an older cousin Mom's family would visit during the summer, and the stories my mom had recounted about their adventures over the years were epic. Such as the time Billi Apa dressed up as the local imam and gave a sermon about the importance of buying your wife expensive weekly gifts. She knew how to shoot a gun and only ever wore pants. She was so wild her parents had sent her to an English boarding school, where she learned to swear in French, English, and German.

Her parents were wealthy landowners and she was their only child. Billi Apa had been my childhood hero, and I had dreamt of one day meeting her. Except I would have had to travel to New Delhi because, my mother assured me, she never left her massive property. Until now.

"Did you know she was coming?" I asked Mom.

"She is always welcome." A polite way of saying no.

"What about the new restaurant opening up? What are we going to do?"

This time Mom stopped chopping coriander and chilies and wiped her forehead with the back of her hand. Wisps of greying hair escaped her black hijab. "We don't have to do anything. There is enough business here for everyone. They will attract attention at first, but things will settle. You will see, Hana *jaan*. It will all work out."

Her eyes looked around at the kitchen as if she were trying to reassure herself. We were all counting on her—Baba, Fazeela, Fahim, me, and the cantaloupe. I thought back to Lily's assurances that Mom was the smartest, most hard-working person she knew. We would survive. Inshallah.

"I'm sure you're right," I said to Mom, and then asked if Rashid and I could go to the BOA meeting.

She nodded. "Fazeela usually goes, but you can take her place. It will be good for Rashid to come along and see how we do things here. Make sure you take notes on the festival. I want to know what they are planning this year."

Every year the Golden Crescent BOA put together a summer street festival for the neighbourhood. It was pretty low-key stuff. The businesses all chipped in for bouncy castles for the kids and set up tables outside to sell food and merchandise. Mr. Lewis gave away free coffee and doughnuts, Luxmi Aunty served a variety of homemade snacks, and Three Sisters offered food for sale. It was a fun, intimate community event. I promised to take copious notes and report back.

AS EXPECTED, MY ALLEGED AUNT/NEWLY revealed childhood hero commandeered my bedroom as easily as she had claimed shotgun on the ride home. The couch was even more uncomfortable than I had anticipated.

I woke up for the pre-dawn fajr prayer at four-thirty a.m. without having to set an alarm, thanks to the lumpy cushions. Baba was already sitting at the dining table, the light low. On the nights he had trouble sleeping, he stayed up to read the newspaper, work on his puzzles, or listen to the radio. I gave him a side hug when I passed by to make *wudu*, the ritual purification before prayer, and he looked up in surprise, removing his headphones.

"What are you doing up at this hour, Hana?" he asked.

"There is an intruder in my room," I whispered.

His eyes widened, then relaxed at my mischievous smile. "Your mother and I were very close to Kawkab Apa when we lived in Delhi as newlyweds. She helped us quite a bit when we first settled in Toronto. She is a wealthy woman. Your mother borrowed money from her to open the restaurant."

I hadn't known that. *Maybe she's here to help out again*, I thought hopefully.

"She hasn't left Delhi in years," he continued. "Whatever has brought her all the way to Canada must be very important." Baba looked at me and smiled. "I am glad you got a chance to meet. You are so alike. We are lucky she has agreed to stay for a while."

I groaned inwardly. *A while* could mean weeks, maybe months.

"You are being a good host, and I am happy to have the company," my father said. "The house hasn't felt this lively in a long time." With my aunt, Rashid, and Fazeela, he was right; we were full to bursting. Maybe the company would be a welcome distraction during my father's isolated days.

After I made *wudu*, I prayed fajr in the living room. The couch was more comfortable when I returned to bed—someone had added extra cushions. Baba's head was bent over the local news section.

"Thanks, Baba," I said drowsily. I wanted to tell him some good news. "Thomas pitched a show to Marisa that she liked. He wants me to help him with it."

The smile on Baba's face wiped away my doubts. "Alhamdulillah!" he said. "What will your show be about?"

"We're still figuring that part out," I hedged. "But it will be about faith, culture, and identity and the role it plays in the city."

My father nodded, thoughtful. "If you do this and your superiors like it, perhaps you will get a full-time job. Security is important, Hana. Don't discount a job with a steady paycheque, some health insurance; you can begin to plan your future. And more opportunities will come, especially if you are pleasant and cooperative. I already know your talent will shine."

"I hope you're right," I said, settling more deeply into the cushions.

"How many customers at the restaurant yesterday?" he asked.

"So many people," I said, eyes firmly shut. "The place was packed."

"Good," he said quietly, and turned back to his newspaper. I turned to face the back of the sofa, but it was a long time before I fell asleep again.

Brace yourselves, listener friends, because I'm about to go on a Brown Girl Rambles rant. Which is quite difficult to do without getting into specific details, but I'll try my best.

I said in my first episode that this podcast would be about nothing but my truth. Today I want to talk about truth's evil twin—deception. Lies. Untruths.

Who do we hurt when we lie to ourselves, and to our families? Lying serves an inherently selfish function. We lie because we don't want to deal with the truth, because it's uncomfortable, or maybe it's more expedient to make something up. But what happens when you lie to spare someone's feelings? Worse, even, when they know that you are lying but go along with it. Are they sparing your feelings even as you spare theirs?

There are some lies that make life more comfortable. Lies like "Yes, I'm fine," when really we mean "I don't want to talk to you about this." Or "Yes, this is the best decision for me," when we mean "I don't know what to do, but this would be easier," or maybe "This is the best decision I can make with the information I have right now," when actually it's despair and inertia leading you on.

When I lie to family and friends to reassure them, who benefits? No one, really. When I tell myself I will pursue a project I never wanted because I might be able to do some good, or because it might lead to something better, is that the truth?

A few things have happened in my life recently that have made me afraid. I'm afraid they collectively signal that the other shoe is about to drop. You know what I mean? When that thing you've been bracing for all your life in a low-key way slowly starts to unravel everything? That might mean I've paid in advance for a cynicism as yet untested by real trials, and now I'm about to see what happens when things really start to go wrong.

Because things are starting to go wrong.

I've lived a calm, mostly sheltered life. I'm not saying I'm living large, you understand. Just a . . . sometimes difficult, but overall good life. As a result, I tend to trust people. When they let me down or disappoint me in some way, I feel foolish, though on some level I'm always expecting that disaster to unfold. On the other hand, perhaps foolishness is the price you pay for lessons learned.

As a Muslim, I have faith that things will work out the way they were meant to. But I also know I will be tested in this life, and I worry about those tests. I spend too much time wondering what will happen if I fail, too. I guess we're all just stumbling around in the dark, hoping the stories—and occasional lies—we tell ourselves will bring us closer to our light.

StanleyP
Just listened to your latest podcast. I guess you decided to do that project in the end.

AnaBGR
I'll see where it leads. Thanks for the advice.

StanleyP
Not sure it was the right advice. You sound sad.

AnaBGR
Just got some unexpected news about my family business.

StanleyP
What sort of news?

AnaBGR
The sort I should have seen coming. We haven't cornered the
market the way I thought.

StanleyP
Competition isn't a bad thing. It's a way to rethink old ways and
try something new. That's the fun, right?

AnaBGR
I think we have very different ideas of fun.

Chapter Twelve

The BOA meeting was held in the basement of Yusuf's grocery store, a low-ceilinged, forbidding space that smelled vaguely of bleach and overripe produce. Brother Musa, Yusuf's father, had tried to make it more welcoming by placing a platter of fruit on a folding table next to the cramped staircase. The room was set up with two dozen folding chairs and another folding table at the very front for Brother Musa and Mr. Lewis, the owner of the Tim Hortons coffee shop—the association's president and vice-president respectively.

I knew Yusuf didn't always get along with his father. A dour man in his early sixties with an impressive grey moustache and sharp blue eyes, Brother Musa had high expectations for everyone in his life, especially his elder son. When we were younger, he would push Yusuf to study harder, to play more sports. He never quite approved of his son hanging out with me and Lily, and his disapproval only deepened when he realized that Yusuf was in love with Lily. Things had always been strained between the two, though Yusuf was loyal to his family and worked at the store without complaint. He also happily involved himself in the goings-on of the BOA and any other neighbourhood issues that came up.

This was the first meeting I had attended, but I recognized many of the local business owners. I greeted the familiar faces and introduced Rashid to Brother Musa before we claimed a seat beside Yusuf in the front row. Rashid had decided to forego the Mughal finery for a plain shirt and jeans. My teenage cousin was turning out to be entirely different from what I had imagined.

"Where are the owners of the new restaurant?" I whispered to Yusuf.

He frowned. "They're not here yet. Dad hates it when people are late."

Brother Musa called everyone to attention. He had a slight Syrian accent, dulled by thirty years of living in North America. "We have a few items on the agenda. First up: our annual summer street festival. We need a volunteer to take charge, as Fazeela will not be able to manage this year. Any takers?"

Opening up my notebook, I began to take the notes Mom had requested.

Rashid fidgeted next to me as the meeting droned on, with details for the street festival followed by a discussion of the new parking regulations and neighbourhood security. Once I had recorded the agenda items, I turned to a new page and wrote *New halal restaurant?*

Rashid leaned over. "You said this would be fun. If I wanted to sit in a room full of old people talking business, I would have attended my parents' accounting parties."

I wondered what an accounting party looked like. "Don't worry. They're getting to the best part," I whispered.

Rashid tilted his head. "What's the best part?"

"The drama."

Fazeela had told me that every meeting of the Golden Crescent

Business Owners Association ended with someone losing their temper and getting into a yelling match with someone else. One time a fist-fight had broken out over the garbage collection schedule. Fazeela described the BOA as *Survivor*, except with more Brown people. I think that was why Mom usually sent my sister; she was allergic to drama. Fazeela, on the other hand, could have worked for the White House. Intrigue was her oxygen.

I heard the basement door open and heavy footsteps clomped down the stairs. Aydin was about to make his big entrance, thirty minutes late.

"Now for the final item on our agenda," Brother Musa said, irritated. "Despite their late arrival, let us welcome Junaid Shah and his son Aydin Shah, owners of the new Golden Crescent restaurant, Wholistic Burgers and Grill."

Polite applause as the dozen BOA members turned towards the back of the room, where Aydin stood with his father. A few uneasy glances were also thrown my way, and my face burned.

I realized some part of me had hoped I was wrong, that Aydin hadn't been spying, that he and his father weren't actually opening a rival halal restaurant in Golden Crescent, in direct competition with Three Sisters. His father had treated me like dirt when they visited our restaurant, and then I had handed our competition a free plate of biryani. I closed my eyes, reliving the humiliation of Aydin's comments about our faded decor and imminent closure.

Aydin and Junaid Uncle made their way silently through the crowd and took seats in the row behind us. Aydin leaned forward and muttered a quiet salaam in my ear. So polite when people were present to witness his actions. I wasn't as prepared to be civil.

I turned around to glare at him. "You've got some nerve," I hissed.

Aydin blinked in surprise. "I'm sorry?"

"Showing up with your dad the other day. Commenting on our food, the lighting, the floors," I said in a heated whisper. "*The only thing you can count on is change*," I mimicked, and Aydin flushed. Good. I hoped he was embarrassed.

In my anger, I hadn't realized I'd raised my voice. The BOA members craned forward, trying to catch every word.

"You were spying on us," I continued flatly. *Let them hear. Everyone should know how our newest members operate.*

Rashid looked from my angry face to Aydin's startled one. He stood up, glaring at father and son. "Yes, how dare you spy on my cousin!" he announced loudly. He ruined the impact by leaning down to whisper loudly, "This is the drama, right?"

Junaid Uncle spoke up, his face contorted with anger. "*Spying* on you? Why would we waste our time spying on your dirty, insignificant little business?" he said loudly.

The shocked silence that greeted his rudeness jolted me out of my temper. We were causing a scene; my mother would not be pleased.

Aydin's face was pale. "Dad, calm down. You said you would let me handle this."

Junaid Uncle turned to his son, and from my close vantage point I could see Aydin flinch. "As usual, you are not handling anything," his father said. He cast an imperious eye around the room. "I don't know why you insisted on coming here. I refuse to be bullied by the local yokels."

From the front of the room, Musa asked his son loudly, "What is this *yokel*? Is that man calling us eggs?"

Junaid Uncle ignored everyone else, his eyes fixed on my face. "This entire neighbourhood is nothing but an ethnic slum," he announced.

That did it. *Drama, consider yourself embraced.* I stood up slowly, fists clenched at my sides. "In case you haven't noticed, you're Brown!"

Aydin turned to his father and, in one last effort to broker peace, said in perfect Urdu, "This is not the time or the place. We came here to meet the community, not to make enemies."

Rashid took a step towards Aydin, and for a moment I thought my cousin was going to punch him. Instead he clasped Aydin's arm. "Bhai, your Urdu is very good. Did you grow up in Pakistan?"

"No, but I took weekend language classes," Aydin said, smiling at him.

Junaid interrupted before they could exchange phone numbers or start following each other on Twitter. "There is no point making friends with the people we will soon put out of business." He glared at the rest of the BOA members. "Your neighbourhood will become gentrified soon. The signs are already there. Rents will rise beyond your profit margins, and every last one of you will be bankrupt within five years."

Aydin closed his eyes. "Dad," he said.

"You disgust me," I said to Junaid Uncle, but my eyes were filled with angry tears. I quickly walked out of the room, hands shaking as I climbed the stairs. I would not cry in front of them.

Outside it was twilight. I took deep, gulping breaths. My eyes were drawn to Golden Crescent, to the commercial strip where my mother had so proudly started her own business, to the neighbourhood where we had set down roots and built a life. I noticed how shabby it looked under the street lamps, the grime and the disrepair. And I hated Aydin and his father even more.

I WASN'T ALONE FOR LONG.

"That wasn't how I wanted our first BOA meeting to go. My father can be . . . difficult," Aydin said stiffly.

Difficult. He thought what Junaid Shah had said inside had been "difficult," that I was upset because his unpleasant father had hurled a few insults at some strangers. He really had no clue.

I took a deep breath. "That hundred-dollar bill you paid, the first time you came to our restaurant. Was that pity for your competition?"

"You're not really my competition."

"Ass." We stared each other down. When he looked away first, I wanted to pump my fist in the air, as if I had won something.

But when he spoke, I realized he hadn't backed down an inch. His voice was wintry. "Your mother's restaurant is in trouble, and the best biryani in the world won't help her. Whatever happens between our stores is just business, nothing more. If you want to keep up with me, I will enjoy the competition. If you can't, and your restaurant closes as a result, that will be your family's choice."

He meant my family's fault. "Your father said we'll all be gone in five years. Are you planning to help that process along?"

Aydin shrugged. "There's incredible growth potential for a well-run halal restaurant. Even my father recognizes that."

A well-run halal restaurant. He clearly did not include Three Sisters in that description. My fist tightened at my side. He hadn't answered my question, I noticed. "Do you and your father plan to shut down every business in Golden Crescent, or just mine?" I asked.

Aydin again sidestepped my question. "Have you heard of Shah Industries?"

The name rang a distant bell. So he was a spoiled rich kid from a rich family. I already knew that.

"Dad wants me to follow in his footsteps. Mergers and acquisitions, property development in target markets—basically grown-up Monopoly."

Grown-up Monopoly. Target markets. He sounded like Marisa, intent on exploiting a new demographic. "Is this all a game to you? You're playing with my family's livelihood. We don't have another business or family money to fall back on if you force our doors closed. You're a suit with deep pockets. We're a local fixture in an *ethnic slum.*" The anger must have been clear on my face, because his gaze dropped. "Why are you really here?" I demanded, stepping closer.

"I like food," he said simply, and his words finally felt honest. "I like the idea of building a business, a lasting brand. Something that will bring halal food into the mainstream. Your mom's biryani really did remind me of my mother's. She died when I was five."

I remembered how vulnerable he had looked that first time we met at Three Sisters, the gentle surprise on his face as he ate Mom's biryani and talked about his mother. I would not feel sorry for him. Lots of people have dead mothers and dick fathers. That didn't mean he got a pass for being arrogant and underhanded.

Aydin's voice was soft in the descending darkness. "Shah Industries buys and sells companies, but we don't hold on to them for very long. We don't build anything real. I wanted something real."

He stood so close I could smell his aftershave, a subtle cologne tinged with sandalwood—and money. I inhaled deeply. So this was what deception smelled like.

Footsteps, and then beautiful Yusuf eased his long body next to mine. He glared at Aydin. "You and your father are no longer welcome in the Golden Crescent Business Owners Association. I'm going to petition City Council to revoke your food licence. We don't need big business trying to pave over the character and traditions of our neighbourhood." He put his arm around me and squeezed my shoulder.

Aydin looked at Yusuf's arm and then at me. "I'm not the villain

here, Hana," he said, ignoring Yusuf. "I've worked too hard and sacrificed too much to stop now."

I shook off Yusuf's arm. "You know nothing about sacrifice," I said.

"You presume too much," Aydin shot back, a trace of anger in his
voice now. "If you're determined to play the victim, there's not much I
can do. My restaurant isn't going anywhere, and you will have to live
with that."

I glanced down the street, at the storefronts that had guarded the
entrance to Golden Crescent for a generation, and then to Wholistic
Burgers and Grill, still under its construction tarps. Something that
felt a lot like fear made my chest tighten. "You mean live with it until
you and your father put my family out of business?"

Junaid Uncle walked past our little group and came to a stop a few
metres away, his back to us. At the sight of his father, Aydin's expression shut down even further. "If it wasn't Wholistic Grill, it would be
another halal restaurant. Consider this as motivation to work on your
competitive skills." His face was immobile. "Assuming that you have
any," he added.

Rashid, who had followed Yusuf, was standing a few feet away. He
waved at Aydin. "If you're free tomorrow, let's play baseball in the
park," he called over in Urdu. Then he caught my eye and his expression turned sheepish. "I'll kick your ass!" he yelled in English.

At this unexpected about-face, Mr. Silver Shades smiled slightly. He
joined his father, and together they walked down the darkened street
towards their new restaurant.

Chapter Thirteen

I knew my family would hear about the Business Owners Association meeting before I got home. The second favourite pastime of the BOA, aside from forming *Survivor*-style alliances, was to gossip. The story of Ghufran's bad-tempered, scene-causing younger daughter would be carried to my family lightning-fast, and I didn't even have a bedroom to hide in.

I slipped into our backyard, stumbling through ankle-high weeds. Mowing the lawn had been my job, but when I became busy with my internship during the past year, I had resigned from yard-care duties. The rest of my family were always working, so the position had yet to be filled.

I dragged one of the rusty lawn chairs from the side of the house and placed it near the back fence. Now it felt almost like my Thinking Wall at Radio Toronto.

Our backyard edged onto a small ravine, and I let the quiet envelop me as I leaned against the fence, tilting my head up towards the inky darkness. The velvet air brushed against my loosened hijab and the dull buzz of nocturnal insects kept me company. *Maybe I should just sleep out here until everyone leaves.*

I heard the click of a cigarette lighter and saw Kawkab Khala's face illuminated beside the patio door. I tried to shrink against the fence, but she had seen me. She stood a foot away and blew smoke into the night.

"Ghufran and Ijaz are worried about you," she remarked. "Rashid said you were going for a walk." No judgment in her voice, only interest. "I used to take night walks too, in Delhi. I waited until my family fell asleep and then I would sneak out. Nobody bothered me, because they all knew who I was—the crazy daughter of the local *nawab*," she said, using the Urdu word for a wealthy landowner. "Nighttime is the best time to think."

"What did you think about?" I asked, intrigued despite my wish to be left alone.

"Love, marriage, my future." She smiled. "I'm sorry to disappoint you with my ordinary thoughts. But then, the young are often very predictable."

"Were you in love with someone?"

She took another deep puff on her cigarette. "Only with my solitude. Love came later. It surprised me, and everyone else too. I married in my forties, but we never had children."

I didn't know what to say to that. I had heard about Billi Apa's wild youth, but not about her adulthood. I was happy to hear she had found love and happiness later in life, even if I wasn't entirely sure what to think of the person before me. She had always been a character from a story until now.

"You shouldn't have attacked that young man and his father today at the meeting. That's not the way a girl should behave."

Right. There she was, my caustic Kawkab Khala.

"In North America, women are encouraged to speak their minds," I answered.

The glow of the cigarette illuminated Kawkab's amused expression. "I only meant that an intelligent young woman—I assume you are intelligent—would not lay all her cards on the table. Gather information, consider your options, and then act accordingly."

"What would you have done?" I asked. Despite my annoyance, I wanted to know.

She dropped the cigarette butt into the grass, ground it with her foot. "I am still gathering information on the situation."

What situation? Our restaurant, the new restaurant, or something else altogether? Perhaps my aunt was the real spy.

As if reading my thoughts, Kawkab Khala said, "Have you asked anyone about me?"

"I grew up hearing stories of your adventures."

Kawkab's brown eyes glittered in the dark night, long fingers pale blue shadows. "Do you know why they called me Billi?" she asked.

"I assumed it was your middle name, short for Bilqis," I said. It was a common Muslim name.

"*Billi* is Urdu for cat. And what do cats do best?"

I waited for her answer, now thoroughly confused by this conversation.

"Cats climb when they are in danger," she said, walking back towards the house. "I will tell Ghufran you are outside."

What was all that about? I sighed, pulled out my phone and messaged StanleyP.

AnaBGR

I need some more advice, oh wise one. You managed to get
your dream project green-lit while I haven't managed to do
anything right lately.

I pressed Send and waited for an answer. After a few moments, I
wrote again.

AnaBGR

I'd like to hire you as a consultant on how to stop fearing and
learn to love competition. You would be doing me a huge
favour. I can offer as compensation one hilarious meme on one
of the following topics: classic '90s movies, vintage stationery,
or Hollywood icons. Reply now—this offer won't last!

Nothing from StanleyP. Vaguely disappointed, I sent him a meme
of Tom Hanks wearing a sweater vest, then headed inside.

Thankfully, the rest of my family had retired for the night, so I could
delay further awkward conversations about the BOA until tomorrow. I
got ready for bed and was settling on the sofa when my phone pinged.

StanleyP

This is going to sound strange but . . . what business is your
family in? I know we said no personal details, and you can keep
it vague, but I've been having a few weird days. That's my price.

AnaBGR

This feels like extortion.

StanleyP

Furniture? Automobiles? Manufacturing? Tech? World domination? I have to know.

AnaBGR

World domination, via the exciting world of tech.

StanleyP

Thank God.

AnaBGR

What's going on?

StanleyP

Nothing. I'm only losing my mind. Don't mind me. As for your question: I have suggestions, I have battle plans, I have a militia of eager bots standing by. I will send them all your way soon. Things have become complicated with my own dream project, so working on that first.

I wished him good luck and signed off. I wasn't sure why I had lied about my family business. I suppose I didn't want anyone, not even my loyal listener and friend, to know the truth about me and Three Sisters. I wasn't ready to feel that vulnerable, not over a situation that had only begun to feel dire in my own mind.

As I drifted off to sleep, I felt better knowing that StanleyP had my back. Even if his suggestions were ludicrous, they would at least make me laugh. He was slowly becoming a necessary part of my life. I could admit that to myself, at least.

Chapter Fourteen

I planned to corner my cousin the next morning over breakfast and get him to spill every last detail he knew about Kawkab Khala and what she was really doing in town. I was confident Rashid would crack quickly—the boy had zero game.

Except, when I emerged from the shower, Rashid had disappeared. I resolved to catch him at Three Sisters, after I had made my father and Fazee breakfast.

My sister was awake when I knocked on her bedroom door. She hadn't had much of an appetite lately, but I urged some toast and fruit on her anyway. The small television was on, and her eyes remained on the morning news as she absently answered my questions. Yes, she felt fine. Yes, she had slept well. No, she didn't feel like chai this morning.

I was worried about her. Then again, I was worried about a lot of things. And I still had to speak to Rashid. I set off for the restaurant.

I was so wrapped up in my thoughts I didn't notice Yusuf on the sidewalk behind me until he tapped me on the shoulder. "Ready for that coffee?" he asked.

I really wanted to talk to Rashid, but talking to Yusuf about the new restaurant was important too. We walked to Tim Hortons.

The Tim Hortons coffee shop was smaller than Three Sisters, but it was filled with neighbourhood folk grabbing caffeine or a snack before work, young moms seeking a sweet treat for their kids, seniors socializing with friends. I went to order while Yusuf snagged a table at the back, far away from the quartet of retired uncles engaged in a deadly game of gin rummy.

Mr. Lewis was at the counter, and he smiled at me when I joined the line. My answering smile faded as I recognized the man standing beside him—Junaid Uncle. Aydin's father ignored me, spoke a few quiet words to Mr. Lewis, and left.

"What did he want?" I asked Mr. Lewis when it was my turn to order. A cheerful white man in his late fifties, Mr. Lewis, balding and slightly overweight, was dressed in his usual white polo and dark pants. He shrugged at my query.

"Wanted to know if I was willing to sell the store. I told him no, thank you, and offered him a complimentary drink, which he turned down. Not the friendliest guy, that Junaid fellow," Mr. Lewis said, filling two cups with fresh coffee and handing me a cookie, my usual order. "He was willing to pay over market value, but I told him this is home and I plan to stay. Heard he's been hitting up all the stores, kicking the tires to see who he can shake loose. Patel at the convenience store might sell; he's been thinking of retiring."

Mr. Lewis's chatter masked my pounding heart. I remembered Junaid Uncle's words from the BOA meeting the night before: *every last one of you will be bankrupt within five years*. If the Shahs started throwing money around Golden Crescent, how long would people hold out before folding?

I returned to Yusuf, disturbed. "Tell me what you know about the Shahs and Wholistic Grill," I said abruptly, setting his coffee before him.

Yusuf didn't know much, only that the restaurant would be opening soon, that it was a gourmet diner, and that the menu would offer things like upscale halal burgers, fries, and shakes. He also told me that Brother Musa had not been impressed with Aydin and Junaid Uncle's behaviour at the meeting. I was sure he hadn't appreciated my contribution either.

"The whole street is behind your family, Hana. The last thing we want is big business gentrifying Golden Crescent. I'm going to organize a protest during their launch and try to get some traction for this story with local media."

Clearly Yusuf and his father hadn't heard about Junaid Uncle's attempts to buy out the other businesses on Golden Crescent. I filled him in, and he promised to tell his father. I wasn't confident Brother Musa would be able to do much. Offering to buy businesses wasn't illegal.

I took another sip of my coffee and glumly broke the cookie in half, offering Yusuf the larger portion. I was too sad to enjoy the snack.

My friend had no such compulsion; he finished his piece in two bites and then leaned back, sighing. "It's been so long since we just sat around and talked. I used to see you almost every day on the way to school. Now it's a quick hello when we pass on the street," he said.

I felt a pang at his words and filled in the image of the person Yusuf was careful not to name. Lily would be with us on the bus downtown, hanging out with us as we ate lunch. Our recent late-night conversation had been the first time I talked to her in months.

"I guess this is part of growing up. No time for friends when there's money to be made," I said lightly. We looked at each other and giggled, and just like that, we were kids again, laughing at an inside joke.

"I'm thinking of doing something big," Yusuf said after a moment. He reached into his pocket and pulled out a small jewellery box. I straightened, eyes flying to his face. "You're the only person I can talk to about this," he continued. "Do you think Lily and I have a shot?"

"Shouldn't you have figured that out before you bought a ring?" I reached across and opened the box. A small diamond ring winked back.

"I want her to know I'm serious, that I want to be with her forever. Do you think she will say yes?" Yusuf asked.

I sighed. "I think the two of you are in different places right now."

"Because she's going to be a doctor and I'm in social work? I don't care about that."

"No," I explained patiently. "Because your parents don't approve, and neither do hers. Not now, maybe not ever. Are you okay with that?"

Yusuf shrugged. "They'll come around, once they realize we want to get married."

"You don't know if that's what she wants! You have to talk to her. Be honest about how hard things will be. You might have to leave Golden Crescent, start over somewhere new."

"But do you think it will work out?" Yusuf persisted. He had always been like that, had always needed repeated reassurances before he did anything.

"If it doesn't, Fahim thinks you should marry me," I answered with a straight face.

We looked at each other and burst out laughing.

"Your mom loves me, and your dad doesn't hate me," I pointed out.

"Definitely makes sense. Let's do it. Hana, will you marry me?" Yusuf got down on one knee and batted his lashes at me.

I laughed and looked around the restaurant, hoping no one had noticed our silliness. Aydin stood in the doorway of the Tim Hortons, hands frozen at his sides. His eyes moved from Yusuf, on bended knee, to my face. He quickly exited the shop, and I motioned for Yusuf to get up.

"We can't get married. You're too pretty for me," I said. I hoped my friend hadn't noticed our unintended audience-of-one rival business owner, or I would never hear the end of it.

"If it's not me, I'm sure there will be plenty of other offers. Maybe a stranger with a murky past or something." Yusuf said, looking suspiciously innocent.

We made our way out of the coffee shop towards our respective stores. It was time to corner Rashid.

RASHID WAS BUSING TABLES, TAKING orders, and making conversation with our few customers as if he had been working in a restaurant all his life. I finally got him alone when he went outside to throw out the trash.

"I have to talk to you," I said.

Rashid instantly looked guilty. "You should hear my side before you jump to conclusions."

"Just tell me the truth. You owe me that much."

Rashid closed his eyes tight. "Fine, I admit it. I played baseball with the enemy this morning—and I liked it! Please don't be angry. At least, not until I make a few more friends. I don't handle loneliness very well."

I blinked. "You played baseball with Aydin?"

"Yes. He was terrible. He kept dropping the ball and asking if you and Yusuf are an item. I told him you're too smart to fall for that *ullu*."

Ullu was Hindi for "owl," which was a total burn in India. I would have to work on redeeming Yusuf in my cousin's eyes. "He's not so bad," I said, but Rashid misunderstood me.

"I'm so glad you feel that way. I think Aydin might have a small crush on you, and as the object of many unrequited crushes, I know the important thing is to let your admirers down gently."

My cousin thought Aydin had a crush on me? Not possible after the way I had yelled at him. I dragged my mind back to the real reason I had sought out Rashid. "I want to talk to you about Kawkab Khala. She mentioned something about her nickname last night. I think I'm missing some family history here."

Rashid's face instantly shut down. He hefted the garbage bag into the Dumpster and dusted off his hands. "I should get back inside. The Imam was about to tell me a funny joke about Friday prayer and the difficulty of keeping *wudu* after eating channa."

"What about Kawkab Khala?"

"Kawkab Khala is here to visit with family. That is all." He went back inside the restaurant.

My cousin was hiding something. Well, he wanted to visit Canada, and around here we believe in a little thing called snooping.

I followed Rashid into the dining room and watched as he laughed at Imam Abdul Bari's jokes. Nalla was wearing a beautiful green abaya with white embroidery down the front and on the cuffs of her sleeves. The Imam waved me over and I hugged his wife in greeting. Her shoulder blades felt sharp beneath the dress. I wanted to hold her even closer, but I was afraid I might hurt her. Years ago, Nalla had been my Sunday School teacher. She had told the best stories about the Prophets, acting out all the parts and even bringing in props.

After a few moments of conversation with the Imam and Nalla, I grabbed a water jug and filled glasses, smiling and making small talk with our regulars. In the far corner, an older woman wearing a pale yellow cotton salwar kameez sat in front of an untouched plate of biryani.

"Are you enjoying your food?" I asked when I filled her glass. She jerked, large brown eyes flying to my face as fingers clutched the folds of her cotton dupatta shawl.

"I'm sorry, Aunty, I didn't mean to startle you. Can I get you anything else?"

The woman looked away. She seemed to be my mom's age, maybe older, but unhappiness had been carved into her drooping shoulders. Her voice was so low I had to stoop to hear. "I am waiting for Kawkab," she said in Urdu.

"My aunt?" I asked, surprised.

Again she knotted her fingers in her dupatta. "Please, can I have some more water?" she said.

Her glass was full. "How do you know Kawkab Khala?"

"*Meri dost*," she said. My friend. "Please bring Kawkab?"

My aunt was in the kitchen, chatting with Mom. She rose instantly when I told her about Sad Aunty.

In the dining room, Kawkab enveloped her friend in a hug that lasted a long time. They spoke quietly, their voices too low for interested parties to overhear. My curiosity only grew.

My phone pinged. StanleyP was back, ready to offer advice on how to crush Wholistic Grill.

StanleyP
Since I don't have more specific details about your business,

here's some general advice to drive your competition into the ground. I come from a family of canny entrepreneurs, so heed my words. Step 1: Know your enemy. Find out who you are working against. Observe them in their natural habitat, among friends, family, strangers, enemies. Step 2: Hit them where it hurts. Are they afraid of public humiliation? Losing money? Worried about their family? Once you figure this out, then you can decide how best to make them bleed. Step 3: Be gracious in victory. Always offer to compromise, but make sure you're left with the better hand.

AnaBGR
I'm actually scared right now.

StanleyP
I stand at your service, milady. Go forth and conquer.

AnaBGR
Did you manage to fix that complication slowing you down?

StanleyP
I think I have a better handle on the situation. I plan to implement my own plan of attack soon. Stay tuned. I anticipate success.

Chapter Fifteen

I spent the commute to Radio Toronto brainstorming ways to subtly, anonymously sabotage Wholistic Grill, according to StanleyP's three-step plan.

After I had come up with a few options, I focused my attention on ideas for the show Thomas and I would be pitching to Nathan Davis. We had worked out a plan already, but I wanted to have a few extra ideas ready to go. Perhaps an episode on public schools versus private schools and how students from marginalized backgrounds navigated both worlds. Or we could do a show about the way government census data was used to set policy that impacted everyday life for Brown, Black, and Indigenous populations.

A tiny flare of excitement ignited in my chest. Maybe our show would actually change something or start important conversations. And any of those stories would help secure my place as a respected journalist, not just another token ethnic voice repeating outdated, same-old narratives.

When I arrived in our office, Thomas was at his desk, twirling a pencil. He straightened when he caught sight of me. "Davis arrived early," he said. "We have a window in about fifteen minutes. If you had arrived any later, I would have had to pitch without you."

"Why didn't you text me?" I asked, scrambling to gather my notes.

"Things move fast in the world of broadcasting, Hana. There's no point in having your habitual tardiness ruin our odds. We have a real chance here. You know how rare that is."

Radio stations—and media in general—had been facing criticism lately for their lack of diversity. As Thomas had said in his initial proposal, a writer-producer duo who looked like us would have a greater chance of attracting attention and funding. So why wasn't he meeting my eyes?

I made sure my voice remained calm. "Great timing. I came up with a few other ideas for episodes that I think will add to our pitch."

A knock on the door, and Marisa joined us in the office. She was wearing a crisp white blouse, her hair straightened and blown out for the occasion. A cherry-red Hermès scarf was draped around her neck and over one shoulder. She squeezed my arm. "I have a good feeling about this! The outline Thomas put together is stellar."

Her words gave me pause, but I decided to share my own story pitches before asking what Thomas considered "stellar"—and why he hadn't included me when he drafted this document.

Marisa and Thomas listened to my ideas, brows identically furrowed. "Sweetie, I think it's great that you want to do some serious investigative journalism, but I'm worried you don't have the expertise or the name recognition to go after those issues," she said when I had finished. "When you go into a pitch meeting with a senior executive, you must have an idea that is truly exceptional."

"What exceptional ideas does Thomas have?" I asked. My co-intern still wouldn't meet my gaze. In a distant corner of my mind, alarm bells were sounding.

Marisa placed a hand on the door handle. "Similar to what you two discussed, only with wider audience appeal. We should go. They're waiting for us." Her heels were loud in the hallway as she walked ahead, Thomas close behind. I followed, trying to ignore the queasy feeling in my stomach.

THE CONFERENCE ROOM WAS LARGE and airless and resembled a basement bunker. Metal filing cabinets surrounded a large oval desk banked by a dozen executives in black leather swivel chairs. Nathan Davis was listening intently to a man in front of a projected Excel spreadsheet, and I took the opportunity to study him.

Davis was in his fifties, dressed in a dark suit, striped shirt, and muted tie. He looked like a career executive, a man who had spent most of his working life carefully marshalling other people's ambitions to meet shareholder expectations. His business acumen was legendary; he was responsible for a portfolio of profitable regional and indie radio stations all over the province.

When he met my gaze, I realized I was staring. "Marisa, I hear your interns have a proposal for us," he said, voice gravelly.

Thomas stood up immediately, clutching a tablet in hands that trembled slightly. I had thought we would be pitching together, and I experienced a moment of sinking realization. A quick glance at Marisa confirmed my suspicions. She was looking at Thomas the way a parent does their child at a school play, practically willing his success into being. Thomas and Marisa didn't want me to speak at all.

"Dear members of the executive group, thank you for this thrilling opportunity to present our exciting ideas. My name is Thomas Matthews, and I am an intern at Radio Toronto. My partner, Hana Khan, and I have a proposal for a new show that will explore race, religion, and identity in the Greater Toronto Area. We are both South Asian and have unique backgrounds that will allow us to delve into this topic. I am eager to discuss Indian food, Bollywood movies, and cultural traditions. In addition, as a Muslim woman, Hana's stories will allow listeners to 'peer behind the veil' and learn about important Islamic issues such as radicalization versus assimilation and why Muslim women wear the hijab."

I stared at Thomas, speechless. He had designed the pitch exclusively around everything I had said I didn't want our show to be about. I had been so intent on sharing my ideas that I hadn't pushed Thomas on his game plan—the plan that didn't include me as anything other than a mute figurehead.

Marisa leaned forward. "Nathan, Hana and Thomas have a unique perspective that reflects the changing demographics of our city. They'll bring in new listeners and new stories."

Davis's eyes started to gleam. Corporate loved the idea of untapped markets.

I had to say something. I stood up and forced a laugh. It sounded more like a strained cough but succeeded in capturing everyone's attention. From my new vantage point, I realized Thomas and I were the only people of colour in the entire room.

"Thomas was just joking. Our show aims to be different, not to retread tired storylines about diverse communities. I'm sure we don't need the same old narratives about South Asians and other groups . . ." My voice trailed off as Marisa furiously made *cut it* motions with her hand. I took a deep breath and ignored her. "I have a few other story pitches that would interest a wide range of people instead of a single target demographic," I said, and outlined my ideas.

"We already have people doing those stories," Davis said. "What we don't have is an insider's view on why immigrant communities have resisted adopting mainstream Canadian values. It would also be great to have the occasional Bollywood movie review. And I'm sure everyone wants to know where to find the best ethnic food."

The men and women around the table chuckled at that, and even Marisa smiled weakly. Davis's words had thawed Thomas, who began to nod vigorously.

"Why don't you put together two episodes and let's see what happens. Marisa can send me your formal proposals," Davis said, and turned away from us. We had been dismissed.

"You will love what Thomas and Hana come up with," Marisa said. "Not to mention the uptick in ad revenue. It's win-win, Nate."

StanleyP's advice floated back to me, and for one crazy moment I wondered if Thomas was my anonymous radio friend. His behaviour had closely mirrored StanleyP's words: *Get to know your enemy. Hit them where it hurts. Make them bleed.* Thomas knew what I most wanted to avoid in any radio show we did about race and culture, and he had gone straight for the kill.

At least now I knew StanleyP's advice really worked.

I HEADED OUT TO THE Thinking Wall, except someone had beaten me there.

"It's Hana, right?" Big J said. "I thought I was the only one who knew about this spot."

"There are no secrets," I said. "There is no loyalty."

Big J laughed, eyes closed and head tilted back against the sun-warmed brick. "Welcome to the cutthroat world of radio broadcasting. It's *Game of Thrones* with microphones in there." When I didn't respond, he continued, "Marisa told me you and your friend were planning to pitch a show to Nathan."

"He's not my friend."

An unreadable expression crossed his face. "I see."

"Friends don't use their friend's identity to sell out."

Big J was standing a respectful three feet away, but I spotted the amused sympathy on his face.

"Are you Muslim?" I asked suddenly.

He smiled, and I realized he was kind of cute. He was sporting a Blue Jays baseball cap pulled low over his wide face. His blue eyes were fringed with lashes so dark his eyes looked as if they had been lined with kohl.

"My parents are from Yemen, but we're Jewish. My full name is Jonathan Sharabi."

I smiled at him. He was one of my people after all.

"When I first started in radio, I worked at this small college station in Manitoba. My producer was named Luanne. She was great, really open-minded and interested in including all sorts of voices at the station. She wanted me to talk about what it was like to be Arab and Jewish, as if it were strange to be both." His voice was magnetic, warm and captivating. "I did it, because I was new and I wanted to make her happy. I interviewed my parents and some other people at synagogue. It was okay."

"But," I prompted.

He shrugged one shoulder. "After the story ran, they asked me to do another one just like it. I think it was about kosher food or something. I said no. Life's too short, you know?"

I wiped my eyes and stared at the sky. Big J leaned against the wall and closed his eyes again. After a moment, I did the same thing.

I liked that Big J hadn't asked what was wrong or why I was crying. He didn't try to cajole me to look at the bright side of things or to be grateful for any opportunity received. He just got it.

"Tell me what you really want to talk about on a show," he said quietly.

I launched into my pitch about schools, small business, and census data, but he put out his hand. "I'm talking about the story in your heart. The one that got you into this business. The one bursting to get out. After I left my first job in radio, that story kept me going."

I paused, uncertain. How had he known my other ideas were attempts to make the race and culture show into something meaningful to me? I opened my mouth to tell him I didn't know, but instead I blurted out, "I want to talk about family. Not my family. Just . . . family. The way different families work, the dynamics behind relationships, the way that family can both help and screw you up. I want to talk about secret family histories, the stories we keep hidden from the people closest to us, even though they hold the key to everything."

It was true, I realized. That was what I wanted to talk about, research, obsess over, and find the perfect stories to narrate. Family is everything, and we are all defined by our secrets.

I opened my eyes. Big J looked at me, inscrutable. "Who's stopping you?" he asked.

I opened my mouth to say *Everyone*, but then shut it. We went back to contemplating the sky.

Chapter Sixteen

The next day I had a rare day off. A text message from Lily jerked me from my fitful sleep at nine a.m.

Ice cream for breakfast? Please say yes!

I stared at the screen, blinking. Who could think of ice cream at that godforsaken hour? I had planned to continue researching ways to shut down Wholistic Grill, but I had had trouble falling asleep, my mind spinning in circles because of Thomas and Marisa's betrayal. I turned off the screen without replying to Lily.

Kawkab Khala came clomping down the stairs, immaculately dressed in a pink and cream silk salwar kameez. I shifted irritably on the sofa, burrowing beneath the blanket. I could feel her gaze contemplating my fake-sleeping form, but she said nothing.

Ten minutes later, the smoke from green chilies roasting in a pan made me cough. I threw off the blanket, walked into the kitchen, and turned on the exhaust fan.

Kawkab Khala wordlessly passed me a mug of milky tea. Boiling hot and rich with the taste of cardamom, cloves, and ginger, the brew was strong and sweetened with a heavy hand. It was also delicious. I took another, more appreciative sip.

"Made from real Indian tea leaves, not that brown water you call chai in Canada," she said. "By the end of that cup you will be hooked."

"Why don't you drink coffee if you want something stronger?" I asked.

"In Delhi we drink chai. Also, I own a tea plantation."

Of course she did. I rubbed the back of my neck, knotted from a week of sleeping on the sofa, and tried to think gracious-host thoughts. I didn't get too far beyond *I gave you my bedroom, why do I have to make small talk too?*

Kawkab Khala added three eggs to the pan of green chilies before turning down the heat. Then she buttered toast and carefully divided the scrambled eggs between two plates. She nodded at the tiny kitchen table.

"I don't usually eat breakfast," I said.

"And I don't usually cook. Sit down. I have spent time with your sister, but not you."

I should have checked on Fazeela. I wondered if she was up or listlessly watching a screen again. I resolved to check on her later and took a single, cautious bite. The scrambled eggs were creamy, spicy, and somehow fluffy.

Kawkab handled her fork and knife with the precision of a surgeon. "Thank you for being kind to my friend at the restaurant yesterday," she said.

I realized she was speaking of Sad Aunty. "How do you know her?"

"An old school friend from India. It was a coincidence that we both planned to visit Canada at the same time. I told her to call me once she arrived, so I could introduce her to my family. We are thinking of working on a mutual project together," Kawkab Khala said.

I couldn't imagine my sarcastic aunt working with someone so shy and withdrawn. "Is that why you came to Toronto, to work with your friend?" I asked, remembering my father's words from a few nights ago.

My aunt was silent as she chewed, eyes steady on my face. "So suspicious, Hana *jaan*. The project is a side interest only. I wonder why you cannot fathom that I am here to visit my family. You have the instincts of a journalist."

She was changing the subject, but I appreciated the flattery. Besides, she was right. I had no real reason to be suspicious of her motives—just because she hadn't bothered to let my parents know she would be coming until she arrived with a half-dozen suitcases and vague plans to stay indefinitely.

"Have you heard anything new about that Junaid Shah?" Kawkab Khala asked, and I shook my head no. I hadn't talked to Aydin or his dad since our confrontation at the Golden Crescent BOA meeting.

"Junaid has not changed from when I knew him in Delhi," she added casually.

I was surprised. "You know Junaid Uncle?"

"Everyone in India knows each other," she said, slanting her eyes at me.

She was joking, but as I watched her sitting at our ancient IKEA table, a regal, sharp-eyed witch, I wasn't completely sure.

"Don't underestimate Junaid," she said, taking a sip of her chai. "If one wishes to get the better of such a man, one must be prepared to stoop to his level." She skewered me with a hard look. "Your mother is an intelligent person, Hana, but she has not accepted the gravity of your situation. She still has hope. You are a few steps ahead of everyone in that respect, I think."

I smiled wanly. My pessimism was coming in handy after all.

My aunt neatly aligned her now empty mug and plate. "Our social circles are small, back home in Delhi," she said quietly. "Just like in this neighbourhood. There have been whispers about the Shah family for years, about Junaid's business practices from when he first started out. He bribed government officials in Delhi, then razed a tenement to the ground so he could sell the land at a profit. I heard he only grew worse once he'd moved to Canada." She picked some lint from an immaculate cuff. "No doubt he has raised his son in his image," she added.

My aunt stood to clear our plates, and I joined her, thinking about her warning. If Kawkab Khala was right, how far was I willing to go to stop Junaid Uncle and Aydin before they burrowed even deeper into my neighbourhood?

I thanked Kawkab for breakfast and locked myself in the bathroom. StanleyP had advised me to hit my enemy where it hurt most. At the radio station yesterday, Thomas had given me a first-hand demonstration of the element of surprise. I couldn't wait any longer. I had to act now, to show Aydin that Three Sisters was willing to do anything to survive. Or at least I was.

Aydin put great store on appearances. He had needled me about our restaurant's shabby interior enough times for me to know that. He also cared about his reputation. Why else would he have tried to ingratiate himself with the BOA, despite his father's surly personality? To destroy Aydin, first I had to dismantle his reputation. And through Aydin I would get to Wholistic Grill and his father. I would keep my family safe.

I looked up the phone number for the municipal Workers Health and Safety Centre and dialled. I chose from a menu of options before reaching a receptionist. I explained that I wanted to anonymously report a workplace safety violation, and I was transferred to the right department.

I explained to the sympathetic woman at the other end of the line that I was the sister of one of the contractors hired by Wholistic Grill, a new restaurant in the Golden Crescent neighbourhood. My poor brother had been seriously injured on the job the day before, and though he was too scared to call in the complaint himself, he had described his work environment as hazardous. I was worried he would be more seriously injured if he returned to work, and I was also concerned for the rest of the crew. I improvised the extent of his injuries—severe but not life-threatening—and painted a vivid picture of a worksite that flagrantly flouted municipal regulations.

"I'm pretty sure this construction is being conducted without the proper permits as well," I said, then rattled off the address of Wholistic Grill and spelled out Aydin's full name. The woman promised to look into my complaints. After thanking her profusely, I hung up.

I was doing the right thing, I reassured myself. Somebody had to fight back against Aydin and his deep pockets. So, then, why did I feel queasy?

Next I texted Lily and accepted her invitation to go out for ice cream after all. Talking to her would help me remember what I was fighting for. I sent another text, inviting Yusuf to join us. I needed both my best friends around, and if they managed to patch things up between them, that would be a bonus—and proof that I could also put some good into the world.

• • •

ISCREAMS WAS A GOURMET DESSERT shop that sold the best ice cream brand in the world, Kawartha Dairy. It was a fifteen-minute walk north in a newer plaza, one that contained a Starbucks, an upscale grocery store, and a craft supplies chain. Lily was already there, nursing Moose Tracks, her favourite flavour—vanilla and chocolate and mini peanut butter cups. I gave her a side hug and ordered my usual, Death by Chocolate.

"How's Fazee?" Lily asked when I sat down. "Tell her she can call me anytime. I know being on bedrest can be lonely." I assured her that my sister was doing well, overall.

Lily reached out to squeeze my hand before changing the subject. "Tell me you know mystery boy's real name by now."

I didn't want to talk about StanleyP, his advice still vivid in my mind. I felt guilty enough about what I had done to Aydin. Instead I asked her for a life update.

Lily took a deep breath, as if coming to a decision. "I interviewed for the residency position. I found out yesterday I got the job," she said.

I whooped loudly and enveloped her in a hug, almost crushing her ice cream cone. "Yes, Doctor Moretti! I am so proud of you!" When I let her go, my eyes had welled up with tears. I knew how hard my friend had worked to get there, how much she had worried and fretted.

Lily remained quiet, toying with her ice cream. "It's in Timmins," she said. "That's more than halfway to James Bay. A seven-hour drive north in good weather. I'll be working for the Weeneebayko Area Health Authority. My patients will be from the Kashechewan First Nation and surrounding area."

I was speechless. Lily had never lived anywhere but in our neighbourhood with her parents. She hadn't even gone away for undergrad or medical school. She was the most determined homebody I knew.

The shock must have been clear on my face, because she began talking rapidly, holding my gaze. "I want to make a difference, Hana, not just here but for vulnerable populations. It will be for two years, and I'll learn so much."

"Two years?" I repeated.

Lily looked uncomfortable. "That's why God invented Skype, right?"

"You don't believe in God," I said, taking another bite of Death by Chocolate. It tasted like ash in my mouth. I saw so little of her as it was. She would return changed, with new experiences and new friends.

I forced a smile onto my face. "If you're happy, I'm happy," I said. Then the smile turned into something more genuine, and I hugged her again. "Promise you won't be too busy flirting with the other doctors and nurses to text me," I said, and she laughed.

The door of IScreams dinged and Yusuf entered the store. "My favourite people and my favourite breakfast," he said, eyes crinkling. He looked at Lily. "Hey, stranger."

I mouthed an apology to Lily while he went to order his usual two scoops of vanilla. I could tell she was annoyed, but she only told me to stay quiet about the new job and her imminent move.

Yusuf took a seat beside Lily and finished his cone in a few bites. He started regaling us with a funny story about his father and a mix-up with the weekly order of berries that soon had us giggling at his spot-on impression of Brother Musa.

Lily even laughed when Yusuf snuck a bite of her Moose Tracks. "Hey," she said, holding her cone away from him, "get your own!" When Yusuf reached around and took an even bigger bite, Lily gave him a playful punch on the shoulder. I felt pleased with my handiwork.

Yusuf then turned to me. "I almost forgot, I talked to my dad about

Junaid Shah. We're going to bring up his threats with City Council, see if we can get them involved over his comments about gentrification and evicting local businesses."

I filled Lily in on recent events. By the end of my narration she was horrified. "Junaid Shah sounds like a monster!" she exclaimed.

"His son is even worse," Yusuf said. "Right, Hana?" I nodded mutely and he continued. "I can't stand these corporate types. All that matters is their bottom line. We can't let them throw their money around and try to sabotage Golden Crescent."

I flinched at *sabotage*. Yusuf's social justice spirit had been activated. Unfortunately, his words had also reactivated my guilt.

"Aydin is only trying to open a business, if you think about it," I started, hating the meekness in my tone. Why couldn't I fight back, and actually feel good about it? I shook my head, and both Lily and Yusuf stared at me.

"Aydin isn't simply a businessman, Hana," Yusuf said slowly, as if he were speaking to a young child. "He's a colonizer. He and his father have their sights set on our neighbourhood, our home. Don't be fooled by his pretty face and expensive clothes. The father is nasty, but the son is the real predator."

I flushed at Yusuf's words. They closely resembled my own thinking, and it was strange to hear them spoken out loud. I was starting to regret coming out for ice cream after all.

Yusuf turned his attention back to Lily and began telling her about his latest passion project, a free medical clinic for refugees. They were looking for doctors willing to volunteer. Would she have time to take a quick tour today?

He gave me a significant look, and I snapped to attention. "We can catch up later, Lil," I reassured her. "You should spend some time with Yusuf on this very worthy cause."

We all agreed to dinner in the next few weeks. My two best friends exited, leaving me with an uncomfortable swirl of feelings. Was my aunt right about the rumours surrounding Junaid Uncle? Was Aydin really a colonizer, as Yusuf had put it? Was Golden Crescent slated to be the next stop on his eastward march from Vancouver? If so, why did I feel so awful about making a fake complaint against his business? This was war, after all. *Because you lied. Aydin never lied to you.*

As if my thoughts had conjured him up, the doorbell chimed and Aydin walked into IScreams, his gorgeous publicist-fiancée on his arm.

Chapter Seventeen

Correction: Aydin and Zulfa walked into IScreams accompanied by my cousin. Rashid spotted me and glanced guiltily at Aydin. There was a lot of that going around.

"Stop following me!" Rashid said loudly. Aydin looked startled, then noticed me. The expression on his face turned stony, but Zulfa smiled and made her way over.

"Hana, right?" she said in a sweet, singsong voice. She was dressed in an emerald green jumpsuit with a cinched waist that emphasized her Barbie doll proportions. Her hair swished around her shoulders like a very expensive curtain, and she walked confidently in three-inch stilettos. Next to her I felt frumpy in my old jeans and black sweatshirt, faded jersey hijab thrown carelessly over my head.

"And you're Zainab, right?" I asked, playing dumb.

"Zulfa," she said, smiling brilliantly.

Gag. She was beautiful *and* nice. "Zalfu?" I repeated, eyes wide.

"You're so lucky you have a name that's easy to pronounce," Zulfa said, sighing prettily. "I've started just spelling my name when I introduce myself. 'Hi, I'm Zed-you-ell-eff-ay.' I still get a blank look, but at least that way they can visualize it in their heads first."

Nice, beautiful, and smart. Damn. "My full name is Hanaan," I muttered. "Nobody can pronounce it either, so I go by Hana."

Rashid sat down beside me. "They followed me here, I swear it," he said.

"You asked us to come with you when we met outside your aunt's restaurant," Zulfa said. A mischievous smile danced on her lips. "Something about feeling lonely in a strange land?"

Rashid shot her a look before turning back to me. "It was most difficult to get rid of them, Hana Apa. You understand how hard it is for an Indian to be rude. The politeness gene has been bred and beaten into me quite intensely."

I rolled my eyes, but Zulfa's musical laughter made my cousin smile broadly. "What did you say your name was again?" she said to my cousin.

"R-A-S-H-I-D," he said, smiling. "And you are the beautiful Zulfa, fiancée to the silent usurper Aydin."

"We're here for ice cream," Zulfa said.

"I thought you were here for the steak and mashed potatoes," I said, cutting my eyes at Aydin, who stood behind Zulfa. His arms were crossed and he looked uncomfortable. A delicious feeling of mischief bloomed in my mind.

Zulfa laughed again. "Aydin said you were funny! I hope it's okay if we join you." Not waiting for an answer, she took a seat and then turned to Aydin. "That Black Raspberry Thunder sounds interesting. Order me a scoop?"

"I'm sure Hana wants to be left alone," Aydin said shortly, still not looking at me. "There are plenty of empty tables."

"No, please have a seat," I said. What was I doing? The politeness gene had clearly been bred into me too.

Aydin caught my eye. "You don't have to pretend to like us."

"I like Zulfa just fine," I answered, and Aydin flushed.

Zulfa laughed. "Ooh, burn." She turned to me. "I had a feeling we would be friends."

Mr. Silver Shades walked to the counter, joined by Rashid.

Maybe she really was only Aydin's publicist. Zulfa's eyes were clear and unassuming, her face empty of guile. I supposed beautiful people have no need to be underhanded. People just give them whatever they want, whenever they ask for it. I sank even lower in my seat and considered my options. I wasn't in the mood to eat ice cream with Aydin. I contemplated making a run for it. If Rashid weren't there, I would have, except his words had made me feel bad.

My cousin had been in Canada for over a week, and he had been the perfect guest. I, on the other hand, had not been the perfect host. I had tried to pump him for information about Kawkab Khala and then ignored him the rest of the time. Yet he hadn't complained once, had even come to the BOA meeting and stood up for me, though we barely knew each other. The least I could do was stay and watch him eat ice cream.

Aydin returned with two cups, Black Raspberry Thunder for Zulfa and Mint Chip. He handed the Mint Chip to me and took a seat beside his fiancée. Rashid was still at the counter, holding three different sample spoons and pointing at yet another flavour.

"Aydin has been working at his restaurant non-stop," Zulfa said, leaning towards me conspiratorially. "I've barely seen him all week. You're coming to the opening, right? We've been running ads on social media, giving away coupons, and distributing flyers. Please say you'll be there. Bring Rashid too. Your cousin is fun."

"Hana's not going to be there, Zulfa," he said. "Just drop it."

Zulfa's brown eyes were puzzled. "I'm sorry to hear that. Aydin told me how much he enjoyed your mom's food. I thought she might want to attend as well."

I looked over at Aydin, then back at the ice cream he had handed me, and took a cautious bite. It was pepperminty and cold, the chocolate chips crunchy and sweet. I felt his eyes on me as I took another taste. "Thanks for the ice cream," I said.

"It's not a peace offering." He looked grumpy. "Mint Chip is my go-to when I'm upset. If you don't like it, I can get you another flavour."

"I'm not upset," I said. Then, more quietly, "This is fine. It's one of my favourites too."

"I don't know how you can eat that," Zulfa said to Aydin. "It tastes like toothpaste."

Aydin's stony expression softened. "We can't get married if you don't like Mint Chip. Irreconcilable differences."

Zulfa laughed again, and I swallowed thickly. Married. These two were engaged to be married, and Aydin wanted to put my mother out of business. I stood up. "I should go."

Aydin stood too. Still seated, Zulfa gave me a tiny wave. "Please try to make it to the opening. I'm lonely in a strange land too, and could use the company." She winked at Rashid, who was looking over at us from the ice cream counter. From the heart emojis in his eyes, I could tell my cousin was a goner.

I hurried to the door, but Aydin easily kept pace. "You don't have to run away. We would have left you alone if you wanted," Aydin said.

"Does your offer extend to the neighbourhood too? Will you leave if I ask nicely?" I asked sweetly.

Aydin's brows drew together at my words. "I told you I'm not leaving Golden Crescent," he said. "You might as well stay and fight, if you think Three Sisters has a chance to survive. Though I'm positive your restaurant hasn't turned a profit in months. Ask your mom how much debt she's had to take on."

Stung by his harsh words, I leaned close, not wanting to make another scene. "There are other ways for a restaurant to fail," I hissed. "Nobody thought David would win against Goliath, and look how that turned out."

"Are you threatening me?" Aydin took one step closer, eyes hard on my face. His gaze dipped lower, to my lips, before looking away.

"Yes," I said, heart pounding.

"You don't want me as your enemy," Aydin said.

"Well, we can't be friends, so where does that leave us?" I asked.

Aydin swallowed. The ice cream shop had grown quiet around us, as if we were inside an intimate bubble. I flashed back to the first time we had met, the way his father's words had affected him, and I felt sorry for him all over again, and then guilty about what I had done to sabotage his store. Without thinking, I handed him my ice cream. He took a large bite, face relaxing as he swallowed. Our eyes met once more, and the ice cream shop resumed breathing. Or maybe that was just me.

He had a smear of Mint Chip at the corner of his mouth. His chin was prickly with stubble, smoother near his lips. The urge to run my fingers along his jaw, to feel that scratchy-smooth skin, was suddenly overpowering. I had to leave.

"Hana," he said, voice low, eyes completely black.

Shit. "There's something on your face," I said, and stumbled out of the store.

• • •

I HAD IMAGINED IT. AYDIN was my sworn nemesis. That jolt of electricity between us was nothing more than old-fashioned burning hatred. Easy to mistake for that other emotion I definitely wasn't feeling.

"Hana Apa, wait!" Rashid jogged up to me. He held an enormous sundae in his hands, at least five different flavours loaded into an oversized bowl, the entire concoction covered with sprinkles, nuts, chocolate chunks, and caramel syrup, topped by a single cherry. It looked like something a sugar-deranged five-year-old might order.

"I was talking to Brother Musa about the summer street festival," he said, taking a giant bite of his sundae. "I told him that you and I would volunteer to organize this year. It might help business at Three Sisters. I told Aydin about the festival as well," he added as an after-thought.

What? "Why would you do that without asking me?"

Rashid said innocently, "It is a street festival for Golden Crescent. His restaurant is part of the neighbourhood. And he said Zulfa would be there." My cousin got a dreamy look on his face. "She looks just like Sridevi," he said, referring to the late Bollywood superstar. "I don't think Aydin and Zulfa have been engaged for very long. They barely look at each other. Do you think I might have a chance?"

I rolled my eyes and we walked home in silence. Now I had the street festival to contend with along with everything else. Aydin would want to be included in any planning. My stomach churned at the thought of talking to him again after that strange moment between us at IScreams—and my recent attempt at sabotage.

Once back at Three Sisters, I sat in my usual booth to wait for customers and did what I should have done a long time ago: I googled "Wholistic Burgers and Grill." A professional-looking website was the first hit, and links to the restaurant's menu had already been posted on Facebook. I noticed its page had over a thousand followers, and when I clicked on its Instagram account, a barrage of artfully arranged white plates heaped with glistening baskets of hand-cut fries, perfectly round and crispy onion rings, and artisan gourmet burgers topped with avocado slices, alfalfa sprouts, fried egg, and crispy halal beef bacon greeted my stunned eyes. The meat was organic and hand-cut, sourced from a local farm, an advertisement claimed. "The way zabiha halal was meant to be!"

Another picture displayed a parade of milkshakes in pastel colours, each topped with whipped cream and artful decorations such as creamy chocolate shavings and luscious fresh fruit. The French vanilla came with silver and gold sprinkles, and the vibrant green mint chip shake was studded with bright red-and-white candy cane. All were offered in lactose-free and vegan varieties.

Each picture had been liked hundreds of times, and the comments were positive and slavering:

Can't wait!
omg loooooove where do I line up?
gourmet halalz in Golden Crescent? Finally! SIGN ME UP BROTHER!

My mouth began to water, even as I felt an overwhelming wave of jealousy mingled with panic. I closed the apps. We were screwed.

The last time Three Sisters had bothered to advertise had been . . . never. My attempts at making a website had been nothing but wishful thinking so far. No one in the family had even thought to marshal the power of social media to post beautifully curated, well-lit pictures of our food, or to distribute flyers and coupons. We didn't even have a menu posted online.

I checked my phone for messages from StanleyP. He had sent me a meme of an army of spider robots attacking a fortress.

It was time for the next phase of my plan. I couldn't let Aydin win. Not when my family had so much to lose.

THAT NIGHT I SIGNED ON to Facebook using an anonymous account I had created and proceeded to write unflattering comments under a dozen professional photographs on the Wholistic Grill page. "Halal gourmet? More like halal not," I wrote, wincing. My attacks didn't have to be clever, only damaging. "I know where this so-called halal restaurant buys its meat, and they aren't halal. The owners aren't Muslim either. STAY AWAY!"

On the carefully curated Wholistic Grill Instagram account, I spent half an hour planting more seeds of doubt about the restaurant's authenticity. Muslims who care about the halal provenance of their meat take that designation very seriously. If there was any suspicion the owners were lying about the authenticity of halal on offer, the results could be disastrous. Ours was a close-knit community, and rumours spread quickly. I hoped.

I logged out of my fake accounts. My queasiness had now turned into actual nausea. *For my family*, I reminded myself, but the thought wasn't as comforting as it should have been. If Mom or Baba knew what I had done, they would be horrified. But someone had to fight dirty.

I texted StanleyP. He would be on my side, surely.

AnaBGR
Checking in. You said you would soon be anticipating success.
How goes the campaign to vanquish your foes?

StanleyP

Not as well as I'd hoped.

AnaBGR

What happened? Were you double-crossed? Is there a spy in
your midst?

StanleyP

The more I get to know my competition, the harder it is to hurt
them.

AnaBGR

This is business, not personal. Repeat after me: NOT personal!

StanleyP

Except it would be personal, for both of us. I can't stop thinking, is this what I really want to do? There has to be a better
way. What is the point of destroying your enemy if it leaves you
all alone?

AnaBGR

No matter what happens in the kitchen, never apologize.

A long pause. Then:

StanleyP

Where did you get that from?

Julia Child said it, obvs. You've never heard it before? It means take control of your domain and own your actions.

StanleyP

No, I've heard it before. I thought your family was in the tech business.

AnaBGR

Techies like to cook too.

StanleyP

I have to go.

Chapter Eighteen

Secret Family History. Family Fodder. Family Fandom.

I was wide awake after fajr and decided to drag myself and my laptop into the backyard to watch the sunrise. I had been trying to work on the story in my heart, as Big J had suggested. So far, typing possible titles for my possible podcast was as far as I had gotten. The backyard was quiet in the post-dawn hush, the sky lightening slowly.

The click of a lighter brought me back to the present, along with the sharp scent of tobacco. Kawkab Khala leaned back against the fence beside me, blowing smoke up into the pale morning sunlight.

"Second-hand smoke is almost as dangerous to bystanders as first-hand smoke is to smokers," I said.

"Feel free to move. I won't be offended."

I edged my chair a few feet away as Kawkab watched with amusement. "Did you look me up on the internet?" she asked, shifting closer to me.

"Yes," I said, irritated. I had searched up my aunt after looking up Wholistic Grill the previous night, with little success. I had tried every combination of my aunt's full name, her family name, even

"Billi Apa." My search had yielded nothing.

"And did you ask Rashid about me?" There was a hint of a satisfaction in her voice.

I didn't answer.

"Cats climb," Kawkab Khala said, blowing more smoke into the air.

I coughed dramatically, waving a hand in front of my face. "As you said."

In response, Kawkab took a deep drag before changing the subject. "Your sister married so young. Have your parents tried to marry you off as well?"

My hands stilled over the keyboard. "Fazeela and Fahim fell in love and decided to marry. I guess my parents assume I'll do something similar. I'm only twenty-four, so there's no rush."

"Yet you have no suitor on the horizon. Unless you are interested in that vapid but undeniably handsome friend of yours, the grocer's son. Or perhaps you would prefer to have a more comfortable life and have set your sights on Junaid's son."

"You implied that Aydin is just like his father," I said. "Greedy and manipulative."

My aunt smiled evilly. "Young women enjoy the bad boys and the beautiful boys," she said.

"I'll take neither, thank you," I answered, and returned to my laptop. I googled "podcasts about family" and started reading. My aunt crept closer, and I could feel her looking over my shoulder. I snapped the cover closed and sighed deeply.

My irritation must have been highly entertaining for my aunt; she was regarding my face with a thinly masked grin. "In my day, twenty-four was ancient for a woman," she said.

I scowled, but then the back of my neck prickled with sudden awareness. My aunt was trying to tell me something, I realized, in her eccentric Kawkab Khala way. "But you said you didn't get married until you were in your forties."

"For years my parents tried very hard to find me a husband, from my seventeenth birthday until the year I turned twenty-four."

Silence as I absorbed that information. "What happened when you turned twenty-four?" I asked.

Kawkab Khala smiled slowly, flicking her half-finished cigarette to the ground. "Let me tell you a story," she began.

TWENTY MINUTES LATER, MY FACE was frozen in a mask of amazement. "You . . . that didn't . . . what . . . ?"

My aunt played with the button of her white silk salwar tunic.

"Why did you tell me this?" I asked after a few seconds of incoherent babbling. I was still processing the remarkable story Kawkab Khala had told me. The details made my head spin, especially considering their context in 1970s India.

She shrugged. "Everyone already knows the story. It is a badly kept secret back home. And I know you are a storyteller, so I thought you would enjoy it. Can you guess the lesson?"

"Always carry a gun?" I said weakly.

Kawkab Khala gave me a look.

"Learn to climb trees?"

"I was thinking of something more relevant, such as 'Find your principles and see your story through to the end, no matter what.'"

I looked down at my closed laptop, my abandoned attempt at finding a story worthy to launch my broadcasting career, and then back up at her. My aunt was a woman ahead of her time, I realized. She hadn't been afraid to make bold decisions and carry them out with little worry for the consequences. I wanted to live like that.

I took a deep breath and whispered, "*Bismillah*"—in the name of Allah—to steady myself. "Kawkab Khala, how would you like to be on the radio?"

THOMAS WAS IN MARISA'S OFFICE when I arrived at the station later that afternoon. He poked his head into the hallway when he heard my footsteps. "I was just about to text you. Glad you could join us," he said loudly.

I was late again, and he wanted to make sure Marisa knew it. I tried to muster the energy to be angry at him, but I was too excited about the story Kawkab Khala had told me. It would make a perfect episode for our radio show, if only I could convince Marisa and Thomas.

As I took a seat, they exchanged a glance. "I know you're not happy with the way things went down with Nathan Davis," Thomas said.

I frowned at his understatement.

He continued. "Even though it accomplished our goal of getting funding and the executive team's attention. Marisa and I were thinking, maybe you could tackle something fun and light for our first episode. How about a story about henna designs and the way they've changed over the years? We could talk about entrepreneurs and focus on women-run businesses. It would be positive representation, something quirky and relatable."

I blinked at Thomas. The idea wasn't terrible, even if it was on the list of stereotypical topics I had expressly told him to avoid. Perhaps it meant they would be open to my ideas after all. "Actually, there's another story that I think would work really well. I'd like to talk about families in the GTA, the way that family background moulds us, hurts us, helps us. The theme would be secret family histories. I would interview parents, grandparents, and kids about a defining experience in their family."

Thomas and Marisa exchanged another glance, but I barrelled on, full of ideas and excitement. If only they could hear Kawkab Khala's story, they would understand. "I'd like to start off by interviewing my aunt. She's visiting from India, and she has the most amazing story from when she was a young unmarried woman." I quickly filled them in on the remarkable story Kawkab had shared. When I finished, I waited for their enthusiastic response.

Instead, my boss and fellow intern remained quiet. "How do we know this story is true, Hana?" Marisa asked carefully. "Forgive me, but that does not sound like something a young woman growing up in India would actually do, does it? It all sounds quite . . . progressive for such a conservative country. We don't want to be accused of fabrication."

My boss had never travelled to Asia. Was Marisa accusing me, or my aunt, of making up the story? I glanced at Thomas to see if he agreed with her assessment, and he shifted uncomfortably.

Marisa continued. "I suggest we start small and build our audience. Tell our listeners the stories they want to hear, not the ones we wish were true. With two young, diverse hosts, it is important to avoid anything that might be seen as propaganda."

My head reeled at her words, and again I turned to Thomas, suddenly suspicious. "What story will you be working on while I research the one on henna?" I asked.

Thomas cleared his throat. "That other story Nathan wanted. The one about radicalization."

"You mean Muslim radicalization, right? Not radicalization among other groups, like the rise of the alt-right, for instance? Or about how the word *radicalization* has been used to justify war and the curtailment of civil rights for marginalized populations around the world?"

Thomas shrugged uneasily. "He seemed to be interested in a story that was more . . . focused and timely."

I exhaled. "You're not even Muslim," I said.

"You could fact-check, darling," Marisa said. "Make sure he gets the tone right."

"Yes, we wouldn't want Thomas to get the *tone* wrong," I said. My eyes pricked with tears and I stood up.

"Hana, please," Marisa said. Her voice was so gentle I had to bite my lip to keep from bursting into sobs. "A story about something fun, such as henna, will be more palatable to our listeners, less likely to offend. You could talk about the way henna art has been embraced by regular Canadians. Leave the political topics for later. The key to success in this business is to camouflage the message in bite-size, easily understandable chunks. You understand, yes?"

In her own way, Marisa was eager to make amends, and I felt my fury drain away at her words. She had no idea what she had suggested, I realized. How her words had minimized me and the stories I wanted to tell, the ones that didn't fit with her tidy understanding of what would appeal to our audience. She thought my story ideas needed camouflage to appeal to our listeners. Except I couldn't hide who I was—something always gave me away.

I thought about Baba. He had advised me to be pleasant and amenable at work so that I could start to plan my future. I knew how much my security mattered to my parents, and to Baba in particular. The accident had left him vulnerable, and he had few options for future work. I couldn't disappoint him too.

"I'll start doing research on the henna story," I said.

If Marisa refused to see the potential in Kawkab Khala's story, I would work on it myself. I recalled my aunt's words from the night before: *Find your principles and see your story through to the end, no matter what.*

...

Welcome to another episode of Ana's Brown Girl Rambles.

We spend our lives working, hoping, planning, and—if you're religious like me—praying for opportunity. I come from a family of entrepreneurs, people who aren't afraid of risk, but who have also paid a price for throwing themselves out of the plane without a parachute. I love that about them, and I recognize that trait in myself. I am heedless sometimes, and I say things I don't mean when I'm angry, or if I think the people I love have been hurt. I suppose that makes me human.

I don't have a lot of family in Canada. Like many immigrants, my parents moved here and made a life for themselves far from where they grew up. No cousins or aunts and uncles to hang out with during Eid. No grandparents to spoil me on my birthday or to tell my parents to chill when they disciplined us. But now I have some family around me, here on a visit. They feel like strangers, yet we are linked in unexpected ways. I see traces of my own features on their faces, or they smile like my mother. They know my stories, and my parents' stories, and their parents' before them. It is the strangest thing to have felt alone in the world for so long, and then to find you have roots that run so deep they are anchored in the bedrock, leading back to a place I have only ever visited as a tourist.

But I am made up of more than my roots; I have grown above ground as well. My branches reach out in different directions. My limbs have faced wind and snow and ice and rain. My leaves open to the sun and close in the dark. I guess what I'm saying is I'm grateful for every new root I have discovered lately, and for every new bud that sprouts, despite everything.

I was pleased with the episode, but for the first time since I had started the podcast, StanleyP didn't leave a comment. Strange.

Chapter Nineteen

When I checked Wholistic Grill's Facebook page a few days later, I discovered I had sparked a lively debate. My smear campaign was clearly hitting its mark; Wholistic Grill had even posted a response to my anonymous attack.

Wholistic Grill Management

Thank you for your continued interest in our restaurant. We are very excited to serve the Golden Crescent neighbourhood, and we would like to reassure customers that all meat served at our restaurant will be hand-cut halal. Once we open, the official certificate from our halal supplier will be displayed and available for inspection.

I had a feeling Zulfa had had a hand in that carefully crafted message. As I read the comments, I could see the damage I had inflicted was extensive. The rumour mill was doing its predictable thing, and guilt sparred with pride inside me.

YusraTK

Halal is really important to me and my family. I'd rather spend my money in a restaurant where I'm sure about the meat.

Dawud Kamal

Who cares about halal

Zeeshan R

Dude, she said she did, wtf.

Dawud Kamal

Halal, zabiha, not halal, who cares. Eating meat is cruelty

YusraTK

Wrong forum, Dawud Kamal. Personally, I'd like more assurances that the owners are Muslim. These so-called halal certificates can be easily forged. Who knows the owners?

AhmadKhan

Not local, I heard.

YusraTK

They're just trying to capitalize on halal because it's trendy. Big corporations want to make money off our community. Where were these big greedy companies 10 yrs ago? I'm not eating there.

Dawud Kamal

You all dumb.

AhmadKhan

You make some good points YusraTK.

Zeeshan R

Not giving them my money either.

Hating myself, I logged into the anonymous Facebook account I had created and added new comments to the fire. I had settled on my course of action, and though I didn't like the way it made me feel, it was also clearly having an impact. Maybe Aydin would take his father and his restaurant and slink away to another part of the city, far away from Three Sisters. I started typing, improvising as I went.

InsiderScoop

Heard Wholistic Grill is in some trouble with the Workers Health and Safety Centre as well. Unsafe working conditions.

YusraTK

That's shameful. I'll spread the word, thanks for sharing. I refuse to support a company that exploits their workers and our community. #CancelWholisticGrill

Zeeshan R

Agreed. Keep us posted @InsiderScoop. #CancelWholisticGrill

Instagram was calmer, but similar sentiments had sprung up on that platform as well, with people latching onto my rumours—okay, libel—and adding their own fuel. My initial comments had been liked several hundred times each, and none of the comments refuted my allegations except for the official statement from Wholistic Grill. Too many people were willing to believe the worst. Clearly I had tapped into a sore spot in the community: who should benefit and capitalize on niche food markets like halal meat. If online sentiment were anything to go by, Wholistic Grill was in for a rough start.

I couldn't resist one final dig before I logged off.

InsiderScoop

I know the local community is not happy. They're planning a protest when—or should I say IF—Wholistic Grill opens. I'll post details here. The Golden Crescent neighbourhood deserves better. #CancelWholisticGrill

I was good at this, and I wasn't sure what that said about me. I knew what I was doing was wrong. My parents had raised me to be honest, to accept that everything would work out if only I had faith. But they had also taught me stories from the life of Prophet Muhammad, peace be upon him. One time the Prophet witnessed a Bedouin man leaving his camel untethered in the desert. When he asked the Bedouin why, the man replied that he trusted God to take care of his animal. The Prophet's advice? "Trust in God, but tie your camel."

I was simply tying my camel, righting the scales of justice in an impossible situation, I rationalized. I almost believed it.

I WAS WORKING ON THE henna story at home on the couch when Kawkab Khala came downstairs, dressed in a starchy white salwar kameez with delicate pink embroidery at the hem and sleeves. Her hair was up and she had a heavy gold chain around her neck and matching gold ear bobs.

"Talking to yourself again?" she asked. She was referring to my podcast. I flushed, but that reminded me.

"I'd like to continue to interview you for that radio story about your life," I said.

"I've already told you the story, Hana. I thought you were good at your job," she said.

I had gotten to know my aunt in the past few weeks, so I was pretty sure she was teasing. "I need a few more details about that period in time and your reflections. I want to make sure I get a sense of your world so I can do this story justice in the edits," I explained.

My aunt smiled thinly at me. "Justice is not for this life, Hana *jaan*."

I jerked at her words. Had she somehow figured out what I was doing to Aydin online?

Kawkab Khala peered at me. "What have you been up to? No, don't tell me. You are just like your mother. Terrible liars both, and I haven't the time for whatever poorly conceived story you'll invent."

"I didn't do anything," I muttered.

"Pity. I hoped to be a bad influence on you. Come on, get dressed. My friend will be visiting shortly, and I cannot have both nieces still in their pyjamas," she announced. I looked back at my laptop with longing but obediently got up to change. I needed my aunt to be in a good mood when we continued the interview.

Fazee was in her room, and she waved me away when I asked if she wanted to come downstairs. She seemed engrossed in a YouTube tutorial, which was a relief after her past few listless days. When I returned downstairs, Sad Aunty was seated in our living room.

Kawkab Khala did not think highly of my black yoga pants and white T-shirt. She looked me up and down and sniffed. "Do all Canadian children dress as if they lived inside a dark cave, Hana, or is it just you?"

I ignored her and greeted her guest. Kawkab Khala introduced me to Sad Aunty, whose real name was Afsana. We settled down before mugs filled with my aunt's signature strong chai, milky and sweetened with a heavy hand.

I took a sip and watched my aunt converse with her friend. She was much gentler with Afsana than she was with me. They spoke of common acquaintances in Delhi, where they both still lived. Afsana was married, with two teenage daughters; she must have married in her late thirties—not common for a woman of her generation. And she had made this first trip to Canada alone, which struck me as strange. Perhaps my aunt enjoyed surrounding herself with unconventional women like herself.

"What a coincidence you both decided to visit Canada at the same time. Girls' trip?" I interrupted to ask.

Kawkab Khala and Afsana Aunty exchanged a look. "Naturally," my aunt drawled. "And if I have anything to do with it, also a shopping trip for you."

She was changing the subject. I turned my attention back to Afsana Aunty. "Do you have family in Toronto?" I asked her.

Afsana looked to Kawkab for help. "Yes," she answered, voice a near whisper. Then, more firmly, "No."

Curiouser and curiouser.

"While you're in town, you should make sure to check out some of the famous sights, maybe go to a musical," I said, trying to make conversation.

Afsana Aunty looked bemused. "I come from the land of musicals. Do you enjoy *filmi* songs?" she asked, referring to the popular music in Bollywood movies.

"I used to watch Bollywood films with my sister when we were younger. I love the dances," I answered, and Sad Aunty smiled slyly at me.

"In Delhi your khala and I would sneak into the theatres late at night. She was in love with Rishi Kapoor," she said, referring to the famously baby-faced actor from the 1970s and '80s.

I burst out laughing, and Afsana Aunty's eyes danced with her revelation of my acerbic aunt's long-ago crush. I was beginning to understand how those two could be friends.

"That was a different life," Kawkab Khala said, smiling indulgently.

Afsana Aunty nodded and played with her empty cup. When she looked up, I could see that Sad Aunty was back. "Thank you for the suggestion, Hana," she said finally. "But I am not here to play tourist."

"Then why did you come to Toronto?" I asked, unable to help myself, knowing I was being rude.

"Because I could not forget," she said, her voice sure.

Afsana's words must have meant something to my aunt, because Kawkab Khala smiled grimly. "Fetch us some of those biscuits from the cupboard, Hana *jaan*, and then you can go. I'm sure you have far more interesting things to do than spend the afternoon with two old ladies," she said. "Perhaps you can work on your poker face. I suggest you practise lying to the men in your life—they tend to be the most gullible."

"I'm not a liar," I grumbled as I set down the tin of sugar cookies between the women.

Kawkab Khala raised an eyebrow at me. "Good choice, *beta*. I doubt you have the constitution for deception."

In a battle of wits with my alleged aunt, I was starting to realize, she would always get the last word. I grabbed my hijab and my phone and left the house.

Chapter Twenty

As I walked into Golden Crescent looking for a man to lie to, I noticed that Wholistic Grill was not surrounded by its usual bevy of trucks, contractors, and construction equipment. An official-looking man with a clipboard stood with Aydin and his father by the entrance. Junaid Uncle noticed me and turned to say something to his son. When Aydin looked up, I gave him a little wave. He didn't wave back.

What was I doing? I shook off my guilt. Maybe the man with the clipboard was their architect. Maybe they were having a perfectly normal meeting at their extremely empty worksite, right before their launch. Sure.

It was lunchtime, but our restaurant was empty. Mom was in the kitchen, talking to Fahim, when I poked my head inside to greet them. Rashid leaned against a wall near the sink, looking serious for once.

"What's going on?" I asked Mom. She glanced at Fahim, who nodded.

"It is time you knew. Hana *jaan*. I'm sure you are aware that things have been difficult lately. Unless something changes, we will be forced to consider our options by the end of summer," she said.

I inhaled sharply. "Do you mean close the restaurant?" Mom nodded. "Why didn't you tell me things were this bad?" I asked.

I watched a parade of emotions cross my mother's face: sadness, fear, and then resignation. She had lived with the knowledge for months, I realized. She was prepared for this, even if she had stayed positive for the rest of the family.

"We're not making enough money to cover basic expenses, and I'm afraid once the other restaurant opens ..." She trailed off. "Your father and I talked it over last night, after looking at our accounts. I had hoped we would be okay, but we are not."

Rashid piped up. "Hana Apa and I have volunteered to organize the summer festival this year, and I am certain it will be a success. Allow us to work on advertising and publicity, and I am sure the increased attention will turn things around for the restaurant. We will rise to the challenge like the Chicago Cubs in the World Series." He tapped his nose. "We must think as they did in *Moneyball*."

We all looked at him blankly.

Rashid focused on my mother. "Please don't make any decisions until after the street festival. We will get the word out more widely, advertise through print and on social media. Let us not forget the lessons of *Field of Dreams*."

We looked at him blankly again, and he threw up his hands. "Haven't you watched *any* baseball movies?"

"We're more of a soccer family," Fahim said. "Fazee loves *Bend It Like Beckham*."

Rashid ignored him. "We need to get everyone excited and take advantage of the widespread animosity against Junaid Shah. No one likes him right now, and they will support each other. Next week, who knows who the villain will be?"

He reached behind the counter and pulled out two large stacks of flyers printed on brilliant goldenrod paper: advertisements for the street festival. Rashid grinned at my surprised expression. "You have no idea how vicious the accounting business can be in Delhi. My parents trained me to attack first and think later."

I made a note to ask Kawkab Khala about Rashid's parents. I wondered what type of "accounting" business they were actually involved in.

Rashid showed off his handiwork, and we all dutifully admired the flyers.

"Hana Apa and I have already made much progress in planning," he lied effortlessly to my mother. "We have another meeting this evening at the Tim Hortons, to work on all the details." My cousin looked at me for confirmation, and I had no choice. I nodded.

Now I allowed myself to hope that the man with the clipboard in front of Wholistic Grill had been sent for a surprise inspection after all. Maybe it would slow Aydin down and give us time to regroup. He was the reason this was happening to my family.

That faint flicker of hope in the eyes of my mother and Fahim was worth any price. I resolved to shelve my guilt and double down on my efforts.

IN THE BOOTH AT TIM HORTONS that evening, Rashid tucked into his order of a half-dozen assorted doughnuts. "When I return to India, I will miss doughnuts very much. Promise you will mail a dozen every two weeks, Hana Apa. I ask for no other payment for all the advice and mentorship I have provided."

I smiled and tried not to think about Rashid leaving. In the short time since his arrival, my cousin had wormed his way into my affections.

I didn't want him to return to India in a year, or four; I would miss his antics and his sense of humour too much. His loyalty had been unflinching, and I had grown used to having an ally on the street.

"Do you miss your family very much?" I asked.

Rashid wiped his face and nodded. "I miss my ammi's parathas. And my abba and I used to drink chai together every morning before he went to the office. There were always people coming in and out of our house; we didn't bother locking the front door."

So much family togetherness sounded wonderful, and suffocating. As if reading my mind, my cousin grinned at me. "Everyone is always in each other's business," he added. "I could barely talk to a girl without everyone asking me when the wedding would be."

"That must have been difficult for you," I said drily.

Rashid nodded solemnly. "But do not worry about the beautiful Zulfa. Once committed, I am a loyal partner."

I smothered my laugh. "I wish you both the best of luck—once you get Aydin out of the way, of course," I teased.

Rashid only waved his hand as if swatting a mosquito.

I took out my notebook and turned to a new page. We had discussed a few ideas already, and I wrote them down while Rashid finished off the doughnuts.

"We cannot call our meeting to order yet," he said, mouth full of glazed goodness. "We are waiting for the rest of the planning committee."

I pinned him with a look. "What have you done, Rashid?"

"I told you that I invited Aydin to the street festival, Hana Apa," he reminded me. "In turn, he informed me that the beautiful Zulfa would help out." So this was all a ploy for Rashid to flirt with Zulfa. I had to have a serious discussion with him about priorities, as well as family loyalty.

Aydin and Zulfa chose that moment to enter the coffee shop. They took their seats, Aydin across from me and Zulfa across from Rashid. She immediately took a small tablet from her designer tote, her tone businesslike.

"I'm so glad Rashid reached out to me. I love local street festivals, and this will really help out Wholistic Grill," Zulfa said.

"Have you encountered problems recently?" I asked innocently. I know, I know.

Aydin and Zulfa exchanged a look. "Everything is proceeding as anticipated," Aydin said shortly.

Zulfa poked his shoulder. "We're among friends, silly." She leaned forward. "There have been rumours circulating online that the restaurant isn't really halal, and that the construction site is unsafe, but we're dealing with it. You know how people love to talk. All part of opening jitters."

Rashid made sympathetic noises while I tried not to smirk. "That must be really difficult," I said. "Rumours like that can devastate a new business."

It was fun to watch Aydin's face turn to stone. His eyes bored into mine. "Nothing I can't handle," he said, jaw clenched.

"You're an experienced restaurateur. I'm sure you'll be fine." I resisted the urge to bat my lashes at him. I was enjoying myself, I realized. Teasing Stone Aydin was turning out to be the highlight of my day. "If you need any advice, feel free to talk to my mom. She's been running Three Sisters on her own for fifteen years."

"Your mom is an inspiration to entrepreneurs everywhere," Zulfa gushed.

"I thought we were here to plan the street festival," Aydin said tightly.

Zulfa straightened, her tone businesslike once more. "You're right. We don't have a lot of time and there is a lot to get done. Aside from food and merchandise, what makes the Golden Crescent street festival different from any other festival in the city?" she asked me and Rashid.

I looked at Rashid, impressed by Zulfa's immediate insight. "We're a local event, meant for people in the Golden Crescent. We're hoping to attract a bigger crowd this year, considering the dire situation both of our restaurants are facing." I nodded at Aydin.

"Wholistic Grill is doing just fine," he said.

"There's no shame in struggle," I said. "Running a restaurant is a really complicated process, with plenty of unexpected traps."

Aydin caught my gaze and held it. "This trap wasn't unexpected," he said softly. The low menace in his voice caused a delighted shiver to run down my spine. He suspected I had something to do with the online rumours, but he had no proof. I bet it was driving him crazy.

Rashid looked from me to Aydin. "When my parents had trouble with their major competitors, the Patel Accountancy Collective, they solved the problem by agreeing to each carve out their own territory. Less profit for both, but also less bloodshed." He paused. "Metaphorical bloodshed, of course. Accountants always wish to stay out of the red."

Aydin and I both stared at my cousin. Zulfa brought the conversation back to the topic at hand and asked if we had confirmed participation of the other businesses on the street. Rashid said he had already spoken to them, showing excellent initiative.

Zulfa nodded and made a note on her iPad before turning back to me. "I saw the flyers for the festival and the Facebook event page Rashid set up. Great work, but you need more. Have you thought about taking out a full-page advertisement in the community newspaper? What about reaching out to the Hindu mandir and the Orthodox church to advertise? Or local radio announcements—can you arrange for a discount on air time at your work, Hana?"

I nodded slowly. "I can ask," I said, impressed. Zulfa knew what she was doing. No wonder Wholistic Grill was flourishing under her public relations guidance.

"People love to support local events. If we can tie the festival to some sort of fundraising drive, that would be even better. You want to empower your attendees and vendors, make them feel they are building community and contributing to an important cause."

"My friend Yusuf is active in a local charity that helps homeless and runaway youth," I said. "There's also a medical clinic for refugees he helps run, and they can always use funds."

"Yusuf is a saint," Aydin said, looking at the ceiling. "What a catch."

"*Ullu,*" Rashid muttered.

I ignored them.

"If we want to brand, we could turn this into a halal food festival," Zulfa suggested, thoughtful. "In the United States, halal food is a twenty-billion-dollar business, and worldwide it's worth seven hundred billion."

"I don't think we should label it a halal food festival," I said after turning the idea over in my mind. "We have businesses on Golden Crescent that cater to a variety of people, not just those who eat halal meat."

Zulfa made a note on her tablet. "What about corporate partners or sponsorship?" she asked. "Most of my contacts are in Vancouver, but let me see if I can find local resources."

Aydin broke in. "Most festivals have live entertainment. My friend Abas will be in town that week. He's part of a bhangra dance troupe called Desi Beat. We could book them."

I blinked in surprise. It was a good suggestion, and here I had assumed he had shown up to intimidate me.

Zulfa looked at my cousin. He had a dreamy expression on his face, hand cupping his chin as he stared at her. "Anything you want to add, Rashid?" she asked.

"With your brains and my looks, our children will be beautiful geniuses. Will you consent to be my wife?" he said.

Zulfa laughed, shaking her head. "No. But can you show me the baseball diamond? I want to see if the park is big enough to accommodate other performers. Live entertainment is always a big draw." She threw me a quick smile as she left, Rashid trailing after her like a besotted puppy.

Aydin and I were alone. An awkward silence descended.

"Zulfa is really good at her job, very competent," I said.

"Don't dodge the subject, Hana. I know what you've been doing online," he said abruptly.

I made my eyes wide. "Are you a fan of RPG gaming too? We have so much in common! Let me guess—your avatar is an ugly, stupid troll."

Aydin looked away, lips twitching. I felt a thrill run through me, as if I had earned points by making him laugh. Disconcerted by my reaction, I stood up to leave, but I couldn't resist a parting shot. "I'm truly sorry to hear your business is in trouble. As you know, Three Sisters has been facing its own crisis lately, so I know how it feels to be attacked by bullies."

Aydin stood up quickly, and I realized I might have gone too far. "Stop spreading rumours about my business online," he growled.

"I don't know what you're talking about," I said, taking a few steps back. My face felt hot and flushed. Why was Aydin even more attractive when he was angry? There was something wrong with me.

He kept pace with my steps. "I mean it. All I've done is open a restaurant on the same street as Three Sisters. What you're doing is sabotage. I could press charges for mischief and libel. Take down those posts."

"Plenty of people are talking about your restaurant online. Are you going to threaten them all with legal action?" I asked.

"If I have to. Take down the posts, Hana."

I held up my hand and he halted instantly, though he continued to glare. "First, I admit nothing," I said, ticking off my fingers. "Second"—I pinned him with my sternest expression, channelling Kawkab Khala and the rest of the badass women in my family—"did you honestly think I wouldn't fight back?"

This time his expression held grudging acknowledgement. "I guess I didn't."

"Now you know better." I picked up my bag from the table and made for the door. He followed, casting quick glances at me as we made our way out of the coffee shop. I waved at Mr. Lewis as Aydin held the door open.

We faced each other on the sidewalk. "Maybe if you had tried to get to know me first—I mean, get to know Three Sisters and the rest of the neighbourhood—you wouldn't be in this mess," I said.

"I'm in this mess because of the lies you spread about my business," he replied.

"Then you should have known better than to piss me off."

Aydin leaned forward. "Maybe I enjoy pushing your buttons."

Sandalwood cologne and intense dark eyes made me dizzy. Our conversation was veering wildly off the rails. I didn't like Aydin, I reminded myself. I wanted him gone, his restaurant a pile of rubble. So what was I doing still talking to him?

He must have realized the same thing, because he pulled back and put his hands in his pockets. "Yusuf picked an unromantic place to propose," he said casually.

I looked at him in surprise. "What?"

Aydin flushed and ran a hand through his hair. "Nothing. It's none of my business."

"Yusuf and I are friends. Like you and Zulfa," I said.

"But not like you and me."

We stared at each other again, and my fingertips tingled with that feeling—the one that always seemed to show up when I talked to this man. I willed away the current, but it only travelled up my arms to my neck, warming my face even as his gaze rested once more on my lips. "You and I are lifelong enemies," I said, my voice raspy.

"To the bitter end," Aydin agreed. We continued to stand there, both reluctant to leave.

"Do you still listen to the radio?" I asked him on impulse. "When we first met, you said you did."

"All the time," he said, surprised. Then, "Have you ever thought about doing a podcast?"

Puzzled at the abrupt change in topic, I instinctively lied. "I'm strictly radio. I know nothing about podcasting. Why?" That came out so naturally my aunt would have been proud.

Aydin shrugged. "I can't make you out," he said.

"Likewise," I said.

His accompanying sigh was resigned. "Take down the posts. Please, Hana," he said quietly.

There was something about the way he said my name that made me feel . . .

"No," I said, and forced my legs to start moving away from him. He might have watched me leave, but I didn't look back. Even though I wanted to—badly.

Chapter Twenty-One

StanleyP
I have a question for you.

AnaBGR
Yes, I am your smartest and most conventionally attractive friend.

StanleyP
I already knew that. With your business, what are you fighting for? Is it simply survival or something else?

Such a serious query from the usually bantering StanleyP, but the question was interesting. I was on my break, seated on a bench on the Golden Crescent strip, enjoying the sunny weather. I typed my reply.

AnaBGR
I guess I don't want to be collateral damage on someone else's march to victory.

StanleyP
Yes, but why? Does it come down to money?

AnaBGR

In the way that everything comes down to money, yes. But it's more than that. Imagine if someone knocked on the door of your home and demanded you leave. Could you abandon it without fighting?

StanleyP

But what if your home was old and falling apart? Maybe it's time to adapt or die.

AnaBGR

Only someone who judged my home from the outside would say that. I know that what's inside is worth the fight. That being said, I'm firmly Team StanleyP. Crush your competition and make them beg for mercy.

StanleyP

I don't think my competition is the begging sort.

AnaBGR

Well, my campaign is going well. I've got them on the run.

StanleyP

I'm proud of you. Don't do anything you regret later.

AnaBGR

I regret nothing.

StanleyP

Take it from this battle-hardened bot: the biggest regrets take a while to manifest, but they get you every time.

I pictured Aydin's face the previous night, before I walked away. Was StanleyP right? I didn't want to talk about it anymore. It was bad enough that I could think of little else.

AnaBGR

What else is happening in your life? Tell me something interesting.

StanleyP

Nothing. You are the sole source of light in the barren wasteland of my life.

AnaBGR

Exactly as it should be. Now tell me what's really up.

StanleyP

Nothing . . .

AnaBGR

Uh-oh. Are you cheating on me with another podcast? Traitor.

StanleyP

Never. But I might have met someone IRL.

I straightened and reread StanleyP's words. He had met someone out in the real world? I wasn't sure what to think. *What about me?* I wanted to write. *We met first.* But my virtual friend hadn't made me any promises, and I had actively discouraged him. Now that I thought about it, the frequency of our texting had slowed down recently. We seemed to have settled into a less flirty, more friend-zone banter. Still, his admission hurt. I wondered if I had read more into the relationship than he had, and my face grew hot with embarrassment. His next message reassured me.

StanleyP
This is weird, right?

AnaBGR
A little.

StanleyP
Forget I said anything.

AnaBGR
It must be something if you mentioned it in the first place.

StanleyP
Have you ever felt a spark for someone almost despite yourself?

I pictured Aydin's face. Nope, I didn't know what that was like at all.

AnaBGR
Sounds serious.

StanleyP

More frustrating. I'm sure it will pass. Tell me more about your plans for routing the enemy. Will there be confetti cannons when you win?

A good friend wouldn't just let it go like that. A good friend would say something. But was that all we were now? I hated being an adult.

AnaBGR

I could have ignored you the first time you messaged, but I responded instead, and that turned out pretty awesome.

StanleyP

It is true that I am both pretty and awesome.

AnaBGR

I'm serious. You're my favourite virtual person.

StanleyP

Likewise.

AnaBGR

And I'm not friends with cowards.

StanleyP

Ouch. Okay, I'll think about it. Thanks.

When I looked up, Zulfa was emerging from the florist shop, a bracelet of jasmine flowers curled around her slender wrist. After our meeting the night before, I felt a lot more comfortable around her. She was genuinely nice, unlike her moody, aggravating friend.

"Pretty flowers," I called, and she made her way over to me.

"The florist gave it to me as a gift. Everyone on this street is so kind. I just put in a big order, for the grand opening," Zulfa said. "Aydin asked me to shop locally whenever possible."

That was surprising. I didn't think our local resources would be good enough for Mr. Silver Shades. "That's considerate of him," I said cautiously.

"He's planning to source all the meat from the halal butcher on Golden Crescent, and the vegetables and fruit from Brother Musa."

Not the actions of a man whose goal was to evict every single business on the street. Though maybe that had been more Junaid Uncle's hyperbole than Aydin's actual plan. I made a noncommittal noise and then redirected the conversation.

"How long are you in town?" I asked Zulfa.

"A few weeks only. I'm here to help out with the launch, mainly. I should say, Aydin and I are helping each other out." A slight blush stained her cheeks, making her look even more delicately beautiful.

"I can't imagine Aydin helping anyone but himself," I said, then wished I had kept my mouth shut. Whatever my personal feelings, he was Zulfa's friend.

But she only laughed. "Don't let that serious face fool you. Aydin is one of the most generous people I know. He's helped me out a lot recently, but he has his demons, just like everyone else." Zulfa hesitated. "Aydin is usually quiet around people he doesn't know. He doesn't seem to have that problem with you."

"We seem to bring out the worst in each other," I said. "Which makes sense. We can't stand each other."

Zulfa shook her head. "I can't speak for your feelings, of course, but Aydin doesn't hate you. You know he's an only child, right? His mom died when he was really little and his dad never remarried. He's always tried to live up to who his father wants him to be—this really focused, profit-driven businessman. I think he's probably more like his mother. My parents say she was creative and gentle. It's sad when people twist themselves up to be someone they're not, isn't it."

"He's lucky to have a fiancée as understanding as you. When is the big day?" I asked, hating myself. I didn't care. I *didn't*.

"We're still working out the details." She winked at me. "I like that you call him on his bullshit, Hana. Maybe you both need someone who gives as good as they get."

She left me at Three Sisters to continue her tour of Golden Crescent businesses. I tried to imagine what growing up with Junaid Uncle must have been like without the balancing effect of another, softer parent. Every time Aydin had turned cold, I realized now, his father had been nearby, or at least present in his thoughts. And Junaid Uncle had been the one to hurl threats at the neighbourhood and try to buy out the other businesses, not Aydin. The son had tried to talk down his father. He had tried to talk me down too, I acknowledged ruefully. Had I been wrong about Aydin all along?

Back at Three Sisters, the few customers finished their meals and I helped with cleanup before setting the tables for dinner. During the lull before dinner, Rashid insisted that we take advantage of our lack of customers to paste more summer festival flyers around the neighbourhood. Together we zigzagged down the street, taping up flyers on storefronts and lamp posts, at the mosque, church, and temple, and on the neighbourhood bulletin board in the community centre. We left a stack of flyers with Mr. Lewis and another at the halal butcher shop.

As we neared Wholistic Grill, I slowed down. Aydin was outside the restaurant, talking on his phone. My face grew hot.

"Why are you turning red?" Rashid asked, looking at me.

"It's really warm out today," I said, waving my hands in front of my guilty, blushing face. I looked around for a place to hide. There were no stores near us, so I ducked behind a tree.

"Why are you turning even redder?" Rashid asked, following me. He had a sudden thought. "Do Canadians get heatstroke if the weather rises above twenty-one degrees Celsius? Or are you trying to avoid Aydin?"

"I'm not avoiding him," I said, contorting my body so Aydin couldn't see me.

Too late. He was walking towards us.

"As my accountant parents always say, it's better to deal with issues directly instead of cowering. Be the blade in the hand, not the snake in the grass," Rashid said.

I was starting to wonder if *accountant* was a New Delhi euphemism for "mafia."

"We had a strange conversation yesterday," I explained, desperate. "Can you please handle him?" I paused, not wanting him to misunderstand what I meant by "handle," given my newly birthed suspicions.

"I did notice tension between the two of you during the meeting," Rashid said. "I was unsure if you wanted Zulfa and me to leave or if you wished to make use of my concealed dagger."

I really needed to talk to Rashid about his jokes. "Just go see what he wants," I clarified.

Rashid shrugged and set off to intercept Aydin. They talked for a long time, heads bent close together. My cousin returned with a big smile.

"Aydin gave me these!" He waved two tickets under my nose. "Two tickets to a Toronto Blue Jays game tomorrow! You must accompany me as my guest."

"Those tickets are expensive."

"He knows I'm a baseball fan, and he said they would go to waste otherwise."

Rashid was so excited. I realized I still hadn't spent a lot of time with my cousin, or even shown him around the city as I had planned. Mom had asked me in particular to take care of Rashid, but so far he had been taking care of us.

"My schedule is completely free tomorrow," I said impulsively. "Why don't we make a day of it? I can show you around downtown Toronto."

Rashid grinned like a little boy who had just learned he could have another piece of rasmalai. "Aydin will be so happy to hear you can make it," he said. My stomach sank at his words. "Back home, when two accountant bosses are unhappy with each other, it is always best if they meet and talk things over. Fewer bodies on the ground that way." Rashid looked at me. "I mean metaphorical bodies."

Why did I get the feeling I had just been bamboozled by the son of a New Delhi mob boss? "Aydin is coming to the game with us, isn't he."

Rashid shrugged. "It would be a bit strange if he didn't join us. These are his expensive tickets, after all." His fingers moved quickly over his phone, texting. "He says he has time for the sightseeing too. What luck!"

Chapter Twenty-Two

When we set off for the bus stop the next morning, Rashid had a list of things he wanted to see in downtown Toronto. "The CN Tower, Kensington Market, Graffiti Alley. Oh, and Imam Abdul Bari said I must visit the aquarium and ponder the majesty of creation in front of the jellyfish tank."

It was nine a.m. and Yusuf was setting up a display of oranges at his father's store. He spotted us and walked over.

"Oh, great, the *ullu*," Rashid muttered. I nudged my cousin in the ribs.

"Where are you off to?" Yusuf asked. He grinned at Rashid, who gave him a small smile and turned away, fingers flying on his phone.

"I'm taking Rashid downtown."

Yusuf frowned. "Just the two of you?"

"Aydin Bhai will also to be accompany us," Rashid said, putting on his fake Indian accent, and I gave my cousin a warning look.

"Why is that guy going with you?" Yusuf asked, eyebrows drawing together.

"Very much we must discuss a business deal of grave import," Rashid said.

"Cut it out," I said to my cousin. "He doesn't talk like that," I explained to Yusuf.

"Talk like vhat?" Rashid blinked at me. "Is there something comical about the vay I am taaaaalking?"

"No, no, of course not, Rashid," Yusuf jumped in. "I can understand everything you say. YOUR ENGLISH IS VERY GOOD!" he said loudly, beaming at my cousin.

I gave Rashid my best *do not mess with me* look and turned back to Yusuf. "I wanted to show Rashid around the city, and Aydin had Blue Jays tickets, so . . ." I trailed off at the sight of Yusuf's unhappy expression.

"You should be careful around him, Hana," Yusuf said, arms crossed. "I don't trust that guy. Make sure he doesn't try anything."

I faltered. *Try anything?* "He's already trying to shut down my mom's restaurant. I don't think he'll have time to try anything else. Besides, Rashid likes him."

Yusuf looked over my shoulder at Rashid, who was still busy texting. "If I didn't have work today, I'd come with you."

A retching sound behind us, quickly masked by a cough. Rashid's head was still bent over his cellphone.

I rounded on my cousin after Yusuf returned to the store. "What's wrong with you? Yusuf is one of my oldest friends."

"He started it. *Ullu.*"

"Who's your friend?" Aydin walked towards us, dressed more formally today in a blue shirt, slim black pants, and white Gucci sneakers. His eyes were hidden behind his silver shades.

"We were talking about Yusuf," I replied, and Aydin frowned slightly.

"You have a thing for pretty boys," he said, removing his sunglasses.

"They have a thing for me," I shot back.

His eyes darkened and he stepped closer. "Oh, look, a tree," he said flatly. "Would you like to hide behind it?"

I blushed and walked quickly towards the bus bench. A minute later, white Gucci sneakers appeared in front of me. I didn't look up.

"I'm sorry," Aydin said. "I was trying to be funny. I'm not as good at teasing as you. Maybe we could call a truce. Just for today?"

I stood up, closing the gap between us. He smelled faintly of soap and that sandalwood cologne I liked, which annoyed me so much that I leaned forward and very carefully stepped on his right foot, pressing down on the soft white leather.

When I lifted my foot, there was a clear black imprint on his formerly pristine shoe. "Truce," I said sweetly.

RASHID WAS DEEPLY UNIMPRESSED WITH THE BUS. "It's no fun without people hanging from the sides," he complained. "Where's the danger? Where's the sense of adventure?" I was almost positive he was joking.

The subway disappointed him too. "No wonder Canadians are so boring. Nobody talks to each other. No boys trying to pick up girls and getting smacked with chappals. Where's the entertainment?"

"It's not so entertaining for the girls being harassed, believe me," I replied. Aydin and I exchanged a glance, then quickly looked away. We hadn't talked too much on the ride. After he had furiously wiped his shoe clean, we had stayed out of each other's way.

Rashid perked up when we arrived at Union Station, craning his head at the imposing beige brick building with its distinctive Beaux-Arts architecture. He bounded ahead as we emerged from the station. "This is more like it!" he said, smiling at a pretty brunette in a floral sundress.

We walked to the CN Tower from the station in silence, Rashid taking videos and narrating his impressions to share with family and friends in Delhi. At the ticket desk Aydin tried to pay for all of us, but I had already bought the tickets online, so we skipped the traditional desi game of *Please let me pay, as my honour depends on this show of generosity.* I've seen grown men almost come to blows when denied the joy of treating everyone. Aydin put away his credit card without a word, and my respect for him grew—slightly.

There was a line for the elevator to the viewing platform. Rashid continued to take pictures while Aydin continued to wear his sunglasses and ignore me. I should have stomped on both shoes when I had the chance.

At the front of the line a perky tour guide with bright red lipstick greeted us. "Welcome to the Canadian National Tower!" she said, grinning at the small crowd clustered in front of the elevator. "The CN Tower was constructed in 1976 and held the record for world's tallest freestanding structure for thirty-two years. It is 553.3 metres tall and is also used as a radio and communications tower. From the top viewing platform you will be able to see all around the beautiful city of Toronto and beyond!" She ushered our group inside the elevator.

My eyes drifted to Aydin, beside me at the back of the elevator. I noticed he had turned an unhealthy shade of Pale White Man. His head was ducked low, arms crossed tightly across his chest. Concerned, I leaned forward and noticed a trickle of sweat snaking from brow to chin. His eyes were closed tightly beneath the sunglasses, and his breathing was shallow. "Aydin," I said softly. "Are you all right?" My hand hovered over his arm.

He didn't respond. But then, it was a stupid question. He was clearly not okay.

The elevator began its supercharged ascension to the LookOut level, 346 metres from the ground. As the other passengers exclaimed over the speed and peered through the partial glass floor of the elevator, I kept my eyes on Aydin, who seemed to be shrinking more into himself the higher we rose. He swayed slightly, and I rested my hand firmly on his arm as his shallow breaths grew ragged.

After what felt like an hour but was probably no longer than sixty seconds, we arrived at the LookOut level. Rashid was at the very front, and he waved as the crowd pulled him out. I exchanged a look with the cheerful elevator operator. Without a word, she shut the door and we began a rapid descent to ground level.

Aydin managed to walk out of the elevator without help, making it through the main door before sinking to the concrete ledge at the entrance. I took a seat beside him and quietly passed him a bottle of water. He removed his sunglasses and took a long sip.

"I'm terrified of cats," I said after his breathing had settled somewhat.

Aydin grunted. "Don't do that," he said. "I don't need your pity."

I ignored him. "Yusuf had a cat when we were kids. Whenever I went to his house, she would wait at the top of the stairs for me to walk past. And then she would jump on me, flying through the air like an avenging tabby angel."

Aydin smiled weakly. His face was starting to look less green.

"Yusuf said his cat loved me, but I knew she just liked to hear me scream."

We sat in silence for a few more minutes. Rashid sent me a selfie from the observation deck, a huge grin on his face.

"You paid for your ticket. You should go back up there," he said.

"Are you kidding me? I'd pay money not to go up that elevator ever again. Every time someone visits from out of town, we take them to the CN Tower. I've been here approximately two hundred times. I should be thanking you." I was babbling. Aydin's reaction had taken me completely by surprise. His arrogant self-possession was one of the most consistent—and irritating—things about him.

"I haven't been here since I was five years old," Aydin said, breaking my nervous silence. "I came with my mother and father. I was so excited. But on the way up, Mom had a panic attack. I think she was afraid of heights too."

I looked at Aydin. His colour was back to its usual warm brown, but there was something glazed about his eyes. I scooted over slightly. He was speaking into his lap, hands curled into tight fists. I wanted to reach over and loosen that grip.

"I didn't know what was happening," Aydin continued. "She started gasping for air as soon as we got on the elevator. I don't think I'll ever forget the look on her face. My dad was so embarrassed."

My eyes were fixed on his, but he wasn't looking at me, or anyone else. His gaze was fixed on the past.

"That's awful." I didn't know else what to say.

"She tried to enjoy herself for my sake. I was so obsessed with the tower. My father kept scolding her. Finally I started to cry and we left. It happened so long ago, but the minute we got on that elevator, it all came back."

This time I did reach over and gently squeezed his hand. We sat in silence, not looking at each other. Rashid sent me another picture of him walking on the glass floor, his face glowing with excitement. I showed Aydin the photo and he took a shaky breath.

"I'm sorry I ruined this for you," he said in a small voice.

I imagined five-year-old Aydin, caught between his terrified mother and his stern father. I wished Junaid Uncle were there, so I could slap his disdainful face. "Don't," I said. "Please don't apologize."

We lapsed into silence once more. I glanced over at him and saw that his ears were slightly pink with embarrassment. "I'm sorry I stepped on your shoe," I said.

He smiled, relieved. "I'm sorry I criticized Three Sisters when we first met."

"That's okay," I said, looking out at the nearly empty pedestrian walkway. "Rashid and I are hatching a plan to destroy you."

Aydin laughed out loud, startling a pigeon perched beside us. "There's the Hana I know. You were being so nice I was starting to worry."

"I do have a reputation to maintain."

His breath was warm, and his dark brown eyes crinkled at the corners. "I like it when you're mean to me," he said.

I stood up abruptly. "I think Rashid is going to be a while. Want to get some ice cream?"

Aydin blinked, then nodded. "Sure, but I'm paying. Don't argue."

IT WAS AN EIGHT-MINUTE WALK to the Dairy Queen from the base of the CN Tower. Given his easy, loping stride, no one would have guessed that the tall man in silver sunglasses beside me had just suffered a panic attack.

Aydin looked at me as we walked, and I saw twin versions of Hana staring back. I was much shorter than his six-foot height, the reflections distorted. I adjusted my bright blue hijab and white tunic. Something had changed between us on the ride down the CN Tower, leaving me feeling raw and a little shy.

We stopped in front of the Dairy Queen. Both of us started to speak at the same time, and I laughed and gestured for him to go first.

Aydin shifted uncomfortably and reached into his pocket. "I bought you something," he said, handing over a small velvet pouch.

Mystified, I opened the drawstring and a heavy metal object fell into my palm. As I examined the tiny cube, he coughed in embarrassment.

"It's a radio keychain. When I saw it at the Golden Crescent convenience store, I thought of you. Mr. Patel says it really works."

The mini radio had an old-fashioned dial and was painted a delicate gold and white. It looked expensive, like something you would buy at a boutique, not our local convenience store. I fiddled with the tiny knobs on the side and then looked up at Aydin. His ears had turned pink again, and he had trouble meeting my gaze.

"It's beautiful," I said gravely. His face lit up with the first genuine smile I had seen since I gave him the free plate of biryani. "Thank you." I carefully pocketed the keychain.

"Consider it partial reparation for past behaviour," he said, and my heart lurched.

"Mom says we won't last the summer," I blurted, desperate to change the strange vibe between us and return to our usual hostile roles.

Aydin stilled, and I continued. "You were right. She has debts. We aren't making the money we need to stay open."

Silver lenses reflected the sunlight, blinding me. I needed to see his face. I reached up and removed his sunglasses, my fingers brushing his hair.

His brown eyes were stricken. "I didn't want to be right," he said. "I didn't want this to happen."

I knew Aydin wasn't opening his fancy halal restaurant simply to put my mother out of business, but the result was the same. He was on one side and I on the other. My loyalty was clear, even if my feelings had become less so.

I liked him. He was smart and funny, hard-working and focused. When he looked at me now, I saw acceptance and an easy affection that just felt right. But it didn't make a damn bit of difference.

"We're Muslim, Aydin," I said. "We believe that all this is exactly what was supposed to happen. Even if we weren't looking for any of it."

In the Dairy Queen I let him buy me a chocolate sundae. It was cold and sweet and I didn't say thank you. On the walk back he held out his hand for the sunglasses, but I had tucked them into my bag. Maybe a part of me wanted something that belonged to him.

We walked in silence to the base of the CN Tower. There we met up with Rashid, and the three of us headed to the aquarium.

Chapter Twenty-Three

The jellyfish tank was ethereal—a wide glass tube that extended to the ceiling, illuminated by a haunting blue light against which giant jellyfish floated like ghostly tentacled aliens. The Imam was right. It was glorious.

"Cool," Rashid said after thirty seconds. He snapped a picture for his Facebook page before walking off in search of the seahorse tank.

Aydin remained beside me. The light from the glowing tank reflected off his face so that he glowed too. "Aquariums make me sad. All these animals caught or bred for captivity, living their life in cages for our amusement. It's a metaphor for life."

The jellyfish couple in front of me had their tentacles entwined as they danced around each other with slow, practised movements. I wondered how long they had been stuck in that tank together. I wondered if they hated it and yearned for freedom. Or did they even realize they were trapped?

"Sometimes I wish we weren't enemies," Aydin said, his gaze intent on the jellyfish. "I wonder how we'd be if things were different. Do you think we could have been friends?" His eyes focused on mine in the reflection.

"Maybe," I replied, though I knew the answer was *yes*. It would be easy to be friends with Aydin. We would just stop fighting against everything and simply . . . be. It would be the easiest thing in the world, if only things were different.

WE HAD AN HOUR BEFORE the gates opened at the stadium. Feeling a sudden hunger, we decided to grab some pizza. I wondered what Aydin was thinking, if he was regretting what he had said.

Rashid walked ahead, oblivious to both of us. He was taking videos again, of the CN Tower, the aquarium exterior, and downtown Toronto street life.

A beefy white man in a dark T-shirt planted himself in front of Rashid. My cousin looked up, and smiled. "Hello, brother," he said.

"Hey, terrorist," the man said, voice booming.

The man was flanked by two other large men. One had his head shaved, and the other wore a shirt with a raised white fist against a black background.

My heart began to pound. "What did you call him?" I said, and my voice shook.

The man looked at me, dismissive. "I wasn't talking to you, bitch. I was talking to your little Brown friend here. Why are you taking videos of the tower? Where are you from? You got a passport, buddy?" The man took a step closer to Rashid.

Aydin stepped up, subtly moving me back. "Take it easy," he said, hands out in a calm-down motion. "We're just walking around, enjoying our city."

"Enjoying *my* city. It's not your city, asshole!" The man's face turned an ugly shade of red and spittle flew from his mouth. "Stay in your own fucking country!"

A small crowd had gathered around us, but they were silent, watching the drama unfold. A few had phones out, filming.

"*This* is my country," Aydin said quietly. "This is her country," he said, nodding at me. "And this man is our guest. Maybe you should stand down."

Blood pounded in my veins. What had we done to attract this type of attention? I reached up and fingered my hijab, a bright blue and cream patterned chiffon that matched my blue jeans.

The man with the shaved head pointed at Rashid, who was still filming. "Turn that thing off *right now*! You planning an attack on Toronto, that why you're taking all this video?" The man stepped closer to Rashid and reached for his cellphone.

"No English," Rashid said in his cultured Indo-British accent. "Many apologies, but I cannot understand a single word you are saying." He backed up a few steps.

The three men followed. "You don't belong here!" the first man yelled. "Give me that phone!"

Rashid leaned back and threw his phone in a perfect arc to Aydin, who caught it one-handed. "What phone?" Rashid asked, all innocence.

Everything began to happen in slow motion.

"FUCK YOU!" the first man roared, and lunged at Aydin. Frightened, I yanked on his shoulder, pulling him away from the man's fist, but the momentum made me lose my balance. I fell, landing hard on my back, the breath knocked out of me.

"Hana!" Aydin yelled, crouching beside me.

Despite the sharp pain in my hip, I noticed the second man charge. At the last second Rashid neatly sidestepped, then pushed the man forward so that he toppled face-first onto the concrete a few feet away.

While our would-be attacker was being helped up by his friends,

Rashid signalled to me. "We should go." My cousin's voice was quiet and unwavering. How could he be so calm?

My hands were shaking. I caught the eye of a young woman in the small crowd that surrounded us, and she looked away. A glance at Aydin reflected my own mix of emotions back at me: shock and fear.

Aydin helped me up, hands grasping my elbows. I was dazed, blood pulsing in a drumbeat through my veins, my back and left leg already sore as I processed what had just happened. We had been attacked on the streets of downtown Toronto. Those men had tried to assault both Aydin and Rashid, yet somehow I had been the one who ended up sprawled on the ground.

We hurried around the corner, all thoughts of lunch forgotten. I looked back, but the men seemed uninterested in giving chase. Or maybe they were waiting for backup. What if they came after us, armed?

I touched my hijab again, wishing I had chosen a colour that blended in better. The thought made me want to laugh and cry, and I realized I must be in shock.

Aydin was still holding Rashid's phone. "I'm calling the police," he said.

"For what?" my cousin asked.

Aydin and I looked at him. "Those men attacked us!" I said.

Rashid started to laugh. "They were probably drunk. If I called the police every time someone called me a bad name or tried to steal my phone, I would never get anything done. Come on, we can buy lunch at the stadium. I heard they sell halal hot dogs."

Aydin and I exchanged worried glances but followed. "I still think I should call the cops," Aydin said to me in a low, tense voice. "They were looking for trouble. They might do something worse to someone else next time. And we should take you to the hospital. Are you sure you can walk?"

"Nobody said anything," I said, my voice cracking. "There were people all around us, and nobody spoke up."

Rashid walked ahead of us, eager to enter the massive fifty-thousand-seat Rogers Centre, known as the SkyDome to long-time residents, with its signature retractable roof. "Let's get some popcorn too," he called over his shoulder.

Aydin and I exchanged another glance and followed him inside.

Chapter Twenty-Four

The pitcher talked to the catcher. The batter took a single swing before spitting on the ground. The first baseman leaned on one leg and made a complicated hand motion to the shortstop. Play paused while the first-base coach and batter conferred.

Three more hours of this. I was vibrating with so much adrenaline I couldn't sit still, though my back, hip, and left leg throbbed painfully. I shifted, and Aydin caught the movement, worry clear on his face. He abruptly got up and left.

"How did you know they wouldn't come after us?" I asked Rashid, seeking a distraction from the pain. My cousin was shovelling popcorn into his mouth, eyes riveted on the field as if he were watching a tense Hollywood blockbuster instead of a sleepy mid-week baseball game.

"His buddies were hanging back after he fell. If they really wanted to start something, they would have attacked again. When they saw you fall down and the crowd form, they backed off. Besides, I didn't look scared enough to make it worth their time. Men like that enjoy the fear on people's faces most of all."

I raised my eyebrows, impressed at his analysis. "How many fights have you been in?" I asked.

My cousin took a bite of his second halal hot dog. "I only fight if I know I'm going to win. That's the accountant way." His parents were definitely part of the New Delhi mafia.

I settled back in my seat. It was comfortable, and we had an excellent view of the game. The stands were only half filled, mostly with school kids on a class trip, retirees, and tourists. I shifted again, and pain shot along my thigh, making me inhale sharply.

"Here, use these." Aydin appeared beside me with two ice packs. He placed one carefully behind my back and went to press the other against my hip, then changed his mind and handed it to me instead. He had been fussing over me ever since the attack, first insisting we go to the hospital and then, when I demurred, fetching me water from the concession stand and arguing with someone about getting me a heating pad. Now he handed me some ibuprofen, which I accepted gratefully. He took the empty seat beside me, dark eyes filled with concern.

"I'm fine," I repeated. I wasn't.

"You fell because of me," Aydin said. He blinked and then looked away, a muscle in his jaw tightening.

"I fell because that crazy racist tried to punch you and I pulled you out of the way. I guess you could say I saved you."

"You should have let him hit me. Then I could have called the police and pressed charges." His fists were balled in his lap, knuckles white.

"And ruin our perfect outing?" I said, keeping my voice light. "Rashid would never forgive us if we missed the game because of something so minor."

Beside us my cousin scowled at a call the umpire had made, eyes fixed on the action.

"I don't care about Rashid's feelings!" Aydin burst out. "I can't believe this happened in broad daylight, in the middle of downtown Toronto, and nobody did anything."

Rashid looked over. "They didn't want to get involved. I wouldn't have done anything either, if it had been me."

I wondered if he was right. If I saw someone being abused and harassed, would I step in and offer to help? Or would I ignore what was happening, thinking that they would be fine, that it was none of my business. "What can we do to stop this hatred?" I asked out loud. I wasn't sure there was an answer.

Rashid smiled at me, and I was struck once again by his calm. I was putting on a brave face and Aydin was clearly trying to tamp down his anger, but my cousin seemed completely unfazed. For the first time I wondered what his life was like in Delhi. I had thought him a sheltered rich kid who had come to Canada to have an adventure. Instead, his reactions made me want to check out the motherland.

"My father says that trying to stop hate is like trying to stop the tides," Rashid said. "The best thing you can do is take advantage of it. Don't stop the tide from flowing. Build a hydroelectric dam and make electricity instead, enough to power ten thousand houses. That's how you stop hate."

I wasn't entirely sure what Rashid's dad had meant. How could you take advantage of hate without causing more hate?

Aydin stood up. "I'm going to get nachos."

I stood up, wincing at the spike of pain through my hip. "I'll come with you," I said, waving off his protests. He slowed his long strides to match mine, fingers hovering under my elbow.

In the lineup Aydin fidgeted, moving his hands in and out of his pockets, fiddling with his wallet. "I'm sorry. I should have stood in front of you—"

"You did," I reminded him.

"When I saw you crumpled on the ground, I . . ." Aydin closed his eyes. "I wanted to kill that man." Fear and protectiveness wrestled with guilt on his face.

"And then you would have gone to jail and solved all my family's problems," I said.

"How can you joke about this?" he asked. Fingers raked his hair and he glared at me.

I smiled back. "What else is there to do but laugh? Did you see how fast Rashid moved? And the way that man's face smooshed into the concrete when he fell?" I laughed, but my voice was shaky. I remembered also the blind hatred in the face of the man who had swung for Aydin, his glee when he watched me stumble backwards and fall, how happy he had been to see me hurt.

"I hope he broke his nose," Aydin said, but he sounded less homicidal. "Is your cousin a little . . ." He trailed off.

"Crazy?"

"I was going to say eccentric."

"I can't figure him out. One minute he's quoting baseball movies and doing a really terrible Apu impersonation, the next he's fighting bigots and helping me save the restaurant from you and your dad." I realized what I had let slip and clamped a hand over my mouth.

Aydin sighed. "We can't be friends because you think I'm trying to destroy your family business, and we can't fight because I think your cousin might be Machiavelli reincarnated. Where does that leave us?"

I shrugged. "Why do we have to be anything? I barely know you."

Except that wasn't entirely true. I knew that he missed his mother and feared his father. I knew he wanted to build something of his own, and had chosen to build it far from where he had grown up, which made me wonder what he was running from. I knew that he cared for me, even though he barely knew me. And that he felt familiar and comfortable, even before I knew any of those other things.

"Why did you come today?" I asked after Aydin paid for his nachos.

He stopped walking, and this time he looked embarrassed. "Because Rashid said you wanted me here."

I was going to slap my cousin so hard . . .

He was still standing there, holding the tray of nachos. "Did you?" he asked. He cleared his throat. "Did you want me here today?"

Yes. Why couldn't I say it? It was the truth. But it would also be an admission, one I wasn't yet ready to make.

We headed back to our seats.

Chapter Twenty-Five

The cure for recovering from an Islamophobic attack, it turned out, was junk food and baseball. I felt almost normal when we walked out of the Rogers Centre at six p.m., though I kept an eye out for three enraged white men in dark T-shirts. Rashid remained completely oblivious, chatting about the home run at the bottom of the third and the spectacular catch that won the Blue Jays the game at the top of the ninth, as if we had nothing to fear. I envied his calm, and I couldn't wait to get back to Golden Crescent, where things were familiar and safe.

"I called a cab," Aydin informed us as I turned towards the subway. A yellow car idled in front of the stadium. He opened the door and motioned for me to get in, then clambered in beside me. Rashid sat beside the driver, a friendly man from Romania. They talked baseball while Aydin adjusted a fresh ice pack behind my back. He gently tugged on my sleeve and our eyes met in the dark interior.

"Okay?" he asked, as the cab merged onto Toronto's perennially congested streets. I noticed a small scar on his jaw amid the dark stubble. I nodded, and he leaned back and closed his eyes.

Rashid sighed with happiness. "What a perfect day," he said. He turned around to face us. "Hana Apa, have you spoken to Aydin about our mutual problem?"

Now what was my cousin up to? "I don't know what you're talking about," I answered, a warning in my voice that Rashid proceeded to ignore.

"Why do you think I invited Aydin on our trip downtown? It is clear we must join forces to fight against a common enemy."

Aydin and I looked at each other. "We don't have a common enemy," he said.

"Yes, we do. Junaid Shah."

Aydin froze. "My father is not my enemy."

Rashid shrugged. "Any fool can see your dad is trying to sabotage you. He spoke out during the business association meeting even though you asked him to stop. He's made enemies of your neighbours by threatening them. For some reason he does not want you or the restaurant to succeed. Your only choice is to join forces with us. The enemy of your enemy is your friend."

Aydin and I exchanged glances. *Machiavelli*, he mouthed.

"Actually I prefer Chanakya, the fourth-century teacher who pioneered political science in India. His teachings helped me with my baseball strategy," Rashid said serenely.

I crossed my arms. "I don't trust him," I said, jerking my head towards Aydin. "He's an opportunist."

"I'm sitting right here," Aydin said.

Rashid ignored him. "Which is why he will make the best ally. As soon as the summer festival is done and all our fortunes have improved, we will return to our former battle stations."

I mulled over his words. Rashid wasn't just my eighteen-year-old cousin from India anymore, I realized. He stood up in the face of hate and talked about building dams. His parents were "accountants" who knew how to fight for their turf. Rashid was not what he appeared.

But then, neither was Aydin. The cold, arrogant man I had first met didn't tally with the vulnerable, protective person I had spent the day with. Maybe it was time to let down my defensive walls, or at least lower them a fraction. I shrugged casually. "Fine, we can work together until after the street festival. I told Yusuf I would help with the protest anyway," I said.

Aydin blinked. "What protest?"

Rashid clapped his hands. "I knew you would see reason. This will all work out, Hana Apa. You'll see."

AYDIN GENTLY SHOOK ME AWAKE; I had fallen asleep on his shoulder during the cab ride. He helped me out of the car and then followed us up the pathway to my house.

Delicious smells wafted through the front door. "What are you doing?" I whispered when he moved to follow us inside.

"Walking you home." His ears were tinged pink again. "I'd like to say salaam to your parents. And, um, to apologize. For what happened today."

I steered him to the side. "We're not telling them," I said firmly, arms crossed.

Aydin looked confused. "Won't they notice that you're hurt?"

"I tripped and fell in the subway but I'm fine." I glared at him. "They have enough to worry about, and I never want to think about what happened downtown again. Understand?"

He nodded. When he still moved to follow me inside the house, I raised an eyebrow.

"It would be rude if I didn't at least say hello. I promise I'll behave."

We were greeted by the aromas of spicy chapli kebab—seasoned minced beef patties studded with whole coriander seeds—and fresh tandoori chicken, served with homemade naan and lots of fresh mint yogurt chutney. I wondered if the opportunity to eat my mother's cooking was the real reason Aydin was eager to visit.

I was happy to see Fazeela dressed and seated on the couch, her feet in Fahim's lap. She looked tired. Her black hijab was draped casually around her head, and her baby bump protruded under an oversized Toronto FC jersey.

"Did you have a fun day?" she asked, smiling at me. Her eyes narrowed when she caught sight of Aydin lurking behind.

"Assalamu alaikum," he said. "Hana invited me."

I shot him a dark look. "He insisted on coming inside," I clarified.

I plopped down on the couch and handed her a tiny Toronto Blue Jays onesie. "For the cantaloupe."

"Cantaloupe is going to play soccer, not baseball," Fazeela said, but her eyes softened as she held up the tiny garment.

"With you and Fahim's genes, Cantaloupe will play everything. Where is Kawkab Khala?" I asked, knowing my aunt would get a kick out of Aydin.

Kawkab had gone out with her friend Afsana for the night, Fazeela informed me as Aydin took a cautious step into the living room. I tried not to feel sensitive about our unfashionable furniture, the framed prints of Quranic verse on the walls, and the plain Corelle dishes on the small kitchen table. Aydin's presence made me instantly re-evaluate everything through his eyes.

As if he knew what I was thinking, he said, "I like your home. It feels warm and welcoming." He put his hand out for Fahim to shake, and they did that bro thing where they flexed their biceps and talked about the Toronto Raptors. Fazeela rolled her eyes at me.

"My parents are outside," I said. The whole thing felt weird. "You wanted to say salaam," I added meaningfully.

Aydin took the hint and wandered out to the back patio, but not before stopping to peek inside the galley kitchen. I hoped it was clean, with no dishes in the sink. He left the patio door open.

I appreciated that Fazeela and Fahim weren't making a big deal out of Aydin's being there. Once he was gone, Fahim sat down again and tugged my sister's feet into his lap, gently massaging them. She leaned back, letting the tiny onesie rest against her rounded belly.

"What's this I hear about you and Rashid organizing the street festival?" Fazeela said, voice drowsy. "You've never organized anything like that before. Is it because of what Junaid Shah said at the BOA meeting? Mom says he's all thunder, no rain."

"Three Sisters is your future. I want to help you fight for it," I said.

Fazeela straightened up and pulled her feet out of her husband's hands. "Maybe I don't want it to be my future."

Fahim froze. "What do you mean, babe?"

Fazeela sighed, the shadows under her eyes even darker. I could see the beginnings of fine lines fanning out around her eyes and mouth. "Maybe I want to do something else. I've had a lot of time to think in the past few weeks, sitting alone in my bedroom," my sister said. "Maybe this was supposed to happen. Maybe this is a sign from Allah that it's time to consider our options—all our options."

Fahim looked at his wife and they conducted one of those silent conversations couples have.

"I'm going to help you fix this mess," I said, interrupting their subliminal dialogue. "It's time to climb a tree holding a gun, not to fold and surrender."

Fazeela smiled at me. "You've been talking to Kawkab Khala."

"We should at least let Hana and Rashid try to help," Fahim said, pulling his wife's feet back into his lap. "They've already put up flyers and canvassed the neighbours. We'll be okay, but what about your mom? This is all she's ever done." His fingers were working on Fazeela's toes as he talked, and she winced when he pressed too hard. "Sorry," he said, letting go.

She reached across, squeezing his hand, and I felt a sudden pang at their easy affection. I wondered what it would be like to have someone on my team like that, someone to massage my feet when they ached and talk through life decisions when I was confused. To tell me I was fearless but who stood beside me when I was afraid. Because after looking into those men's eyes today, I *was* scared, no matter what I had said to Aydin about laughing through the pain.

I left my sister and Fahim and made my way to the patio door. Aydin was standing near the barbecue, stooping over my father's diminutive form. Baba was having a good day; his hand rested lightly on his four-pronged cane, face animated as they chatted. I didn't know if he realized who Aydin was, but Mom seemed relaxed as she rotated chicken pieces on the grill.

Aydin noticed me by the door and smiled tentatively. For a moment I was struck by déjà vu, his hesitant expression was so familiar. I combed through my memories trying to place it but came up short.

"Your father and I were debating the merits of NPR, CBC, and BBC radio shows for style and technique," Aydin said.

"My Hana is a gifted storyteller," Baba said. "Did you know she will soon have her own radio show?"

Aydin raised an eyebrow at me. "I'll be sure to listen," he murmured, before turning back to my dad. "She's lucky to have your support.

Not all parents are happy when their children want to pursue a non-traditional career, especially in the arts."

Baba shook his head. "Parents are happy when their children are happy. My Hana must tell stories. That is who she is."

"Aydin doesn't want to hear this, Baba," I said, mortified. My father didn't realize what he was saying. He had never met Junaid Uncle and couldn't know how sharply his comments would land.

I caught a shadow of something in Aydin's brown eyes, something that wasn't quite jealousy, wasn't quite sadness. A puzzle piece slotted into place and I realized who he reminded me of—Sad Aunty, the first time I had seen her, sitting in Three Sisters waiting for Kawkab Khala and looking as if she had all the world's sorrow resting on her narrow frame.

Aydin swiftly rearranged his expression to a smiling neutral, and the resemblance vanished, so quickly I wondered if I had seen it in the first place.

We ate, and Aydin was perfectly behaved, as promised. I even over-heard him asking my mother for business advice. After dinner I walked him to the backyard gate. He lingered, glancing back at my father.

"Car accident, two years ago," I said. "He loves talking to people, but it's hard for him to get around these days."

Aydin's eyes were on me now, assessing. "You don't look like your father, but you have the same energy. Your mom is a lot more ... calm." He grinned at my frown, then sobered. "It must have been hard on your family, after the accident."

"Lots of things have been difficult lately."

"Like me?" he asked. There was a hesitation in his voice that made me want to take his hand again.

"Yes," I said, and his face fell. "And no. I'm not sure what I would have done today without you."

Aydin liked that, but he tried to appear modest. "Rashid had matters well in hand."

"Don't mess with my cousin."

We grinned at each other. With a final wave, Aydin unlatched the gate and walked out into the night.

. . .

When I want to reassure myself, I think about space. As in outer space. Did you know that the universe is ninety-three billion light years across? That number is difficult to visualize. One light year—how far light can travel in a year—is something like 9.4 trillion kilometres. Let me put that into a bit more perspective: Voyager 1, the space probe NASA launched way back in 1977, will reach our next-door neighbouring star in about forty thousand years!

Yet at the same time, our own little solar system, the collection of planets and asteroids and moons we call home, is well hidden. Beyond gas giant Neptune is an enormous field of asteroids called the Kuiper belt that keeps our little neighbourhood nice and snug. Out beyond that—much, much farther out—is the Oort cloud. Nobody has seen it yet, because it would take Voyager 1, travelling at a speed of seventeen kilometres per second, about three hundred years to reach it, and maybe thirty thousand years to travel through it!

And even the Oort cloud is a tiny part of our much larger galaxy, which in turn is part of a much larger local group of galaxies, and in turn part of a local supercluster, which in turn is part of another cluster . . . In the end there are one hundred billion galaxies in the known universe, and who knows what beyond.

I like to think of our tiny-speck-of-dust Earth wrapped inside its snug little Kuiper belt, cocooned somewhere inside the massive Oort cloud, completely undetectable inside a universe so massive there is no comparison. And here we are, living and dying, completely unaware of all that lies beyond. Terrifying, but also comforting, especially when things happen that are hard to understand.

The first chapter of the Quran is called Surah Al-Fatiha, or "The Opening," and Muslims recite it with every prayer. One of the verses translates to "Praise be to God, lord of all the worlds."

Worlds, plural. There's a metaphor in there. Some solid advice too.

The world is vast, but not as vast as you think. The worlds are plentiful, but you happen to be stuck on this one, with little chance of escape.

After some recent events, I'm even more determined to make my time on this globe count, to fight harder for what I want and against anything that may hold me back.

Chapter Twenty-Six

During my shift at Radio Toronto the next day, I continued to research henna artists for my story. I associated henna with happy occasions; it was applied for weddings or the night before Eid and other celebrations. But it was difficult to focus on joy; my thoughts kept spiralling around fear, anger, and sadness.

I had told Aydin I never wanted to think about the downtown attack ever again, but I could think of little else, my thoughts centred on the day we had spent together. Aydin had shown me another side of himself, a kindness and vulnerability I had only caught glimpses of before. And I didn't know how to respond. What could I say when I was still trying to destroy his business by spreading rumours online? What could I say when the tiny radio keychain he had given me lay in my pocket like a talisman? Things were murky and complicated, which was fine when I thought it was just me. It felt much worse now that I knew he was equally as confused by what was happening between us.

Marisa tapped me on the shoulder, and I jumped. "Everything all right, darling?" she asked. She wore a brilliant green scarf tied around her neck. I remembered when I first started at Radio Toronto, how much I had wanted to be just like her.

I nodded yes, but my body betrayed me and tears threatened. Alarmed, Marisa asked what was wrong, and then the story of the attack came spilling out in a giant emotional wave.

Afterwards, Marisa perched on the edge of my desk, concern and sympathy etched on her face. "I just can't believe that happened in Toronto!" she said. "People come here from all over the place. Maybe those men were from the United States."

"They made sure to tell my cousin that he was taking videos of *their* city."

"It's your city too, Hana. You've lived here for years," Marisa said.

"I was born here," I said.

Marisa blinked. "Of course, that's what I meant." She stood up, thinking. "Imagine how often this type of harassment happens to people and it doesn't make the news. I think we should devote one episode of your show to discussing what happened to you. We could start a conversation that might help others. What do you think?"

I didn't know what to say. I hadn't confided in Marisa to take advantage of the incident. "I'm not sure I would be comfortable doing that," I said.

Thomas had joined us in our tiny office, and he looked at me carefully, gauging my reaction.

"Consider it your responsibility as a journalist," Marisa said. "Just run us through the day, what you were doing downtown. Talk about how you were showing your cousin around the city, how scary the attack felt. Maybe you could post a picture of yourself, to give listeners some context," she said, warming to her theme.

My heart sank at her words. I pictured the blue hijab I had been wearing, one of my favourites. A very poor choice of camouflage. I should have worn a red and white maple-leaf hijab instead.

Marisa reached out and squeezed my shoulder, taking my silence as reticence instead of discomfort. "People will be interested in hearing your side. They want your perspective. They will be sympathetic, Hana. This will be a *good* story about your community."

"Because this time the Muslims were the victims?"

"Exactly!" Marisa beamed at me. Behind her, Thomas's face remained neutral, but I could feel his unease. "Please just think about it. Okay?" Marisa asked.

I looked down at my shoes. Sneakers today—great for running. "I'll think about the story," I said.

Hemingway allegedly said there's nothing to writing. "All you do is sit down at a typewriter and bleed." Being a visible Muslim felt a bit like that too, sometimes. This time.

AT THE THINKING WALL, THOMAS eased beside me, adjusting his body so that his hands were folded behind him, digging into the brick at the small of his back.

"Marisa was trying to be kind," he said. "Her intentions are good."

"Her intentions are always above reproach," I said. "It's left for others to deal with the impact of those good intentions."

Thomas looked at his feet and the breeze ruffled his dark, curly hair. "I wasn't born here," he said. "I immigrated with my parents and sister when I was eleven, from Chennai. I had to take ESL classes for years because I didn't know any English. I still don't understand the spelling rules, your obsession with the silent *g*." He smiled. "I used to watch TV constantly, to mimic the way Americans spoke."

"Is that why you're such a sellout now?" I asked.

"Yes," he said. He caught my eye and we laughed. "You don't have to tell this story. Not if it's too painful," Thomas said.

"But my pain makes for good storytelling, right? It makes me more relatable."

Thomas looked away. Our laughter had been spontaneous, a subtle acknowledgement of all that we shared, despite our different outlooks. I liked that we could laugh together. Even if I wasn't sure we were laughing about the same thing.

Chapter Twenty-Seven

Rashid convinced me to accompany him and Fahim to the base-ball diamond on Friday morning, two days after the downtown attack. The restaurant would open late that day, after the jumah prayer, and the weather was fine.

While Fahim and Rashid practised hitting and pitching, I sat in the empty wooden bleachers and worked on editing my *Secret Family History* podcast. I had finally cornered Kawkab Khala and convinced her to finish our interview. As I played over our conversation, I allowed myself a tiny flare of excitement. The rest of my world might be on fire, but this podcast was shaping up to be excellent. Perhaps I would show it to Marisa and Thomas, an example of an introspective program that talked about the everyday experiences of people of colour, without having to turn everything into a painful lesson.

Working on that secret project also gave me something to think about besides Aydin and my plans to sabotage Wholistic Grill. I had studiously avoided checking on the progress of my rumour-spreading. I was too busy, I told myself. Perhaps it also felt strange now, after everything that had happened downtown.

I took out my phone and messaged StanleyP. We hadn't communicated in a while; he hadn't even commented on my last few podcast episodes. My listener count had been rising steadily, but I missed my friend.

AnaBGR

It took me a while, but I think you might have been right.

He replied immediately, as if he had been waiting for me to message.

StanleyP

I usually am. What am I right about this time?

AnaBGR

Feeling bad about something I did re: competition.

StanleyP

Welcome to Regretsville. The rent is high and the amenities are pitiful, but at least you can wallow among beautiful company.

AnaBGR

I blame my Muslim guilt.

StanleyP

The guilt will keep you honest. In fact, I'm tendering my official resignation as your revenge consultant. We're both in uncharted waters now.

AnaBGR

I thought revenge made the world turn.

StanleyP

Pretty sure that's chai.

AnaBGR

You didn't say "chai tea." Now I know you're one of my people.

StanleyP

And you're one of mine. Thanks for the advice the other day.

AnaBGR

Did it work? Are you in luuuuurve?

StanleyP

Please stop. And no. Just . . . invested.

The word stung. *Invested*. My friend had gone from assuring me his feelings would pass to feeling invested. My bot buddy was my friend, my ally, my cheerleader. He had hinted at something more, and I had felt a pull towards him as well. How had those feelings been so easily replaced? Or was he playing with both this mystery girl and me? I quickly typed.

AnaBGR

Investments are good. So long as you don't have a diversified portfolio, if you know what I mean.

StanleyP

Nah, I'm an all-in kind of investor.

Whoever this girl was, I hope she knew how lucky she was to have caught the eye of someone so kind and principled. I thought back to Aydin, the way he had stepped up to defend me without hesitation. He had bought me an ice cream to cheer me up, though he didn't even like me. I thought of his dark gaze on mine, and revised that statement. He didn't want to like me—and yet he did. We had that in common at least.

StanleyP
What about you? Any new investments in your life?

AnaBGR
Not sure how I feel about this metaphor, actually.

StanleyP
Don't change the subject.

AnaBGR
No new investments. But . . .

StanleyP
I knew it!

AnaBGR
. . . maybe some potential profits from an unexpected source.

StanleyP
I have no idea what that means, but I'm intrigued. Keep me posted.

I had no idea what I meant either. I looked up from my phone at my cousin and brother-in-law. Fahim was still pitching, throwing his entire weight behind each throw, while my cousin methodically knocked each one into the green. No wonder Rashid was applying for an athletic scholarship. He was really good.

I caught my cousin's eye and tapped my wrist. It was time for jumah, and I didn't want to be late. We had to stop by the house to pick up Baba; attending weekly congregational prayers at the mosque was the highlight of his week. I was looking forward to Imam Abdul Bari's comforting sermon as well.

THE MOSQUE WAS WALKING DISTANCE from our house, but we drove to make it more accessible for Baba. Yusuf met me in the parking lot as Rashid helped Baba from the car. He shook hands with everyone before leading me to one side.

"Have you heard the rumours about Wholistic Grill?" My friend grinned, barely able to contain his glee.

"What are you talking about?" I asked. My family was waiting for me.

"Apparently one of their workers was injured on the job and has threatened to sue. I heard they also have a rodent problem and they failed their health inspection. And it turns out their meat isn't actually halal."

"Don't believe everything you read online," I muttered, thinking rapidly. I had made up one of those rumours and encouraged two others, but they seemed to be taking on a life of their own. What had I started?

"I thought you'd be happy," Yusuf said, puzzled. "This is great news for Three Sisters. Lots of people have been getting in touch about the protest. People will want to hear from you, as the daughter of the owner of a neighbourhood institution. Could you say a few words? All of this is going to make a real difference, Hana."

"No," I said shortly. "It won't make a bit of difference, actually." I walked away from Yusuf, back towards my family, but he followed.

"What do you mean?" he pressed.

Thoughts buzzed around me. "All these people sharing this 'reliable' information about Wholistic Grill—have they been eating at Three Sisters instead?" I asked slowly. The rumours had been circulating for nearly two weeks and our restaurant had not benefited by one extra cent. If anything, business had gotten worse. "These people, so worried about authentic halal meat or preserving the legacy businesses in Golden Crescent—I haven't seen them at our restaurant. Their outrage hasn't filled our register. Mom is planning to close the store."

Yusuf's eyes widened at my words. "I didn't know things were that bad."

"They are, and attacking Aydin's business hasn't—won't help," I amended. I had thought myself so clever. I had thought I was taking StanleyP's advice. I had expanded on his words and put everything into destroying Wholistic Grill, even after Aydin pleaded with me to take down the online allegations. I had hoped the virtual mob would take up the cause and frequent Three Sisters instead of Wholistic Grill, maybe sink his business before it even opened.

I felt foolish now. Why hadn't I thought to take active steps to help Three Sisters? My time would have been better spent working on our restaurant's website or encouraging my mother to revamp the menu or invest in a modest renovation, or even using social media to engage in targeted advertising. Instead I had delighted in trolling Aydin to give myself some sense of power. It had been for my benefit only; it hadn't helped Three Sisters at all.

With a sinking sense of horror, I realized I had transferred my rage and hate onto someone who was neither the source of my frustration nor responsible for our failure, just as our downtown attackers had done to us. Anger was easier, feeling justified in my tactics more satisfying. Trying to change my world was the harder path, and less likely to succeed. My face burned with shame.

"I'll make sure the protest has a huge turnout," Yusuf vowed now, mistaking my silence for despair. "A thousand—no, *five* thousand people. You'll see, Hana. Wholistic Grill won't know what hit them."

My friend meant well, but I knew his efforts wouldn't help. I sighed and thanked him anyway. Rashid was right—Yusuf really was an *ullu*. But I didn't have to be one.

ZULFA STOOD AT THE MAIN DOORS of the Toronto Muslim Assembly, handing out flyers. She looked pretty in a long-sleeved floral dress that reached to the ground, black hair tucked beneath a tan hijab. She stopped distributing long enough to give me a hug as I passed by.

"How are you holding up?" she asked, sympathetic.

"I'm fine," I said automatically, not sure what she meant.

"If you need to talk or need some advice on how to handle all this attention, let me know," Zulfa said.

What was she talking about? If anything, I should be making sure she was okay, after the extra work I had created for her PR machine with my rumours.

She pasted a cheery smile back on her face and stuck a coupon into my hand. "Free gourmet milkshakes with every artisanal organic burger purchase, for a limited time!" she said, swiftly switching gears. "We're trying to get people excited about our opening. Everyone loves free stuff, right? I hope you'll be able to make it, Hana. I know Aydin would love to see you." Her smile was friendly as she moved on to the person approaching behind me—Rashid. Of course he would be lurking nearby.

My cousin greeted Zulfa with a goofy smile and took one of the flyers. "I will be at the opening," he said. "Will you allow me to buy you a milkshake?"

She laughed and swatted at him with her stack of flyers. "They're free with the purchase of a burger. Are you going to cheap out on me?"

Rashid vehemently shook his head. "For you I would buy a dozen burgers. Or perhaps we could meet later for chai?"

I steered my cousin away. "You're eighteen," I reminded him. "Your mom asked us to keep an eye on you, not send you back with a wife."

His eyes were still trained on Zulfa. "I enjoy the company of older women. My ammi would be relieved that I had finally settled down."

I pushed him in the direction of the men's area of the prayer hall before glancing down at the flyer. More closeups of mouthwatering food set on simple white plates, clearly the work of a professional photographer. Even the advertisement was printed on heavy card stock, giving the restaurant an upscale feel. The care that Aydin and Zulfa had put into the project was clear in every perfectly posed poutine, and I felt even worse about trying to destroy them.

Rashid and Fahim helped Baba find a chair in the prayer hall. Unlike in other mosques, there was no formal separation between men and women in the Toronto Muslim Assembly.

After the adhan, the call to prayer, the congregants settled down to hear Imam Abdul Bari's words. His sermons were usually jovial and punny; today he spoke on the importance of unity. The Imam was wearing a blue robe; I wondered if he had a Hawaiian shirt beneath.

Around me, women dressed in colourful hijabs and dresses, jeans, or skirts sat on the floor, cross-legged or with their knees up, listening. A few of the younger ones nearby glanced over at me and then nudged their friends. I made eye contact and smiled, assuming they were customers I had interacted with in the past, but they looked away. Weird.

"Prophet Muhammad showed kindness and love, even to his enemies," the Imam said. I closed my eyes at his words. *Et tu,* Abdul Bari?

"He was silent in the face of their taunts and with patience cleared the garbage they hurled at him. He stood firm in the face of hostility, intent on his goal: changing his society. While he showed his enemies compassion, he was always just, because he was in the habit of constantly checking his *niyyah,* his intention. Brothers and sisters, I urge you to reflect on the famous words of our beloved Prophet: 'Actions are judged by intentions, so each one will have what they intended.'"

After the sermon, the crowd prayed together, the ritual movements a well-orchestrated dance, each step familiar and comforting. Bow from the waist. Up again. Bow down in prostration. Sit upright, then prostrate once more.

An enveloping peace drifted over me as Imam Abdul Bari recited Arabic verses from the Quran in his deep, melodic voice. "*Assalamu alaikum wa rahmathullah. Assalamu alaikum wa rahmathullah.*" The prayer concluded with the symbolic greeting of the angels that Muslims believe keep us company throughout our lives.

Around me, other young women continued to cast glances my way. I wiped my mouth and fixed my hijab, but the staring continued. What was going on?

The prayer hall emptied slowly, and I spotted Aydin slipping out the side entrance. Our eyes met and he nodded briefly before disappearing. I walked into the hallway to locate my shoes and spotted my cousin standing beside the main entrance.

"Hana Apa, look!" There was barely concealed excitement in Rashid's voice as he passed me his phone. He pressed Play on a saved video.

The image was shaky at first, but as it cleared, I heard a man shout in a tinny voice: "You planning an attack on Toronto?"

I flinched, remembering those words. "What is this?" I asked Rashid.

"I was looking over photos and video to send home when I realized my camera had been recording the entire time when those men tried to attack us. I uploaded the video to YouTube and Facebook last night, and it already has thirty thousand views!"

My heart stuttered. What had he done?

Oblivious, Rashid was scrolling down the comments, reading some out loud. "People are so angry about this video. I've received so many messages of support from strangers."

I read a few of the comments over his shoulder. They seemed to be evenly divided between righteous outrage on our behalf and ugly bigotry. "You don't know what you've started," I said. I looked at the video again, a profile shot of me in my blue hijab, another of Aydin stepping in front of me. The confrontation was there for anyone to see, comment on, and share. I buried my face in my hands.

"This is a good thing, Hana Apa," Rashid said, brows furrowed in confusion at my reaction. "Those men thought they would be able to hide in the shadows, but I have exposed them to the mob. Let's see how much they enjoy the spotlight."

"But people will come after us as well," I said quietly.

Rashid might be the son of a New Delhi mafia boss, but I was a broadcaster-in-training, and I knew how quickly stories like that could spin out of control. What had happened to us downtown had been ugly, but the fallout might be worse.

"Hana! Are you all right?" Fahim asked, coming up to us. "I just heard about the attack. Why didn't you tell us what happened?"

"I'm fine," I said. "It was nothing." The last thing I needed was for my family to start worrying about me.

Fahim looked at Rashid, and for once he wasn't smiling. "You should have been more careful," he said. "Women in hijab are often targeted in Toronto."

A flash of something hard crossed my cousin's face and he folded his arms. "They are often targeted around the world," he said evenly. "In India also. Which is why I posted the video, to show what hatred looks like up close, so we may confront it directly. I had the situation well in hand. Those men were nothing."

"They could have been armed. They could have hurt her." Fahim looked down at me, fear clear on his face. "You have to be more careful when you're walking around the city."

I looked from Rashid to Fahim and back again. "That confrontation would have happened whether I was being careful or not," I said slowly. "It didn't happen because I was wearing hijab. None of it was my fault."

Both men had no answer to my words, but I had more to say to my cousin. I turned to Rashid. "You posted that video without asking my permission. Now you've exposed me too."

"People will be on our side, Hana Apa," Rashid insisted. "We are forming alliances. People want to support communities who have been wronged. Don't you want to help your mother, your sister, and Fahim? This is how you build a dam and counteract hate."

I shook my head. He didn't understand what he had done, but my brother-in-law did.

We helped Baba into the car in tense silence.

Chapter Twenty-Eight

Baba noticed how quiet we were on the ride home. As we helped him up the stairs to the house, he asked what was wrong.

"Nothing, Baba. Everything is fine," I replied, but he wasn't convinced.

I looked up the post on my phone once we settled Baba in the kitchen. Fahim had disappeared into Fazeela's room, Rashid to the basement. I sat on the couch and watched the video in its entirety, reliving a moment I had hoped to forget.

The picture was remarkably clear, but I watched the events as if from a great distance. I noted the surprised and then scared expressions on our faces. A flash of Rashid's calm voice as he mocked our attackers. I relived the impact of my fall, Aydin's fear as he crouched down beside me, the look of malevolent delight on our attackers' faces at my pain.

I put down my phone, shaken once more by the randomness of the attack. My bruises hadn't yet healed, and I realized that trying to ignore the incident hadn't helped either. I picked up the phone again and looked at the view count on YouTube. It hovered near forty thousand already.

Footsteps on the stairs, and Fahim poked his head in. "Come upstairs. Fazee wants to talk to you and Rashid."

I hadn't spent a lot of time with my sister lately. She had mostly kept to her room and I had been busy running around fighting fires. But looking at her now, I realized the cantaloupe had grown a lot and my sister looked more rested. The circles under her eyes had started to disappear; the old fire was back in her eyes.

When my cousin walked into the room, she aimed that fire right at him. "What did you do, Rashid?" she asked in a dangerously pleasant voice.

Uh-oh. I hadn't seen this version of Fazeela in a long time. My cousin was so dead.

Rashid looked at her in confusion. "I posted a video of the fight we had downtown. Didn't your sister tell you?"

Fazeela whipped her head towards me. Shit. Now I was in trouble too.

"It wasn't that bad. I was showing Rashid the city and these guys started hassling us. I fell down but I'm fine," I said, babbling.

"Hanaan, what the hell were you thinking, keeping this to yourself? You were the victim of a hate crime. You should have reported it to the police immediately. Thank God nothing worse happened."

"As I said to Fahim Bhai, we had things well in hand—" Rashid began, but my sister pinned him with a look so full of protective rage I nearly felt bad for him.

"What you did was worse. By posting this video, you have exposed our entire family to possible attack. Instead of it being an isolated incident that could have been dealt with appropriately, you have opened us up to the world. All this without seeking my sister's consent! Rashid, you cannot post videos without permission."

"I was trying to shame those men online, and also to raise attention for Three Sisters."

"Even you can't be that naive. Let me show you what you have done," my sister said, her voice icy. She pulled up the video on YouTube and read a few of the comments posted in the past five minutes. They were vile and threatening.

When she looked up, Rashid had paled. "I am sorry, Apa," he said in a low voice. "I wanted to inform the public about what had happened and use the attention to help our business."

My heart softened at Rashid's motives, and I reminded myself that he was eighteen years old, that he had acted impulsively but with good intentions. He had joined the fight for Three Sisters wholeheartedly and he had been calm in the face of our downtown attackers. Fazee and Fahim hadn't been there to see that, but I remembered.

My sister was less impressed by his words. "I'll be telling the rest of the family about the downtown attack and this video, including Kawkab Khala," she said ominously. "In the meantime, Rashid, if you pull anything like this again, you'll answer to me. Let's just hope we can manage the fallout of your action."

She looked at me next. "And no more secrets, Hana. Staying quiet about our problems is how we got into this mess with Three Sisters in the first place, and I'm sick of it. Now get out. Fahim and I need to talk."

By mid-afternoon the view count had risen to fifty thousand, and I couldn't stop reading the comments. Rashid had been right—many were positive. But many were also negative and scary. I jumped from post to post, from hate to support, from "ban all immigrants, especially Moslems" to allies taking our side. I read until the roiling unease in my stomach forced me to turn off the screen. It was time for my shift at Three Sisters anyway.

Fazee must have called ahead, because Mom cornered me the minute I walked into the nearly empty restaurant. "What is going on, Hana?" she demanded. "Were you attacked when you went downtown with Rashid? Your sister told me about the video, and people have been calling." Her face was full of concern and worry.

I took a deep breath and filled her in, downplaying our encounter with the men. When I finished, she was quiet.

"That doesn't sound so bad," she said. "Are you sure you are all right?"

I nodded, and she shrugged. "When we first moved to Canada, people were unkind all the time. More than once, strangers yelled things at me, obscenities and profanities I didn't understand. One time in the grocery store, a woman rammed me with her shopping cart. I thought she did it by accident and apologized for being in her way, and I bent down to help pick up the apples that had fallen out of her cart. She told me to return to my home country." Mom smiled. "I was so new, so ignorant, I thought she was advising me to visit my mother in India. That was when Nani was sick."

She shrugged again, and I stared at her. "You never told me that," I said.

Mom looked away. "It didn't matter. What they said—what anyone said—it didn't hurt so very badly. Because I was here, you see? By then we had you and Fazeela, we had started our businesses. We knew that things would get better when our roots had gone a little deeper, when we had settled more firmly into the soil of this country."

I tried to swallow past the sudden lump in my throat. "But I *am* settled," I said. "I was born here. And it's still happening."

Mom squeezed my hand. "Only once in so many years? Hana, that is nothing. I know your sister is concerned, and Rashid was wrong to post the video online, but things will calm down soon."

My mom's perspective was based on her expectations as an immigrant. She believed that enduring some hatred was inevitable, that it was the price one paid for living as a minority in a new and sometimes hostile country. I understood her perspective, but I didn't agree. I changed the subject. "Who has been calling?" I asked.

"Some of the neighbours. Also some radio stations and local media. They want to speak with you."

The phone rang and Mom picked up. After listening for a moment, she passed the receiver to me.

A reporter from one of the city's big newspapers was on the line. She asked me about the incident and I related the details as best I could, confirming the video and our names. The next call was from the police station that serviced the downtown core. A polite officer took down details of what had happened and promised to be in touch. A few more newspapers called, and a local radio station asked for an on-air interview, which I declined. I knew Marisa would be upset if I appeared on another station, and I didn't want to talk to her again about the incident. I knew things had become serious when a twenty-four-hour news channel called for more information and said we would be making the evening news.

Rashid had been at least partially right. The journalists were sympathetic about what had happened. But talking about the attack over and over with curious strangers was exhausting. I was grateful the restaurant was empty, as it gave me space to think.

The online comments continued to be polarized. When I checked a few hours later, the view count for the video was close to a hundred thousand, and it had been shared nearly ten thousand times on Rashid's Facebook page alone.

In the afternoon my cellphone rang. It was Marisa; I had been expecting her call.

"Why didn't you tell me there's video of your downtown confrontation?" she said in lieu of a greeting. "Clever girl, uploading the recording to the internet."

"That was my cousin's doing, not mine," I said.

"Oh, the one who threw the phone into the hands of that rather gorgeous young man?" she asked. I didn't know how to respond to that, so Marisa continued. "I'm calling to let you know we can have you on the radio this afternoon. A full interview, where you can relate your side of the story, followed by a phone-in segment. Isn't that exciting?"

"Thank you for calling to check up on me," I said through gritted teeth. "As I told you before, I'm not comfortable talking about this on air."

"Don't tell me you're going to speak to those sharks at the all-news station. Remember, you work for us. Loyalty above all things, Hana."

I watched the evening news on the small TV set we kept in the kitchen. The white male newscaster looked grim as he played Rashid's blurry hand-held footage. The video captured my shocked expression, the determined one on Aydin's face when he stepped in front of me. The report wrapped up with a brief mention about the rise of hate groups in Ontario.

I peeked again at the comments section below the video, and immediately wished I hadn't. The comments were starting to get more personal, questioning what we had been doing walking around downtown Toronto, whether we were actually Canadian citizens, while others wondered why Rashid had been filming in the first place.

The most liked comment was posted by someone with the username Alt_RightDungeon, and it made my heart sink. Somebody had copied into the comments section the flyer Rashid had posted on Facebook, and Alt_RightDungeon was suggesting that the "Brotherhood" visit the neighbourhood, maybe attend the "terrorist-halal-fest" and hold a counter-festival of their own, serving bacon, ham, and pork sausage.

A few comments later, someone named AnarchyNow! had figured out who we were.

AnarchyNow!
Hana Khan, Aydin Shah, Rashid Khan. Aydin Shah is the son of Junaid Shah, CEO of Shah Industries, the man who helped decimate the West Coast housing scene by buying up properties in working-class neighbourhoods, driving up rent and gentrifying. I bet they're in town to do the same thing to Toronto's east end.

"Useless rich immigrants," another poster added, and I shook my head. Either we were being criticized for not fitting in and sticking to traditional beliefs or we were being hounded for chasing capital.

I closed all my browsers, told my mom to take a message if more media called the restaurant looking for me, and left Three Sisters. The day had been difficult and overwhelming. I had been so consumed with handling the backlash for my family, I had completely forgotten about the third victim of the attack. If the media had got hold of my contact information, they were likely calling Aydin as well.

I had to find him and Rashid. We had to discuss what was happening online and the impact it might have on Golden Crescent. Things were spiralling out of control, everything happening too fast, and my head hurt. I needed backup. It was time to close ranks before something worse happened.

Chapter Twenty-Nine

Aydin wasn't at his restaurant. He wasn't at the baseball diamond or the Tim Hortons either, and he didn't pick up his phone when Rashid called. We finally found him at the mosque, speaking quietly to Imam Abdul Bari.

My cousin kept shooting me nervous looks while we waited. "Have I ruined everything, Hana Apa?" he finally asked.

"Everyone makes mistakes," I said shortly.

"I feel terrible about the position I have put you in."

"You exposed Aydin too," I retorted, and my cousin shut up.

Imam Abdul Bari smiled as he walked over, Aydin following behind. "Please let me know if you or your family need anything, Sister Hana," the Imam said, then returned to his office, leaving the three of us to stare at each other.

Rashid broke the silence, surprising Aydin with a hug. "You must forgive me!" he wailed, hanging from Aydin's shoulders. "I thought you would both be pleased I had posted the video. My friends back home are jealous I have gone viral so easily. They thought it would take me at least a few months."

Aydin and I exchanged bemused looks as he disentangled himself from Rashid's embrace. "I know you didn't intend this reaction," Aydin said. "Maybe something good will come out of it."

I filled them both in on the latest news, and Aydin confirmed that he had been getting media requests as well. "It's all been too much," he admitted. "The online rumours about Wholistic Grill, the delay with the construction, and now this . . ." He trailed off, face grim. His usually sleek clothes were rumpled, I noticed. I wondered when he had last slept.

"We need to divide and conquer," I said. "For the next few days, forward all media requests to me. We need to separate the attack from the businesses on the street. I'll keep an eye on the online comments, too. Rashid, you and Aydin continue to work, and let Zulfa handle the PR for the launch of Wholistic Grill. All this attention and sympathy might even help our businesses."

A look of relief washed over Aydin. "You're going to help me?" he asked, voice uncertain.

"We're going to help each other," I said firmly. "If we're very lucky, this will all blow over soon."

A MESSAGE ON AYDIN'S VOICEMAIL forwarded all media requests related to the "CN Tower race attack," as the media had dubbed it, to me, and I spent the next few days responding to queries from all over the province. The constable who had recorded the details of the downtown confrontation was in touch again the next day; the police had not identified our attackers but they were working on it.

Marisa finally convinced me to do a brief on-air account of what had happened to the three of us downtown, but I drew the line at a phone-in segment. Reading the online comments had been painful enough; I had no wish to hear hateful words or mean-spirited conjecture spoken out loud.

I managed to record and post another episode of *Ana's Brown Girl Rambles* and put in more time on *Secret Family History*. When I checked the view count on Rashid's video a few days later, it still hovered around one hundred thousand, and the comments had slowed to a trickle. I had been right—things were finally returning to normal.

I did one last thing. I deleted my fake Instagram and Facebook accounts and scrubbed my timeline of all rumours related to Wholistic Grill. I even posted a few comments under my own profile, refuting the pile-on commenters and their swirling rumours. *The food at Wholistic Grill will be halal*, I wrote. *The owner's family is Muslim, and his restaurant is a welcome addition to the Golden Crescent neighbourhood.* I wasn't sure if it would do any good, but it went some way towards righting my wrongs.

• • •

Listener friends, sometimes your world is a trash fire. This episode will be about how to survive and thrive when things are going up in flames. There are things happening IRL that have made my life more chaotic than normal, and my commitment to remaining an anonymous Brown girl podcaster makes this episode particularly difficult to record.

The reasons for that are complicated. For one, when you are the daughter of "Suck it up, buttercup" immigrant parents, you learn pretty quickly that all your problems pale in comparison to the existential ones they faced when they were your age. Sad about a boy? Try staying afloat in a strange land. Worried about your job prospects? That's nothing compared to facing deep-rooted systemic discrimination, language barriers, a lack of job experience, and no family ties to help you stay off the streets when you first shift continents. You get the picture.

I recently told my mom about a hateful thing that had happened to me. Her response was to casually share a story I had never heard before. When she was new to the country, she was rammed by an irate fellow shopper in a grocery store, a random, race-motivated attack. *Translation: What I had faced was nothing in comparison to how things used to be.* According to my folks, I should get over it, because in the grand scheme of things, I am winning.

But am I? Compared to what she had to face on the regular, yes. Compared to what I dream for myself, no.

It is this personal accounting that gets me every time, listener friends. And here's the truth of it all: things are better for folks like me—the Brown, the Muslim, the Other. But because two truths can exist simultaneously in the universe, things are worse for us too. Real change is a boulder we keep pushing, but don't fool yourself into thinking it doesn't push back. Because it does. And sometimes it pushes back hard.

In my parents' time, simply being acknowledged as worthy of notice, as having your own history and worth, was enough. That's not enough for me. I want to be included and celebrated. I want nuanced and plentiful stories to be told about my people, and I don't want it to mean something when one of us breaks through, because there are so many of us breaking through, all the time, in every field.

When things (because, trash fire) remind me how far we still have to go collectively, it gets me down. And then it makes me mad. I want it to change. But I don't know how to make that happen.

I've learned a few things, though. When you are pushed out of the safety of anonymity and made to stand in the glare of public derision, here's what you should do:

1. *Find allies and gather them close.*
2. *Figure out who your real enemies are.*
3. *Plan out the best course of action over the next few days, and then the next few weeks, before worrying about the amorphous future with a capital F.*
4. *Remember that it's okay to be in survival mode.*

I know this all sounds bleak, but I hope to return to better times soon. In the meantime, if you are the praying sort, pray for me, or send me some of that good energy. I'm thinking of all of us tonight.

StanleyP messaged me soon after I uploaded my podcast. It was good to hear from him after our last awkward conversation.

StanleyP
I'm getting worried now, Ana. Are you okay?

AnaBGR
Not really. It's been a rough week.

StanleyP
Remember our deal?

StanleyP was referring to our long-ago deal that he would send me a picture of his finished project, after which I would decide what to do about us. In the craziness of the past few weeks, it had slipped my mind.

AnaBGR
I remember.

StanleyP

I'll be sending you that pic soon. I hope you know you can share things with me too. Your podcast was intense.

AnaBGR

Maybe I'll tell you about it one day.

StanleyP

I'd like that. Take care, friend.

Chapter Thirty

I had a shift at Three Sisters the next morning and I was late. I made chai and scrambled eggs for Baba's breakfast and toast for Fazee, then threw on black pants, a white shirt, and my green hijab with the pink flowers before sprinting for the door. I would grab something to eat from the restaurant.

It was a cool morning with a hint of warmer weather in the air. I walked onto Golden Crescent towards Three Sisters and spotted one of the festival flyers Rashid and I had posted on a street lamp. Except something was wrong. I walked closer, frowning.

Someone had written something across the front in black Sharpie: **MUSLIM PIGS**.

But we don't even eat pigs, I thought. Then, realizing what I was reading, I ripped down the paper, crumpling it into a ball and stuffing it into my pocket.

I walked faster towards the restaurant. Over a week ago, Rashid and I had taped a dozen flyers side by side to the window of Luxmi's bakery, next door to Three Sisters. Now I saw that someone had spray-painted **MUSLIM TERRORISTS GO HOME** across them, black paint dripping onto the sidewalk below. I tried to rip them down, too, but the painted words had bled through. Now it read **M———ORISTS GO H———**.

Luxmi Aunty spotted me and hurried out. "It happened overnight," she said. Her eyes were round with worry and fear. "They hit nearly every business on the street, the ones that put up flyers. Even the Tim Hortons. I called the police and they said they would send someone."

My face felt numb and she patted my arm. "The police will find out who did this. Probably some bored teenagers."

"N-nobody saw anything?" My teeth were chattering and I was suddenly freezing. I closed my eyes, trying to calm down, but my mind created a picture of the perpetrators. They looked like the angry, red-faced men in black T-shirts who had screamed at Rashid and tried to hurt Aydin and me.

Luxmi Aunty patted my arm again. "I'm so sorry, Hana," she said, and I caught the worried glance she sent towards Three Sisters. My stomach tightened in response, body instinctively readying itself for a punch to the gut, as I walked toward the store.

A large swastika had been spray-painted across the front window of Three Sisters. **SHARIAH LAW? NOT IN MY CANADA!** was written below, an ugly slash of blood-red paint.

My legs felt like jelly. I reached out to support myself, and my hand came to rest on the hate-filled symbol. I jerked away, nearly falling backwards in the process.

Mom appeared in the window and then hurried outside. "Are you all right?" she asked, hands claw-like on my arms.

I nodded, and she tugged me inside the restaurant, onto a plastic chair. "The police are on their way," she assured me, as if that meant something, as if everything would be put to rights now that the powers that be had been summoned. My eyes drifted to the dripping red shadow on our storefront, and I flinched, looking away.

Mom placed a large chipped mug in front of me, sloshing some of the tea over the side. She was never clumsy. I gripped the cup with my hands before I risked a look at her face. She was smiling, but as I looked closer, I realized it was more of a grimace, frozen to her face and stapled to the corners of her mouth. She was trying to hold it together, I realized. Trying not to react.

Rashid came running into the store, eyes wide and panicked. He skidded to a stop before us, breathing hard. "You are okay," he said, and it was not a question. He put a hand on his knee and took a deep breath. "Alhamdulillah, you are both fine."

Mom stood up to make him a cup of tea. What was it about desis and their obsession with chai? As if a hot cup of steeped leaves with milk and sugar can make everything better.

I took a sip, and felt my bones unclench. I took another sip, and my eyes drifted once more to the vandalized window, then beyond. Beautiful Yusuf stood outside his family's store, carefully picking up the remains of a fruit stand that had been strewn across the sidewalk. Ugly words had been spray-painted on the sidewalk in front of the store. His father stood outside, hands on his hips. I had never seen Brother Musa so still. He was usually always moving, refilling bins, barking orders, talking loudly on his phone, scowling at the world. Now his face was blank with shock.

As I continued to sip the scalding-hot tea, my thoughts began to slow down. Mom stayed late almost every night at the restaurant. Sometimes she walked home after midnight, usually alone. What if she had bumped into the people who defaced our street? What would they have done to her?

I put the cup down and reached into my pocket for the crumpled flyer, staring at the thickly lettered words. **MUSLIM PIGS**. Whoever attacked the street the night before had been right. I was a Muslim, and I was bloody pig-headed.

"You used goldenrod for the flyers, right?" I asked Rashid, and he nodded.

I told him I'd be back maybe in an hour, maybe less if I hurried. Back with another thousand flyers on cheerful goldenrod-yellow paper, which I vowed to paste on every available surface of our street, of our neighbourhood, of our home.

As Rashid had said, *Build a dam*.

Chapter Thirty-One

I bumped into Lily on my way out of the restaurant.

"Thank God you're all right!" she said, throwing her arms around me. "Yusuf told me what happened."

In her embrace, I started to shake. "I was late for my shift at Three Sisters," I began.

Lily's laugh was a broken sob. "You're always late, Han."

"I ripped down the defaced flyers on the other stores. Do you think that will slow the investigation when the cops come?" I was babbling, in shock.

She let go of me and reached into her pockets for tissues, handing me one. Dr. Moretti, prepared for every eventuality. "I'm pretty sure the graffiti and death threats are enough to charge someone with something." She wiped her face, eyes skittering past the window of Three Sisters. "Where were you headed just now?"

"To print another thousand flyers."

Lily's laugh was buoyant in the quiet stillness of the street, and the sound made me burst into tears.

"Hey, hey, it's all right," she said softly, leading me to the side of the store, to the alley where we kept the trash and where Lily, Yusuf, and I had played superheroes as kids. I had always been Catwoman because Lily insisted on playing Wonder Woman to Yusuf's Batman. She was better at lassoing.

"Mom comes home late at night. She could have been hurt. They could have . . . People were posting things, but I never thought they would bring it to our doorstep . . ." I said between heaving sobs. Lily rubbed soothing circles over my shoulders and passed me tissues while I cried, murmuring comforting words neither of us believed, but which made me feel better anyway.

After a few moments I stood up. "Thank you."

"Don't thank me. Tell me what I can do to help."

I looked up and down the street, at the defaced storefronts, the trash strewn all over the place, and nearly started crying again.

"I'll organize cleanup," Lily said decisively. "Go print those flyers."

Rashid called while I was in line at Staples. "The police are here," he said in a subdued voice. "They want to speak to you and Aydin about the downtown confrontation. I have already shown them the comments and threats we received online . . . I can't believe this has happened."

I knew my cousin felt guilty and regretful, but none of us could have anticipated the damage to our street. I felt partly to blame as well. I had promised Aydin and Rashid I would keep an eye on the online chatter, and I had missed the signs. Or maybe I hadn't wanted to believe that people could be so hateful.

I paid for my purchase and drove home. Lily had rallied people to clean up, including Fahim, but it was slow work. I gave my statement to the two uniformed police officers sent to interview business owners on Golden Crescent, and then Rashid and I spent the next couple of hours stapling and pasting up flyers everywhere, twice as many as the previous time. I anticipated that the media would show up soon to document the carnage.

It was late morning when we finished, and I couldn't go home. Only a chocolate glazed doughnut and a too-sweet French vanilla cappuccino could make me feel better.

Mr. Lewis stood behind the counter at Tim Hortons. "How is everyone holding up?" he asked as he filled my order, waving away my money.

I shrugged. "How badly did they get you?"

The Tim Hortons had been left relatively unscathed, Mr. Lewis informed me. Just some ripped-up flyers and trash in front of the store. He smiled as he passed over my order. "Your cousin dropped off a stack of flyers, and I'm planning to put up a display. I'll also be handing them out with every cup of coffee."

My eyes filled with tears at his generosity. "What if they come back?"

Mr. Lewis walked with me to an empty booth. "My mother was born in Poland in 1932. Her family was Orthodox Catholic. She was nine years old when the Nazis invaded. Her family fled, saved by the grace of God. But they never forgot what happened to their home, and she told us the stories so we would never forget too."

"Everything is such a mess. I don't know what to do."

He leaned down. "You know you're doing the right thing when you've pissed off the bad guys," he said in a terrible gangster accent.

I laughed shakily. He gave my shoulder a squeeze before returning to the counter, to serve the neighbourhood he had lived in all his life, even as that community grew and changed around him. And he was fine with that. "If the people are changing, that means we're still alive. Only living things change," he always said.

I remembered his mother. Mrs. Lewis had died the previous year.

My family had attended her funeral at the Orthodox church down the street. Mom had made kheer—rice pudding with cardamom—for the wake, and there hadn't been a single spoonful left by the end of the night. Mrs. Lewis would visit the restaurant with her church friends on Sunday, dressed in floral cotton and sensible shoes, eyes milky behind enormous pink-framed glasses. She had always smiled whenever we met.

The bells over the door chimed and I looked up. Aydin.

Was he worried about his restaurant? Maybe now he would finally move to a less exciting neighbourhood, one with a more welcoming business community and targeted by fewer Nazis. If Aydin packed up and left right away, as I had wanted all along, would that solve our problems? Could we return to the careful normality of before?

No. Three Sisters would still be in financial trouble, and there would still be hate. But maybe it wouldn't land on us. Maybe we would be spared. Or maybe we had been spared all along. Muslims believe that when you make *du'a*, or sincere prayer, for something, one of three things happens: (1) you are granted your request, (2) something bad that was headed your way is deflected, or (3) the good thing you asked for is kept for you in heaven.

I watched as Aydin chatted with Mr. Lewis, his face creased in a tired smile. He reached up to run his fingers through the dark hair over his brow, and I remembered that I still had his sunglasses in my purse. I fished them out and tried them on. Camouflage.

Mr. Lewis said something to Aydin, and he turned around and spotted me.

I took a gulp of cappuccino, burning my tongue. "Are you wishing you'd picked a different neighbourhood for your restaurant?" I asked, trying for a smile, but Aydin only shook his head and took a seat.

"If I had opened up somewhere else, I would have missed all this."
He caught my eye and grimaced. "Laugh at the hard stuff, right?"

I nodded, glad he'd remembered my words from the baseball game. That instant of levity felt far away in the face of this disaster. "What else is there to do but laugh?" I repeated. No, really, I wanted to ask him. What else could we do?

He must have understood, because he replied, "Build a dam?"

We lapsed into silence.

"Are you still going ahead with your plans to open next week?" I asked.

Aydin nodded. "I've arranged for extra security. Will you be there?"

"I have my protest sign ready to go." I took off the sunglasses and handed them to him. "Are you all right?" I asked quietly.

"No," he said. "Are you?"

I shook my head. We were being careful, each trying to appear calm in front of the other. I stood up. "I should get back to Three Sisters. My mom probably needs help cleaning off the . . ." I trailed off.

"I'll walk you," Aydin said abruptly.

"It's fine. You're busy."

Aydin gripped the sunglasses until his knuckles turned white. "Please, Hana. Let me walk you back."

I grabbed my bag, and we left Tim Hortons together.

Chapter Thirty-Two

Mom wasn't working on pre-lunch prep as she usually did in the morning. Instead I found her in one of the booths at the back of Three Sisters.

"Are you all right?" I asked her, my voice gentle in the quiet of the dining room.

"I'm just taking a little break," she said.

Mom never took breaks. Breaks were for lesser mortals and shiftless daughters with artistic proclivities. I walked to the kitchen tea urn, the first thing that was turned on at Three Sisters every morning.

"It's empty," Mom called. She was looking around the restaurant with distant eyes. "I didn't bother refilling it after this morning." She might as well have told me she had forgotten how to breathe.

I filled the tea urn with water, tossed in a few cloves, crushed cardamom, whole cinnamon, and tea bags, and set the machine to boil. Mom didn't even look over to make sure I was doing it right.

Next I filled a large bucket with hot, soapy water and retrieved some acetone we kept stored in a cupboard, then dragged the bucket through the kitchen towards the main door. Mom still hadn't moved.

The paint on the window was thick and goopy, caked in some spots as if the vandals had added layers to the original design, but thin in others. Overall, the swastika was sloppily done, almost as if the white supremacists hadn't cared about their handiwork. Nobody had standards anymore. Where was the pride in a job well done?

I started to scrub, reaching as high as I could. We must have been attacked by seven-foot-tall Nazis, or maybe they had a ladder. I could only reach the top of one arm of the swastika. The water was scalding and the acetone burned my eyes as I worked. After ten minutes I had only managed to smear the arm into a dark red swirl.

"Hana, leave it. The BOA or City Council will have funds for this," Mom called. "I sent Fahim home for the day to be with Fazeela. She was so upset, and that's not good for the baby. Leave it, *jaan*."

But I couldn't leave it. This ugly red graffiti was the reason my chai-addicted, workaholic mom was staring at the walls of her restaurant with lifeless eyes. Not even unexpected guests or the threat of losing her livelihood had done that to her. It needed to be dealt with—right now.

I plunged the rag back into the soapy water. Red pigment dribbled down my hands as I scrubbed. The paint crept under my fingernails, caking my fingers in red slime. I paused for a moment to wipe my forehead and looked around. Lunch was an hour away, and across the street Yusuf's store was closed. The profanity on the sidewalk in front of the shop was easy to read. They would have to use a power washer to blast it off.

I returned to the task. Half the swastika was smeared now, so blurry that it resembled a misshapen letter *Y*. My shoulders ached, but I dipped the rag back in the bucket and reached up once more, as high as my arms would go, then higher.

When I looked inside the restaurant again, Mom had disappeared. I wondered if the people who had drawn their crooked symbol on our window knew that the swastika is actually an ancient symbol of good luck, and that it originated in India. I wondered if the person who had so effortlessly demanded that my family return to the home they left decades ago knew that the symbol Hitler had appropriated for the Third Reich was a religious shorthand for positivity. My parents had bought our house from a Hindu family, and they had found tiny "swastiks" in the backs of cupboards and under the kitchen counter, put there to bless the house and its inhabitants.

My neck hurt. I massaged my shoulders and shook out my arms before plunging into the bucket once more. The water was now a dull, chalky red.

"Here, use this." Mom handed me a squeegee. She was holding a razor blade in one hand, stepladder in the other. She carefully climbed up to scrape the top of the window while I wiped the smeared red paint dripping down below. We worked in silence until most of the damage was cleared.

Inside the restaurant, the red light flashed on the tea urn. I poured us both a cup of strong chai while Mom washed her hands and then her face. She looked more awake now, less pale, and we drank our tea in silence. Mom finished her cup quickly, even though it was boiling hot. Years spent cooking had given her a crazy-high heat tolerance; she was nearly impervious to burns.

"I have to make vegetable fry for the lunch special today." She paused by the kitchen door. "Thank you, *beta*. Leave some flyers for the street festival with me. I'll put them in the takeout bags and hand them out to customers."

Chapter Thirty-Three

According to Constable Lukie, the police officer who called me that evening at home, their working theory was that, while the downtown attack may have inspired the Golden Crescent rampage, it was unlikely the two events were directly related. "A hate crime has many qualifiers, and right now we can't be certain this was a targeted attack," she explained, to my dumbfounded silence.

What about the swastika? I asked. The reference to Muslim pigs, the demand that we return home, the profanity on Brother Musa's sidewalk that made reference to his Arab heritage?

"It's too early to tell what the real motivations were in this case," Constable Lukie explained patiently. I knew she was doing her job, staying objective, but my throat tightened just the same. "The video that was posted online likely inspired this act of mischief and vandalism. Luckily there is some camera footage, which we will be reviewing in the next few days, and we will speak to any witnesses who come forward. My deepest regrets to you and your family, Ms. Khan," she continued, voice sincere.

Constable Lukie promised to be in touch as soon as she had news. She signed off with one final admonition: "According to our review of the online comments, there were a number of references to an upcoming festival."

I explained about the Golden Crescent summer festival. With a sigh, she said, "In light of recent events, you might want to consider cancelling."

I thought about the thousand flyers we had distributed and pasted on storefronts that day. "It's a local festival," I said. "The neighbourhood kids look forward to it every year. Parents and grandparents show up. It's a community tradition. We can't—" My voice broke, and Constable Lukie waited until I had regained control. "We're not cancelling," I said firmly.

"You can arrange for some police presence, but you must promise to let me know if you receive any more targeted threats. Our priority right now is finding the people responsible for the vandalism on Golden Crescent, and making sure no one gets hurt," she said.

When I hung up, Baba was standing in the living room. "Fazeela told me about the video and the attack on the street. People have been calling all day. Hana, what is going on?" he asked.

"Nothing to worry about," I said, the lie coming automatically to my lips. I had become so used to protecting him from reality, it had become a habit.

Baba sighed. "Stop, *beta*. I know the restaurant is in trouble. I know that things have not been going well. Your mother is worried, and Fahim has not smiled in days. Keeping things from me will not help."

"I want you to get better. I don't want you to worry about anything except that," I said quietly. My father's receding hair had gone completely grey in the past few years, I noted.

He sat down beside me on the couch and covered my hand with his own. "It is a luxury to worry about my family. I nearly died in that accident, and I am thankful for whatever time I have been granted. You must stop trying to shut me out. I am part of this family as well."

He was right. I couldn't hide things from him anymore, and I didn't want to. Interspersed with my tears and then his tears, I told my father everything. Kawkab Khala joined us during my retelling of the downtown attack and the day's events, settling into the armchair and listening to my narration without interruption.

When I finished, they were both silent.

"You are very brave, Hana," my aunt finally said. I waited for her usual jab, but she was serious.

"My Hana has always been this way," my father said. His eyes were red-rimmed. It felt good to tell Baba the truth. His shoulders had once again become strong enough to handle this worry.

"We will show those cowards we are not intimidated by their clumsy fear tactics," Kawkab Khala said, and there was something in her voice that made me want to stand up and cheer. Knowing what I did about her personal history, my aunt's vote of confidence lit a fire within me.

The doorbell rang and I went to answer it, expecting my cousin or maybe Fahim. Instead, Sad Aunty—Afsana, I corrected myself—stood in the doorway, holding a covered plate. "For you," she said simply, handing it over. A delicious aroma escaped from the foil-wrapped platter.

"Is that Afsana?" Kawkab called from the kitchen, where she was making tea. "Tell her she is late."

Baba had disappeared upstairs to rest after the excitement of the day. Kawkab Khala carried three steaming mugs of chai to the kitchen table and, just like the previous time Afsana Aunty had visited, the three of us sat down to sip and chat. Afsana had brought fresh potato pakoras—fritters seasoned with garam masala, salt, red chili powder, fresh coriander, and green chilies, battered in chickpea flour and deep-fried. The greasy spiciness of the pakoras, paired with hot chai, was comforting.

"I am sorry about what happened on the street today," Afsana Aunty said. "I was so scared when I heard the news. Is everyone . . . fine?" Her voice was hesitant, and I noticed my aunt sit up straighter at her words.

"The vandals attacked late at night, when everyone was home," I reassured her.

"Your mother said there will be a Business Owners Association meeting, to discuss increased security," Kawkab Khala said casually. "I would enjoy attending that meeting." She was telling me, not asking for permission, and I looked at her in surprise. My aunt had shown little interest in the operation of Three Sisters, and I instantly knew she was up to something. My suspicions were confirmed by her quick glance at Afsana Aunty, who gripped her mug tightly, waiting for my response.

"It's just a bunch of old aunties and uncles arguing," I said weakly. I had no wish to make another scene at the BOA, but if my aunt wanted to go, there was also no way I was letting her attend alone. Who knew what mischief she would get up to without my supervision.

"Yes, I can almost guarantee that," she said, her words a sharpened promise.

We drank the rest of our chai in silence. Afsana Aunty left soon after, clutching her washed plate, which we had heaped with sugar cookies. In our family it was unthinkable to return a dish empty.

"You and Afsana Aunty are so close," I commented to my aunt, picking up the empty mugs and putting them in the sink.

"She is my best friend, though I am older. Afsana was always full of life, but occasionally she falls into periods of darkness." My aunt began to wash the dishes, not looking at me. "I understand because I suffered from the same darkness, only I was better at hiding it. People knew who my father was, who my family were. She was not so lucky. Her parents were poor, and everyone knew she was at the school only because of a generous *waqf*, an endowment."

"You protected her," I said, understanding more of their relationship now. Kawkab Khala's protectiveness was very much in evidence when her friend was present.

"We looked out for each other. But yes, she has always treated me as an older sister. Unfortunately she was married too young and left school too soon. But when I saw her, I tried to help."

I processed this. "Did she get help for her . . . dark episodes, after she married?"

"Her first husband never understood her. Allah blessed her with a better man the second time," Kawkab Khala said.

"And two daughters," I added.

My aunt stacked dishes on the drying rack. "They are her stepchildren, but she loves them as if they were her own. When I decided to visit Toronto, I told her to come along, that we would have a grand adventure together. Her husband is generous and her stepchildren nearly grown, so we made arrangements." She reached for the hand lotion we kept on the counter and began massaging the thick cream into paper-thin skin. "What a cold country your family chose. If I were your mother, I would have moved to California."

I smiled faintly. "Mom likes a challenge."

"A characteristic shared by all the women in our family, I'm afraid. Good night, Hana *jaan*." She left me in the kitchen.

My phone pinged while I was getting ready for bed. To my surprise, the text was from Aydin. He must have gotten my number from Rashid.

> If it's not too much trouble, could you come by Wholistic Grill tomorrow night?

I texted back, asking what was going on.

> I'd like to talk. I can bribe you with a peek inside the Evil Empire, and a taste of our menu.

When he put it like that . . . *See you at 6 pm*, I typed. *This better be good.*

. . .

I'm usually all about #blessed. As a Muslim, I was taught to be grateful for my many gifts; I know how lucky I am. I love my family, I'm young and healthy and educated, and I was born in Canada. But lately I've felt weighed down by sadness. A series of unfortunate events has paraded through my life, and I miss the days when I had the luxury to not worry about things I can't control.

I came face to face with hatred recently. I don't want to get into the details because this is supposed to be an anonymous podcast, and the incident is easily google-able. For the first time in my life, I was targeted, and the experience has left me rattled. It has been an unsettling experience too, because for so long I felt invisible. That strange dual existence—of being seen for one thing and dismissed for it at the same time—is just part of regular, everyday life for this particular Brown

Muslim girl, and likely for a lot of people out there. I've lived in this skin for so long it's the only way I know how to be.

Yet for the first time ever, I feel both seen and misunderstood. There is no solution to this feeling, I know, except to learn to grow comfortable with the me on the inside, the one not everyone gets to see or know. So I'm throwing this out to you now, listener friends: if you see someone struggling, don't be afraid to reach out, to show them some compassion and maybe even empathy. Tell them you can see who they truly are, underneath their pain. You might find yourself similarly enveloped by clouds at some point. No one knows when the dark days will descend, only that they come for us all.

Chapter Thirty-Four

It was past six p.m. when I made my way to Wholistic Grill. Aydin's storefront was set back from the street and partially shaded by trees. I pictured couples strolling there on summer evenings, children playing on the patio while friends caught up with their day. He had chosen a good spot for his restaurant. The door was unlocked and I let myself inside, overcome by curiosity. I wanted to see what had been done with the place.

The restaurant was all bright white and soft grey. The centre aisle held a long, communal bench–style table made of reclaimed wood, with chic chrome barstools and hanging lamps overhead. All around the periphery stood booths in grey and red and black leather, visible under clear plastic protective wrapping. They were interspersed with smaller tables with seating for two or four, plus a few large circular tables for bigger groups. The kitchen wasn't hidden in the back like in Three Sisters, but set up at the front of the restaurant, behind glass.

The walls were accented with silver and white wallpaper, and at the far end of the restaurant was a massive flat-screen television surrounded by a bank of comfortable sofas and bar tables. The lighting was tasteful, with hanging crystals winking beneath gauzy black shades. The result didn't look like it belonged on Golden Crescent, I thought, then reconsidered. Our neighbourhood deserved beautiful spaces too.

Aydin was waiting at the counter in front of the kitchen, watching me snoop shamelessly. "What do you think?" he asked after a few minutes.

I could only shake my head. I couldn't explain what I was feeling. It wasn't jealousy or resentment exactly. I looked around again, noticing little details like the salt and pepper shakers shaped like stars, crescents, and hearts, and the floor, a white-and-grey travertine. Everything demonstrated an eye for detail.

My gaze travelled back to his face. He looked vulnerable as he waited for my answer.

"It's astonishing, Aydin. Everything is exactly as it should be," I answered honestly.

His shoulders relaxed and he gave me a cocky smile. "Wait until you see the patio."

The back patio was small but secluded, a patch of sleek grey slate near the parking lot, enclosed by mature pine trees. The furniture was cast iron with heavy, black umbrellas at each table.

I whistled my appreciation. "You know your customers take their bratty kids everywhere, right? They're going to tear this place apart," I teased.

He smiled briefly. "That's why I included a cushion in the price—for repairs. Wait here, I'll be back."

He returned and placed a steaming plate in front of me, cutlery folded into a linen napkin.

Aydin had made me biryani poutine. I looked from his suddenly shy face to the dish, speechless. The pleasure I felt at this gesture was almost overwhelming, so I did the best thing a person can do for a cook. I dug into the oozing gravy-soaked rice and chicken, scooped up fries and cheese curds, and tried not to think too hard about what it all meant.

"It's delicious," I said. "Thank you."

"This dish is more complicated than it looks," he said.

"Don't tell me it's on the menu."

"Only the secret menu, strictly for VIPs." He picked up an extra fork and took a small bite. He grimaced. "I really don't know why you like it. It's like eating puréed baby food, with the flavours all mixed up."

"Not everyone gets my elegant palate."

Aydin smiled and looked around the patio. He seemed nervous, jumpy, and I wondered again why he had invited me. It wasn't to plan the street festival, or he would have told me to bring Rashid. He would get to why in his own time, I reasoned.

I decided to ask him something I had wondered about for a while. "Why did you decide to get into the restaurant business? With your dad's contacts and money, you could have done anything." Running your own business was never easy, but restaurants were notorious for long hours, unruly customers, and razor-thin margins.

I watched Aydin trace circles on the table. I couldn't stop staring at his finger, long and blunt-tipped. "Why do people do anything? Why are you so interested in putting together this street festival?" he asked.

"Because a rich boy moved into my neighbourhood and decided to ruin my life," I said lightly. I smiled to show I was joking—mostly. "You didn't answer my question."

"My mom loved to cook," he started, then stopped. I took another bite and waited for him to find the words.

"I knew my parents didn't get along. It wasn't that they fought. It was more that they didn't really talk. They never seemed to be in the same room at the same time, you know? My dad worked all the time and Mom was alone a lot. I was so young when she died . . . not even six."

My fork paused. I tried to imagine little Aydin, a child with floppy dark hair and huge eyes. I bet he was scrawny.

"I didn't even realize she was sick until she was gone. Nobody told me anything. But when she was alive, she loved to cook. We lived in this massive house in North Vancouver, and she was always experimenting in the kitchen. Dad used to get so mad because she was a careless cook. She'd get *haldi*, that yellow turmeric powder, all over the white marble counters he had shipped from Italy."

The kitchen at Three Sisters looked like that. Indian spices seriously stain your clothes, the walls, the counters.

"She made the best potato pakoras and chocolate chip cookies for me as after-school snacks, but I loved her biryani best of all. She said it was a secret recipe, passed down only through the women in the family. I remember feeling sad because I never planned to get married—I thought girls were gross. When I went to your restaurant, that biryani tasted just like my mother's." He looked up at me and our eyes locked, both remembering his father's words that day. His smile was rueful. "Poor little rich boy, right?"

I shook my head. "I would have liked to meet your mom. I love pakoras."

He laughed. "She would have loved to cook for you."

"I'm a terrible cook."

"You're not great at waitressing either," he said. "Good thing you're going into broadcasting. You know, you never told me why."

"Radio saved my life," I said quietly. "When my father was in the hospital and we were waiting to hear if he would live through the night, and then waiting to hear if he would live through the first surgery, and then the second and the third, waiting to hear if he would ever walk again, radio and podcasts kept me distracted. They kept me upbeat and gave me something to think about other than my life. Later, when he was recovering, Baba and I binged entire shows while he was doing physio or waiting for the pain to pass. Storytelling helped us forget for a little while. That's when I realized I wanted to tell stories for the rest of my life."

Aydin stared at me while I was talking, his gaze moving from my eyes to my lips and back. My face grew hot. "You think that's dumb, right?"

He shook his head. "No," he said. "I was just thinking I never thought I would meet someone like you."

I wasn't sure what he meant. "Did you spend the past year dreaming about an opinionated broadcaster?" I asked. Our conversation had been getting too serious.

"Yes," he said simply. "You're ambitious, independent, loyal, smart. I love your family. You make me laugh. I can't stop staring at you."

The butterflies floating in my stomach were making it hard to finish the biryani poutine. I put down the fork. "Why are you telling me this?" I asked.

Aydin shook his head, and I could see that his fists were balled at his sides. "I've wanted to tell you this for a while. I'm afraid that when I tell you the rest of it, you'll hate me."

"I tried hating you. That didn't work out so well," I said.

"Me too." He took a deep breath, then blurted, "My father wants me to marry Zulfa."

My stomach dropped. "I see."

"I've known her my whole life. I also know she's in love with someone else, in Vancouver, and that her parents have been putting pressure on her to marry me. I offered to pretend to be her fiancé for a few months, to make our parents happy. In exchange, she would help me launch the restaurant."

"Sounds like the plot of a romcom," I said.

His answering smile was bleak. "It isn't that sort of movie," he said. "I'm telling you this because I want you to understand the kind of man my father is. He wants the world to operate in a certain way and he expects obedience and loyalty from the people in his life, especially me. Becoming engaged to Zulfa was one of two conditions he set before he agreed to back my restaurant. I initially agreed because Zulfa needed time so she and Zain could make plans. But the other reason was because I needed my dad's money and support to start Wholistic Grill."

I wasn't sure where he was going with this. "Rashid will be so disappointed," I murmured.

Aydin laughed, shaking his head. "You're not making this easy for me," he said. I knew there was more, that I wouldn't like what came next.

"Am I supposed to make things easier for you?" I asked.

We exchanged a long glance. "Ever since we met, you've turned my world upside down. Just let me get through this first, and then you can decide what you want to do next."

I nodded, wheels turning in my mind. "You said getting engaged to Zulfa was your father's first condition for backing Wholistic Grill. What was his second condition?"

"My dad thinks I lack the killer instinct needed to succeed in business. He said if I wanted his money, I would have to prove I was a worthy investment."

My conversation with Zulfa came back to me now, her insight into Aydin and his strained relationship with his father. I could believe that Junaid Uncle saw his son as an investment, to be held on to until a suitable return was achieved. And I could imagine Aydin tying himself in knots to comply, though his very nature rebelled.

He continued, voice a monotone now, and my heart sped up at this hint of Cold Aydin's return. "I lied to you before. It was no coincidence that I built Wholistic Grill in Golden Crescent."

"What do you mean?" I asked.

"To keep my father's investment, I had to open Wholistic Grill next to another, well-established restaurant. I had six months to put it out of business. I chose Three Sisters. I would prove myself when you closed." He recited the facts slowly, as if they were a confession.

Which I realized they were. It took me a moment to absorb his words. When I had, I slowly stood up. My heart was beating so fast I wasn't sure if I could remain upright. I gripped the table, and Aydin started to move towards me, but I held up my hand. He froze in place, anxious eyes locked on my face.

"Then I guess I was right all along," I said, voice strangely calm. Why was I so calm? "You've been my enemy from the start."

His shoulders slumped. "I'm sorry."

And then I wasn't calm anymore. I was furious. "What are you sorry about, exactly? For working to destroy my family from the first moment we met?"

"It wasn't personal. You were a stranger," Aydin answered, a note of pleading in his voice.

"You would have been fine with putting another family out of business, just to get your father's money and vote of confidence?" I asked, voice rising.

"Your mom was having trouble even before we arrived. I admit I played a part, but you can't put this all on me," Aydin said. He really didn't get it; he didn't understand how much privilege and power he had. He held all the options while my family had to scramble to stay afloat.

"That doesn't make it okay to take away our choices!" I yelled. "We have nothing to fall back on. My entire family will be ruined because you can't stand up to your father!"

"You know how I feel about my father," Aydin said, and he stood up to face me.

"YOU STILL TOOK HIS MONEY!" I roared.

He flinched, stepping back as if I had hit him. His face flushed an ugly red, raw emotion crawling across his cheeks and jawline as if I had slapped him. I wished I had.

"You're not innocent in this, Hana," Aydin said, his voice dark and low. "You spread rumours online about Wholistic Grill. You called Workers Safety and tried to shut down my renovations. At least I told you the truth."

"Eventually! You told me the truth eventually!" I cried. "To think I felt guilty for what I had done. I erased the posts, I even vouched for you online, when you were out to get us from the start. I should have gone with my first instincts and burned your restaurant to the ground!" I was spinning out of control, anger snapping at my heels and urging me forward, even as I recognized the hurt, shame, and guilt on his face. But it wasn't enough. After everything that had happened to us—on Golden Crescent, online, downtown. I had trusted him, helped him, and he had betrayed me.

I could feel the pinpricks of tears, but I held them back. "How could you do this to me?" I asked, hating how small I sounded.

"I wanted to tell you the truth as soon as I realized . . ." He trailed off. Then, more softly, "This wasn't supposed to happen."

"What wasn't supposed to happen? You weren't supposed to feel bad for me? To feel sorry for my family when you pushed us out of our *ethnic slum* and onto the street?"

"No!" he said.

I dared him to explain. I was standing so close I could feel the heat of him, just as he could see that I was trembling. "Then what?" I yelled back.

"I WASN'T SUPPOSED TO FALL FOR YOU!" Aydin shouted.

His words pushed me backwards in shock. We were both breathing hard now, facing off like two exhausted boxers in the final round.

I tossed my head, disbelieving, hurt, and sad—and so very, very sorry. "Don't fool yourself into thinking you actually feel something for me, Aydin. That's not love," I said deliberately. "Love doesn't deceive, or play games, or always take."

Part of me knew that wasn't the whole truth. I had witnessed his kindness; I just didn't know if any of it had been real. My next words were cruel, a direct hit. "What would your mother think of you now?"

I regretted the question immediately. Aydin closed his eyes, and when he opened them again, they were wet. He swore under his breath and walked away.

I forced myself to leave, slipping out by the patio gate, leaving the biryani poutine he had made for me—and what was left of my heart—on the table.

Chapter Thirty-Five

I was still furious with Aydin the next day, and I wasn't sure what to do about his confession. I wondered if I should tell my family. Fazeela and Baba had both asked me to start sharing, but what good would that information do? I didn't want to admit to sabotaging Aydin online, and it might all come out now. I wasn't sure why Junaid Uncle wanted our closing in any case, aside from proof that his son could be shaped by his motives. It seemed like terrible business practice to me, but then I didn't live in the rarified world of corporate plotting. Besides, I could picture my mother's indifferent reaction to Aydin's behaviour: *We were in trouble before he came along. I do not see the issue.*

I also wasn't sure what Aydin had expected the previous night. Some sort of easy forgiveness, perhaps? If so, we had both been surprised by my rage. And I had been even more shocked by his admission that he had feelings for me. *I wasn't supposed to fall for you!* His words echoed in my mind as I got ready for my shift at Radio Toronto.

There had been attraction between us from the start, but love? We were virtually strangers. *How could you do this to me?* Remembering my own words brought a flush of embarrassment to my cheeks. *What would your mother think of you now?* I couldn't stop thinking about the look in Aydin's eyes when I had conjured up his mother. He had deserved my anger, but perhaps not that final cruelty.

I wasn't sure how I would face him again. With swords drawn, pistols at dawn? Or would he wave his white flag, tempt me with some more biryani poutine, and refuse to fight? What would I do then?

One thing was sure: the truth was out between us, all our secrets revealed. In the light of morning, that honesty felt clean and oddly refreshing. I was tired of lying to myself about how I really felt about so many things in my life. I was tired of going along to get along and of ignoring the cost of that deceit in my life. It was time to open the windows and let sunshine stream into the dark corners. It was time to take my story into my own hands, not leave it in the hands of those who didn't respect my words.

I dressed for work, mentally flinging open those windows as I wrapped my most colourful hijab—pink, blue, and purple—and secured it with a straight pin. I put on mascara and bright red lipstick with a heavy hand. And I thought about the women in my family—my mother, Kawkab Khala, Fazeela. Each had faced major challenges, and not one had chosen the easier, less strenuous path. They had all fought for what they believed in, for as long as they could.

I willed that same clarifying light to stream into the conversation I now realized I had to have with Marisa and Thomas.

MARISA LOOKED AT HER WATCH when I walked through the door of Radio Toronto—I was on time for once. "Nice to see you're making an effort, Hana. I know things have been difficult for you lately," she said.

I felt a prickle across the back of my neck. Her words had been designed to put me in my place, but instead they were having the opposite effect. Marisa knew about the Golden Crescent attack; it had made the news, and once again I had been quoted and interviewed, representing my family business and the street, but not by Radio Toronto. I knew she resented my refusal to do another on-air radio segment, about the attack on my neighbourhood. That was probably why she was being so short with me.

She asked if there had been any new developments, and what the police had said. Marisa had never shown an interest in my family before, but now she peppered me with queries. Your mother has run a restaurant for fifteen years? Rashid is new to the country, here on a student visa? Fazeela used to play soccer semi-professionally and now she is on bedrest with a difficult pregnancy? But her interest was fleeting, especially since there would be no accompanying story for the station, and she turned back to the monitor in front of Thomas. On the screen I spotted an outline of the story about radicalization, the one they had pitched to Nathan Davis despite my protests.

"You're not still doing that story," I said flatly.

"Of course we are, darling," Marisa said, not bothering to turn around.

Thomas caught my eye and straightened. "What's wrong, Hana?" he asked.

It was now or never. Channelling my inner Kawkab Khala, I started in. "I've thought a lot about responsible storytelling lately," I said carefully.

"Yes, Hana?" Marisa said, clicking through Thomas's document. She still hadn't turned around.

My nails dug into my palms. "I don't want you to pursue the story about radicalization among young Muslims," I blurted. "It's dangerous. It will incite more hatred against a community already under tremendous scrutiny and suspicion."

I finally had my boss's attention. Marisa stared at me while Thomas shifted position, his hands rising in a subtle motion. *Calm down*, his eyes beseeched. *Don't start anything.*

I ignored him.

"This is an important story that will lead to discussion from interested listeners," Marisa responded, in her best reasoning-with-a-toddler tone. "I know some ugly things have happened to you and your family recently, but as a journalist, you have to learn to separate your personal biases from current events. Your job is to be objective, darling." She returned to the screen.

How had I never noticed the patronizing tone in her voice before? Or maybe I had simply been ignoring it all this time, because that had been easier.

"You can't," I said, and my voice cracked. I was scared, I realized.

Marisa stilled. "I . . . can't?" she repeated, shaking her head. "Hana, you were in the wrong place at the wrong time downtown, and your cousin aggravated a fringe group by posting that video. He made a choice, and the fallout is on him. The fact that the video went viral demonstrates how interested people are in this issue, which is great news for your show. When I chose you and Thomas for this competitive internship, you both agreed to work on assigned projects. This show is important to everyone at the radio station. Good journalism requires you to dig deep and make sacrifices."

I shifted from one foot to the other, contemplating my options. I could back down right away. She had effectively put me in my place. If I folded, she might give in on my next idea or offer me a paid position, because I had proven myself capable of being "objective," of being a team player. Except I didn't want to be on this team. I took a deep breath and acknowledged the truth: I couldn't do it anymore.

"I've never been comfortable with the way you wanted to frame a show about people of colour in Toronto," I began. The moment the words were out of my mouth, out of my head, my shoulders dropped in relief. "I made my concerns clear at the meeting with Nathan Davis, as well as later, but you didn't listen to me."

Marisa's jaw tightened at my words, and two bright spots of colour appeared high on her cheeks. "Do you have any idea what a gift you've been given?" she said. "Working on a show of your own, at this stage of your career, is an incredible opportunity. If you're having trouble making the best of things now, how will you survive in this field? You should be thanking me, not causing further problems."

Her true feelings finally. I should be thanking her. I should feel honoured and privileged to work on the story—any story—she had gifted me. The worst of it was, I knew she was right on one level. It *was* an opportunity. But she was also wrong on a different level, one that held in the balance my sense of self, the history and responsibility I carried, and that balance was not equal.

Thomas stared at me, willing me to reverse my position, to back-pedal.

I closed my eyes. *Bismillah.* Time to go all in.

"I went into broadcasting to tell stories about real people," I said, gaze steady on her face. "Not to reinforce the projections of strangers. I can't be party to perpetuating harmful stereotypes about Brown people and Muslims. Promoting the same old narrative about the dangerous outsider will cause harm to my community. I know, because it already has."

"That's unfair. We want to hear everyone's stories," Marisa said.

"No, you don't," I replied. "You want to hear me retell the stories you tell yourself about people who look like me."

Thomas had remained silent during the entire exchange. He spoke up now. "Hana, let's talk about this. We can work things out."

I felt a deep well of sadness at his words. It was too late, and we both knew it.

"No, Thomas. Hana has made it clear that she can't work here or work on her assigned projects without compromising her moral compass," Marisa said. "She is free to move on to a situation that better aligns with her beliefs."

Was it better in the end to find out where you stood and leave with that knowledge? No matter what I said, Marisa would never understand the experiences that had shaped me. Then again, I found her pretty baffling too.

I held out my hand. "Thank you for the opportunity and for your guidance, Marisa. I hope our paths cross again someday."

She grasped my hand. "Be good, Hana."

I packed up my things from the office. It wasn't until I walked out of the station that the trembling began. I had to place my hands on my knees and take deep breaths until my vision cleared.

I had worked for months to secure that internship. It was meant to be a step towards a better, more secure job in broadcasting. All that work and effort, all those hours of filing and archiving, of holding my tongue or getting my ideas shot down, had come to nothing. The prospect of job security my father wanted for me—that I had dreamed of for myself—had now completely vanished from my life. The restaurant would close, Aydin would win, and my career in broadcasting was over.

What had I done?

・・・

I WOKE UP FRANTIC FROM A SHADOWY NIGHTMARE. The blanket lay in an untidy heap on the floor and I was sprawled out on the sofa, arms and legs splayed. I sat up and looked at my phone. It was late morning. Someone (most likely my mother) had left my favourite breakfast for me on the coffee table: upma, a savoury ground-wheat porridge of rava cooked with onion, mustard seeds, curry leaves, dry-roasted red chilies, and toasted whole cashews.

I microwaved the upma while the kettle boiled for chai, then took both back to the sofa. The first bite burned my tongue, and the fiery red chili woke me up completely. The scalding hot chai did nothing to calm my mouth. Instead, I closed my eyes while my taste buds throbbed.

Had I really quit my internship? Had I really accused Marisa of not listening to the diverse voices on her staff? Where had that fiery Hana come from?

My eyes paused on Kawkab Khala's elegant black cashmere shawl embroidered with orange flowers, draped over the armchair in front of me. This was definitely all her fault. She was an agent of chaos, encouraging me to want more, to expect more, from everyone in my life.

My podcast had shifted also in the past few weeks. *Ana's Brown Girl Rambles* had started as a place for me to record my random thoughts. It had evolved into an audio diary, and judging from my rising listener count, there was active interest in the stories I was telling. The thought warmed me, and I opened the editing software on my laptop.

After I finished working on my latest podcast episode, I pressed Play on what I had so far of *Secret Family History*. Weeks ago Big J had asked what was stopping me from working on the story in my heart.

Now, thanks to my impulsive actions, I had all the time I needed to finish it.

My aunt's voice over the microphone was throaty. "What do you want to know, Hana?" she had asked, impatient. She had been fun to interview, if only because she so clearly thought the enterprise a complete waste of her time.

"That story you told me, Kawkab Khala. Do you remember? When we were outside in the backyard? I thought I had heard all the stories from back home, but that one was new to me."

My aunt snorted. "You North Americans. You hear a few stories from your parents and you think you know everything about people you have never met. When was the last time you visited India, Hana *jaan*?"

I smiled now, remembering how awkward I had felt. "Um . . . when I was twelve? We went for Hamid Mamu's wedding."

"Your Hamid Mamu is a fool. I told him not to marry that girl. Why are men such idiots, Hana? He is dancing attendance on her now. I could have told him he would repent in leisure. The girl had sharp eyes."

"About that story . . ."

Kawkab Khala sighed. "Have you ever interviewed anyone before?" she asked.

"Yes," I replied. "Just not family."

"Family is who you should have thought to interview first," my aunt answered.

"That's what I'm doing, Kawkab Khala, but you keep changing the subject."

"I don't understand how talking into this microphone is considered radio. Where is your antenna?"

On the sofa I laughed out loud and pressed Pause. It was still rough; it needed editing, but there was something there. I could feel it.

By now I was certain that news of my unceremonious firing had trickled throughout the station's small office. I wondered what Big J would think of me when he heard. I wondered if he would still want to help, or would he ignore me now?

There was one way to find out. Muttering a brief prayer, I sent the first five minutes of the recording to Big J with a quick note. Maybe he would like what I had done. He had expressed interest before in the stories I wanted to tell. Perhaps he could help me find another position too. I had nothing left to lose, really.

· · ·

I've been thinking lately about the lies we tell ourselves and the secrets that define us. I mentioned in the last episode that I recently came face to face with hate. I had been hoping things would improve, but instead they've gotten worse, in almost every way possible. Both personally and professionally, I have been targeted and attacked. Worse, the most important people in my life have been targeted as well, which has been painful to watch. We're trying to pick up the pieces now, trying to figure out what to do next and how to move forward.

Strangely, something good has come out of all this pain. I've realized that I have to be more honest about what I truly want. I also need to be brave enough to confront the things that have held me back—in some cases, myself.

What does this have to do with the lies we tell ourselves and the secrets we harbour? During the course of the past few weeks, I've realized that I am guilty of believing soothing lies, the lies that have allowed me to function in my world. I have turned away from things that niggled at my conscience, that went against my principles, and rationalized my behaviour as the price one pays to get ahead. When I finally confronted just a few of those lies, I ended up losing my job.

I don't have much of a safety net, so the consequences of confronting such hard truths are real, and terrifying. Still, I feel lighter for it, better about myself and stronger. I know now what I will and will not tolerate. I know where my line is, and what I am willing to lose to defend my heart.

While I am scared of what the future will bring, the uncertainty has been refreshing in a strange way. I know who I am in a way I never have before, and what I'm willing to sacrifice to stay true to myself. I guess that's not a bad lesson to learn at any age.

Chapter Thirty-Six

My phone was flashing with dozens of messages when my alarm, muffled under the sofa cushions, went off the next day. I swiped, and my eyes landed on a text from Yusuf.

> Nalla died last night. Janazah today after zuhr prayer at 1:30 pm. Spread the word.

Rapid footsteps on the stairs. "Hana!" Mom called, urgent. "Wake up, wake up!"

My fingers were numb. I put my phone face down on the seat cushion beside me.

Imam Abdul Bari's wife had been at Three Sisters just last week, looking weak but luminescent in her green dress, smiling at her husband's jokes. She couldn't be dead.

Mom stood in front of me in her cotton nightgown, face pale. "Nalla—" she started, but I shook my head.

She collapsed onto the couch beside me, breathing hard. "She was my age." Mom's voice was unsteady. "Even younger. *Inna Lillahi wa inna ilayhi raji'un,*" she recited. *Surely to Allah we belong, and to Him we return*, the Quranic verse Muslims utter when hearing of a death, as reflexive as an observant Catholic genuflecting. I echoed her words.

She stood up. "I'm going to the restaurant. They will need food, for after," she said.

She meant after *janazah*, the funeral prayer that's part of the Islamic ritual of burial. Muslims are encouraged to perform funeral services as soon as possible. Nalla had been sick for a long time; we had all known this day would come.

I dressed quickly and headed to the restaurant with her. Mom was right. They would need food to feed the people who came to pay their respects to the Imam at the reception, which would likely be held in the mosque gymnasium.

Mom, Fahim, and I worked quickly. Mom's hands flew as she chopped mint and coriander, mixed a marinade for curry, diced vegetables for the grill. I assembled the biryani, doling out a huge tray of half-cooked basmati rice, then layering the yogurt-and-spice marinated chicken, covering that with another layer of rice. I topped the dish with saffron, ghee, fresh coriander, and browned onions before carefully manoeuvring the covered tray into the restaurant's oven, where the rice and chicken would cook, casserole style. By midmorning the food was assembled.

We drove to the mosque, where the parking lot was already full. News of death spread quickly in the community as people texted and shared the information over social media. Everyone knew that if they wanted to attend the *janazah* prayers, previous plans would have to be rescheduled.

The main prayer hall overflowed with people, spilling into the hallway. Mom, Fahim, and I carried the trays of food past the crowd, moving swiftly downstairs to the cafeteria. I passed the tray to Sister Fatima, a friend of the Imam's. Her face was sombre and her lips trembled as she hugged me and Mom. "She helped so many people, Abdul Bari most of all. I don't know what he will do without her," Fatima said.

We walked back upstairs to the main hallway, where the Imam was greeting people. Dressed in a crisp white robe that reached his ankles, hair neatly brushed, he was smiling, but tears dripped steadily down his face, drenching his grey beard. He hugged Fahim, then clasped his hands together and inclined his head to me and Mom.

"Imam," I said, my eyes filling. "I will miss her so much."

Abdul Bari nodded, mouth trembling. "Her heart is at peace at last. She was in so much pain."

Aydin stepped forward from behind me and clasped the Imam in a long embrace. I hadn't noticed him standing there. The adhan, the call to prayer, began and the crowd moved into the hall. Aydin kept a firm hand on the older man's shoulder as they walked in together.

After zuhr, the crowd waited while the plain pine coffin was wheeled to the front, where the Imam stood. It was covered with an embroidered green velvet cloth, the only flash of adornment in the simple Islamic burial rites. Abdul Bari reached out a hand and gently placed it on Nalla's coffin. He rested it there, eyes closed, the tears streaming freely, while his congregation watched. All around me men and women cried openly, weeping into tissues.

"My mother chose Nalla to be my wife," Abdul Bari said, his voice reed-thin through the microphone. "We were strangers to each other, but Allah placed love in our hearts, and we nourished it for over twenty-eight years with affection, laughter, and respect. We were never blessed with children, our fondest wish, but our faith helped us. My dearest Nalla, my love, I will miss you every day I have left on this Earth. Wait for me at the bridge to the afterlife, so that we may enjoy one another's company again, dearest one. So that we may live with the children who went before you, the ones who are keeping you company now."

My nose stuffy from crying, I closed my eyes as the Imam began the *janazah*. As one, we raised our hands to our shoulders and the brief prayer began.

It was over too soon. There were too many people. It was hard to breathe. When the Imam had recited the last *Assalamu alaikum wa rahmatullah*, I edged my way out of the prayer hall and quickly walked through the seldom-used ornate glass front doors, hurrying down the main stairs, which faced a busy intersection. I collapsed on the bottom step, head in my hands.

Someone sank down next to me. I didn't need to look up to know it was Aydin. He must have spotted me leaving. "I couldn't stay inside either," he said.

"I can't imagine losing someone you love that much," I said, wiping my eyes. "Abdul Bari will never forget what that felt like, watching his wife die."

Aydin's hands were tangled in his lap. "I don't remember my mother's funeral. Dad says I was there, but I don't remember it at all. I must have wiped it from my mind. Maybe the Imam will forget too, after some time."

My eyes were fixed on the traffic in front of the mosque—cars speeding towards various destinations, pedestrians on sidewalks, everyone immersed in their own world, ignorant of the quiet, everyday heartbreak unravelling inside the mosque.

"I wonder if I will ever love someone the way Abdul Bari loved Nalla," I said. I wasn't sure if I was asking Aydin or myself.

He reached over and gently clasped my hand, his touch warm. His hand was large, and more callused than I would have expected. It felt right, holding his hand, and I saw it now: we fit together somehow. Despite the grief that lay behind us and the murky future ahead, we just fit.

THE HEARSE WAS OUTSIDE, AND Nalla's plain pine coffin was loaded into the back by the Imam and a few other men. Burial was traditionally done as soon as possible, preferably within twenty-four hours of a death.

I made my way to the mosque's kitchen, where Mom and some other women were putting away the food for the funeral reception that night. I picked up a tray of salad and placed it in the fridge.

"Aren't you heading back to Three Sisters?" I asked. "Lunch crowd."

Mom shook her head, wiping her forehead. "We closed for the funeral. I'm needed here."

I couldn't remember any other time Mom had shut the restaurant. Our family vacations had consisted of quick two-hour trips to the mall.

"Let's go to the cemetery. They have this covered."

Mom didn't want to, but I insisted. Nalla had been our friend.

There was no Muslim-owned cemetery in the city, so our mosque had bought a small piece of land in an existing Catholic cemetery, to the east of the city, where we buried our dead.

Muslim burial rites are simple. Coffins are plain pine, bodies wrapped in a cotton shroud after being given *ghusl*—ritual purification—by community volunteers. Graves are traditionally unmarked by anything more than a number. Some families have plots with simple engraved plaques bearing names and dates, but many graves don't even have that. The Muslims in our community who cared about being buried among their brethren tended to be those traditional enough to eschew the ornate symbols of death that adorned the Catholic part of the cemetery.

A fleet of cars was already there, and at least a hundred people milled around outside. The sky was overcast but the sun sat high, shining determinedly through the clouds. It was warm, and I could see the Imam wipe a light sheen of sweat from his forehead before he dabbed his eyes with the same handkerchief. He had removed the long robe he usually wore in front of the congregation, revealing a bright pink Hawaiian shirt, two flamingos in a heart-shaped embrace on the front. Nalla had told me once that he wore those shirts for her, because he knew she loved them, because they made her laugh. A secret message of hope for his wife. I turned away from the crowd as grief rose once more.

Mom gripped my shoulder before pulling me close. I allowed myself to be held for a moment, breathing in the faint smells of turmeric and garam masala that always seemed to cling to her, no matter how much she used her favourite Clinique perfume or kept her nicer clothes away from the restaurant. It was as if the spices had sunk into her skin. The fragrance of those spices had always been synonymous with *Mom* and *home*.

We faced the crowd now, edging closer to the coffin. Imam Abdul Bari had his hands up in *du'a* and I raised mine too, joining in the group prayer as he recited slowly in Arabic. I spotted Fahim behind the Imam, his usual grin replaced by a serious expression.

"Ameen," the congregation murmured as the *du'a* ended. The people at the front of the crowd gathered handfuls of dirt and one by one dropped them onto the coffin, which had already been lowered slightly into the grave.

When it was our turn, Mom moved forward, picked up a clump of dirt, and dropped it gently on top of the coffin. She lay a hand on the pine lid and closed her eyes. "*Khuda hafiz*, my friend," she said softly. I followed suit.

The crowd slowly returned to their cars, a wave of people receding from the shore, leaving behind a lone figure in a pink Hawaiian shirt, saying his final goodbye.

Chapter Thirty-Seven

Though I spent the next few days continuing to deal with media inquiries about the Golden Crescent attack, my heart was heavy. Nalla's death had put a damper on everything. At the same time, I felt a greater sense of urgency.

Constable Lukie and I were in almost daily contact, but thankfully the chatter online had stopped almost completely. The rest of my free time was spent working on *Secret Family History*. Big J had loved the small segment I sent him and wanted to hear the rest when I finished.

Between working on my podcast and the new show and my shifts at Three Sisters, I was busy, but my mind kept wandering back to Aydin. Things between us were so tangled up I didn't know how to begin to loosen the threads. Instead we avoided each other. I hadn't seen him on the street all week, though he had been on my mind constantly.

The work on Wholistic Grill had intensified in preparation for their launch. The day before, balloons were secured near the restaurant's entrance and placards announcing the festivities were placed strategically around Golden Crescent. If Rashid's excitement was any indication, Wholistic Grill could expect a full house. The rumours I had started online had been overshadowed by more recent events, and the community was eager for a reason to celebrate.

Kawkab Khala had no interest in attending the grand opening, and Mom and Fahim were busy at Three Sisters. Mom waved away my excuses. "You must take Rashid," she said. "He will not let us have any peace otherwise." She smiled at her nephew, who was bouncing with excitement—at the prospect of seeing Zulfa again more than anything else. I hadn't had the heart to tell him that his efforts in that direction were in vain, that her heart belonged to the perfectly named Zain. *Zainfa*—even their couple moniker was cute.

As Rashid and I approached Wholistic Grill, I realized there was something else I had forgotten about, namely Yusuf and his promise to protest the launch of Aydin's restaurant. Though the turnout was less than his promised five thousand, my friend had managed to round up a few dozen protestors on the sidewalk in front. Lily was in attendance, and my friends held handmade signs: SUPPORT LOCAL BUSINESS, NOT CORPORATE SELLOUTS! and THERE'S NOTHING HOLY ABOUT WHOLISTIC GRILL! As I watched, Lily leaned close to Yusuf, her hair brushing against his cheek. I guessed they had made up. I wondered if Yusuf had proposed yet. Probably not; he would have told me.

"Hana, we made a sign for you," Yusuf called at my approach. The placard in his hands read THREE SISTERS NEEDS YOUR HELP! SUPPORT LOCAL BUSINESS, NOT BULLY BUSINESS! Three stick figures in hijab stood arm in arm above the message. "We can make one for you too, Rashid!" he yelled when he caught sight of my cousin. Lily smacked Yusuf's arm, but my cousin only smiled and went inside the restaurant.

"I'm going to scope out the enemy first," I said, and followed Rashid.

Although we were early, a sizable crowd was already present, and I nodded at people I knew. The crowd skewed young and Muslim, but there was plenty of diversity. Three chefs in kitchen whites chopped and prepared meals amid the whir of blenders whipping up frozen concoctions. The smell of burgers and poutine made my mouth water. Zulfa was running around welcoming people, handing out goody bags to small children, calling for extra chairs, and directing overflow to the patio outside.

I realized I was looking for Aydin when my eyes snagged on his familiar form. I had something I needed to say to him, I realized.

Aydin was dressed for the occasion in a slim-cut black suit that emphasized his broad shoulders. His crisp white shirt set off his warm brown skin. He was in the middle of the crowd, making small talk with customers, joking around with kids and parents. He looked happy. Until he spotted me, and his expression turned to wary resignation.

"Assalamu alaikum," I said. *Peace be with you.* My voice was steady, not like the angry whip I had used to berate him when we fought.

He nodded. "Walaikum assalam," he replied. *And upon you be peace.* Tension marked every inch of his body, as if he were bracing for a punch.

"You look nice," I said, eyes perusing his suit once more. *He's falling for me,* my mind whispered. *He's destroying Three Sisters,* another voice reminded me. *I tried to put him out of business too,* the first voice countered. "Congratulations on the launch," I said instead.

Aydin's lips quirked. "It was a close thing for a while there."

A young child jostled me, and he suggested we move to his office. I followed him through the crowded space to a tiny room in the back set up with a desk, chair, and filing cabinet. Words bubbled up as he half-closed the door.

"I shouldn't have said that about your mother," I blurted. "If she were alive, I know she would be proud of the man you've become."

"You mean the coward who can't stand up to his father?" His lips twisted and he looked down. I saw how my words were haunting him, as his own haunted me. "Everything you said was true, Hana. I would have put your family out of business without another thought . . . if I hadn't gotten to know you first."

His words didn't make me feel vindicated, and I realized I wasn't there to continue our argument. I peered into his lowered face. "Pity party, table for one?" I said, and Aydin smiled wryly. "So you're a shitty disappointment. So you've made mistakes. At least you can acknowledge doing wrong. You stood there and took my abuse without flinching."

"I deserved it," he muttered.

"Yes, you did. Now do better," I countered.

His eyes searched mine. "I was afraid I had blown the only shot I had with you. I meant what I said before. Not that I didn't mean to fall for you, but that I already had."

Things were complicated between us, but I couldn't deny that his words sent a thrill through me. There was something drawing us together, something stubborn that refused to give way, despite everything pushing against it. I shook my head at the strangeness of it all. "Of all the halal joints in the world, you had to walk into mine."

Aydin didn't laugh. "You were right, Hana. I can't move across the country to lead my own life if my dad still stands behind me calling the shots." He took a deep breath. "I am sorry for the hurt I caused you. I respect you and your family very much, and from now on I would like for us to be cordial business allies."

I laughed at his formal phrasing. "A cordial business ally? Is that all I am?"

Aydin's eyes darkened. "I'll start wherever you want. Do you accept my apology?"

"That depends on the actions that accompany your words," I said, matching his formal diction. I was only half joking, but Aydin nodded as if he had anticipated my response.

"I have some savings and investments from my time at Shah Industries. I'm going to cash it all in and then beg the bank for a loan. I plan to return every cent my dad lent me, immediately. I want to be free and clear of his money and his interference."

I raised my eyebrows, impressed by the changes he was prepared to make. The fire in his eyes was inspiring. And also . . . okay, pretty hot.

"What happens after that?" I asked softly, daring him to say more.

"Then you tell me your favourite colour so I can send you flowers, your favourite place so I can take you there, your favourite book so I can read it just so we can argue about it. I know you want to work in radio, and I plan to cheer you on every step of the way. I might even listen to TSwift, if you insist."

I started laughing, but he wasn't done.

"You hold all the cards, Hana. What happens next is up to you."

"We barely know each other—" I started, but he shook his head.

"It doesn't feel that way to me. I feel like I've known you for much longer," he said.

I recognized the truth of his words. That strange familiarity had been at the root of our instant connection from the very start. And while I wasn't sure about our future, I could at least start by answering his questions.

"My favourite colour is leopard print," I said. "My favourite place is Three Sisters, my favourite book is *Persuasion* by Jane Austen, and you need to listen to *1989* to appreciate the genius of Taylor Swift. Also, I hope you don't have a problem with ambitious women, because I have big plans."

"Ambitious women are my favourite kind," he said. The smile that broke across his face reached from his lips to the crinkly corners of his eyes.

I finally let go of my fear and distrust and let myself fall too. I reached out my hand and gently cradled his face. He gripped my wrist tightly, the promise of more in his eyes, before he let go.

We were both smiling as we exited his office, having decided on nothing and everything.

OUTSIDE, THE PROTESTERS HAD GROWN slightly in number, and they cheered as I walked up to them.

"Here comes Hana, daughter of the hard-working owner of Three Sisters Biryani Poutine!" Yusuf roared through the megaphone. "Hana, please share your story with your supporters!"

I accepted the megaphone. "Go home," I said to the group. "Or better yet, go inside and support Wholistic Grill, because they have reason to celebrate. Three Sisters Biryani Poutine is happy to finally have some company providing quality halal meals to our neighbourhood, especially after the hatred unleashed on Golden Crescent last week. And then come back tomorrow and support my mother's restaurant. She's been running it on her own for fifteen years, and I think some of you have been taking her for granted."

I handed the megaphone back to a stunned Yusuf and walked away. Lily recovered first, falling into step beside me. "Yusuf was really looking forward to that protest. He wanted to do something for you."

"Half your protesters were holding takeout containers from Wholistic Grill," I said, and we smiled at each other.

"You're really okay with Wholistic Grill opening?" she asked.

I paused, thinking. "No."

"You want it gone?"

"No," I said immediately. Not anymore.

Lily grinned beside me. "I'm going to miss you when I'm in Timmins," she said. "Especially that fuzzy logic of yours."

"You're the science-and-facts girl. I'll stay with my feelings. Have you told Yusuf you're leaving?"

"There's a lot I need to catch you up on." Lily looked back at the protest, and I understood. She wanted to be where Yusuf was, and from the look on my best friend's face, he felt likewise.

I would always be the third musketeer in our trio, but that was okay. I was learning to find my own place.

Chapter Thirty-Eight

Things settled into an uneasy sort of rhythm for the rest of the week. Mom sent food to Abdul Bari every day, but I suspected the Imam didn't have much of an appetite. When I saw him walking down the street, he looked thin and grey, though he mustered a smile for me and asked how my radio career was coming along.

I hadn't spoken with Aydin. Things still felt raw and strange between us, but he had been clear that he was waiting for me to make the next move.

I could see the lineup at Wholistic Grill from our front window, while our own dining room remained empty. Mom had taken up working on the crossword in the newspaper while we waited for customers, and I continued to edit.

"What were you talking to Kawkab Khala about this morning?" I asked, fingers drumming on the counter. Their heads had been bent close together when I came downstairs.

"She offered me money. I turned her down," Mom said.

"I thought she wasn't rich anymore."

A faint smile crossed my mother's face. "That's because she keeps giving away money to any family member who asks. I told her to save it for herself. She can use it to visit again soon."

"Why didn't you take the money? Just until things get better . . ."

But Mom shook her head. "I won't borrow money I can't pay back," she said firmly.

"You can pay her back," I said. "In a few months, maybe a year."

Mom looked around the dining room. "No other woman in my family has ever started her own business. Everyone in India thought I was crazy, except Kawkab Khala. Her father was a *nawab* and she was always wealthy, but she was born a rebel. She appreciated that I wanted to swim against the current. You're like us both in that way, Hana." She smiled at me, and I was touched by her acknowledgement of my wayward instincts. "But I'm not sure I want to do this anymore," she added softly.

"What about Fahim? What about Fazeela and the cantaloupe?" I shook my head. "We have a lot of interest and sympathy going for us right now, after the attack on the street."

She only smiled at me and returned to her crossword.

I looked around the dining room. I could ask Kawkab Khala for the money myself, buy some new chairs, invest in proper tablecloths and new cutlery. A coat of paint, maybe some pretty decorations, better light fixtures . . .

"Carry with difficulty," Mom said out loud, interrupting my train of thought.

"What?" I said, distracted.

"Six letters," she said. "Carry with difficulty."

"Schlep," I said.

She filled in the word and continued working on the puzzle. Grey strands of hair escaped from the black cotton hijab she always wore when working and dangled over the newspaper. She tucked them back with blunt fingers, dry and cracked after a decade and a half spent chopping, stirring, cutting, nourishing.

I had grown up in the restaurant. A part of my heart would remain right there: crouching behind the chairs when Fazeela and I played hide-and-seek as children; watching my mother prep and cook while I did homework in elementary school; taking orders for the first time as a server and sharing the meagre tips. Who would my mother be if she weren't peering into the pots of boiling water that had kept her face clear and unlined, presiding over her kingdom like a powerful, stoic queen? Three Sisters was home.

I straightened. We would make it through, even if I had to schlep her through this trial myself.

Kawkab Khala joined us at lunchtime to remind me that the Business Owners Association meeting was scheduled for that night. As if I could forget. I still didn't know why she wanted to attend.

Rashid, who had come with her, perked up at that. "Will the *ullu* be there?" he asked.

I shrugged. "His name is Yusuf. Wait, why?"

"No reason," he replied.

I was instantly suspicious. "You're both up to something," I said.

My aunt and Rashid looked at each other. "A healthy amount of suspicion is the key to long life expectancy, Hana Apa, but in this case your fears are misplaced. I simply wish to make amends with the *ullu*," Rashid said.

"I hope you aren't planning on causing a scene," I grumbled.

Kawkab Khala smiled grimly at my words. "Not everything is about you, Hana *jaan*."

Hmph. I returned to editing *Secret Family History*.

I listened on my headphones to the introduction I had recorded. My voice sounded throaty. "India in the 1970s was still reeling from the effects of war with neighbouring Pakistan, still haunted by memories of Partition. In that world lived my aunt, Kawkab Fazeela Muzamilah Khan. She was the twenty-four-year-old daughter of the local *nawab*, a wealthy landowner. And it was high time she was married."

THE BUSINESS OWNERS ASSOCIATION MEETING was scheduled for nine p.m. Kawkab returned to Three Sisters with Afsana Aunty at her side. I raised an eyebrow but my aunt didn't offer an explanation for her uninvited guest.

The bigger surprise was Rashid. He had gone home at eight o'clock, ostensibly to fetch something, and when he returned with my aunt, he was completely transformed. Rashid was dressed in a long cream sherwani jacket decorated with seed pearls, a large cream-coloured turban on his head. Pointy-toed *khoosay* slippers embroidered with gold thread adorned his feet. He was dressed as a Mughal prince, and I shook my head in amusement.

We crossed the street to Brother Musa's grocery and made our way to the basement, where the meeting was being held.

The other shop owners mingled by the snacks beside the stairs, Yusuf among them. Catching sight of my cousin, he burst into laughter.

"All right, all right, I get it," Yusuf said after he had calmed down. "Can I show you to your chair, Your Majesty?"

Rashid nodded regally. "That's Supreme Rajah to you, peasant."

My aunt and Afsana found seats at the back while I made small talk with Sulaiman Uncle, who owned the halal butcher shop. Footsteps down the stairs, and then Aydin joined the meeting. A few of the other business owners nodded, but no one moved to speak to him except me. He was still an outsider.

"I'm surprised to see you here," I said, teasing. "I thought we had run you off after the last meeting."

"I heard the BOA is the place to be." He leaned close to whisper. "*Because of the drama.*" He straightened, casting a rueful eye across the room. "Actually, the drama has already happened. Machiavelli was right: my dad had his own plans all along. He was financing the restaurant for his own reasons. He wanted to bully the neighbourhood, buy up properties cheap so he could build condos and gentrify." He shook his head. "Everyone turned him down."

"They did?" I was surprised. Money was an attractive inducement, especially for Golden Crescent business owners. None of them were wealthy.

"Only one or two businesses were interested in selling. The rest were worried about what he would do to the neighbourhood, because they live here. My plans have upset him even more. He's used to getting his way in everything."

I wanted to give Aydin a hug but settled for a sympathetic smile. No need for more gossip to get back to my family before I could speak to them about us first. "That must have been a difficult conversation," I said.

"He's furious and has cut me off completely," Aydin said cheerfully. "But it's not all bad. I'm cautiously optimistic that Golden Crescent will provide a few perks." He raised an eyebrow at me, and I blushed. "I meant easy access to your mom's biryani," he intoned solemnly, and I laughed again.

Rashid and Yusuf looked up from where they were chatting, and Aydin nodded at them both. Rashid waved enthusiastically, and after a moment Yusuf nodded stiffly. Baby steps.

Brother Musa called the meeting to order as we took our seats at the front of the room. Mr. Lewis had just taken the floor, discussing the property damage caused by the attack, when we heard sharp thuds from above. Conversation ceased as everyone looked towards the stairs, though I had a pretty good idea who was about to crash the party.

And then Junaid Uncle stood before us, a malevolent warlock, upset because he hadn't been invited. Aydin's father stalked into the cramped meeting space. People parted as he moved forward until he stood in front of his son.

"Aydin has just informed me that he has thrown in his lot with the rest of you," Junaid Uncle said loudly. "But I will not stand aside and watch while he is swayed by a pretty smile." He glared at me.

Aydin stood up. "Dad, we discussed this. I'm buying you out—" he started, but Junaid Uncle ignored him and continued to address the room.

"I have been more than reasonable," he announced, his voice echoing from the concrete basement walls. "Sell your businesses to me by the end of the week, and you will be compensated fairly. If you do not, none of you will enjoy what comes next. Particularly the wounded birds among you." Junaid Uncle was looking directly at me.

Aydin and I looked at each other in confusion, unsure what to do with that information. Why was Junaid Uncle behaving like the villain in a Pakistani drama?

Aydin closed his eyes. "Dad . . ." he said, resigned. I had seen the same interaction play out before, at their first BOA meeting. It had ended with the father stalking out and the son following.

Except this time Kawkab Khala was there. From the back of the room, my aunt approached us. "Assalamu alaikum, Junaid," she said. I watched Junaid Uncle freeze.

My aunt's chin was raised high, so that she appeared to be looking down on us all. She contemplated Aydin's face, Junaid Uncle motionless beside him. "You look so much like your mother," she said slowly, enunciating every word so the entire room could hear. "I wonder how your father can stand to look at you. Today I brought someone here who might wonder the same," she added.

The blood drained from Junaid Uncle's face, and he followed my aunt's pointed glance, straight towards Afsana Aunty. A dawning realization crawled across my skin, making my blood burn hot. I looked from Aydin to Afsana. How had I not connected the dots before?

Junaid Uncle caught my flash of understanding. His posture stiffened further, as if he was wondering if he should stand his ground and fight or grab his son and run.

Not everything is about you, my aunt had warned me that afternoon, and I hadn't understood. I had never understood.

Affable mask on tight, Aydin answered my aunt. "Most people tell me I look like my dad, but thank you for seeing my mother in me," he said. I wanted to cry at that most Aydin of responses, at his instinctive need to calm everyone down after his father had rampaged into a room. He hadn't figured it out either.

Aydin couldn't remember his mother's funeral because there hadn't been one. She hadn't died when he was five years old. In fact, I had met her several times. We had shared chai and eaten her potato pakoras, the ones her son had loved, and I had watched her avoid questions about what she was doing in Toronto. Afsana Aunty was there to see her son, Aydin, who had absolutely no idea his mother was still alive.

Junaid Uncle's mouth opened and shut. Then, after one last glare at Kawkab Khala, he turned on his heel and bounded up the stairs. With an apologetic glance towards me, Aydin followed his father out of the BOA meeting, into the dark night.

It was Rashid who broke the silence. With great dignity he brushed cracker crumbs from the front of his sherwani. "Shall we continue? I have an update on the street festival. I have a strong suspicion this year's event will be the best one yet."

Everyone settled into their seats and Brother Musa called the meeting back to order.

Chapter Thirty-Nine

I hope you will forgive me for hijacking your meeting, Hana *jaan*. It was time to deal with my friend's unfinished business." Kawkab Khala was perched on the edge of my bed. We had walked home in brittle silence and I had followed her upstairs to demand an explanation.

I had so many questions for my khala, but mostly I was burning with fury at once again being left in the dark. "Why didn't you just tell Aydin the truth?" I asked tightly.

"I meant to warn Junaid only—that we were here, and ready to tell his son if he didn't do it first. I am not a monster, Hana. I only want justice for my friend."

"What justice is that?" I asked.

"I told you before that Afsana and I are close and that she married too young. Her parents were pleased with the match; Junaid Shah came from money, and Afsana was lucky to get him. After the nikah, they moved to a city I had never heard of—Vancouver."

My aunt was silent for a few minutes. Outside it had started to rain, a light sprinkling that tapped against my bedroom window. I took a seat on the wooden chair by my desk.

"She was happy at first," my aunt continued. "It is hard to lie in letters—too easy for teardrops to mark the page. It is easy to dissemble online, but paper doesn't lie. Shaky handwriting doesn't lie. He treated her well, she said. But she was lonely, and Junaid was busy growing his empire in Canada. When she became pregnant with Aydin, he let her return to her mother to have the baby. Two months of being coddled at home should have made her happy, but when I went to visit her, I knew something was wrong."

There was another silence, longer this time. My aunt dabbed her eyes with a handkerchief.

"What was wrong with your friend?" I asked, my voice gentle now.

"You would call it postpartum depression, but back then it was seen as a woman's weakness. All I knew was that she was not herself, not during the pregnancy or afterwards. She didn't want to hold the baby and she cried often. If it wasn't for her mother taking care of everything, I am sure she would have deteriorated quite badly. The neighbourhood women claimed it was normal, and as the weeks passed, she seemed to improve. I visited her once when she was nursing Aydin. She had the sweetest expression on her face; it told me how much she loved him. After two months, her family sent her and Aydin back to Vancouver.

"The letters came less frequently after that. I told myself she was settling in, that she had a child to fill her days. Perhaps five years after Aydin was born, Afsana's mother told me she was pregnant again. Not long after, Afsana called me long distance. She was crying so hard I couldn't understand her, and I grew frightened. The very next day I spoke with Junaid." Her voice warmed with anger. "He said his wife was simply upset because he had refused to send her home to have the second baby. A week, maybe two weeks later, I heard there had been an accident. She lost the child."

I tried to imagine Afsana Aunty, how desperate she must have felt, how hopeless in an unfamiliar country, isolated from family and with only her young son and a cold, absent husband for company.

"Junaid brought her back to India a few months later, and he was a changed man. It wasn't until much later that Afsana confided she had tried to kill herself. I suppose Junaid thought their son would be better off without his mother in his life. By then she was so broken, she actually believed that too." My aunt's words were sharp as glass. She was disgusted, and I was horrified.

"He gave his wife money and made her sign a piece of paper she barely understood. She showed it to me once. It was a legal document that awarded sole custody to him. Aydin was five years old at the time."

"He abandoned Afsana when she was at her most vulnerable, and took away her son?" I said.

My aunt's voice was venomous. "He excised her like an infected boil. He refused to allow contact between them, and today she is a stranger to her son. It took her years to recover. Afsana was lucky; she married again, to a kind widower, and she loves his daughters. But she has never forgotten. I made it my business to keep track of Junaid and Aydin. She was so afraid of returning, but I finally persuaded her when we learned that Aydin had made plans to move to Toronto. When I found out that he meant to open a restaurant in Golden Crescent, I knew it was a sign."

My aunt's words left me chilled. I knew she meant every syllable, but all I could think about was Aydin. How would he react to the news that his mother was still alive, that she had been banished from his life and that his father was responsible? Junaid Uncle was a hard man, but I knew Aydin loved his father. What would this do to their already strained relationship?

And how would he feel about the person who told him the truth? I knew I couldn't keep that secret from him. "Who else knows about this?" I asked. I couldn't think of anything else to say.

"Everyone does, back home. Why do you think Aydin has never visited India? His father didn't want the information to slip out through some busybody relative or neighbour."

Another thought occurred to me. "Is that the real reason you came back? It wasn't for my mother or the restaurant at all, was it."

She didn't answer for a long time. "We are so far away in India. You didn't even know my real name when I arrived. Tell me, Hana, how strong can blood ties remain when they stretch across an ocean?"

Chapter Forty

I didn't sleep well, and the next morning I dressed automatically, my attention scattered. I needed to find Aydin and tell him.

Hurrying, I pulled on a plain blue hijab and ran out of the house, rounding the corner towards the Golden Crescent strip at a dead run and nearly colliding with a man who stepped into my path. Junaid Uncle.

In the morning light, my neighbourhood's nemesis seemed older than he had the night before, as if he had lost some of the malevolent fire that gave him life. Before my aunt had taken a metaphorical sword to his knees, he had once again threatened everyone, including his son. Now that I knew what he had done to Aydin, I could barely look at him.

"Can I help you?" I asked stiffly.

His face wavered. "Your aunt told you," he said, almost to himself.

"Is it true?" I asked him. "Is Afsana Aunty really Aydin's mother?"

Junaid Uncle laughed, the sound hollow. "That is one version of the truth, yes. The version that will damn me—and destroy him."

I didn't need to ask who he meant. My temper snapped. "How could you do such thing to your only son!" I hadn't wanted it to be true, hadn't wanted to think even Junaid Uncle capable of such cruelty.

"I will not explain my actions to you," he said.

"Are you planning to explain them to your son?" I shot back.

"I did what I thought best for Aydin," Junaid Uncle said.

I realized he had somehow convinced himself he was in the right. For all those years he had believed his comforting lies. Now he wasn't prepared to deal with the fallout.

As if in confirmation of my thoughts, a calculating gleam appeared in his eyes. "A clever person might turn this situation to their advantage," he said.

"What are you saying?" I asked slowly.

"I've made no secret of my interest in Golden Crescent. I will pay double the market rate for your mother's restaurant—if you can guarantee your family's silence. I know from your antics online that you're not as innocent as you pretend, Hana. Let us come to an understanding."

A few weeks before, I had been the one trying to sabotage Aydin, by spreading rumours about his business online, by questioning his faith, by doing anything in my power to ensure that his dream of opening a restaurant was ruined. Like Junaid Uncle, I had convinced myself that I was in the right, and I felt sick all over again at my duplicity. But, unlike Aydin's father, I had learned from my mistaken actions. Junaid Uncle must have been truly desperate if he thought I would agree to lie to his son. It would be like making a deal with the devil.

Misunderstanding my hesitation, he pressed his advantage. "If Aydin stays, what will happen to your mother, your sick father, your pregnant sister?" he asked, his voice a menacing hiss. "They will end up on the street, and it will be all your fault, for choosing a man you barely know over your own blood. Talk to your aunt; convince her not to say anything to Aydin. I will tell him myself, in my own time. What is the point in resurrecting forgotten ghosts? Our secrets are none of your concern."

He stalked off, so confident of my answer that he didn't bother to wait for it.

FAZEELA HAD SAID THAT STAYING quiet about our difficulties was what had led to the problems in our family, and she was right. After my confrontation with Junaid Uncle, I returned home and went straight to my sister's bedroom. She was lying in bed, watching YouTube videos on her laptop.

"I need help," I said.

She shut the computer. "Finally. Your eyebrows have been driving me crazy."

I blinked. "I mean I need some advice."

Fazeela motioned for me to pass her a plastic basket from under her bed, full of brushes and lotions and lipsticks.

"When did you learn how to apply makeup?" I asked, momentarily distracted. My sister had never cared about that stuff before.

"Since I've been stuck here with nothing to do but watch online tutorials." Fazeela shrugged at my surprised expression. "I have other interests besides soccer and cooking Indian food."

"No, you don't," I said, nudging her gently.

Fazeela shifted over, making room for me beside her on the twin bed. She grunted slightly as she scooted. "I feel like I'm carrying a bowling ball," she groused.

I kept still while Fazeela carefully plucked my eyebrows, then applied primer to my eyelids and face, her fingers quick and gentle. The motions were so soothing I relaxed under her touch.

"What did you want to talk to me about?" she asked, reminding me why I was there. It had been so long since we had simply hung out together.

I considered my words. I didn't want to get into specific details about the relationship between Afsana and Aydin; he deserved to know about his mother before anyone else did. "If you knew something that would help Three Sisters but hurt someone else, would you act on that knowledge?" I asked.

Fazeela reached for a small beauty blender and started to dab concealer under my eyes, around my nose, and along my jawline, blending it with the sponge. "I'm not thrilled about Wholistic Grill either, Hanaan, but there's no reason to put out a hit on Aydin."

"I'm serious."

She applied a light layer of foundation, smoothing the liquid over my blemishes with a deft hand, before picking up a container of blush, intent on her work. "Fahim and I are thinking of moving to Saskatoon after the baby comes." She passed a fluffy brush over my cheeks as I stared at her, astonished.

"What happened to no more secrets?" I asked.

She smiled at me. "It's not a secret—I just told you. Mom and Baba moved continents when they were our age. We can move a few provinces. His mother said she would help with the baby and we're thinking of opening a restaurant of our own. Maybe a restaurant like Wholistic Grill." She reached for a peachy golden pressed powder and dabbed it onto my cheekbones, nose, chin, and forehead as I processed her words.

"Everything ends, and maybe this is the right time for Three Sisters to close," my sister said. "Mom is getting tired; she could use a break.

Things aren't so dire. We can always sell the store or liquidate our assets and try something new."

Fazee was right, I realized. We did have options, beyond what Junaid Uncle had so callously offered. But that left me with an even greater dilemma. "I'm worried about Aydin," I said, almost to myself.

Fazee grinned up at me, pulling back to look at my face. "We're talking about some guy you met just a few weeks ago, someone we're not supposed to like. Or is that the problem? Do you liiiiike him?" She tickled my ribs as she elongated the word.

I flushed and swatted away her hands.

Fazeela was laughing now. She motioned for me to close my eyes so she could apply eyeshadow. "From what I hear, you're always talking about Aydin and Wholistic Grill. Fahim would be happy to send a rishta for you."

"Don't you dare," I said, and my sister laughed again. She brushed something over my brows and then motioned me to half-close my eyes while she applied mascara.

My smiling, easygoing brother-in-law and my serious, intense sister. He was the ying to her yang. I was so glad they had found each other. "How did you know Fahim was the right person for you?" I asked, curious. "Getting married is the biggest decision people can make."

My eyes rested on Fazeela's swollen belly. She was almost six months pregnant now, her cantaloupe more like a small watermelon. She rested a bottle of finishing spray on her stomach. The sight was so adorable I wanted to take a picture.

She snapped her fingers at me. "My eyes are up here," she said. "Deciding to marry Fahim was easy. He's kind and smart and we love and support each other. It wasn't a hard decision at all. No, the biggest decision I ever made was to quit playing soccer after the hijab ban went into effect. I could have made pro, but there was no way I was going to take off my scarf. So I left. I miss it every day."

"You could have kept playing house league or pickup," I said. The FIFA headgear ban had eventually been lifted, but too late for my sister to realize her dreams of turning pro.

Fazeela glared at me, her movements jerky, and I realized it was still a painful subject, so painful she rarely talked about it. "If soccer couldn't accept all of me, I wouldn't let it have any of me." Her shoulders drooped. "I was punishing myself too, really, because I loved it so much. Walking away from soccer changed me. I got married and started working at the restaurant with Fahim. And when this bowling ball came along, I couldn't stop thinking about the kind of world my daughter would be born into."

"You could be having a boy."

"It's a girl. Trust me."

We were both silent, and my eyes travelled back to her stomach, where a fragile new life had sprouted only a few months ago. In another few months' time, a tiny person would join our family. I was still wrapping my head around that. No wonder my sister was wondering who she was and who she wanted to be after the new addition arrived. Aydin had been right; he wasn't the cause of our family's identity crisis. But he hadn't helped, either.

"Do you regret not taking off the hijab and continuing to play soccer?" Fazeela and I had never really talked about this. She had never wanted to.

"Yes," she said simply. "And I hate them for putting me in that position. I hate that I was a pawn in some stupid political game. I just wanted to play."

Fazeela placed a small mirror in my hand. A more polished version of me stared back. I admired her handiwork: my eyes seemed larger, the smoky effect dramatic above nude lips. She had somehow unearthed my cheekbones, highlighting them with a subtle glowing blush.

She gathered her tools, putting them neatly back in the bin. "The reign of Three Sisters is coming to an end, and it's time to think about what you want to do next. It's okay to be selfish sometimes, Hanaan." Fazeela grinned at me. "And it would be really awesome to have a filthy rich brother-in-law willing to invest in an exciting new restaurant in western Canada."

Feeling lighter than I had since I learned Afsana's secret, I left for my shift at the restaurant. I texted Aydin on my way, asking if he was busy and if we could meet that night. I needed some time to figure out how I would tell him about his mother, how best to reveal a secret that had been concealed from him for decades. I knew that, no matter how carefully I told him, the knowledge would upend his entire world.

Except Aydin didn't respond to my text, not in the next hour and not that night. Instead, I received word from an unexpected quarter.

> Soufi's, tomorrow 9 am. Heard what happened with Marisa.
> Let's talk about next steps. Bring your podcast.

Big J was ready to talk.

Chapter Forty-One

Soufi's was a tiny, quirky, family-run Syrian café located near the radio station. I was so nervous about meeting Big J that I was fifteen minutes early.

He must have heard all about the unceremonious way I had left Radio Toronto. What if he had written me off as flaky and unreliable? But then why would he want to meet? Maybe he wanted to remind me that walking away in a huff doesn't help one's career path, especially considering that I was an intern with no money or useful contacts.

I hadn't yet told my parents I had quit my internship; I was afraid of disappointing them, especially Baba. Kawkab Khala, on the other hand, would probably wonder why it had taken me so long to grow a backbone. Then again, she was the rich daughter of a *nawab*. Access to ready money has a way of smoothing the path of dissidence.

Soufi's was mostly empty when I arrived. I claimed a table at the front, near the window, after ordering an orange blossom latte and knafeh, white cheese topped with phyllo pastry soaked in a sweet rose-flavoured syrup.

I spotted Big J through the window as he walked towards the café. He wasn't alone. Thomas was walking beside him, hands stuffed deep into jacket pockets, stride loping. My former fellow intern caught my eye through the window, then looked away.

THEY SHARED EARBUDS, LISTENING TO the podcast I had finished editing late the night before. A quick smile slipped across Big J's face a few times, and his thick eyelashes fluttered in amusement as he listened to my aunt berate me. He was still working on his beard, which was in the awkward, wispy phase. I wondered if he used conditioner and beard oil.

My eyes moved to Thomas. Big J hadn't explained why he was there, only throwing out a casual "You don't mind, right?" before striding to the counter to order for them both. Thomas had made polite Brown-boy conversation, asking about the restaurant and my parents, until Big J returned with two steaming cups of coffee with generous dollops of cream.

I didn't want to stare while they listened, so I went to the bathroom to splash cold water on my face. When I returned, Thomas and Big J had removed their earbuds. One smiled at me; the other did not.

"You made this episode yourself?" Thomas asked. Rude.

"You have a unique style. Impressive work," Big J said.

"This is the sort of stuff I want to work on—remarkable, nuanced stories and diverse experiences. Every time I tried to suggest something like this, I was never supported." I glanced at Thomas. Was he spying for Marisa? I shifted, uncomfortable, and addressed Big J. "I could use some help trying to get my work aired elsewhere."

Big J leaned back, hands running through the whiskers on his face.

"Marisa went ahead with your former show. The first episode, about radicalization in the Muslim community, ran a few days ago."

I tensed, glancing at Thomas. Had he come here to gloat? "Congratulations. How was it?" I asked flatly.

"Marisa and Nathan had a lot of . . . input. The episode wasn't exactly what I had envisioned," Thomas said, fiddling with his phone. "After the episode aired, we got a lot of coverage and online comments. Radio Toronto doesn't usually get that kind of attention. One of the local TV stations even invited us on their evening program, to talk more about Islamization."

"A topic you know so much about," I said.

"I thought you were crazy when you quit, Hana," Thomas said, ignoring my snipe. He couldn't meet my gaze. "I thought we were starting a conversation, that we would make a difference. Marisa told me the show received so much attention they've approved another five episodes." He finally looked at me, but there was no smirking exultation on his face. Instead, I recognized deep remorse. "They didn't have to read the emails, tweets, and posts from listeners. The things people said were . . . I've never had to . . ." He trailed off, then swallowed. "I told them they had to make some changes, and they refused. I quit yesterday. You were right, Hana. It did more harm than good."

I was surprised. I would have guessed that Thomas would step on whoever he needed to, do anything required to get ahead. Perhaps our many conversations had made an impact on him after all. Still, he needed to understand that his privilege was different from mine, that his experiences didn't give him a free pass from acknowledging that he had hurt me—and others he might never meet. "We had a real chance to change Marisa's mind, to bring a new perspective to Radio

Toronto," I said slowly. "Instead of backing me up, you chose to stab me in the back and push me out."

He dropped his gaze. "I'm sorry, Hana. I was wrong. I made a mistake."

Choice. My mother was big on choice. I could choose to carry a grudge; Thomas did deserve my anger. Or I could choose to give him another chance. I nodded once, acknowledging his words.

Minority Alliance (shakily) reactivated. Though I wouldn't let him off the hook until he had demonstrated more than a superficial wish to change his behaviour.

"Your podcast is great, but you need a sound engineer, and maybe a co-host," Big J suggested gently. "Maybe you and Thomas were meant to work together after all."

"I'll think about it," I said. After making Thomas stew for a bit first.

I ordered another latte while they ran through my podcast again.

Chapter Forty-Two

The decision to work with Thomas on *Secret Family History* was easy in the end. With his help we would have our pilot episode ready by the end of the week, and Big J promised to work his contacts for us.

When I returned to the restaurant that evening, Mom was at the counter while a few customers finished their meals. She looked more tired than normal. She had been working constantly for weeks, her only day off Nalla's funeral. I told her to leave a little early.

"It will be good to have dinner with your baba," she agreed, giving me a hug. "We have barely spoken these past few days." She had been doing that a lot, ever since the attack—making sure she hugged me and Fazee, noticing how much time she was spending away from the family. Almost as if something had tipped within, a shift in her personal accounting.

The bell on the door jingled as Mom gathered her things, and Imam Abdul Bari stepped inside. "Assalamu alaikum, Sister Hana, Sister Ghufran," the Imam greeted us as he reached the counter, his voice soft. Grief had stolen his usual strong tenor.

I reached behind the counter for the Imam's order: butter chicken, basmati rice, and a special serving of his favourite dessert, carrot halwa, which Mom had made for him. I waved away his money and handed him the bag.

Rashid emerged from the kitchen, where he had been putting away supplies, and the Imam lingered to chat. The house must have felt so lonely without his Nalla.

"Everyone is looking forward to the festival in a few days. I hope you are not worried about this latest development," Abdul Bari said.

My cousin and I exchanged swift glances. I asked the Imam to explain, and he pulled out his phone. A simple flyer, plain white with a stark black border, was displayed in his browser: "PROTEST SHARIAH LAW IN TORONTO! HALAL FOOD FEST = CREEPING SHARIAH LAW! JOIN THE CONCERNED CITIZENS COALITION FOR AN ANTI-HALAL PROTEST. FREE CANADIAN BACON, HAM, AND PIGS IN A BLANKET!" There was a graphic of a man with a long beard dressed in a white robe and brandishing a wicked-looking scimitar. He was pointing a finger, Uncle Sam–style, at the reader. The date and time were listed below. Unsurprisingly, the protest was scheduled for the same date, time, and location as our street festival.

I took a deep breath, trying to stay calm. It didn't work. "It's not a halal food festival!" I burst out.

"Maybe we should cancel," Rashid said. I was sure he was remembering the video he had uploaded so gleefully, and the graffiti and vandalism that had resulted.

What if we held the street festival and things got out of hand? Golden Crescent had been through enough.

"We will not cancel." Mom stood behind us, eyes flashing, her exhaustion gone. "We live here. Our friends live here. I will not be threatened by strangers." She turned to me. "I will talk to Brother Musa. Put it to the rest of the businesses if you want, but Three Sisters will participate, even if we are the only stall on the entire street."

Mom walked the Imam out. They were discussing who they would talk to in the neighbourhood to encourage a better turnout, and how to drum up more community support. I quickly texted Aydin to let him know what had happened. Surely he would respond to the message, even though he had ignored the other three I had sent. I was starting to worry about him.

Rashid reached for his jacket and wallet. "I will go to the police station right now and inform Constable Lukie about the planned protest." He paused. "Will you be okay to return home on your own tonight after closing?"

I waved him off, trying not to think about the dark walk back and the hateful flyer. This was my home. I was safe. Besides, one shriek and five people would come running.

The last customer left after ten o'clock. I wiped down the counters, ran the dishwasher, and stacked cutlery, plates, and other supplies before turning off the lights. It was after eleven when I turned on the security alarm and flipped the deadbolt.

I checked my phone. Still nothing from Aydin, but there was a message from Lily.

Where are you?

Walking home, I typed back.

Meet you on the corner.

Lily was waiting for me at the edge of Golden Crescent, just before the street emptied into our residential neighbourhood. She wore a white hoodie over tights, her hair tightly wound in a braid. Her face was pale under the street lamp, and I hugged her, happy she had thought to text me. I was relieved to have some company in the dark quiet of the neighbourhood, and I was eager to update her about Aydin and the restaurant and to ask for some advice.

I opened my mouth to speak, but hesitated. Lily had drawn her arms tightly around herself and ducked her head into the warmth of her sweatshirt hood. She wasn't there to catch up or hear my latest gossip, I realized. Lily had come to tell me something, and she was working up her nerve. Silence stretched taut between us, an elastic band ready to snap.

"Yusuf and I . . ." Lily started, before trailing off and trying again. "He's coming with me to Timmins. He wants to get involved in First Nations advocacy, to see if he can set up a Muslim–First Nations cooperative."

I smiled at her in the darkness. Some good news, finally. "Did you like the ring?" I asked.

Lily nodded, and I knew there was more.

"We eloped last week," she said softly. "Yusuf and I are married."

Chapter Forty-Three

Over breakfast the next morning, Rashid filled me in on his conversation with Constable Lukie, but I wasn't paying attention. My mind was stuck on a single thought: *Married. Yusuf and Lily are MARRIED! And they didn't tell me!*

I had spoken to Yusuf recently and he hadn't said a word. Lily and I had talked during the protest at Aydin's launch, and she hadn't hinted that they were even back together, let alone joined by a more permanent bond. My two best friends had taken that huge step without telling me, the keeper of their confidences.

On top of the other secrets everyone had kept from me, it felt like a betrayal. Things were changing all around me: Fazeela and Fahim's plans to move halfway across the country for a fresh start; the idea that my mother might close the restaurant; my self-imposed ouster from Radio Toronto; and now my two best friends leaving me behind. Rashid would eventually return to India, and Kawkab Khala's departure would come even sooner than that. All I would be left with was a rapidly changing Golden Crescent, my jumbled feelings for Aydin, and my life in the middle of a massive upheaval, whether I welcomed the change or not.

I remembered Fazeela's advice from a few nights before, while her careful hands smoothed and shaped my face. *It's time to think about what you want to do next. It's okay to be selfish.* I had filled my heart and hands with everyone else's burdens, had accepted their worries as if they had been my own, assuming they were all doing the same for me—but they weren't. The thought made me feel lonely, and my eyes filled with tears.

Rashid stopped talking instantly, stricken at my reaction. "I didn't mean to worry you. I know it has been difficult lately, but things will work out for the better. You will see."

I sniffed, wiping my eyes. "Don't you mean work out for the best?"

Rashid looked puzzled. "Best is not for this world, Hana Apa. Better is all we can hope for in this life."

He was right. No matter what happened next—with Aydin, with Three Sisters, with my family and my career in broadcasting—I could only keep working and hope for better. In the case of Aydin, I could also confront his silence on his own turf.

THE CHEF AND MANAGER OF Wholistic Grill, Gary, was taking orders at the cash when I entered the busy restaurant. I asked if Aydin was around and free to talk.

A frown crossed Gary's face. "He had to rush back to Vancouver."

Aydin had left? "Did he say why?" I asked.

Gary shrugged. "His dad had some sort of emergency. Aydin told me I was in charge and that he'd be back." He smiled at the next person in line.

I felt more confused than ever. I was glad Aydin was okay, but why wasn't he replying to the—I checked my phone—half-dozen messages I had sent over two days? Was I being ghosted?

BROTHER MUSA CALLED AN EMERGENCY meeting of the BOA after hearing of the latest threat to Golden Crescent. This time my mother—a popular, though mostly absent, member—was in attendance. Everyone was curious to hear what she had to say, and they weren't disappointed. She had even prepared a handwritten speech.

"We have lived here and raised our families in this neighbourhood for decades," she said, clutching her lined paper, voice steady. "I have known most of you for over fifteen years, and though we come from different parts of the world, we know what hatred can do. Many of us have witnessed first-hand the effects of anger, violence, and bloodshed back home. We cannot allow that same hatred here on our street. We must push back against those who want us to feel afraid in our own homes. We are a part of this neighbourhood, this city, this country, just as much as anybody else. It is time to make our presence known."

By the end of the meeting, a dozen businesses had confirmed their participation in the street festival. A few held back, particularly the newer ones, but the response was better than I had dared hope.

I hugged her afterwards. "You're amazing," I said.

Mom shrugged. "Might as well end our time here with a big splash."

My heart sank. I knew what she was hinting at, and wondered what new secrets were about to be revealed.

I sent Aydin another text, filling him in on the challenge ahead. I wasn't sure if he would receive or respond, but I wanted him to know anyway.

I MESSAGED STANLEYP—I missed him and wanted to hear his thoughts.

AnaBGR

How do you know if someone is ghosting you?

StanleyP

Uh-oh. Did Mr. Unexpected Source mysteriously vanish? Or perhaps . . . HE NEVER REALLY EXISTED AT ALL!

AnaBGR

I'm so glad we're friends.

StanleyP

You're lucky to have me. Now back to your imaginary boy toy . . .

AnaBGR

He's not my boy toy, or my boyfriend, or anything like that.

StanleyP

This sounds more and more like a stalker/stalkee situation. Are you positive he didn't go into witness protection?

AnaBGR

I'm logging off.

StanleyP

Wait, I'll be serious. You're being ghosted if he drops off the planet without a word and doesn't respond to texts or phone calls, no matter how dire. If some guy did this to you, I need his name. He's got a strongly worded email heading his way. Also some malware for good measure. Mess with a bot's best friend, you get the virus.

Thanks, Mr. P. I like you too.

StanleyP
Stop it, you're making the bot blush.

AnaBGR
You're in a good mood.

StanleyP
The world is full of unicorns and rainbows. Have you heard of a writer named Jane Austen?

AnaBGR
Tell me you're joking.

StanleyP
Don't be embarrassed if you haven't. My girl is well-read.

AnaBGR
Maybe he's not ghosting me. Maybe he's dead.

StanleyP
That's my positive Anony-Ana, always looking on the bright side. Back to Persuasion. This Captain Wentworth needs to get over himself.

StanleyP logged off before I could reply. I stared at the screen, puzzling over our conversation. *Persuasion*?

Chapter Forty-Four

The next morning the kitchen was empty except for my cousin, who was sipping his morning chai and scrolling gleefully through his phone. "The online trolls are still threatening to show up and cause trouble, but now they will have company."

Rashid showed me his phone, the browser open to the Facebook page he had set up. Someone had called for a counter-protest against the anti-halal protestors.

"There's going to be a 'No Halal Food' protest and a 'Support Halal Food' protest, all at a festival that isn't about halal food at all?" I asked skeptically.

Rashid smiled widely. "Now you are getting it! In Hyderabad there is an enormous annual festival called Numaish. My family attends every year. It attracts millions of people, and everyone comes out— the aunty and uncle-jis, the nanas and nanis, the hoodlums, pick-pockets, and con artists, young married couples, old married couples, teenagers pretending not to be couples, misbehaving children—all are welcome. The same thing will happen at our festival. Everyone will argue with each other and then they will become hungry and buy our tasty food. It will all work out. Believe me."

I must still have looked dubious, because my cousin patted me on the arm. "It will be fine. And if it is not, it will soon all be over. What was it that famous man said? 'What's past is prologue'?"

"Shakespeare."

Rashid frowned. "I thought it was Shah Rukh Khan."

"Maybe SRK said it better, but not first. What else is left to do before the festival?"

Rashid shrugged. "Continue to advertise. And, of course, pray."

I THOUGHT OF NALLA WHEN I entered the mosque. I wondered if the Imam had resumed his duties or if he was still in mourning.

I could pray just as easily at home, but somehow sitting inside the Toronto Muslim Assembly's hall made me feel closer to God, or at least to the God I remembered from my childhood—a warm, fuzzy being who would grant me a new pair of running shoes or an extension on my essay if only I prayed hard enough. As an adult, my prayers had become more complicated, my wishes more vague, but I had never stopped asking for help.

The women's section was empty except for an older woman: Afsana Aunty. Aydin's mother sat cross-legged on the beige and olive striped carpet, head bent low. She held *tasbih* prayer beads in her hands and was worrying them quickly, eyes tightly closed. I nearly turned around and left at the sight of her, but I had come there seeking peace and a chance to think. I couldn't deny Afsana Aunty the same thing.

I prayed zuhr quickly, then two extra *nafil* prayers. I sat down cross-legged on the floor a few spaces over from Afsana and raised my hands in *du'a*. I prayed for my parents, for Fazee and Fahim and the bowling ball, for Three Sisters and Kawkab Khala and Rashid, and finally for Aydin and his mother.

When I opened my eyes, Afsana Aunty was observing me, and I returned her perusal. Aydin looked so much like her; he had her clear brown eyes and full mouth. Kawkab Khala had been right. I too wondered how Junaid Uncle could look at his son and not think of Afsana, and of the trauma he had unleashed upon his family.

"Assalamu alaikum, Aunty. I hope you've been well," I said, and she smiled shyly. She looked more at peace than any other time we had met. I felt awkward; I knew this woman's intimate secrets, yet we were strangers. I felt as if I should acknowledge that somehow, or apologize for knowing information I wished I wasn't privy to.

I opened my mouth to say something, but she reached out and took my hand, pressing it tightly. "Your khala is my good friend," she said in her heavily accented English. "I am happy my—Aydin has you as his friend too." She said her son's name slowly, enunciating every syllable; it was clearly a word she didn't say out loud very often.

I remembered how Aydin had said *mom* in the same tentative way when we first met. I had wondered then how a single word could hold so much loss. He deserved to know the truth. I had to get through to him somehow.

BIG J TEXTED ME ON my way back to Three Sisters.

> I know where we can play Secret Family History. Tune in to The Wrap-Up tomorrow.

I texted back immediately.

HanaK

Marisa will fire you for this. You're not supposed to go off script.

Big J

Just got a job with one of the big players. She can consider this my two weeks' notice.

I was touched by Big J's generosity. Having the first episode of *Secret Family History* air on *The Wrap-Up* would mean a huge audience, more than I had dreamt of for my first solo venture.

HanaK

Thank you. For this and everything else.

Big J

Make sure your whole family listens. It's going to be great. Keep chasing the story in your heart, Hana, and you'll go far.

Chapter Forty-Five

"Baba, I have a surprise for you," I announced the next afternoon. I was vibrating with excitement, and Fazeela, seated on the sofa, looked up from her book.

My father had been having one of his okay days. He had had some trouble getting up that morning, but the colour was back on his face after lunch.

"What's going on?" Fazeela asked, standing up. Her belly hung low, and she put a hand to her back, rubbing.

I leaned across and switched on the radio, turning up the volume. "My work will be featured on *The Wrap-Up* today!" I announced.

Baba smiled widely and clapped. "Alhamdulillah! Wonderful news, *beta*. Fazee, you must inform your mother, Fahim, and Rashid. Tell them to listen. How can we record your show? Where is Kawkab Apa? She will not want to miss this!"

My sister texted Fahim while I called my aunt to come downstairs and join our impromptu listening party. Kawkab Khala settled into the armchair. This was her story too.

Big J's voice, deeper and richer through the microphone than it was in person, came on the air. "Welcome to *The Wrap-Up*," he said. "I have something extra special for all you listeners today. I'm going to devote the entirety of today's episode to a new show, produced by one of the most talented interns I've ever met, Hana Khan. Even though Hana has left the station for bigger and better things, I want to share the first episode of her new series. It's called *Secret Family History* and it's about different families that have lived and loved all around the world, and the secrets they keep from each other—sometimes for decades. *Secret Family History*, a new series from Hana Khan, coming up right after the break."

"It's about Kawkab Khala and the Billi story," I explained.

I adjusted the volume before leaning against a wall in the corner of the room. I wanted a good view of everyone as they listened. That was what had been missing from *Ana's Brown Girl Rambles*, I realized. As freeing as it had been to stay anonymous, I had given up something to preserve my privacy. One year ago I had been unsure about my abilities, still learning my craft and finding my voice, and I had needed that protective shell.

I didn't need it anymore. Now I wanted to be recognized for my work. I was ready to move out from the shadows, to let the harsh light of other people's opinions strike me as it would. Whatever they thought, or didn't think, I would deal with it, and keep creating and improving. I knew that now.

I could tell from the studied quiet in the living room that I had my family's undivided attention. I hoped my mom, Rashid, and Fahim were listening at Three Sisters too.

I made a quick *du'a* and my show began.

• • •

Secret Family History, created by Hana Khan. Episode One: The Bride in the Tree.

Welcome to Secret Family History, the storytelling podcast about the secrets that families keep from one another. I'm your host, Hana Khan, and for our inaugural episode I'm going to share a secret I recently learned about my own family. Here is my Aunt Kawkab, who will narrate the rest of this show:

[Kawkab] It was 1972. We lived in Hyderabad, India. My father was a nawab, a very rich man, from a long line of titled property owners. I was his only child and he let me get away with pretty much anything I wanted, so long as I left him alone. Ammi was busy with her charity projects, and she too let me do as I liked. I grew up riding horses, going to the British clubs, playing poker with my friends, and taking lessons in horseback riding, classical dance, and shooting. Every proper young lady should know how to handle a firearm.

Everything changed once I turned twenty-four. Until then I had no idea what I wanted to do in the future; I was too busy having fun in the present. One day my father asked to speak to me.

"Kawkab Fazeela Muzamilah Khan," my father said, addressing me by my full name, "it is time for you to marry. You will marry the boy I have chosen for you. He is rich and comes from a good family. Your marriage will take place after Eid. No need to be shy, daughter. I know this is what you want." Eid was eight weeks away. In hindsight, I suppose I shouldn't have laughed out loud at his words. He grew quite red in the face. When I refused outright, he called in the heavy artillery: my mother.

She quickly advised me that my single status, at the ancient age of twenty-four, was a sign of her progressive thinking, something she had even boasted about to her friends. But to have her only daughter remain single beyond that age was inconceivable. "Hameed is a good boy, from a good family," my mother informed me. "This marriage has been arranged for a long time. Hameed is about to leave for Oxford, and his family wants the nikah to take place before he goes to that rain-soaked land and, God forbid, falls in love with a white woman."

Hameed was the son of one of my father's friends. We had never exchanged more than five words altogether. And now I was supposed to report to my wedding as if I were going to Dr. Aziz for an immunization shot? I would sooner eat a bottle of turmeric.

My mother was upset by my proclamation that I would remain single, and I learned that the other aunties had been giving her a hard time. Ammi was a strong woman, but deep down she was also a traditionalist. She understood and accepted the world she lived in. Her rebellions were small in scope, while mine contained multitudes. She wanted to see me settled, but I was unsettled by nature. She thought I would come around eventually, so she began to plan my wedding without me. Of course a nikah is not valid without the bride's consent, but my parents were certain I would change my mind, once I realized how much it would mean to them both.

I had thought I had the perfect life, yet in that moment I felt as if I didn't know my parents. As if I had woken from a pleasant dream to find I lived in a nightmare. It wasn't until the engagement ceremony that I realized they considered me their property.

The wedding date was fixed and invitations soon dispatched. Ammi looked through her jewellery collection and went shopping for my jahaz, my trousseau. I stayed at home and refused to eat. I stopped playing cards and going riding, and the rifle-range coach was so concerned he came to the house to assure himself that I was still alive.

Yet no one in the family seemed to care. They thought I was playing the part of the shy, reluctant bride. As you know, Hana, I have never been shy in my life. Instead, I was plotting.

Over a thousand people had been invited to witness my nikah ceremony. We had many guests staying from out of town, including at least a dozen of my giggling girl cousins. I could hear them downstairs, singing wedding songs about shy brides and confident grooms, manipulative mothers-in-law and clever daughters-in-law. I had been left by myself to prepare for the wedding night and make the necessary prayers before the ceremony. The du'as that a bride makes on her wedding day are said to be particularly potent. But so are the prayers of the oppressed, and I was planning my escape.

I was dressed in a heavy red lengha decorated with delicate gold embroidery. The pearl and diamond maang tikka swung against my forehead as I manoeuvred out of the bedroom window. Thankfully I had decided on two heavy gold bangles instead of the usual glass bracelets, which would have made too much noise during my escape. The gold chains on my feet did have tiny bells on them, but everyone inside the house was too occupied to hear them tinkle. My thin gold nath nose ring swayed with the weight of pearls and rubies and kept getting caught on the large red dupatta draped over my head.

I was lucky. The only people who spotted me were the caterers and the people hired to put up the enormous wedding tent in our backyard. They weren't being paid to question why the bride was climbing out a first-floor window hours before the nikah. Or why I then ran towards the nawab sahib's mango orchard. For all they knew, I was feeling peckish. A bride should always be humoured on her wedding day.

Beside the mango orchard, a large banyan tree had stood on the very edge of our property for generations. A small bench had been built beside the tree. I had done target practice from that bench since I was old enough to hold a gun.

The rifle I now held in my hands was large. I had to shift it and the box of ammunition to one arm to hike the full skirt of the lengha to my knees. I threw off my embroidered slippers and began to climb the gnarled branches, not stopping until I had a clear view of the wedding festivities. Then I lay the rifle across my lap and waited.

My outfit was itchy, and the branch I sat on was hard. I snacked on the pakoras and barfi I had brought with me. I had to keep my strength up for the scene I knew was coming.

Finally, around nine p.m., with the nikah set to begin, my parents realized they were short one bride. I could see the alarm spreading quickly through the house. Some of my more high-strung relatives began to wail and lament, convinced I had been kidnapped and held for ransom. By this time the groom's baraat, his entourage, had arrived: Hameed, garlanded with flowers, was perched unsteadily on a horse, while his family followed behind on foot, accompanied by hired drummers. They had arrived to claim their bride, but I was nowhere to be found.

One of the tent wallahs must have tipped them off, because it wasn't long before my father, in his regimental dress uniform, and my mother, in a dark blue silk sari with silver zari embroidery, approached the banyan tree, a substantial crowd behind them. I raised my gun, took careful aim, and shot at the ground before my father's feet.

My father was so shocked he was rendered mute. I had done the worst thing a child could do: I was Making a Scene in Front of Family.

"Beti, come down this instant!" Ammi said. Naturally I refused.

One of my boy cousins made a big show of approaching the tree. "Don't worry mamu-ji, I'll get her down," he said.

I shot at the ground by his feet too, and then smiled sweetly. "I'm fine where I am, Ladoo," I said. He hated that nickname.

I don't think my parents had fully realized the lengths I would go to stop that wedding. I laid my terms before them: "Ammi, Baba, I will come down if you cancel the nikah."

"But the baraat is here already!" Ammi wailed. I saw the full realization of what I had done hit her like a tidal wave. We would be the laughingstock of the entire neighbourhood. The servants would compose mocking songs about us behind our backs. We were ruined.

Even so, I did not waver. They had made their choice when they refused to listen to me, and now I was making mine. I cocked the rifle and pointed it at the crowd.

"If you bring that drip Hameed anywhere near me, I'll shoot his left foot and then his right foot. And then I will move higher," I vowed. The men in the crowd instinctively cupped their privates and exchanged uneasy glances.

Meanwhile, Hameed, his face covered by a veil of jasmine flowers, had dismounted from that ridiculous horse and made his way to the front of the crowd. Hameed's mother caught the tail end of my threat. Shrieking, she threw herself in front of her son.

"Batameez! Pagal!" she screamed up at me. Ill-mannered, crazy. "That bastard whore witch will never get anywhere near my son. The wedding is cancelled!"

This pronouncement was followed by several minutes of yelling and arguing. I took advantage of the confusion to climb down from the tree. By the time I had straightened up, the groom and his baraat had disappeared.

My family went inside, though a circle of aunts stayed behind for a long time to berate me. After a while they left too. It was dark by then, and I watched the tent wallahs dismantle the wedding venue. I wondered if they would get paid even though the bride had threatened to shoot the groom. I asked the person in charge, a gruff older man dressed in a simple white lungi and dress shirt. He patted me on the arm when I asked. "Don't worry about it, beti," he said.

It was the first kind word anyone had spoken to me in so long, I burst into tears. I stood there sobbing while they removed the tent, the hanging lights, the tables and food. Once I had stopped crying, I went inside the house, changed out of my wedding finery, and went to sleep.

I had won, but I had also lost. My parents didn't talk to me for almost an entire year afterwards. I never received another rishta proposal from anyone else.

My father died when I was thirty-five. My mother died when I was forty-two. I didn't meet Mohammad, the love of my life, until I was forty-five. We had fifteen wonderful years together before Allah called him to Jannah. I know he's waiting for me there, but I also know I have many good years left on Earth, and I want to make the most of them.

Chapter Forty-Six

"hank you for sharing your story, Kawkab Khala," Radio Hana said. "And thank you all for listening to my brand-new show, *Secret Family History*. What's *your* secret?"

The question, the trademark handle I had brainstormed with Thomas and Big J, landed like a thunderclap in the living room. Fazee, Baba, and Kawkab blinked as if they had been released from a spell.

I imagined Marisa's face at that precise moment, the colour of her cherry-red Hermès scarf.

I glanced at my aunt, who was placidly folding her silk dupatta, and a wave of admiration swept over me once more. In an era when women around the world were still being routinely belittled and silenced, when feminist activism was only in its infancy, my aunt had felt no qualms about refusing to do as she was told. In the best of ways, she was truly a radical.

I wondered if Fazee and Baba were thinking about their own marriages. Fazee and Fahim had fallen in love first and then married, but my parents had an arranged marriage. Mom once told me that she only saw a picture of Baba before their wedding day, her shy silence being interpreted as consent. In her case, it had been. In the case of Kawkab Khala, whose parents were far richer than my family, her loud and repeated protests had fallen on deaf ears. "Cats climb," she had told me.

In the living room now, the chai in front of Baba had grown cold, and my sister had not reached for her phone once while my show was playing. Even my aunt had been caught up in the story she had lived through, and a flare of pride ignited in my chest. I had done this. I had kept my family entranced. *Follow the story of your heart.* I had done so, and the results were before me, in the contemplative bubble that only good storytelling inspires.

Baba rose from his seat and kissed my cheek, enveloping me in a hug. He smelled like starched linen and cinnamon, and I drank it in. "Mubarak ho," he said. "Allah has blessed you with a gift. You will be a star one day." Fazeela congratulated me as well, and then they both made their way to their bedrooms, leaving me alone with my aunt.

"Why was this story a secret for so long?" I asked Kawkab. I hadn't asked her on air, but I was curious.

"Shame, I suppose. My parents were embarrassed by my behaviour. They died with that shame. I'm sure I became a cautionary tale of the dangers of raising a willful girl." My aunt smiled crookedly. "Of course, my extended family were afraid that their daughters would find inspiration in my story and learn to climb trees of their own. I believe some of them did. Look at your mother, at yourself, even your sister. You all possess that same spirit of adventure and risk-taking, in your own way. Perhaps your mother and sister lost that feeling recently, and the only way for them to get it back is to begin anew. Just as you are about to do, Hana *jaan.*"

I acknowledged the truth of my aunt's words. Her story had remained an open secret in some ways. Most people back home in

India knew the details, so it wasn't much of a secret at all; in fact, it had turned into a family myth. In turn, she had turned that mythology to her advantage. My aunt had chosen her fate, though it came with consequences. We hadn't elaborated on it during the show, but her relationship with her parents had been severely damaged. Yet she had accepted her lot and worked within the parameters of her decision. Her eventual marriage, later in life, had been a choice freely made. My aunt valued her independence above all else.

I was grateful to have learned my aunt's secret family history, even if it wasn't so secret. Our secrets expose what we most deeply fear, or most fervently want. I could understand that now. Yusuf and Lily were ready to be together, despite the obstacles. Fahim and Fazeela had on some level felt trapped by the restaurant, and our financial difficulties had offered the freedom to make a new, independent move. Aydin and Afsana had been heading back towards each other ever since they were torn apart. And maybe Aydin had been looking for his true home all along, one that he had found in Golden Crescent.

Aydin said he had chosen my community, my neighbourhood, on purpose as the site of his long-dreamed-of restaurant. I began to contemplate the possibility that he hadn't come to unleash chaos and destruction. Maybe some part of him had known that he was approaching a nexus point, and he had been looking for the strength to throw off his father's expectations and take a different path.

If my aunt could climb a tree holding a rifle, if she could deliberately set fire to her life based only on a clear, unwavering vision of her future; if my mother had the courage to start again; if Aydin had the nerve to take a chance on love and community—then I could do it too. It was time for me to throw off my own anonymous alter ego and embrace the Hana I had become over the past year.

Assuming Aydin ever came back from Vancouver. But even if he didn't, I would be okay. I came from a long line of unstoppable women.

I texted StanleyP, eager to share with someone who would understand, someone who had been with me from the start.

AnaBGR

Rethinking this whole anonymous thing.

StanleyP

You're ghosted once and suddenly you're questioning everything.

AnaBGR

Not sure I need the mask anymore, and even if Mr. Unexpected Sources did ghost me, I'll be all right.

StanleyP

Don't tell me you just realized you've been in Oz all along.

AnaBGR

I'm ready to face my audience as myself, and use any hate or love that comes my way as fuel and inspiration. As my cousin once said, Build a dam.

A long moment. Then—

StanleyP

Your cousin said that?

Yes, during this thing that happened to me a while ago . . .
Never mind. I just think of his words sometimes, when life gets
especially difficult. He's just a kid, but one of the smartest
people I know. Build a dam means to use the negativity in your
life to power good. You know?

StanleyP
I think I know it all now.

I texted Big J. *Did you get into a lot of trouble?*

My phone rang. "Pretty sure Marisa was about to break down the
door to the studio, until the calls and texts started pouring in," Big
J said. "People wanted to tell us their secrets, they wanted to know
what happened to your aunt, they demanded pictures to go with the
story. And they wanted to know when the next episode would air. We
got plenty of hate too, but people have to listen to get pissed, right?
Marisa was so angry she had to leave the room. Davis called me right
after, wondering if we should replace the old show with this new one,
especially since Thomas has quit."

"I wish I could have seen that," I said.

"I turned Davis down, of course. Even when he offered you a permanent job and a pot of money," he continued.

"Wait, what?"

Big J laughed. "Just kidding. He said he'd give you back your unpaid
internship, but you would be on probation for three months and
would report directly to Marisa. I politely declined on your behalf. I
hope that's okay."

I thanked him again for taking a chance on me, and we discussed plans for the next episode. With any luck, this would lead to more opportunities.

In the meantime, the street festival was the next day, and I had to make sure we were ready for whatever happened.

Still no response from Aydin.

Chapter Forty-Seven

The day of the summer street festival dawned like any other. Mom and Baba were already in the kitchen, drinking their morning chai. They made space for me at the table, and Rashid joined us a few minutes later.

My apprehension must have been apparent, because Mom placed an arm around me. "I will be there. Fahim will be there. Rashid will be there. Your father and Yusuf and Brother Musa will be there. We won't let anything happen to you, *beta*." With a final squeeze, she stood up. "Besides, you never know. Sometimes people can surprise you."

Usually in the worst possible way, I added silently.

I SPENT THE REST OF the morning setting up tables for vendors, mostly local businesses and some others who had rented booths to sell clothing, jewellery, or snacks. Rashid had secured a permit to close Golden Crescent to traffic for the afternoon. We blocked off one end of the street with makeshift wooden barricades, festooned with signs and streamers advertising GOLDEN CRESCENT ANNUAL SUMMER STREET FESTIVAL! FAMILIES WELCOME!

Constable Lukie arrived and began to direct traffic. The Golden Crescent business owners who had agreed to participate set up folding tables and canopies outside their stores, nearly a dozen stalls in total. Rashid caught my uncertain glance around the street, and reassured me. "Don't forget there will be food and entertainment, and Mr. Lewis has donated a bouncy castle. It will be fine, Hana Apa."

I remembered that Aydin had promised to invite his desi dance group friends to perform. I didn't know if that would still be happening.

We started stringing up the huge banner Rashid had had printed at the south end of Golden Crescent, but he nearly dropped his side when he caught sight of Zulfa. She was dressed in a colourful salwar kameez, dark hair loose around her shoulders. He ran after her as soon as the banner was in place, and I saw him taking out his phone for a selfie.

The business owners began to bring out their merchandise, though the table we had reserved for Wholistic Grill remained empty. Mom emerged from Three Sisters carrying an enormous pot filled with meat biryani. She was followed by Fahim and Rashid with massive containers of haleem, a thick stew made with lentils, grain, and beef, and a fragrant lamb korma. They disappeared back into the restaurant and returned with a large tray overflowing with freshly made tandoori naan, plus a large barbecue grill. They had made enough food to feed hundreds.

Mom expertly lit the charcoal grill and shut the lid so it could heat up. She looked up and threw me a quick smile, that same reflexive expression I had seen so many times before, and I was filled with a sudden gratitude for my hard-working mother. I hoped that I would one day be as good at what I had chosen to pursue as she was right then.

The other stalls were slowly starting to get busy. The air was filled with conversation and a hum of excitement. Brother Musa had moved his vegetable stall out onto the street and was setting up a juicer. Luxmi Aunty had prepared two gigantic cauldrons. In one she was making fresh jalebi, a bright orange dessert made from dough piped into thin pretzel shapes and deep-fried, then soaked in sweet syrup. The other pot was filled with peanuts boiling in salted water.

A few stalls had beautiful salwar kameez and hijabs for sale. Another booth showcased a henna artist, who was laying out patterns and mehndi cones filled with dark green henna paste. A few curious neighbours were waiting for the festival to officially start.

I spotted Gary setting up at the booth reserved for Wholistic Grill. "You made it!" I said, going over to him.

"Special instructions from the boss man. He told me to close the store and put up a sign directing traffic here." He issued a few quick orders to his helpers. "It's going to be great," he said.

"That's what everyone keeps telling me," I said. For the first time all day, I actually believed it.

Which was when the first protestor showed up.

Chapter Forty-Eight

DOWN WITH SHARIAH LAW!"

My attention jerked from Gary to a heavy-set man standing in the middle of our cordoned-off street. His black T-shirt displayed the now familiar raised white fist, and he held a placard emblazoned with the words MY CANADA DOESN'T INCLUDE: MUSLIMS/GAYS/IMMI-GRANTS/YOU!

Arms folded across his chest, Gary contemplated the man. "Impressive penmanship," he said drily. "I like the way he's covered all his bases with that last word."

My eyes locked on the man's face. His eyes were cold and flinty, even as his face glistened with sweat. He glared at festivalgoers and stall vendors alike, who, after a few curious glances, ignored him. In response, he shook his sign and bellowed, "WE DON'T WANT YOU HERE! GO BACK TO ARABIA, TOWEL HEADS!"

Mom glanced over at me from the Three Sisters table, one eyebrow raised. She shook her head, then returned her attention to the grill.

I hurried over to Black T-Shirt. "Can I help you?" I asked politely.

"Yes, you can help me. You can LEAVE MY COUNTRY! WE

DON'T WANT YOU HERE!" he roared in my face. A few people looked over again, their unease rising.

I took a deep breath and channelled my mom—Angela Merkel in a black hijab. "You don't make the rules. This is my street and my festival, and you are not welcome here."

"You mean your HALAL food festival! The ISLAMIST TAKE-OVER of CANADA will be PUT DOWN by FORCE if necessary!" The man's eyes were bulging now, and spittle flew from his mouth. "You can't make me leave! I have a RIGHT to protest! FREEDOM of SPEECH hasn't been outlawed in this country!" He stepped closer.

Fahim eased up beside me, Rashid flanking him, and their silent presence gave me courage. "True, but you can't protest on this side of the street," I said, my voice measured. "We have a permit."

Black T-Shirt predictably refused to leave, so I left him shaking his sign and yelling and went to find Constable Lukie. She was near Wholistic Grill with her partner, a tall white man with massive biceps and full-sleeve tattoos. By the time we returned to Black T-Shirt, he had been joined by a few other people, three men and one woman, all dressed the same and holding similarly worded placards. After a heated debate with Constable Lukie and her partner, the small group of protesters moved to the other side of the street, though they didn't let up with their taunts. They continued to yell and heckle stall holders and festival attendees alike, and the mood instantly dimmed.

I kept an eye on the protestor numbers, which slowly swelled from five to ten, and then from fifteen to twenty-five people. There was some diversity in their ranks: mostly men, but a few women too; mostly white, but also a few Brown and olive faces, all yelling, chanting, and stomping their feet. Constable Lukie called for backup, and soon there were four officers, two of whom kept a close watch on the group across the street. The other two watched our side just as carefully. Who had the police been assigned to protect? I wondered. Especially since the protestors now outnumbered the festival participants. I looked around and my heart sank. No children, no teenagers. Most of the people who remained seemed to be related to the business owners. The protestors had accomplished their purpose: people coaxed outside by the promise of food, shopping, and family fun had been scared off by Black T-Shirt and friends.

"Go home, terrorist, or we'll make you leave!" a brown-skinned woman yelled as she made eye contact with me. She glared, mouthing profanities. I wondered what had driven her to that. Did she truly hate me, or had she been hurt so badly by something or someone that she had to lash out at others?

I looked around and locked eyes with Rashid. Zulfa stood beside him, and she gave me an encouraging smile. My cousin made a motion with his hands. *Be easy, Hana Apa. The day is not over yet.*

But the wave of despair that had washed over me at the sight of the swelling crowd of black T-shirts and the dwindling crowd of Golden Crescent families peaked and broke. I hurried to find comfort. Inside the empty Three Sisters Biryani Poutine, I fell into a booth in the corner and dropped my head. It would never be enough. No matter how much we planned and wished and tried, it would never be enough to stop the tide of hatred.

My phone pinged, a message from StanleyP.

StanleyP
I promised you a picture.

A photo accompanied the message, and I stared at it. A solemn-looking Aydin stood in front of Wholistic Grill. He had a half-smile on his face.

StanleyP
Last secret, though to be fair, I finally sorted this one out yesterday. I had my suspicions all along, but it seemed too crazy. I think you suspected too. Don't feel bad that I figured it out first. I had a slight head start in the clue department: in your first podcast you said you were a twenty-something Muslim woman who lived in Toronto.

My face was flushed and I felt faint. I kept returning to the picture he had sent. StanleyP was Aydin Shah? My friend and confidant, my first listener and biggest supporter, the man who had advised me on battle tactics, who had teased me mercilessly and encouraged my dreams, had been my competition all along? I recalled the way he had talked about his "girl." Was that me? If so, why had he left without a word and ignored all my messages? I continued to read, head spinning.

StanleyP
The coincidences kept piling up, and when you mentioned your cousin and building a dam, I had my proof. Finally.

I closed my eyes and tried to breathe. Of course my cousin was somehow behind this mystery. Rashid might as well change his name to Loki, or maybe Shaitan. I looked more closely at the photo and realized that it was more than recent. There were stalls and tables set up in the background, and I could make out the signs for the street festival. *He's here, right now.*

StanleyP

I have the advantage at this point, so let me officially introduce myself. My real name is Aydin Shah. I'm a 27-year-old Muslim man who used to live in Vancouver but recently moved to the centre of the universe, Toronna. I have no siblings, my mother died when I was five, and my father is a jerk who somehow blocked all your texts in the past few days. Also, I recently opened up a restaurant on the same street as the most perfect girl in the world. Hello, Hana.

Aydin/StanleyP had returned home. And he still didn't know about his mother. I wrote back, not sure what else to do: *Salaams, Aydin.* It was time to rejoin the fight outside.

I HAD BEEN GONE FOR less than thirty minutes, but when I emerged from Three Sisters, the festival was completely transformed. The street was now bustling with people browsing stalls and munching on snacks. The number of protesters had grown as well, to about forty people, all yelling, chanting, and holding up hateful messages.

Except now they had company. The counter-protestors had shown up as promised, about two dozen in total. They waved placards of their own that read: ALL ARE WELCOME! and WE SAY NO TO HATE! Though they were outnumbered by the black T-shirt army, they were just as loud. I spotted Yusuf in the middle of the throng, clutching a megaphone and working the crowd, Lily by his side. My do-gooder friends simply couldn't help themselves. Lily caught my eye and gave me an uncertain smile, which I returned.

Imam Abdul Bari stood on the fringes. When he caught my gaze, he smiled beatifically. The sight of his silent courage, despite his recent devastating loss, made me stand a bit straighter.

A trio of little girls skipped past, clad in dresses paired with sneakers, trailed by their parents. A couple walked hand in hand, the woman in hijab, the man in jeans and a T-shirt. They were followed by a larger family, a teenage boy trailing his elderly grandparents, the grandfather in starched white salwar kameez and a brown felt prayer hat, grandmother in a neatly tied sari.

The Three Sisters booth wasn't as busy as Wholistic Grill's, but a steady stream of customers lined up for our specialities. Mom stood beside the stall, nursing a cup of strong chai. I hugged her from behind, startling her. "What are you thinking about?" I asked.

"How long it has been since your father and I visited India," she said. "Kawkab Apa reminded me that I have not been back since your nani died." I remembered that—the call in the middle of the night, my mother's quiet weeping at the news of her mother's death, the scramble to find a plane ticket so she could get back to India in time for the *janazah*, how we had all pulled together and split her shifts for the five days she had been away.

"We might go back, for a few weeks this time," she added.

"What about Fazeela?" I asked.

"She's got a few months before the baby comes. And she has Fahim, and you," Mom said. She looked around again, sipping her chai. "I didn't want to participate in the street festival this year, but I'm glad we did. It has been . . . nice, despite our unwelcome guests," she said, nodding at the protestors. She paused, and I knew what she was about to say before she spoke. "I have decided to sell the restaurant, *meri jaan*. It might not be what you want, but it is my choice and I am at peace with it."

Mom had been telling me, in so many different ways, for weeks. She waited while I absorbed the news. I took a deep breath, pulling myself together. I would be all right, and my mother deserved to think about herself for once. It was time she got to choose.

Choice. That's what my parents had gifted me. There is nothing more powerful than being able to make up your own mind about something. Nothing headier than reaching out your hand and saying: *This. I choose this.*

Across the lane, a young man near the Wholistic Grill booth caught my eye. He was dressed in a white T-shirt and dark jeans, silver sunglasses tucked into the neckline of his shirt. As our eyes locked, I realized I felt another, equally powerful sentiment: *You. I choose you.*

Chapter Forty-Nine

Aydin didn't walk over right away. Instead he held up one finger, motioning for me to wait. I watched him cross the street, to where the protestors and anti-protestors were busy yelling at each other, on the verge of violence. It was difficult to stand still and watch. My need to talk to him, to discuss our relationship as StanleyP and AnaBGR, and most especially the last remaining secret between us—that his mother was alive and wanted to meet him—was overwhelming.

The mood across the street had grown uglier. Screaming and red-faced, original Black T-Shirt was facing off against Yusuf now. As I watched, he reached forward and grabbed Yusuf by the shirtfront, pulling his hand back to swing. I had a sudden memory of the man who had tried to hurt Aydin downtown before I pulled him away from harm. Across the street now, Lily did the same, yanking Yusuf back; they stumbled together, a near parody of the downtown attack. Constable Lukie stepped forward just as I started running towards my friends. Our street festival was about to descend into an ugly brawl.

"NOBODY WANTS YOU HERE, ISLAMIST SCUM!" Black

T-Shirt yelled, just as Aydin reached the vanguard of the racist protestors. From my vantage point I could see that Aydin wore a small smile, his demeanour calm. The protestors surrounding Black T-Shirt began to jeer and yell at him, but he didn't react. Instead he turned briefly and scanned the crowd, almost as if he were waiting for something.

I watched his smile widen slightly, and then I heard it too. A drumbeat. It came from the Golden Crescent neighbourhood. Everyone in the hateful tableau swivelled their heads, searching for the source of the noise.

The first drumbeat was joined by a second, and then a third. Three young men emerged from the other end of the street, each dressed in a vibrant red salwar and cream-coloured kameez pants, golden turbans perched cheekily on their heads. The drumming originated from the *dhols* the men carried; the barrel-shaped, double-headed drums were supported by long lanyards looped around each drummer's neck and across the chest, leaving their arms free. Using curved drumsticks, the musicians hammered out a beat that grew steadily louder as they marched towards Aydin, until the noise was deafening.

"What's happening?" Rashid shouted beside me. "Was this part of the plan?" He took out his phone and began to take a video of the unfolding scene.

I shook my head, bewildered. "Aydin said he would invite some performer friends, but I didn't know any details."

My cousin broke into a grin. "He is using war tactics to intimidate the enemy. Look how they cower in fear."

The black T-shirt army and even the counter-protestors seemed more confused than scared, but they had all stopped yelling. In fact, everyone had stopped what they were doing, including the festival attendees and vendors. All eyes were riveted on the scene in front of us, transfixed by the sight and sounds of the musicians in their colourful clothing.

The three drummers stood in a line behind Aydin, their hands flying as they hammered out a heart-pounding rhythm. The beat rose to a crescendo as it came to a climax. Then they all stopped and executed a neat flip of their drumsticks in unison, catching them as they turned around to face the festivalgoers.

"GOLDEN CRESCENT!" the man in the centre bellowed. "Are you ready to PARTY?" This was greeted by only a smattering of cheers and claps, but the drummers were undaunted. They began to play once more, a lively, danceable beat this time. Six dancers, dressed casually in track pants and T-shirts, burst from the crowd as raucous, cheerful bhangra music began to pound from speakers set up surreptitiously around the edges of the street. The dancers began to execute an elaborate, high-energy choreographed routine, their movements broad and punchy, jumping into the air and landing in tandem, arms flailing and legs skipping and leaping. The festival attendees and vendors went wild, clapping and hooting and stomping their feet to the pounding, bass-heavy beat.

They thought it had all been planned, I realized—the protests, the dancers—all working together like a flash mob. I noticed that Aydin was dancing too. He tried to keep up as best he could, but he was obviously an amateur, and the effect was hilarious. He was a few beats off, his movements wild and erratic. When I caught his eye, he winked at me, just as the music changed and a familiar Taylor Swift tune began to play.

The dancers turned around, facing the festival area, their backs to the black T-shirts. And then Aydin and the dancers started awkwardly twerking, bums shaking and jerking in the protestors' confused faces.

I burst out laughing. Around me, the street festival participants laughed as well. Tears were falling down Rashid's cheeks as he filmed, he was laughing so hard, and beside him Zulfa giggled. We watched Aydin try to execute a shimmy, followed by jazz hands, before breaking into an awkward running man, while the rest of the dancers continued to shake their bums in time with the beat.

Black T-Shirt and friends looked around at the laughing crowd, dazed and irritated by the unexpected turn of events. By the middle of Queen T's flip-off anthem, they had started to peel away, leaving in pairs and singles. By the end of the song, only Original Black T-Shirt and a few of his friends remained. His face was still red, but I suspected more from embarrassment at the backside salutes than anything else. I heard him yell something at Aydin, a final hateful, profanity-laced parting shot, before he too hefted his sign and left.

The counter-protestors seemed to have the same idea. A few of them joined the impromptu dance party in the middle of the street, but most of them had realized that both the rally and the show were over. Rashid had disappeared with Zulfa.

Aydin sank down onto a plastic folding chair beside me. Our eyes met and we started to laugh, small giggles at first, but soon we were howling. His shoulders shook with great convulsions of hilarity. Tears streamed down my face and it was hard to breathe.

I knew I loved him. And that I had to tell him about Afsana Aunty.

"Hana," he managed between bouts of laughter.

"Yes?" I gasped. I was nearly hysterical, half laughing and half crying.

"I never want to leave this place."

"Neither do I," I said, wiping my eyes. His mother was likely in the crowd. Would he hate me for revealing the awful secret?

"I don't want to leave you either," he continued, his breath warm and sweet on my cheek. "Ana ... Hana ... whatever and whoever you want to be, can we please start over?"

I breathed in his scent—cedarwood chips and sandalwood cologne—and closed my eyes. "I'll think about it, Stanley Park."

When I opened my eyes, I saw Kawkab Khala standing nearby, at the very edge of the festival. From the knowing look on her face, I guessed she had overheard some of our conversation. Afsana Aunty stood behind her, a look of muted terror on her face.

I stood up, and Aydin rose too, following my gaze. I took a deep breath, channelling the courage he had shown in front of the enraged protestors. I couldn't let anything else happen until he had learned the truth about himself.

"But first," I said, heart pounding, "you have to talk to my aunt."

Chapter Fifty

Aydin flashed me a smile before he turned to face Kawkab Khala and Afsana Aunty. I saw my aunt place a gentle hand on his shoulder, then turn towards her friend and motion her forward. I watched him walk away with the women in the direction of Wholistic Grill. Even from a distance I could see the unsteadiness of Afsana's steps. She walked as if she were in a dream. How long had she waited for that moment? How would Aydin react?

A muffled cry, and then Aydin stumbled backwards, landing heavily on the wooden bench in front of his restaurant. He shook his head from side to side and then buried his head in his hands, shoulders jerking. I stood frozen to the spot, fighting the urge to run to him, unsure what comfort I could provide.

Together, Kawkab Khala and Afsana Aunty helped him up and they all went inside Wholistic Grill.

An hour later, my phone buzzed with a text.

Did everyone know but me?

I didn't hesitate. No more hiding things from each other. *Yes,* I typed. My hands did not shake.

I guess we're finally even, he wrote back.

Chapter Fifty-One

I t had been Rashid's doing all along. Mom told me after the festival that my cousin had bought the restaurant. When I cornered him outside Three Sisters, heaving three bags of trash into the Dumpster, he said, "Family is like the Mafia, Hana Apa. Once you join, you're in it for life. Besides, my parents were looking for an investment opportunity in Canada."

"Is your family part of the New Delhi mafia?" I blurted. What if he had bought Three Sisters to launder money, or as a place to meet his underworld contacts?

Rashid started laughing. "Are you plotting the next episode of *Secret Family History* already? The restaurant will be safe with me. Don't worry, Hana; I paid your mother a fair price, only slightly offset by a family discount."

He hadn't answered my question, but I decided to leave that worry for another day.

"Zulfa told me she is engaged to someone else," Rashid continued, his voice mournful. "But who am I to stand in the way of true love?" His face brightened. "And she told me she has a younger sister. Hana Apa, how far is Vancouver from Toronto?"

"Very far, especially for a newly minted restaurateur," I assured him. But, knowing Rashid, he would find a way.

Given Aydin's message, I didn't expect to hear from him anytime soon. His entire life had been upended, and he would need time to process the new information. I kept myself occupied by helping with festival cleanup efforts. Things had wound down around sunset, and most of the protestors and counter-protestors had scattered by then, leaving their litter behind.

Imam Abdul Bari was picking up discarded coffee cups and take-out containers. He paused as I passed him a pair of disposable gloves and a garbage bag. "Congratulations, Hana. The festival has been a resounding success," he said.

I smiled weakly at the Imam and continued to sweep up trash, stopping only at Brother Musa's store. Beautiful Yusuf stood outside, waiting for me.

"Hi, Hana. What's new?" he asked, smiling easily, as if he hadn't just eloped with my best friend without telling me.

"Go to hell, Yusuf," I said evenly.

His face fell. I realized I had never before spoken to him like that, in anger rather than with my usual affectionate mockery. I didn't feel any urge to make him feel better, either. Rashid was right: beautiful Yusuf was an *ullu*, and it was time for all of us to grow up.

"Be kind to Lily," I added. "Or else."

WHEN I RETURNED HOME a few hours later, shoulders and knees aching from bending, stooping, and cleaning, I half expected to see my aunt seated on the couch, dressed in fine silk and calm vindication. Instead she was nowhere to be found. I went upstairs, but my bedroom was empty. Worse, it had been cleared out.

Kawkab Khala's expensive leather suitcases were gone from under my bed, neatly folded outfits and jewellery removed from my dresser. She had also done a thorough rummage through my closet and drawers, piling all the clothes she deemed "unsuitable, unflattering, or just plain ugly" (according to the Post-it note she left) into four garbage bags at the foot of the bed. And then she had taken it upon herself to rearrange my remaining clothes. She had also moved around my furniture so that the airless bedroom felt more than twice as big.

There was a long note left on the bed, written on heavy, expensive cream stationery.

My dear Hana jaan,

Your room was not comfortable at all. I suggest you make a bonfire of your lumpy mattress and deflated pillows, as I will probably be back to visit sometime before I die. Don't worry, I'll make it a surprise, so you can't think of an excuse and run away before I arrive. I'll expect a new double bed, and for God's sake, get rid of that leopard-print hijab!

If you ever come to Delhi, I will take you shopping and try to teach you how to coordinate your clothes so that they will distract from the scowl on your face.

I flipped the page, grinning.

I saw what you did at the festival today. I'm not sure if it was one of the bravest things you have ever done or the stupidest. Doubtless you would like to know how my conversation with your admirer went. For that, you will have to ask him. I am sure, once he gets over the shock of learning that he has been lied to all his life, he will forgive you for participating in his deception, however briefly.

I never got a chance to tell you that I enjoyed your radio programme. It was the first time I had heard my story being told to me instead of about me, and it was an interesting experience. I think perhaps you made me seem a bit more adventurous than I am. After all, it took me this long to visit you all in Canada.

I think also that you are not so terrible at this thing you have decided to do with your life, Hanaan. Perhaps the next time we meet, I will tell you a few more stories. The "bride in the tree" tale is the one that everyone knows, but it is not the most interesting, by far.

Do you know that Hameed never married? He was too scared to have his mother arrange another marriage after my little stunt, and too timid to look for his own wife. I found him on Facebook. He still has all his hair and he lives alone in Mumbai. I might pay him a visit on my way back home. I hope he doesn't have a heart attack when he recognizes me.

Khuda hafiz, *my love,*
Kawkab Khala

The room still smelled like her—a mixture of Yardley English Rose powder and the musky Chanel perfume that would have overpowered a lesser personality. I folded the letter and put it in the pocket of my jeans. Then I carefully closed the door to keep her scent inside the room a little longer, and went downstairs to sleep on the couch.

Chapter Fifty-Two

Aydin knocked on the door of Three Sisters two days later, while I was cleaning in preparation for the renovations slated to begin in a few days. I nearly dropped the rag in my hand when I spotted him.

His hair wasn't neatly combed and his face seemed harder somehow. But when he caught my eye through the glass, his shoulders dropped and he leaned against the door. *Please?* he mouthed, motioning. As if there had been any doubt.

When I let him inside, he handed me a bouquet of bright yellow daisies. Our eyes tangled, his gaze hot on my face.

Taking a deep breath, I said, "I should be giving you flowers. I'm so sorry. I should have told you about your mother right away, as soon as I figured it out. I didn't know what to do, I didn't think it was my place, and your father . . ." I trailed off. I wasn't sure if he knew that Junaid Uncle had tried to buy my silence, or if it even mattered anymore. "I'm sorry for the way things ended between us at the festival."

Aydin removed the bouquet from my hands. "Things haven't ended between us," he said. "They've barely begun. Why do you think I'm here?" He smiled, and I recognized forgiveness and a delicate tenderness in his eyes. It made me want to put my arms around him and cry. Or laugh. Maybe both.

"I did put your mom out of business," he added.

He hadn't heard. "Mom has sold the restaurant to Rashid. He's shutting down to do some renovations and upgrades. A coat of paint, maybe some tablecloths, and bigger, brighter lights to perk up the place," I said, echoing his suggestions from long ago. "Three Sisters should be open again in a month."

A smile tugged at the corners of his mouth. "Machiavelli will be my competition?"

"I should warn you, Rashid plays dirty. He's hired Zulfa to manage his publicity campaign."

Aydin threw back his head and laughed out loud. My heart lifted. I wanted to hold on to that joyful laughter. I wanted to bottle the sound and play it back on demand. I wanted to listen to him laugh for the rest of my life.

Now he leaned in close. "I knew I wanted you from the very beginning. From the moment we first met, I was intrigued, and then I was fascinated, and then I was in love. I just needed to figure out some things first. Hana, Anony-Ana, are you ready for this?"

He was teasing and he was serious. I knew him well enough to understand what he was really asking. Was I ready to stop playing games and let this beautiful untested thing between us unspool?

His eyes darkened as he looked at me, and I flushed. Yes. Yes, I was ready.

"Nice to meet you, Aydin," I said. "My name is Hanaan Khan. I'm the daughter of Ghufran and Ijaz Khan, sister to a soccer star, niece to a warrior queen, cousin to Machiavelli. I am a wielder of microphones and slinger of stories. It's been a rough few months but I'm ready to face whatever comes next, together. What about you?"

"Yes," he said simply. "For as long as we both shall live, my answer to that question will always be . . . *yes*."

· · ·

Here are the rules:

This is no longer a single-person podcast. That means there might be interviews, a co-host, and possibly, if I'm feeling up to it, some comedy.

Also, this whole anonymous thing isn't working for me anymore. So, listeners, here we go.

My name isn't Ana; it's Hana Khan. I'm twenty-four years old and I live in Scarborough, an east-end suburb of Toronto, Canada. My parents immigrated from India before I was born, and until recently we ran a small halal restaurant called Three Sisters Biryani Poutine. My mom let me name the place when I was nine years old, because she didn't care about things like market research or worry about confusing her customers. My cousin Rashid runs the restaurant now, and you should definitely check it out. The food is great, and it's definitely not a front for the New Delhi mafia.

The other halal restaurant on our street is Wholistic Burgers and Grill. It's owned and run by my husband, Aydin Shah. We first met because of this podcast. Later he tried to shut down Three Sisters, and then I tried to shut down his restaurant. After a few months we decided it would be better if we got married instead, since it was obvious he was madly in love with me. We plan to live mostly happily ever after, which is the best anyone can hope for in this life, according to my cousin.

When I started this podcast a year ago, I promised nothing of substance and nothing but the truth. This is my truth:

The First Law of Thermodynamics states that energy is neither created nor destroyed, but it can be transformed from one form to another. That law will get you every time, so make sure the energy you put out into the world is positive. Otherwise it will turn the other way and then turn on you.

Newton's Third Law of Motion states that every action has an equal and opposite reaction. Everything that happened to me this year has been proof, whether I wanted it to be or not. Luckily, the hatred aimed at me and mine was met with an equal and transformative amount of love.

Rashid's Second Law of Enthusiastic Fresh Starts is to build a dam—and then a hydroelectric power station right beside it to make money while your world is changing.

Kawkab Khala's Eternal Law of "Stop Being Ridiculous, Hana jaan" is to dress with intention, keep tabs on your enemies, and always take care of your friends. Also, intelligent women play the long game.

Aydin's Law of Final Words is to accept that crazy coincidences really do happen in real life, and that love keeps to its own schedule.

And finally, Hana's First Law of Living states that everything is better told as a story, and mine is still unfolding. I hope you tune in again soon for all the adventures that await.

Newport Community
Learning & Libraries

Acknowledgements

*B*ismillah. I feel nervous and a little shocked to be writing the acknowledgements for my second novel already. While *Hana Khan Carries On* didn't take as long to write as my first book, *Ayesha at Last*, it was just as difficult. Writing is a lonely occupation for the most part, but it would have been impossible without my community:

Many thanks to my wonderful agent, Ann Collette. Your advice is spot-on and your support unflagging. The way we met is a meet-cute of its own. Huge thanks also for steering me away from that particular plot line we'll never talk about again!

Thanks also to my amazing editor, Jennifer Lambert at HarperCollins Canada. Your wisdom and insights always blow me away. Thank you for believing in *Hana Khan* and for encouraging me to dig deeper, to the heart of this story. I wouldn't have arrived here without you!

So much thanks to the stellar team at HarperCollins Canada for hyping my writing on the socials and for supporting my funny Muslim romcom in every way. I am thrilled to be part of the family.

To my #SisterhoodOfThePen, the talented writers Sajidah (S.K. Ali) and Ausma Zehanat Khan, thank you for reading my earlier drafts, offering honest feedback, and cheering me on. I couldn't do this without the support of our "staff room."

Thank you to my first readers, Aminah and Nina. Your suggestions are always excellent, and I live for your unfiltered reactions.

Many thanks to Radiyah Chowdhury, Shireen Ahmed, and Aaron Reynolds for answering my many questions about the world of radio and podcasting. Thanks also to Fasiha Khan for talking to me about family law. Any mistakes are mine entirely.

Heart emojis to my #Robarts friends: I've known most of you since I was a kid obsessed with books. Thanks for being my people.

Many thanks to my parents, Mohammed and Azmat Jalaluddin, and the rest of my family in Toronto and around the world. Your absolute delight at having a writer in the family has meant the world.

For my sons, Mustafa and Ibrahim: Your continued indifference to my writing career is a great reminder of what is truly important in life. I am so proud of the compassionate and kind people you are growing into. Sorry for being such a distracted mom.

For my husband, Imtiaz: None of this would have been possible without your help, love, advice, and cheerleading. You read every draft I write and tell me what you truly think. You listen to my complaints, put up with my distracted musings, and support every dream. I'm not sure how I got so lucky. Thank you.

And finally, a big shout-out to you, reader. This book wouldn't exist without you! I hope you enjoyed *Hana Khan Carries On*, and if you did, please spread the word and consider reviewing on the platform of your choice—it really helps.

HD 9715 COR

QM Library

23 1345083 0

WITHDRAWN
FROM STOCK
QMUL LIBRARY